THE WITCH-KING LIVES!

Entreri went for his sword, but when the lich reached out with bony fingers, the assassin instead thrust his gloved hand out before him. Again Entreri screamed—in defiance, in denial, in rage—as another lightning bolt blasted forth.

Spots danced before his eyes, and waves of dizziness assailed him.

The floor and walls began to tremble with a low, rolling growl.

And he heard the taunting cackle of the lich.

FORGOTTEN REALMS®

R.A. SALVATORE

THE SELLSWORDS

Servant of the Shard
Promise of the Witch-King
Road of the Patriarch
October 2006

THE LEGEND OF DRIZZT

Homeland
Exile
Sojourn
The Crystal Shard
Streams of Silver
The Halfling's Gem
The Legacy
Starless Night
Siege of Darkness
Passage to Dawn
The Silent Blade
The Spine of the World
Sea of Swords

THE HUNTER'S BLADES TRILOGY

The Thousand Orcs
The Lone Drow
The Two Swords

FORGOTTEN REALMS®

R.A. SALVATORE

PROMISE OF THE WITCH-KING

THE SELLSWORDS

BOOK II

Wizards of the Coast™

The Sellswords, Book II

PROMISE OF THE WITCH-KING

Published by Wizards of the Coast, Inc. FORGOTTEN REALMS, WIZARDS OF THE COAST, and their respective logos are trademarks of Wizards of the Coast, Inc., in the U.S.A. and other countries.

Printed in the U.S.A.

Cover art by Todd Lockwood
Map by Todd Gamble
Original Hardcover Edition First Printing: October 2005
First Paperback Printing: September 2006

9 8 7 6 5 4 3 2 1

ISBN-10: 0-7869-4073-5
ISBN-13: 978-0-7869-4073-8
620-95015740-001-EN

U.S., CANADA,
ASIA, PACIFIC, & LATIN AMERICA
Wizards of the Coast, Inc.
P.O. Box 707
Renton, WA 98057-0707
+1-800-324-6496

EUROPEAN HEADQUARTERS
Hasbro UK Ltd
Caswell Way
Newport, Gwent NP9 0YH
GREAT BRITAIN
Save this address for your records.

Visit our web site at www.wizards.com

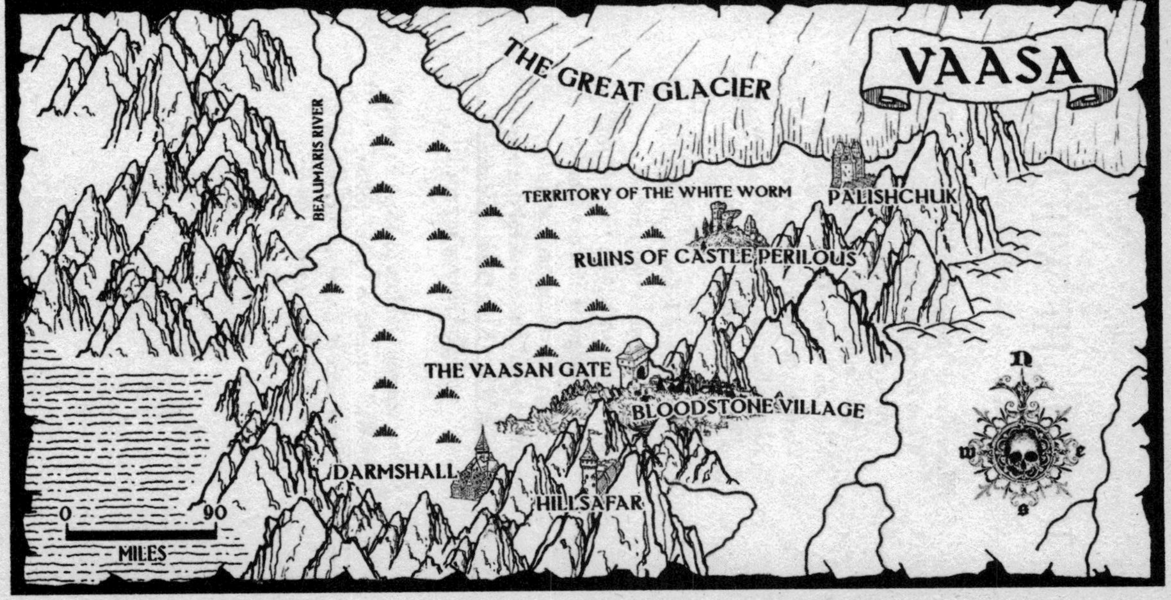
VAASA
THE GREAT GLACIER
BEAUMARIS RIVER
TERRITORY OF THE WHITE WORM
PALISHCHUK
RUINS OF CASTLE PERILOUS
THE VAASAN GATE
BLOODSTONE VILLAGE
DARMSHALL
HILLSAFAR
0
90
MILES
n
w
e
s

TO KILL THE WITCH-KING

When Gareth's holy sword did flash on high
When Zhengyi's form was shattered.
A blackened flame of detritus
His corporeal form a'tattered.
When did victory's claim ring loudly
When did hearts of hope swollen pride
Rejoice brave men, at Gareth's blow
The pieces of Zhengyi flung wide.

But you cannot kill what is not alive
You cannot strike a notion
You cannot smite with force of arm
The magic of dark devotion.
Thus Gareth's sword did undo
The physical, the corporeal shattered.
The Witch-King focus was denied
The magical essence scattered.

So hearken you children to Mother's words
Walk straight to Father, follow.
For a piece of Zhengyi watches you
In dark Wilderness's hollow.

PRELUDE

The smallish man skated along the magically greased, downward sloping corridor, his feet moving in short stabs to continue scrabbling ahead and keep him upright—no easy task. Wisps of smoke rose from his battered traveling cloak and a long tear showed down the side of his left pant leg, with bright blood oozing beneath.

Artemis Entreri slid into the right hand wall and rolled along it, not using it to break his dizzying dash, for to do so would be to allow the lich to catch sight of him.

And that, above all else, the assassin did not want.

He came around from one roll and planted his arms hard against the wall before him, then shoved out, propelling him diagonally down the narrow hallway. He heard the sound of flames roaring behind him, followed by the strained laughter of Jarlaxle, his drow companion. Entreri recognized that the confident dark elf was trying to unnerve the pursuer with that cackle, but even Entreri heard it for what it was: a discordant sound unevenly roiling above a bed of complete uneasiness.

Few times in their months together had Entreri heard any hint of worry from the collected dark elf, but there was no mistaking it, and that only reinforced his own very real fears.

He was well beyond the illumination of the last torch set along the long corridor by then, but a sudden and violent flash from behind him brightened the way, showing him that the corridor ended abruptly a dozen feet beyond and made a sharp right turn. The assassin took full note of that perpendicular course, his only chance, for in that flash, he saw clearly the endgame of the lich's nasty trap: a cluster of sharpened spikes sticking out from the wall.

Entreri hit the left hand wall and again went into a roll. On one turn, he sheathed his trademark jeweled dagger, and on the next he managed to slip his sword, Charon's Claw, into its scabbard on his left hip. With his hands free, he better controlled his skid along the wall. The floor was more slippery than an icy decline in a windless cavern in the Great Glacier itself, but the walls were smooth and solid stone. His hands worked hard each time he came around, and his feet skidded and spun in place as he rolled his shoulders to keep himself upright. He approached the sharp turn and the abrupt, deadly ending.

He yelled as another thunderous explosion rocked the corridor behind him. The assassin shoved off with all his strength as he came around, timing it perfectly for maximum effect. Turning, he threw his upper body forward to strengthen the movement, cutting him across the hallway to the side passage. As soon as his feet slid off that main corridor, he stumbled, for the magical grease abruptly ended. He caught the corner and pulled himself back to it, going in hard, face up against the wall. He glanced back only once, and in the dim light could see the sharp, barbed tips of the deadly spikes.

He started to peek around, back the way he had come, but he nearly cried out in surprise to see a flailing form charging past him. He tried to grab at Jarlaxle, but the drow eluded him, and Entreri thought his companion doomed on the end of the spikes.

But Jarlaxle didn't hit the spikes. Somehow, some way, the drow pulled up short, whipped to the left, and slammed hard into the wall opposite Entreri. The assassin tried to reach out but yelped and fell back behind the corner as a bolt of blue-white lightning streaked past, exploding in a shower of stinging sparks as it crashed against the back wall, shearing off several of the spikes in the process.

Entreri heard the cackle of the lich, an emaciated, skeletal creature, partially covered in withered skin. He resisted the urge to sprint away down the side corridor and growled in defiance instead.

"I knew you'd get me killed!" he snapped at Jarlaxle.

Trembling with fury, Entreri leaped back into the middle of the main, slippery corridor.

"Come on then, spawn of Zhengyi!" the assassin roared.

The lich came into sight, black tattered robes fluttering out behind it, lipless face, rotted brown and skeletal white, grinning wide.

Entreri went for his sword, but when the lich reached out with bony fingers, the assassin instead thrust his gloved hand out before him. Again Entreri screamed—in defiance, in denial, in rage—as another lightning bolt blasted forth.

Entreri felt as if he was in a hot, stinging wind. He felt the burn and tingle of tremendous energies bristling around him. He was down on his knees but didn't know it. He had been thrown back to the wall, just below the spikes, but he didn't even register the firm footing of the base of the back wall against his feet. He was still reaching forward with the enchanted glove, arm shaking badly, sparks of blue and white spinning in the air and disappearing into the glove.

None of it registered to the assassin, whose teeth were clenched so forcefully that he couldn't even yell any louder than a throaty growl.

Spots danced before his eyes, and waves of dizziness assailed him.

He heard the taunting cackle of the lich.

Instinctively, he shoved off the wall, angling back to his left and the side corridor. He got one foot planted on that non-greased surface and sprang back up. He drew his sword, blinded still, and scrambled along the side passage's edge, then leaped out as fast and as far as he could, swiping Charon's Claw wildly and having no idea if he was anywhere near the lich.

He was.

The dark blade came down, sparks dancing around it, for the glove had caught the bulk of the energy from the lightning bolt and released it back through the metal of its companion sword.

The lich, surprised at how far and how fast the opponent had come, threw an arm up to block, and Charon's Claw sheared it off at the elbow. Entreri's strike would have destroyed the creature then, except the impact with the arm provided the conduit for the release of the lightning's energy.

Again the explosion sent Entreri sliding back to the wall to slam in hard and low.

The shrieking of the lich forced the assassin to reach out and retrieve his scattered senses. He turned himself around, his hand slapping the floor until he once again grasped the hilt of Charon's Claw. He looked up the corridor just in time to see the lich retreating, cloak aflame.

"Jarlaxle?" the assassin asked, glancing back to his right, to where the drow had been pressed up against the wall.

Confused to see only the wall, Entreri looked back into the corner, expecting to see a charred lump of drow.

But no, Jarlaxle was just . . . gone.

Entreri stared at the wall and inched himself into the corridor opposite. Off the greased section, he regained his footing and nearly jumped out of his boots when he saw two red eyes staring at him from within the stone of the opposite corridor.

"Well done," said the drow, pressing forward so that the outline of his face appeared in the stone.

Entreri stood there stunned. Somehow Jarlaxle had melded with the stone, as if he had turned the wall into a thick paste and pressed himself inside. Entreri didn't really know why he was so surprised—had his companion ever done anything within the realm of the ordinary?

A loud *click* turned his attention back the other way, up the hall. He knew it immediately as the latch on the door at the top of the ramp, where he and Jarlaxle had met up with, and been chased away by, the lich.

The floor and walls began to tremble with a low, rolling growl.

"Get me out of here," Jarlaxle called to him, the drow's voice gravelly and bubbly, as if he was speaking from under liquid stone, which, in fact, he was. He pushed forth one hand, reaching out to Entreri.

The thunder grew around them. Entreri poked his head around the corner.

Something bad was coming.

The assassin snapped up Jarlaxle's offered hand and tugged hard but found to his surprise that the drow was tugging back.

"No," Jarlaxle said.

Entreri glanced back up the sloping, curving hallway and his eyes went so wide they nearly fell out of his head. The thunder came in the form of a waist-high iron ball rolling fast his way.

He paused and considered how he might dodge, when before his eyes, the ball doubled in size, nearly filling the corridor.

With a shriek, the assassin fell back into the side passage, stumbled, and spun around. He glanced at Jarlaxle's form receding into the stone once more, but he had no time to stop and ponder whether his companion could escape the trap.

Entreri turned and scrambled, finally setting his feet under him and running for his life.

The explosion behind him as the massive iron ball collided with the end wall had him stumbling again, the jolt bringing him to his knees. He glanced back to see that the impact had taken most of the ball's momentum but had not ended its roll. It was coming on again, slowly, but gathering momentum.

Entreri scrambled on all fours, cursing at Jarlaxle yet again for bringing him to this place. He got his feet under him and sprinted away, putting distance between himself and the ball. That wouldn't hold, he knew, for the ball was gaining speed, and the corridor wound along and down the circular tower for a long, long way.

He sprinted and looked for some way out. He shouldered each door as he passed but was not surprised to discover that the trap had sealed the portals. He looked for a place where the ceiling was higher, where he might climb and let the ball pass under him.

But there was nothing.

He glanced back to see if the ball hugged one wall or the other, that he might slide down beside it, but to his amazement, if not his surprise, the ball grew yet again, until its sides practically scraped the walls.

He ran.

The shaking made his teeth hurt in his mouth. Inside the stone, every reverberation as the sphere smashed the wall echoed within Jarlaxle's very being. He felt it to his bones.

For a moment, there was only blackness, then the ball began to recede, rolling along the adjacent corridor.

Jarlaxle took a couple of deep breaths. He had survived that one but feared he might need to find a new companion.

He started to push out of the stone again but stopped when he heard a familiar wheezing laughter.

He fell back, his eyes gazing out through a thin shield of stone, and the lich stood before him. The drow didn't dare breathe or move.

The lich wasn't looking at him but stared down the corridor, cackling victoriously. To Jarlaxle's great relief, the powerful undead creature began moving away, gliding as if it was floating on water.

Jarlaxle wondered if he could just press backward out of the tower then simply levitate to float to the ground and be gone from the place. He noticed the obvious wounds on the lich, though, inflicted by Entreri's reversal of the lightning bolt and the heavy strike of Charon's Claw, and another possibility occurred to him.

He had come with the idea of treasure after all, and it would be such a shame to leave empty handed.

He let the lich glide down around the bend. Then the drow began to push out from the wall.

"It has to be an illusion," Artemis Entreri told himself repeatedly. Iron balls didn't *grow*, after all, but how could it be? It was so real, in sound, shape, and feeling . . . how could any illusion so perfectly mimic such a thing?

The trick to beating an illusion was to set your thoughts fully against it, Entreri knew, to deny it, heart and soul. He glanced back again, and he knew that such was not a possibility.

He tried to block out the mounting thunder behind him. He put his head down and sprinted, forcing himself to recall all the details of the corridor before him. No longer did he try to shoulder the doors, for they were closed to him and he was only losing time in the futile effort.

He pulled the small pack from his back as he ran. He produced a silken cord and grapnel and tossed the bag to the floor behind him, hoping against hope that it would interrupt the gathering momentum of the stone ball.

It didn't. The ball flattened it.

Entreri didn't allow his thoughts to drift back to the rolling menace, but rather, worked the cord frantically, finding its length, picturing the spot in the corridor still some distance ahead, gauging the length he'd need.

The floor shook beneath him. He thought every step would be his last, with the sphere barreling over him.

Jarlaxle had once told him that even an illusion could kill a man if he believed in it.

And Entreri believed in it.

His instincts told him to throw himself flat to the floor off to the side, in the prayer that there would be enough room for him between the sharp corner and the rounded edge of his pursuer. He never found the heart to follow that, though, and he quickly put it out of his mind, focusing instead on the one best chance that lay before him.

Entreri readied the cord as he sprinted for all his life. He bounded around the next bend, the ball right behind. He ran past where the wall at his right-hand side dropped into a waist-high railing, opening into the center of the large tower, with the hallway continuing to circle along its perimeter.

Out went the grapnel, expertly thrown to loop around the large chandelier that was set in the top of the tower's cavernous foyer.

Entreri continued to run flat out. He had no choice, for to stop was to be crushed. The cord was set firmly in his hands, and when the slack wore out he let it force him to veer to the right. It yanked him right over the railing as the rolling iron sphere rushed past, ever so slightly clipping him on the shoulder as he swooped out into the air. He spun in tight circles within the larger circles of the rope's momentum.

He managed to watch the continued descent of the ball, thumping down along the edges, but was quickly distracted by a more ominous creaking from above.

Entreri scrambled, hands working to free up and drop the rope below him. He started his slide with all speed, hand-running down the rope. He felt a sudden jerk, then another as the decorated crystal chandelier pulled free of the ceiling.

Then he was falling.

The door stood slightly ajar. Given the trap he'd set off, there was no reason for the "innkeeper" to believe any of the intruders would be able to get up to it. Still, the drow drew out a wand and expended a bit of its magic. The door and the jamb glowed a solid and unbroken light blue, revealing no traps, magical or mechanical.

Jarlaxle moved up and gingerly pushed through.

The room, the top floor of the tower, was mostly bare. The gray stone walls were unadorned, sweeping in a semi-circle behind a singular large, wide-backed chair of polished wood. Before that seat lay a book, opened atop a pedestal.

No, not a pedestal, Jarlaxle realized as he crept in closer. The book was suspended on a pair of thick tendrils that reached down to the floor of the room and right into the stone.

The drow grinned, knowing that he had found the heart of the construction, the magical architect of the tower itself. He moved in and around the book, giving it a wide berth, then came up on it beside the chair. He glanced at the writing from afar and recognized a few magical runes there. A quick recital of a simple spell brought those runes into better focus and clarity.

He moved closer, drawn in by the power of the tome. He noted then that there were images of runes in the air above it, spinning and dipping to the pages below. He scanned a few lines then dared to flip back to the beginning.

"A book of creation," he mumbled, recognizing some of the early passages as common phrases for such dweomers.

He clasped the book and tried to pull it free, but it would not budge.

So he went back to reading, skimming really, looking for some hint, for some clue as to the secrets of the tower and its undead proprietor.

"You will find not my name in there," came a high-pitched voice that seemed on the verge of keening, a voice held tenuously, like a high note, ready to crack apart into a shivering screech.

Jarlaxle silently cursed himself for getting so drawn in to the book. He regarded the lich, who stood at the open door.

"Your name?" he asked, suppressing his honest desire to scream out in terror. "Why would I desire to know your name, O rotting one?"

"Rot implies death," said the lich. "Nothing could be farther from the truth."

Jarlaxle slowly moved back behind the chair, wanting to put as much distance and as many obstacles between himself and that awful creature as possible.

"You are not Zhengyi," the drow remarked, "yet the book was his."

"One of his, of course."

Jarlaxle offered a tip of his hat.

"You think of Zhengyi as a creature," the lich explained through its ever-grinning, lipless teeth, "as a singular entity. That is your error."

"I know nothing of Zhengyi."

"That much is obvious, or never would you have been foolish enough to come in here!" The lich ended with a sudden upswing in volume and intensity, and it pointed its bony fingers.

Greenish bolts of energy erupted from those digits, one from each, flying through the air, weaving and spinning around the book, the tentacle pedestal, and the chair to explode into the drow.

That was the intent, at least, but each magical bolt, as it approached, swirled to a specific spot on the drow's cloak, just below his throat and to the side, over his collarbone, where a large brooch clasped his cloak. That brooch swallowed the missiles, all ten, without a sound, without a trace.

"Well played," the lich congratulated. "How many can you contain?"

As the undead creature finished speaking, it sent forth another volley.

Jarlaxle was moving then, spinning away from the chair, straight back. The magic missiles swarmed at his back like so many bees, but again, as they neared him, they veered and swooped around him to be swallowed by the brooch.

The drow cut to the side, and as he turned halfway toward his enemy, his arm pumped feverishly. With each retraction, his magical bracer fed another dagger into his hand, which he promptly sent spinning through the air at the lich. So furious was his stream that the fourth dagger was in the air before the first ever struck home.

Or tried to strike home, for the lich was not unprotected. Its defensive wards stopped the daggers just short of the mark and let them fall to the ground with a *clang.*

The lich cackled, and the drow enveloped it in a globe of complete and utter darkness.

A ray of green energy burst from the globe and Jarlaxle was glad indeed that he had moved fast. He watched the ray burrow through the tower wall, disintegrating the stone as it went.

Entreri tucked his feet in tight and angled them to the side so that when he hit, he spun over sidelong. He drew his head in tight and tucked his shoulder, allowing himself to roll over again and again, absorbing the energy of the fifteen foot drop.

He continued to roll, putting as much distance as possible between himself and the point of the chandelier's impact, where glass and crystal shattered and flew everywhere.

When he finally came up to his feet, Entreri stumbled and winced. One ankle threw sharp pains up his leg. He had avoided serious injury but had not escaped unscathed.

Nor had he actually "escaped," he realized a moment later.

He was in the foyer of the tower, a wide, circular room. To the side, high above, the stone ball continued its rumbling roll. Before him, beyond the shattered chandelier and just past the bottom of those perimeter stairs, sat the sealed doorway through which he and Jarlaxle had entered the magical construction. To one side stood the great iron statue the pair had noted when first they had entered, a construct Jarlaxle had quickly identified as a golem.

They had to take care, Jarlaxle had told Entreri, not to set off any triggers that would animate the dangerous iron sentry.

Entreri learned now that they had apparently done just that.

Metal creaked and groaned as the golem came to life, red fires appearing in its hollow eyes. It took a great stride forward, crunching crystal and flattening the twisted metal of the fallen chandelier. It carried no weapon, but Entreri realized that it needed none, for it stood more than twice his height and weighed in at several thousand pounds.

"How do I hurt that?" the assassin whispered and drew forth his blades.

The golem strode closer and breathed forth a cloud of noxious, poisonous fumes.

Far too nimble to be caught by that, Entreri whirled aside. He saw an opening on the lumbering creature and knew that he could get in fast and strike hard.

But he ran instead, making all speed for the sealed doorway.

The golem's iron legs groaned in protest as it turned to pursue.

Entreri hit the door with his shoulder, though he knew it wouldn't open. He exaggerated the impact, though, and moved as if in terrified fury to break through.

On came the golem, focusing solely on him. He waited until the last second and darted along the wall to the left as the golem smashed in hard against the unyielding door. The sentry turned and pursued, iron arms reaching out for the assassin.

Entreri held his ground—for a few moments, at least—and he launched a barrage of swings and stabs that had the golem confused and standing in place for just . . .

. . . long enough.

The assassin bolted out to his left, out toward the center of the room.

The rolling metal sphere thundered down the last expanse of stairs and crashed hard against the back of the unwitting iron golem, driving the construct forward and to the floor, then bouncing across it, denting and twisting the iron. The ball continued rolling on its way, but most of its momentum had been played out on the unfortunate construct.

In the middle of the room, Entreri watched the twitching golem. It tried to rise, but its legs were crushed to uselessness, and it could do no more than lift its upper torso on one arm.

Entreri started to put his weapons away but paused at a sound from above.

He looked up to see many of the ceiling decorations, gargoyle-like statues, flexing their wings.

He sighed.

His darkness globe blinked out and Jarlaxle found himself once again facing the awful undead creature. He looked from the lich to the book and back again.

"You were alive just a few short tendays ago," the dark elf reasoned.

"I am still alive."

"Your existence might stretch the meaning of the word."

"You will soon enough know what it does and does not mean," the lich promised and it raised its bony hands to begin casting another spell.

"Do you miss the feel of the wind upon your living skin?" the drow asked, trying hard to sound truly curious and not condescending. "Will you miss the touch of a woman or the smell of springtime flowers?"

The lich paused.

"Is undeath worth it?" Jarlaxle went on. "And if it is, can you show me the path?"

Few expressions could show on the mostly skeletal face of the lich, of course, but Jarlaxle knew incredulity when he saw it. He kept his eyes locked with the creature's but angled his feet quietly to get him in line for a charge at the book.

"You speak of minor inconveniences against the power I have found," the lich roared at him.

Even as the creature howled, the drow sprang forward, a dagger appearing in one of his hands. He half-turned a page, laughed at the lich, and tore it out, confident that he had found the secret.

A new tear appeared in the lich's ragged cloak.

Jarlaxle's eyes widened and he began to work furiously, tearing page after page, driving his knife into the other half of the tome.

The lich howled and trembled. Pieces of its robe fell away and chips appeared in its bones.

But it wasn't enough, the drow realized, and he knew his error when the torn pages revealed something hidden within the book: a tiny, glowing violet gem in the shape of a skull. That was the secret, he realized, the tie between the lich and the tower. That skull was the key to the whole construction, to the unnatural remnant of Zhengyi, the Witch-King.

The drow reached for it, but his hand blistered and was thrown aside. The drow stabbed at it, but the dagger splintered and flew away.

The lich laughed at him. "We are one! You cannot defeat the tower of Zhengyi nor the caretaker he has appointed."

Jarlaxle shrugged and said, "You could be right."

Then he dropped another globe of darkness over the again-casting lich. The drow slipped on a ring that stored spells as he went. Considering the unearthliness of his foe, he thought to himself, hot or cold? then quickly chose.

He chose correctly. The spell he loosed from the ring covered his body in a shield of warm flames just as the lich blasted forth a conical spray of magical cold so intense that it would have frozen him solid in mid-stride.

Jarlaxle had won the moment, but only the moment, he knew, and in the three choices that loomed before him—counter with offensive magic, leap forth and physically strike, or flee—only one made any practical sense.

He pulled the great feather from his cap and dropped it with a command word that summoned from it a gigantic, flightless bird, an eight-foot avian creature with a thick neck and a deadly and powerful hooked beak. With a thought, the drow sent his summoned diatryma into battle, and he followed its course but broke off its wake as it barreled into the darkness globe.

Jarlaxle prayed that he had angled himself correctly and prayed again that the lich hadn't shut the door. He breathed a lot easier when he came out of the darkness to find himself in the corridor once more, running free.

And running fast.

Oily liquid, the blood of gargoyles, dripped out from the channel along the red blade of Charon's Claw. One winged creature flopped about on the floor, mortally wounded but refusing to stop its futile thrashing. Another dived for Entreri's head as he sprinted across the floor. He ducked low, then lower, then threw himself forward in a roll, fast approaching another of the creatures as it set down on the floor before him.

He came up at full speed, launching himself forward, sword leading.

The gargoyle's stonelike hand swept across, parrying the thrust, and Entreri lowered his shoulder and barreled in hard. The powerful creature hardly moved, and Entreri grunted when he took the brunt of the damage from the collision himself. The assassin's dagger flashed hard into the gargoyle's gut. Entreri growled and leaped back, tearing his hand up as he did and opening a long gash. He started to strike with Charon's Claw again but at the last moment leaped off to the side.

A swooping gargoyle went right past him, slamming headlong into its wounded companion.

Entreri slashed back behind the flying creature, drawing Charon's Claw hard across the passing gargoyle's back. The creature shrieked, and its gutted companion grunted and stumbled backward. Entreri couldn't pursue the tangled creatures, however, for another gargoyle came down fast at him, forcing him back.

He threw himself into a sidelong roll, going right under a table and hard into the base of a long rectangular box standing upright against the wall. He came up with the table above him, lifting it and hoisting it away.

The box creaked open behind him.

The assassin shook his head and glanced back to see a fleshy humanoid creature peering out at him from inside the box. It was larger than he, larger than any man ought to be.

Another golem, he knew, but one of stitched flesh rather than sculpted iron.

The creature reached out and the assassin scrambled away, turning back just long enough to slash Charon's Claw against one of the golem's forearms.

The golem stepped out in pursuit, and behind it, Entreri saw the back of the box, the false bottom, swing wide to reveal a second flesh golem.

"Lovely," the assassin said, diving yet again to avoid another swooping gargoyle.

He glanced up and saw more gargoyles forming, growing across the high ceiling. The tower was coming to life and hatching an army to defend itself.

Entreri sprinted across the foyer but pulled up short as he saw another form coming down at him. He skipped back a few steps and readied his sword, then he recognized the newest opponent.

Jarlaxle tipped his hat, all but stopping his rapid descent, and he gently touched down to the floor.

Entreri spun around and drove his sword again across the outstretched arms of the pursuing flesh golem.

"Glad you found your way here at last," the assassin grumbled.

"But I fear I did not come alone," Jarlaxle warned, his words turning the assassin back around.

The dark elf's gaze led Entreri's up to the high balcony where the lich ran toward the descending stairs.

The lich stopped at the top of the steps and began waggling its bony fingers in the air.

"Stop the beast!" Entreri cried.

He launched a more forceful routine against the golem, slashing Charon's Claw across and using its magic to bring forth a cloud of black ash. With that optical barrier hanging in the air, Entreri rushed by the first golem and stabbed the second one hard.

"We must be leaving," Jarlaxle called to him, as Entreri dived again to avoid a swooping gargoyle.

"The door is sealed!" Entreri shouted back.

"Come, and be quick!" replied the dark elf.

Entreri turned as he went and watched a series of green bolts soar out from the lich's fingers, weaving and darting down. Five struck Jarlaxle—or would have except that they were gathered up by the magic of his brooch—while the other five soared unerringly for Entreri.

The assassin tossed Charon's Claw into the air and held forth his gauntleted hand, absorbing the missiles one after another. He caught his sword and looked back to see Jarlaxle's slender fingers beckoning to him. Up above, the lich charged down the stairs.

Entreri ducked at the last moment, barely avoiding a heavy swipe by one of the golems that would have likely torn his head from his shoulders. He growled and ran at the drow, sheathing his sword as he went.

Jarlaxle grinned, tipped his hat, bent his knees, and leaped straight up.

Entreri leaped, too, catching Jarlaxle by the belt as the drow's levitation sped him upward, dragging Entreri along.

Below, the golems reached and swung futilely at the empty air. From the side came the attack of a gargoyle, the creature clawing hard at Entreri's legs. The assassin deftly retracted, just ahead of the claws, and kicked the gargoyle hard in the face.

He did little damage, however, and the gargoyle came back fast and hard—or started to, but then turned upright, wings beating furiously as Entreri reached out with his gauntlet and sent forth the missiles the lich had just thrown his way. The magic darts crackled into the gargoyle's black skin, making the creature jerk this way and that.

It started right back at the levitating pair, however, and from above came the shrieks of more gargoyles, already "grown" and ready to swoop down from on high.

But the companions had reached the railing by then, and Jarlaxle grabbed on and pulled himself over, Entreri coming fast behind.

"Run back up!" the drow cried. "There is a way!"

Entreri stared at him for a moment, but with gargoyles coming from above and beyond the railing and the lich reversing and running back up the stairs at them, Jarlaxle's order seemed fairly self-evident.

They sprinted back up the sloping corridor, gargoyles flapping at their heels, forcing Entreri to stop with practically every step and fend the creatures off.

"Quickly!" Jarlaxle called.

Entreri glanced at the drow, saw him with wand in his hand, and could only imagine what catastrophe might be contained within that slender item. The assassin bolted ahead.

Jarlaxle pointed the wand behind Entreri and spoke the triggering command word.

A wall of stone appeared in the corridor, blocking it from wall to wall, floor to ceiling. Behind it, they heard the thud as a gargoyle collided with it then the scratching noises as the frustrated creatures clawed at the unyielding stone.

"Run on," Jarlaxle told his companion. "The golems can batter through it in time, and it won't slow the lich at all."

"Cheery," said Entreri.

He sprinted past Jarlaxle and didn't wait for the drow to catch up. He did glance back as the corridor bent out of sight of the wall of stone, and he saw Jarlaxle's warning shining true, for the lich drifted into sight, moving right through the stone barrier.

The door to the tower's apex room was closed but not secured and Entreri shouldered through. He pulled up abruptly, staring at the partially torn book and the glow emanating from its central area. He felt a shove on his back.

"Go to it, quickly!" Jarlaxle bade him.

Entreri ran up to and around the book and its tentacle pedestal. There he saw the glowing skull clearly, pulsing with light and with power.

A thunderous retort slammed the stone door, which Jarlaxle had shoved closed, and it swung in, wisps of smoke rising from a charred point in its center. Beyond it and down the corridor came the lich, magically gliding, eyes glowing, teeth locked in that perpetual undead grin.

"There is no escape," came the creature's words, carried on a cold breath that swept through the room.

"Grab the skull," Jarlaxle instructed.

Entreri reached with his left hand and felt a sudden and painful sting.

"With the gauntlet!" Jarlaxle implored him.

"What?"

"The gauntlet!" shouted the drow, and he staggered and jolted to and fro as a series of green-glowing missiles struck at him. His brooch swallowed the first couple, then it glowed and smoked as the remaining missiles stabbed at him. Two quick steps moved the drow out of the lich's view, and Jarlaxle dived down and rolled to the side of the room.

That left Entreri staring through the open doorway at the lich, cognizant that he had become the primary target of the horrid creature.

But Entreri didn't dive aside. He knew he had nowhere to run and so dismissed the thought out of hand. Staring at his approaching enemy, his face full of determination with not a shred of fear, the assassin raised his gloved hand and dropped it over the glowing skull.

The lich halted as abruptly and completely as if it had smacked into a solid wall.

Entreri didn't see it, however, for the moment his magic-eating glove fell over the throbbing skull, jolts of power arced into the assassin. The muscles in his right arm knotted and twisted. His teeth slammed together, taking the tip off his tongue, and began to chomp uncontrollably, blood spitting out with each opening. His body stiffened and jerked in powerful spasms as red and blue energy bolts crackled and sparked through the gauntlet.

"Hold it fast!" Jarlaxle implored him.

The drow rolled back in sight of the lich, who stood thrashing and clawing at the air. Patches of shadow seemed to grab at the undead creature and eat at it, compacting him, diminishing him.

"You cannot defeat the power of Zhengyi!" the lich growled, words staggered and uneven.

Jarlaxle's laugh was cut short as he glanced back at the snapping and jerking form of Entreri, who shuddered on the edge of disaster, as if he would soon be thrown across the room and through the tower wall. His eyes bulged weirdly, seeming as if they might pop right out. Blood still spilled from his mouth and trickled from his ear as well, and his arm twisted, shoulder popping out of its socket, muscles straining so tightly that they seemed as if they might simply tear apart.

Growls escaped the assassin's mouth. He grimaced, strained, and fought with all his strength and all his willpower. Within the resonance of the growls came the word "No," oft repeated.

It was a challenge. It was a contest.

Entreri met it.

He held on.

Out in the hall, the lich wailed and scratched at the empty air, and with each passing moment, it seemed to diminish just a bit more.

The tower began to sway. Cracks appeared in the walls and floors.

Jarlaxle ran up beside his companion but took care not to touch him.

"Hold on," the drow implored.

Entreri roared in rage and clamped all the tighter. Smoke began to rise from the gauntlet.

The tower swayed more. A great chunk fell out of one wall, and sunlight beamed in.

Out in the hallway, the lich screamed.

"Ah yes, my friend, hold on," Jarlaxle whispered.

The skull pulled out of the book, held fast in the smoldering glove. Entreri managed to turn his hand over and stare at it for just a moment.

Then the tower fell apart beneath him.

Entreri felt a hand on his shoulder. He glanced aside.

Jarlaxle grinned and tipped his hat.

PART 1

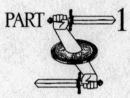

LEGACY OF INTRIGUE

By the time he'd left the crumbling tower, Jarlaxle had already secured the magical skull gem in an undetectable place: an extra-dimensional pocket in one of the buttons of his waistcoat designed to shield magical emanations. Even so, the drow wasn't confident that the item would remain undetected, for it verily throbbed with arcane energy.

Still, he took it with him—leaving his familiar waistcoat would have been more conspicuous—when he went to the palace-tower of Ilnezhara soon after the collapse of the Zhengyi construction. He found his employer lounging in one of her many easy chairs, her feet up on a decorated ottoman and her shapely legs showing through a high slit in her white silk gown that made the material flow down to the floor like a ghostly extension of the creamy-skinned woman. She flipped her long, thick blond hair as Jarlaxle made his entrance, so that it framed her pretty face. It settled covering one of her blue eyes, only adding to her aura of mystery.

Jarlaxle understood that it was all a ruse, of course, an illusion of magnificent beauty. For Ilnezhara's true form was covered in copper-colored scales and sported great horns and a mouth filled with rows of fangs each as long as the drow's arm. Illusion or not, however, Jarlaxle certainly appreciated the beauty reclining before him.

"It was a construct of Zhengyi," the dragon-turned-woman stated, not asked.

"Indeed it would seem," the drow answered, flipping off his wide-brimmed hat to reveal his bald head as he dipped a fancy bow.

"It was," Ilnezhara stated with all certainty. "We have traced its creation while you were away."

"Away? You mean inside the tower. I was away at your insistence, please remember."

"It was not an accusation, nor were we premature in sending you and your friend to investigate. My sister happened upon some more information quite by accident and quite unexpectedly. Still, we do not know how this construct was facilitated, but we know now, of course, that it was indeed facilitated, and we know by whom."

"It was a book, a great and ancient tome," Jarlaxle replied.

Ilnezhara started forward in her chair but caught herself. There was no denying the sparkle of interest in her blue eyes, so the drow let the tease hang in the air. He stood calm and unmoving, allowing a moment of silence slip past, forcing Ilnezhara's interest.

"Produce it then."

"I cannot," he admitted. "The tower was constructed by the magic of the book and controlled by the power of a lich. To defeat the latter, Artemis and I had to destroy the former. There was no other way."

Ilnezhara winced. "That is unfortunate," she said. "A book penned by Zhengyi would be most interesting, beneficial . . . and profitable."

"The tower had to be destroyed. There was no other way."

"Had you killed the lich, the effect would have been the same. The tower would have died, if not fallen, but no more of its defenses would have risen against you. Perhaps my sister and I might even have given the tower to you and Entreri as an expression of our gratitude."

Despite the empty promise, there was more than a little hint of frustration in the dragon's voice, Jarlaxle noted.

"An easy task?" he replied, letting his voice drip with sarcasm.

Ilnezhara harrumphed, waved her hand dismissively, and said, "It was a minor mage from Heliogabalus, a fool named Herminicle Duperdas. Could a man with such a name frighten the great Jarlaxle? Perhaps my sister and I overestimated you and your human friend."

Jarlaxle dipped another bow. "A minor mage in life, perhaps, but a lich is a lich, after all."

Again, the dragon harrumphed, and rolled her blue eyes. "He was a middling magic-user at most—many of his fellow students considered him a novice. Even in the undead state, he could not have proven too formidable for the likes of you two."

"The tower itself was aiding in his defense."

"We did not send you two in there to destroy the place, but to scout it and pilfer it," Ilnezhara scolded. "We could have easily enough destroyed it on our own."

"Pray do, next time."

The dragon narrowed her eyes, reminding Jarlaxle that he would be wise to take more care.

"If we do not benefit from your services, Jarlaxle, then we do not need you," Ilnezhara warned. "Is that truly the course you desire?"

A third bow came her way. "No, milady. No, of course not."

"Herminicle found the book and underestimated it," Ilnezhara explained, seeming as if she had put the disagreement out of her mind. "He read it, as foolish and curious wizards usually will, and it consumed him, taking his magic and his life-force as its own. The book bound him to the tower as the tower bound itself to him. When you destroyed the bonds—the book—you stole the shared force from both, sending both tower and lich to ruin."

"What else might we have done?"

"Had you killed the lich, perhaps the tower would have crumbled," came another female voice, one a bit deeper, less feminine, and less melodious than that of Ilnezhara. Jarlaxle wasn't really surprised to see Tazmikella walk out from behind a screen at the back of the large, cluttered room. "But likely not, though you would have destroyed the force that had initially given it life and material. In either event, the danger would have passed, but the book would have remained. Hasn't Ilnezhara already told you as much?"

"Please learn this lesson and remember it well," Ilnezhara instructed, and she teasingly added, "for next time."

"Next time?" Jarlaxle didn't have to feign interest.

"The appearance of this book confirms to us what we already suspected," Tazmikella explained. "Somewhere in the wastelands of Vaasa, a trove of the Witch-King has been uncovered. Artifacts of Zhengyi are

revealing themselves all about the land."

"It has happened before in the years since his fall," Ilnezhara went on. "Every so often, one of the Witch-King's personal dungeons is found, one of his cellars opened wide, or a tribe of monsters is defeated, only for the victors to find among the beasts weapons, wands, or other magical items of which the stupid creatures had no comprehension."

"We suspected that one of Zhengyi's libraries, perhaps his only library, has recently been pilfered," added Tazmikella. "A pair of books on the art of necromancy—true tomes and not the typical ramblings of self-important and utterly foolish wizards—were purchased in Halfling Downs not a month ago."

"By you, I presume," said Jarlaxle.

"By our agents, of course," Ilnezhara confirmed. "Agents who have been more profitable than Jarlaxle and Entreri to date."

Jarlaxle laughed at the slight and bowed yet again. "Had we known that destroying the lich might have preserved the book, then we would have fought the beastly creature all the more ferociously, I assure you. Forgive us our inexperience. We have not long been in this land, and the tales of the Witch-King are still fresh to us."

"Inexperience, I suspect, is not one of Jarlaxle's failings," said Tazmikella, and her tone revealed to the drow her suspicions that perhaps he was holding back something from his recent adventure in the tower.

"But fear not, I am a fast study," he replied. "And I fear that I—we—cannot replicate our errors with this tower should another one appear." He held up a gauntlet, black with red stitching, and turned it over to show the hole in the palm. "The price of an artifact in defeating the magic of the book."

"The gauntlet accompanying Entreri's mighty sword?" asked Tazmikella.

"Aye, though the sword has no hold over him with or without it. In fact, since his encounter with the shade, I do believe the sword fancies him. Still, our excursion proved quite costly, for the gauntlet had many other valuable uses."

"And what would you have us do about that?" asked Ilnezhara.

"Recompense?" the drow dared ask. "We are weakened without the gauntlet, do not doubt. Our defenses against magic-users have just been greatly depleted. Certainly that cannot be beneficial, given our duties to you."

The sisters looked to each other and exchanged knowing smiles.

"If this tome has surfaced, we can expect other Zhengyian artifacts," Tazmikella said.

"That the tome made its way this far south tells us that someone in Vaasa has uncovered a trove of Zhengyi's artifacts," Ilnezhara added. "Such powerful magical items do not like to remain dormant. They find a way to resurface, again and again, to the bane of the world."

"Interesting . . ." the drow started, but Tazmikella cut him short.

"More so than you understand," she insisted. "Gather your friend, Jarlaxle, for the road awaits you—one that we might all find quite lucrative."

It was not a request but a demand, and since the sisters were, after all, dragons, it was not a demand the drow meant to ignore. He noted something else in the timbre of the sisters' voices, however, that intrigued him at least as much as the skull-shaped remnant of the Zhengyian construct. They were feigning excitement, as if a great adventure and potential gain awaited them all, but behind that, Jarlaxle clearly heard something else.

The two mighty dragons were afraid.

In the remote, cold northland of Vaasa, a second skull, a greater skull, glowed hungrily. It felt the fall of its little sister in Damara keenly, but not with the dread of one who had lost a family member. No, distant events were simply the order of things. The other skull, the human skull, was minor and weak.

What the distant remnant of the Witch-King's godliness had come to know above all else was that the powers could awaken—that the powers would awaken. Too much time had passed in the short memories of the foolish humans and those others who had defeated Zhengyi.

Already they were willing to ply their wisdom and strength against the artifacts of a being so much greater than they, a being far beyond their comprehension. Their hubris led them to believe that they could attain that power.

They did not understand that the Witch-King's power had come from within, not from without, and that his remnants, "the essence of magic scattered," "the pieces of Zhengyi flung wide," in the songs of the silly and naïve bards, would, through the act of creation, overwhelm them and take from them even as they tried to gain from the scattering of Zhengyi.

That was the true promise of the Witch-King, the one that had sent dragons flocking to his side.

The tiny skull found only comfort. The tome that held it was found, the minds about it inquisitive, the memories short. The piece of essence flung wide would know creation, power, and life in death.

Some foolish mortal would see to that.

The dragon growled without sound.

CHAPTER

THE COMPANY

1

Parissus, the Impilturian woman, winced as the red-bearded dwarf drew a bandage tight around her wounded forearm.

"You better be here to tell me that you've decided to deliver the rest of our bounty," she said to the soldier sitting across the other side of the small room where the cleric had set up his chapel. Her appearance, with broad shoulders and short-cropped, disheveled blond hair, added menace to her words, and anyone who had ever seen Parissus wield her broadsword would say that sense of menace was well-placed.

The man, handsome in a rugged manner, with thick black hair and a full beard, and skin browned by many hours out in the sun, seemed quite amused by it all.

"Don't you smile, Davis Eng," said the woman's female companion, a half-elf, much smaller in build than Parissus.

She narrowed her gaze then widened her eyes fiercely—and indeed, those eyes had struck fear into many an enemy. Light blue, almost gray, Calihye's eyes had been the last image so many opponents had seen. Those eyes! So intense that they made many ignore the hot scar on the woman's right cheek, where a pirate's gaff hook had caught her and nearly torn her face off, tearing a jagged line from her cheek through the edge of her thin lips and to the middle of her chin. Her eyes seemed even more startling because of the contrast between them and her long black hair, and the angular elf's features of a face that, had it not been for the scar, could not have been considered anything but beautiful.

Davis Eng chuckled. "What do you think, Pratcus?" he asked the dwarf cleric. "That little wound of hers seem ugly enough to have been made by a giant?"

"It's a giant's ear!" Parissus growled at him.

"Small for a giant," Davis Eng replied, and he fished into his belt pouch and produced the torn ear, holding it up before his eyes. "Small for an ogre, I'd say, but you might talk me out of the coin for an ogre's bounty."

"Or I might cut it out of your hide," said Calihye.

"With your fingernails, I hope," the soldier replied, and the dwarf laughed.

Parissus slapped him on the head, which of course only made him laugh all the louder.

"Every tenday it's that same game," Pratcus remarked, and even surly Calihye couldn't help but chuckle a bit at that.

For indeed, every tenday when it came time for the payout of the bounties, Davis Eng, she, and Parissus played their little game, arguing over the number of ears—goblin, orc, bugbear, hobgoblin, and giant—the successful hunting pair had delivered to the Vaasan Gate.

"Only a game because that one's meaning to pocket a bit of Ellery's coin," Calihye said.

"*Commander* Ellery," Davis Eng corrected, and his voice took on a serious tone.

"That, or he can't count," said Parissus, and she groaned again as Pratcus tugged the bandage into place. "Or can't tell the difference between an ogre and a giant. Yes, that would be it, I suppose, since he's not set foot outside of Damara in years."

"I did my fighting," the man argued.

"In the Witch-King War?" Parissus snapped back. "You were a child."

"Vaasa is not nearly as untamed as she was after the fall of the Witch-King," said Davis Eng. "When I first joined the Army of

Bloodstone, monsters of every sort swarmed over these hills. If King Gareth had seen fit to pay a bounty in those first months, his treasury would have been cleared of coin, do not doubt."

"Kill any giants?" asked Calihye, and the man glared at her. "You're sure they weren't ogres? Or goblins, even?"

That brought another laugh from Pratcus.

"Bah, that one's always had a problem in measuring things," Parissus added. "So they're saying in Ironhead's Tavern and in Muddy Boots and Bloody Blades. But he's not one for consistency, I'm thinking, because if he's measuring now like he's measuring then, sure that he'd be certain we'd given him a titan's ear!"

Pratcus snorted and jerked, and Parissus ended with a squeal as he inadvertently twisted the bandage.

Calihye was laughing too, and after a moment, even Davis Eng joined in. He had never been able to resist those two, when all was said and done.

"I'll call it a giant, then," he surrendered. "A *baby* giant."

"I noted nothing on the bounty charts about age," Calihye said as Davis Eng began to count out the coins.

"A kill is a kill," Davis Eng agreed.

"You've been taking a particular interest in our earnings these last tendays," Calihye said. "Is there a reason?"

Pratcus started to chuckle, tipping the women off. Parissus pulled her hand back from him and glowered at him. "What do you know?"

Pratcus looked at Davis Eng, who similarly chuckled and nodded.

"Yer friend's passed Athrogate," the dwarf priest explained, and he glanced over at Calihye. "He'll be back in a couple o' tendays, and he's not to be pleased that all his time away has put him in back o' Calihye in bounties earned."

The look that crossed between Parissus and Calihye was one more of concern than of pride. Was that honor really a desired one, considering the disposition of Athrogate and his known connections to the Citadel of Assassins?

"And you, Parissus, are fast closing in on the dwarf," Davis Eng added.

Davis Eng tossed a small bag of silver to Calihye and said, "He'll fume and harrumph and run about in a fury when he gets back. He'll make stupid little rhymes about you both. Then he'll go out and slaughter half of the monsters in Vaasa, just to put you two in your place. He'll probably hire wagons out, just to carry back the ears."

Neither woman broke a smile.

"Ah, but these two can pace Athrogate," Pratcus said.

Davis Eng laughed and so did Calihye, and Parissus a moment later. Could anyone truly pace Athrogate?

"He's got a fire inside of him that I've never seen the likes of before," Calihye admitted. "And never does he run faster than when there's a hundred enemies standing in his way."

"But we're there, right beside him, and I mean to pass him, too," Parissus said, allowing her pride to finally spill forth. "When our fellow hunters look at the board outside of Ironhead's, they're going to see the names Parissus and Calihye penned right there on top!"

"Calihye and Parissus," the half-elf corrected.

Davis Eng and Pratcus burst into laughter.

"Only because we're being generous on this last kill," said Davis Eng.

"It was a giant!" both women said together.

"After that," the soldier replied. "You two were dead before you got to the wall, had not Commander Ellery rushed out. That alone should negate the bounty."

"So says yourself, bluster-blunder!" Calihye roared in defiance. "We had the goblins beat clean. Was your own fellow who wanted a piece of the fight for himself. He's the one Ellery needed saving."

"*Commander* Ellery," came a call from the doorway, and all four heads turned to regard the important woman herself, striding into the room.

Pratcus tried to appear sober and respectful, but giggles kept escaping his mouth as he tugged hard to tighten down Parissus's bandage.

"Commander Ellery," Calihye said in deference, and she offered a slight bow in apology. "A title well-earned, though all titles seem to fall hard from my lips. I beg your pardon, Commander Ellery, Lady Dragonsbane."

"Given the occasion, your indiscretion is of no concern," said Ellery, trying not to appear flushed by the complimentary use of her surname, Dragonsbane, a name of the greatest renown all across the Bloodstone Lands. Technically, Ellery's last name was Peidopare, though Dragonsbane immediately preceded that name, and the half-elf's use of the more prominent family name was certainly as great a compliment as anyone could possibly pay to Ellery. She was tall and slim, but there was nothing frail about her frame, for she had seen many battles and had wielded her heavy axe since childhood. Her eyes were wide-set and bright blue, her skin tanned, but still delicate, and dotted with many freckles about her nose. Those did not detract from her beauty, though, but rather enhanced it, adding a touch of girlishness to a face full of intensity and power. "I wanted to add this to the bounty." She pulled a small pouch from her belt and tossed it to Calihye. "An additional reward from the Army of Bloodstone for your heroic work."

"We were discussing whether Athrogate would be pleased when he returns," Davis Eng explained, and that thought brought a grin to Ellery's face.

"I expect he'll not take the demotion to runner-up as well as Mariabronne accepted Athrogate's ascent."

"With all respect to Athrogate," Parissus remarked, "Mariabronne the Rover has more Vaasan kills to his credit than all three of us together."

"A point hard to argue, though the ranger accepts no bounty and takes no public acclaim," said Davis Eng, and the way he spoke made it apparent that he was drawing a distinction between Mariabronne the Rover, a name legendary throughout Damara, and the two women.

"Mariabronne made both his reputation and his fortune in the first few years following Zhengyi's demise," Ellery added. "Once King Gareth took note of him and knighted him, there was little point for Mariabronne to continue to compete in the Vaasan bounties. Perhaps our two friends here, and Athrogate, will find similar honor soon."

"Athrogate knighted by King Gareth?" Davis Eng said, and Pratcus was bobbing so hard trying to contain his laughter at the absurd image those words conjured that he nearly fell right over.

"Well, perhaps not that one," Ellery conceded, to the amusement of them all.

Something just didn't feel right, didn't smell right.

His face showed the hard work, the battles, of more than twenty years. He was still handsome, though, with his unkempt brown locks and his scruffy beard. His bright brown eyes shone with the luster of youth more fitting of a man half his age, and that grin of his was both commanding and mischievous, a smile that could melt a woman on the spot, and one that the nomadic warrior had often put to good use. He had risen through the ranks of the Bloodstone Army in those years during the war with the Witch-King, and had moved beyond even those accolades upon his release from the official service of King Gareth after Zhengyi's fall.

Mariabronne the Rover, he was called, a name that almost every man, woman, and child in Damara knew well, and one that struck a chord of fear and hatred in the monsters of Vaasa. For the ending of his service in the Bloodstone Army had only been the beginning of Mariabronne's service to King Gareth and the people of the two states collectively known as the Bloodstone Lands. Working out of the northern stretches of the Bloodstone Pass, which connected Vaasa and Damara through the towering Galena Mountains, Mariabronne had served as tireless bodyguard to the workers who had constructed the massive Vaasan Gate. More than anyone else, even more so than the men and women surrounding King Gareth himself, Mariabronne the Rover had worked to tame wild Vaasa.

The progress was slow, so very slow, and Mariabronne doubted he'd see Vaasa truly civilized in his lifetime. But ending the journey wasn't the point. He could not solve all the ills of the world, but he could help his fellow men walk the path that would eventually lead to that.

But something smelled wrong. Some sensation in the air, some sixth sense, told the ranger that great trials might soon be ahead.

It must have been Wingham's summons, he realized, for had the old half-orc ever bade someone to his side before? Everything with Wingham—Weird Wingham, he was called, and proudly called himself—prompted suspicion, of course, of the curious kind if not the malicious. But what could it be, Mariabronne wondered? What sensation was upon the wind, darkening the Vaasan sky? What omen of ill portent had he noted unconsciously out of the corner of his eye?

"You're getting old and timid," he scolded himself.

Mariabronne often talked to himself, for Mariabronne was often alone. He wanted no partner for his hunting or for his life, unless it was a temporary arrangement, a warm, soft body beside him in a warm, soft bed. His responsibilities were beyond the call of his personal desires. His visions and aspirations were rooted in the hope of an entire nation, not the cravings of a single man.

The ranger sighed and shielded his eyes against the rising sun as he looked east across the muddy Vaasan plain that morning. Summer had come to the wasteland, though the breeze still carried a chilly bite. Many of the more brutish monsters, the giants and the ogres, had migrated north hunting the elk herds, and without the more formidable enemies out and about, the smaller humanoid races—orcs and goblins, mostly—were keeping out of sight, deep in caves or high up among the rocks.

As he considered that, Mariabronne let his gaze linger to the left, to the south, and the vast wall-fortress known as the Vaasan Gate.

Her great portcullis was up, and the ranger could see the dark dots of adventurers issuing forth to begin the morning hunt.

Already there was talk of constructing more fortified keeps north of the great gate, for the numbers of monsters there were declining and the bounty hunters could no longer be assured of their silver and gold coins.

Everything was going as King Gareth had planned and desired. Vaasa would be tamed, mile by mile, and the two nations would merge as the single entity of Bloodstone.

But something had Mariabronne on edge. Some feeling warned him far in the recesses of his mind, that the dark had not been fully lifted from the wild land of Vaasa.

"Wingham's summons is all," he decided, and he moved back to the sheltered dell and began to collect his gear.

Commander Ellery paced the top of the great wall that was the Vaasan gate a short while later. She hardly knew the two women, Calihye and Parissus, who had ascended so far and so fast among the ranking of bounty hunters, and in truth, Ellery was not fond of the little one, Calihye. The half-elf's character was as scarred as her formerly pretty face, Ellery knew. Still, Calihye could fight with the best of the warriors at the gate and drink with them as well, and Ellery had to admit, to herself at least, that she took a bit of private glee at seeing a woman attain the highest rank on the bounty board.

They had all been laughing about Athrogate's reaction, but Ellery understood that it truly was no joke. She knew the dwarf well, though few realized that the two had forged such a partnership of mutual benefit, and she understood that the dwarf, whatever his continual bellowing laughter might indicate, did not take well to being surpassed.

But all accolades to Calihye, and soon to Parissus, the niece of Gareth Dragonsbane thought. However she might feel about the little one—and in truth, the big one was a bit crude for Ellery's tastes, as well—she, Athrogate, and everyone else at the Vaasan Gate had to admit their prowess. Calihye and Parissus were fine fighters and better hunters. Monstrous prey had thinned severely about the Vaasan Gate, but those two always seemed to find more goblins or orcs to slaughter. Rare was the day that Calihye and Parissus left the fortification to return without a bag of ears.

And yes, it did sit well with Ellery that a pair of women, among the few at the Vaasan Gate, had achieved so much. Ellery knew well from personal experience how difficult it was for a woman, even a dwarf female, to climb the patriarchal ranks of the warrior class, either informally as a bounty hunter or formally in the Army of Bloodstone. She had earned her rank of commander one fight and one argument at a time. She had battled for every promotion and every difficult assignment. She had earned her mighty axe from the hand of the ogre who wielded it and had earned the plume in her great helmet through deed and deed alone.

But there were always those voices, whispers at the edges of her consciousness, people insisting under their breath that the woman's heritage, boasting of both the names of Tranth and particularly of Dragonsbane, served as explanation for her ascent.

Ellery moved to the northern lip of the great wall, planted her hands on the stone railing and looked out over the wasteland of Vaasa. She served under many men in the Army of Bloodstone who had not seen half the battles she had waged and won. She served under many men in the Army of Bloodstone who did not know how to lead a patrol, or set a proper watch and perimeter around an evening encampment. She served under many men in the Army of Bloodstone whose troops ran out of supplies regularly, all on account of poor planning.

Yet those doubting voices remained, whispering in her head and beating in heart.

CHAPTER
LOOKING IN THE MIRROR
2

"You are a weapon of disproportion," Artemis Entreri whispered. He sat on the edge of his bed in the small apartment, staring across the room at his signature weapon, the jeweled dagger. It hung in the wall an inch from the tall mirror, stuck fast from a throw made in frustration just a moment before. Its hilt had stopped quivering, but the way the candlelight played on the red garnet near the base of the pommel made it seem as if the weapon was still moving, or as if it was alive.

It does not satisfy you to wound, Entreri thought, or even to kill. No, that is not enough.

The dagger had served Entreri well for more than two decades. He had made his name on the tough streets of Calimport, clawing and scratching from his days as a mere boy against seemingly insurmountable obstacles. He had been surrounded by murderers all of his life, and had bettered them at their own game. The jeweled dagger hanging in the wall had played no small part in that. Entreri could use it to do more than wound or kill; he could use its vampiric properties to steal the very life-force from a victim.

But beyond proportion, he thought. You must take everything from your victims—their lives, their very souls. What must it be like, this nothingness you bring?

Entreri snorted softly and helplessly at that last self-evident question. He shifted on the bed just a bit, moving himself so that he could see his reflection in the tall, ornate mirror. When first he had awakened, hoisting the dagger in his hand to let fly, he had taken aim at the mirror, thinking to shatter the glassy reminder out of existence. Only at the last second had he shifted his aim, putting the dagger into the wall instead.

Entreri hated the mirror. It was Jarlaxle's prize, not his. The drow spent far too much time standing in front of the glass, admiring himself, adjusting his hat so that its wide brim was angled just right across his brow. Everything was a pose for that one, and no one appreciated Jarlaxle's beauty more than did Jarlaxle himself. He'd bring his cloak back over one shoulder and turn just so, then reverse the cloak and strike a pose exactly opposite. Similarly, he'd move his eye patch from left eye to right, then back again, coordinating it with the cloak. No detail of his appearance was too minor to escape Jarlaxle's clever eye.

But when Artemis Entreri looked into the mirror, he found himself faced with an image he did not like. He didn't appear anywhere near his more than four decades of life. Fit and trim, with finely-honed muscles and the lean athleticism of a man half his age, few who looked upon Entreri would think him beyond thirty. At Jarlaxle's insistence and constant badgering, he kept his black hair neatly trimmed and parted, left to right, and his face was almost always clean-shaven except for the small mustache he had come to favor. He wore silk clothes, finely cut and fit—Jarlaxle would have it no other way.

There was one thing about Entreri's appearance, however, that the meticulous and finicky drow could not remedy, and as he considered the tone of his skin, the grayish quality that made him feel as if he should be on display in a coffin, Entreri's gaze inevitably slipped back to that jeweled dagger. The weapon had done that to him, had taken the life essence from an extra-dimensional humanoid known as a shade and had drawn it into Entreri's human form.

"It's never enough for you to simply kill, is it?" Entreri asked aloud, and his gaze alternated through the sentence from the dagger to his image in the mirror and back again.

"On the contrary," came a smooth, lyrical voice from the side. "I pride myself on killing only when necessary, and usually I find that to be more than enough to sate whatever feelings spurred me to the deed in the first place."

Entreri turned his head to watch Jarlaxle enter the room, his tall black leather boots clacking loudly on the wooden floor. A moment ago, those boots were making not a whisper of sound, Entreri knew, for Jarlaxle could silence them or amplify them with no more than a thought.

"You look disheveled," the drow remarked. He reached over to the dark wood bureau and pulled Entreri's white shirt from it, then tossed it to the seated assassin.

"I just awakened."

"Ah, the tigress I brought you last night drove you to slumber."

"Or she bored me to sleep."

"You worry me."

If you knew how often the thought of killing you entered my mind, Entreri thought, but stopped as a knowing smirk widened on Jarlaxle's face. Jarlaxle was guessing his thoughts, he knew, if not reading them in detail with some strange magical device.

"Where is the red-haired lass?"

Entreri looked around the small room and shrugged. "I suspect that she left."

"Even with sleep caking your eyes, you remain the perceptive one."

Entreri sighed and glanced back at his dagger, and at his reflection, the side-by-side images eliciting similar feelings. He dropped his face into his hands and rubbed his bleary eyes.

He lifted his head at the sound of banging to see Jarlaxle using the pommel of a dagger to nail some ornament in place on the jamb above the door.

"A gift from Ilnezhara," the drow explained, stepping back and moving his hands away to reveal the palm-sized charm: a silvery dragon statuette, rearing, wings and jaws wide.

Entreri wasn't surprised. Ilnezhara and her sister Tazmikella had become their benefactors, or their employers, or their companions, or whatever else Ilnezhara and Tazmikella wanted, so it seemed. The sisters held every trump in the relationship because they were, after all, dragons.

Always dragons lately.

Entreri had never laid eyes upon a dragon until he'd met Jarlaxle. Since that time, he had seen far too many of the beasts.

"Lightning of the blue," Jarlaxle whispered to the statuette, and the figurine's eyes flared with a bright, icy blue light for just a moment then dimmed.

"What did you just do?"

Jarlaxle turned to face Entreri, his smile beaming. "Let us just say that it would not do to walk through that doorway without first identifying the dragon type."

"Blue?"

"For now," the drow teased.

"How do you know I won't change it on you when you're out?" Entreri asked, determined to turn the tables on the cocky dark elf.

Jarlaxle tapped his eye patch. "Because I can see through doors," he explained. "And the eyes will always give it away." His smile disappeared, and he glanced around the room again.

"You are certain that the tigress has gone?" he asked.

"Or she's become very, very small."

Jarlaxle cast a sour expression Entreri's way. "Is she under your bed?"

"You wear the eye patch. Just look through it."

"Ah, you wound me yet again," said the drow. "Tell me, my friend, if I peer into your chest, will I see but a cavity where your heart should be?"

Entreri stood up and pulled on his shirt. "Inform me if that is the case," he said, walking over to tug his jeweled dagger out of the wall, "that I might cut out Jarlaxle's heart to serve as replacement."

"Far too large for the likes of Entreri, I fear."

Entreri started to respond, but found that he hadn't the heart for it.

"There is a caravan leaving in two days," Jarlaxle informed him. "We might not only find passage to the north but gather some gainful employ in the process. They are in need of guards, you see."

Entreri regarded him carefully and curiously, not quite knowing what to make of Jarlaxle's sudden, ceaseless promotion of journeying to the Gates of Damara, the two massive walls blocking either end of the Bloodstone Pass through the Galena Mountains into the wilderlands of neighboring Vaasa. This campaign for a northern adventure had begun soon after the pair had nearly been killed in their last escapade, and that battle in the strange tower still had Entreri quite shaken.

"Our bona fides, my friend," said the drow, and Entreri's face screwed up even more curiously. "Many a hero is making a name for himself in Vaasa," Jarlaxle explained. "The opportunities for wealth, fame, and reputation are rarely so fine."

"I thought our goal was to make our reputation on the streets of Heliogabalus," Entreri replied, "among potential employers."

"And current employers," Jarlaxle agreed. "And so we shall. But think how much service and profit we might gather from a heroic reputation. It will elevate us from suspicion, and perhaps insulate us from punishment if we are caught in an indiscreet action. A few months at the Vaasan Gate will elevate our reputations more than a few years here in Heliogabalus ever could."

Entreri's eyes narrowed. There has to be something more to this, he thought.

They had been in Damara for several months, and had known about the "opportunities" for heroes in the wilderlands of Vaasa from the beginning—how could they not when every tavern and half the street corners of the city of Heliogabalus were plastered with notices claiming as much? Yet only recently, only since the near disaster in the tower, had Jarlaxle taken to the notion of traveling to the north, something Entreri found quite out of character. Work in Vaasa was difficult, and luxuries nonexistent, and Entreri knew all too well that Jarlaxle prized luxury above all else.

"So what has Ilnezhara told you about Vaasa that has so intrigued you?" Entreri asked.

Jarlaxle's smile came in the form of a wry grin, one that did not deny Entreri's suspicions.

"You know of the war?" the drow asked.

"Little," Entreri admitted. "I have heard the glory of King Gareth Dragonsbane. Who could not, in this city that serves as a shrine to the man and his hero companions?"

"They did battle with Zhengyi, the Witch-King," the drow explained, "a lich of tremendous power."

"And with flights of dragons," Entreri cut in, sounding quite bored. "Yes, yes, I have heard it all."

"Many of Zhengyi's treasures have been uncovered, claimed, and brought to Damara," said Jarlaxle. "But what they have found is a pittance. Zhengyi possessed artifacts, and a hoard of treasure enough to entice flights of dragons to his call. And he was a lich. He knew the secret."

"You hold such aspirations?" Entreri didn't hide the disgust in his voice.

Jarlaxle scoffed at the notion. "I am a drow. I will live for centuries more, though centuries have been born and have died in my lifetime. In Menzoberranzan there is a lich of great power."

"The Lichdrow Dyrr, I know," Entreri reminded him.

"The most wretched creature in the city, by most accounts. I have dealt with him on occasion, enough to know that practically the entirety of his efforts are devoted to the perpetuation of his existence. He has bought eternity for himself, so he is terrified of losing it. It is a wretched existence, as cold as his skin, and a solitary state of being that knows no like company. How many wards must he weave to feel secure, when he has brought himself to the point where he might lose too much to comprehend? No, lichdom is not something I aspire to, I assure you."

"Neither do I."

"But do you realize the power that would come from possessing Zhengyi's knowledge?" the drow asked. "Do you realize how great a price aging kings, fearing their impending death, would pay?"

Entreri just stared at the drow.

"And who can tell what other marvels Zhengyi possessed?" Jarlaxle went on. "Are there treasuries full of powerful magical charms or dragon-sized mounds of gemstones? Had the Witch-King weapons that dwarf the power of your own Charon's Claw?"

"Is there no purpose to your life beyond the act of acquisition?"

That rocked Jarlaxle back on his heels—one of the very few times Entreri had ever seen him temporarily rattled. But of course it passed quickly.

"If it is, it's the purpose of both my life and yours, it would seem," the drow finally retorted. "Did you not cross the face of Faerûn to hunt down Regis and the ruby pendant of Pasha Pook?"

"It was a job."

"One you could have refused."

"I enjoy the adventure."

"Then let us go," said the drow, and he waved his arm in an exaggerated motion at the door. "Adventure awaits! Experiences beyond any we have known, perhaps. How can you resist?"

"Vaasa is an empty frozen tundra for most of the year and a puddle of muddy swamp the rest."

"And below that tundra?" the drow teased. "There are treasures up there beyond our dreams."

"And there are hundreds of adventurers searching for those treasures."

"Of course," the drow conceded, "but none of them know how to look as well as I."

"I could take that two ways."

Jarlaxle put one hand on his hip, turned slightly, and struck a pose. "And you would be correct on both counts," he assured his friend. The drow reached into his belt pouch and brought forth a corn bread cake artistically topped with a sweet white and pink frosting. He held it up before his eyes, a grin widening on his face. "I do so know how to find, and retain, treasure," he said, and he tossed the delicacy to Entreri with the explanation, "A present from Piter."

Entreri looked at the cake, though he was in no mood for delicacies, or any food at all.

"Piter," he whispered.

He knew the man himself was the treasure to which Jarlaxle was referring and not the cake. Entreri and Jarlaxle had liberated the fat chef, Piter McRuggle, from a band of inept highwaymen, and Jarlaxle had subsequently set the man and his family up at a handsome shop in Heliogabalus. The drow knew talent when he saw it, and in Piter, there could be no doubt. The bakery was doing wonderful business, lining Jarlaxle's pockets with extra coin and lining his notebooks with information.

It occurred to Artemis Entreri that he, too, might fall into Jarlaxle's category of found and retained treasures. It was pretty obvious which of the duo was taking the lead and who was following.

"Now, have I mentioned that there is a caravan leaving in two days?" Jarlaxle remarked with that irresistible grin of his.

Entreri started to respond, but the words died away in his throat. What was the point?

Two days later, he and Jarlaxle were rode sturdy ponies, guarding the left flank of a six-wagon caravan that wound its way out of Heliogabalus's north gate.

CHAPTER 3
LIFE IN FUGUE

Entreri crawled out of his tent, rose to his feet and stretched slowly and to his limits. He twisted as he reached up high, the sudden stab in his lower back reminding him of his age. The hard ground didn't serve him well as a bed.

He came out of his stretch rubbing his eyes then glanced around at the tent-filled plain set between towering walls of mountains east and west. Just north of Entreri's camp loomed the gray-black stones and iron of the Vaasan Gate, the northern of the two great fortress walls that sealed Bloodstone Valley north and south. The Vaasan Gate had finally been completed, if such a living work could ever truly be considered finished, with fortresses on the eastern and western ends of the main structure set in the walls of the Galena Mountains. the gate served as the last barrier between Entreri and the wilderness of Vaasa. He and Jarlaxle had accompanied the caravan through the much larger of the two gates, the Damaran Gate, which was still under construction in the south. They had ridden with the wagons for another day, moving northwest under the shadow of the mountain wall, to Bloodstone Village, home of King Gareth—though the monarch was under pressure to move his seat of power to the largest city in the kingdom, Heliogabalus.

Not wanting to remain in that most lawful of places, the pair had quickly taken their leave, moving again to the north, a dozen mile trek that had brought them to the wider, relatively flat area the gathered adventurers had collectively named the Fugue Plane. A fitting title, Entreri thought, for the namesake of the Fugue Plane was rumored to be the extra-dimensional state of limbo for recently departed souls, the region where the newly dead congregated before their final journey to Paradise or Torment. The place between the heavens and the hells.

The tent city was no less a crossroads, for south lay Damara—at peace, united, and prosperous under the leadership of the Paladin King—while north beyond the wall was a land of wild adventure and desperate battle.

And of course, he and Jarlaxle were heading north.

All manner of ruffians inhabited the tent city, the types of people Entreri knew well from his days on Calimport's streets. Would-be heroes, every one—men and a few women who would do anything to make a name for themselves. How many times had the younger Entreri ventured forth with such people? And more often than not, the journey had ended with a conflict between the members of the band. As he considered that, Entreri's hand instinctively went to the dagger sheathed on his hip.

He knew better than to trust ambitious people.

The smell of meat cooking permeated the dew-filled morning air. Scores of breakfast fires dotted the field, and the lizardlike hiss of knives being sharpened broke the calls of the many birds that flitted about.

Entreri spotted Jarlaxle at one such breakfast fire a few dozen yards to the side. The drow stood amidst several tough-looking characters: a pair of men who looked as if they could be brothers—or father and son possibly, since one had hair more gray than black—a dwarf with half his beard torn away, and an elf female who wore her golden hair braided all the way down her back. Entreri could tell by their posture that the four weren't overly confident in the unexpected presence of a dark elf. The positioning of their arms, the slight turn of their shoulders, showed that to a one they were ready for a quick defensive reaction should the drow make any unexpected movements.

Even so, it appeared as if the charming Jarlaxle was wearing away those defenses. Entreri watched as the dark elf dipped a polite bow, pulling off his grand hat and sweeping the ground. His every movement showed an unthreatening posture, keeping his hands in clear sight at all times.

A few moments later, Entreri could only chuckle as those around Jarlaxle began to laugh—presumably at a joke the drow had told. Entreri watched, his expression caught somewhere between envy and admiration, as the elf female began to lean toward Jarlaxle, her posture clearly revealing her increasing interest in him.

Jarlaxle reached out to the dwarf and manipulated his hand to make it seem as if he had just taken a coin out of the diminutive fellow's ear. That brought a moment of confusion, where all four of the onlookers reflexively brought a hand to their respective belt pouches, but it was quickly replaced by howls of laughter, with the younger of the men slapping the dwarf on the back of his head.

The mirth and Entreri's attention were stolen when the thunder of hooves turned the attention of all of them to the north.

A small but powerful black horse charged past the tents, silver armor strapped all about its flanks and chest. Its rider was similarly armored in shining silver plates, decorated with flowing carvings and delicate designs. The knight wore a great helm, flat-topped and plumed with a red feather on the left-hand side. As the horse passed Entreri's position, he noted a well-adorned battle-axe strapped at the side of the thick, sturdy saddle.

The horse skidded to a stop right in front of Jarlaxle and his four companions, and in that same fluid motion the rider slid down to stand facing the drow.

Entreri eased his way over, expecting trouble.

He wondered if the newcomer, tall but slender, might have some elf blood, but when the helm came off and a thick shock of long, fiery red hair fell free, tumbling down her back, Entreri realized the truth of it.

He picked up his pace and moved within earshot and also to

get a better look at her face, and what he saw surely intrigued him. Freckled and dimpled, the knight's complexion clashed with her attire, for it did not seem to fit the garb of a warrior. By the way she stood, and the way she had ridden and dismounted so gracefully despite her heavy armor, Entreri could see that she was seasoned and tough—when she had to be, he realized. But those features also told him that there was another side to her, one he might like to explore.

The assassin pulled up short and considered his own thoughts, surprised by his interest.

"So the rumors are true," the woman said, and he was close enough to hear. "A drow elf."

"My reputation precedes me," Jarlaxle said. He flashed a disarming grin and dipped another of his patented bows. "Jarlaxle, at your service, milady."

"Your reputation?" the woman scoffed. "Nay, dark-skinned one. A hundred whispers speak of you, rumors of the dastardly deeds we can expect from you, certainly, but nothing of your reputation."

"I see. And so you have come to verify that reputation?"

"To witness a dark elf in our midst," the woman replied. "I have never seen such a creature as you."

"And do I meet with your approval?"

The woman narrowed her eyes and began to slowly circle the drow.

"Your race evokes images of ferocity, and yet you seem a frail thing. I am told that I should be wary—terrified, even—and yet I find myself less than impressed by your stature and your hardly-imposing posture."

"Aye, but watch his hands," the dwarf chimed in. "He's a clever one with them slender fingers, don't ye doubt."

"A cutpurse?" she asked.

"Madame, you insult me."

"I ask of you, and I expect an honest answer," she retorted, a tremor of anger sliding into the background of her solid but melodious voice. "Many in the Fugue are known cutpurses who have come here by court edict, to work the wilderness of Vaasa and redeem themselves of their light-fingered sins."

"But I am a drow," Jarlaxle replied. "Do you think there are enough monsters in all of Vaasa that I might redeem the reputation of my heritage?"

"I care nothing for your heritage."

"Then I am but a curiosity. Ah, but you so wound me again."

"A feeling you would do well to acquaint yourself with. You still have not answered my question."

Jarlaxle tilted his head and put on a sly grin.

"Do you know who I am?" the woman asked.

"The way you ask makes me believe that I should."

The woman looked past the drow to the female elf.

"Commander Ellery, of the Army of Bloodstone, Vaasan Gate," the elf recited without pause.

"My full name."

The elf stuttered and seemed at a loss.

"I am Commander Ellery Tranth Dopray Kierney Dragonsbane Peidopare," the woman said, her tone even more imperious than before.

"Labeling your possessions must prove a chore," the drow said dryly, but the woman ignored him.

"I claim Baron Tranth as my uncle; Lady Christine Dragonsbane, Queen of Damara, as my cousin; and King Gareth Dragonsbane himself as my second cousin, once removed."

"Lady Christine and King Gareth?"

The woman squared her shoulders and her jaw.

"Cousins in opposite directions, I would hope," said Jarlaxle.

That brought a less imperious and more curious stare.

"I would hate to think that the future princes and princesses of Damara might carry on their shoulders a second head or six fingers on each hand, after all," the drow explained, and the curious look turned darker. "Ah, but the ways of royalty."

"You mock the man who chased the demon lord Orcus across the planes of existence?"

"Mock him?" Jarlaxle asked, bringing one hand to his chest and looking as if he had just been unexpectedly slapped. "Nothing could be farther from the truth, good Commander Ellery. I express relief that while you claim blood relations to both, their own ties are not so close. You see?"

She steeled her gaze. "I will learn of your reputation," she promised.

"You will wish then that you included D'aerthe in your collection of names, I assure you," the drow replied.

"Jarlaxle D'aerthe?"

"At your service," he said, sweeping into yet another bow.

"And you will be watched closely, drow," Commander Ellery went on. "If your fingers get too clever, or your mannerisms too disruptive, you will learn the weight of Bloodstone judgment."

"As you will," Jarlaxle conceded.

As Ellery turned to leave, he dipped yet another bow. He managed to glance over at Entreri as he did, offering a quick wink and the flash of a smile.

"I leave you to your meal," Ellery said to the other four, pulling herself back into her saddle. "Choose wisely the company you keep when you venture forth into Vaasa. Far too many already lay dead on that wasteland tundra, and far too many lay dead because they did not surround themselves with reliable companions."

"I will heed well your words," Jarlaxle was quick to reply, though they had not been aimed at him. "I was growing a bit leery of the short one anyway."

"Hey!" said the dwarf, and Jarlaxle flashed him that disarming grin.

Entreri turned his attention from the group of five to watch the woman ride away, noting most of all the respectful reactions to her from all she passed.

"She is a formidable one," he said when Jarlaxle appeared at his side a moment later.

"Dangerous and full of fire," Jarlaxle agreed.

"I might have to kill her."

"I might have to bed her."

Entreri turned to regard the drow. Did anything ever unsettle him? "She is a relative of King Gareth," Entreri reminded him.

Jarlaxle rubbed his slender fingers over his chin, his eyes glued to the departing figure with obvious intrigue.

He uttered only a single word in reply: "Dowry."

"Lady Ellery," said Athrogate, a dwarf renowned in the underworld of Damara as a supreme killer. He wore his black beard parted in the middle, two long braids of straight hair running down to mid-chest, each tied off at the end with a band set with a trio of sparkling blue gemstones. His eyebrows were so bushy that they somewhat covered his almost-black eyes, and his ears so large that many speculated he would be able to fly if only he learned how to flap them. " 'E's made hisself some fine company already. Be watchin' that one, I'm tellin' ye. Watchin' or killin' him, for if ye're not, then he's to be killin' us, don't ye doubt."

"It is an interesting turn, if it is anything at all beyond mere coincidence," admitted Canthan Dolittle, a studious looking fellow with beady eyes and a long straight nose. His hair, as much gray as brown, was thin, with a large bald spot atop his head that had turned bright red from a recent sunburn. The nervous, slim fellow rubbed his fingertips together as he spoke, all the while subtly twitching.

"To assume is to invite disaster," the third and most impressive of the group advised. Most impressive to those who knew the truth of him, that is, for the archmage Knellict wore nondescript clothing, with his more prized possessions stored safely away back at the Citadel of Assassins.

Athrogate licked his lips nervously as he regarded the mighty wizard, second only to Timoshenko, the Grandfather of Assassins, in that most notorious guild of killers. As an agent of Tightpurse, the leading thieves guild of Heliogabalus, Athrogate had been assigned to ride along with Jarlaxle and Entreri to Bloodstone Village, and to report to Canthan in the Fugue. He had been quite surprised to find Knellict at the camp. Few names in all the northern Realms inspired fear like that of the archmage of the Citadel of Assassins.

"Have you learned any more of the drow?" Canthan asked. "We know of his dealings with Innkeeper Feepun and the murder of the shade, Rorli."

"And the murder of Feepun," Knellict said.

"You have proof it was brought about by these two?" a surprised Canthan asked.

"You have proof it was not?"

Canthan backed off, not wanting to anger the most dangerous man in the Bloodstone Lands.

"Information of their whereabouts since the incident with Rorli has been incomplete," Knellict admitted.

"They been quiet since then from all that we're seein'," Athrogate replied, his tone revealing that he was eager to please. Though he was answering Canthan, his brown eyes kept darting over to regard Knellict. The archmage, however, quiet and calm, was simply impossible to read. "They done some dealin's with a pair o' intrestin' lady pawnbrokers, but we ain't seen 'em buy nothin' worth nothin'. Might be that they be lookin' more for lady charms than magic charms, if ye're gettin' me meanin'. Been known to fancy the ladies, them two be, especially the dark one."

Canthan glanced back at Knellict, who gave the slightest of nods.

"Keep close and keep wary," Canthan told Athrogate. "If you need us, place your wash-clothes as we agreed and we will seek you out."

"And if yerself's needing me?"

"We will find you, do not doubt," Knellict intervened.

The archmage's tone was too even, too controlled, and despite a desire to hold a tough facade, Athrogate shuddered. He nearly fell over as he bobbed in a bow then scurried away, ducking from shadow to shadow.

"I sense something more about the human," Knellict remarked when he and Canthan were alone.

"I expect they are both formidable."

"Deserving of our respect, indeed," Knellict agreed. "And requiring more eyes than those of the dolt Athrogate."

"I am already at work on the task," Canthan assured his superior.

Knellict gave a slight nod but kept staring across the tent city at Jarlaxle and Entreri as they walked back to their campsite.

Tightpurse had been ready to move on the pair back in Heliogabalus and would have—likely to disastrous results for Tightpurse, Knellict figured—had not the Citadel of Assassins intervened. At the prodding of Knellict, Timoshenko had decided to pay heed to the pair, particularly to that most unusual dark elf who had so suddenly appeared in their midst. Drow were not a common sight on the surface of Toril, and less common in the Bloodstone Lands than in most other regions. Less common in Damara, at least, a land that was quickly moving toward stable law and order under the reign of Gareth Dragonsbane and his band of mighty heroes. Zhengyi had been thrown down, flights of dragons destroyed, and the demon lord Orcus's own wand had been blasted into nothingness. Gareth was only growing stronger, the tentacles of his organizations stretching more ominously in the consolidation of Damara's various feudal lords. He had made no secret of his desire to bring Vaasa under his control as well, uniting the two lands as the single kingdom of Bloodstone. To that end, King Gareth's Spysong network of scouts was growing more elaborate with each passing day.

Timoshenko and Knellict suspected that Vaasa would indeed soon be tamed, and were that to occur, would there remain in all of the region a place for the Citadel of Assassins?

Knellict did well to hide his frown as he considered yet again the continuing trends in the Bloodstone Lands. His eyes did flash briefly as he watched the pair, drow and human, disappear into their tent.

There was a different feeling to the air the moment Jarlaxle and Entreri walked out of the Vaasan side of the wall fortress. The musty scent of peat and thawing decay filled the nostrils of the two, carried on a stiff breeze that held a chilly bite, though summer was still in force.

"She's blowing strong off the Great Glacier today," Entreri had heard one of the guards remark.

He could feel the bone-catching chill as the wind gathered the moisture from the sun-softened ice and lifted it across the muddy Vaasan plain.

"A remarkable place," Jarlaxle noted, scanning the sea of empty brown from under the wide brim of his outrageous hat. "I would send armies forth to do battle to claim this paradise."

The drow's sarcasm didn't sit well with Entreri. He couldn't agree more with the dreary assessment. "Then why are we here?"

"I have already explained that in full."

"You hold to a strange understanding of the term. 'in full.' "

Jarlaxle didn't look at him, but Entreri took some satisfaction in the drow's grin.

"By that, I presume that you mean you have explained it as well as you believe I need to know," Entreri went on.

"Sometimes the sweetest juices can be found buried within the most mundane of fruits."

Entreri glanced back at the wall and let it go at that. They had come out on a "day jaunt," as such excursions were known at the Vaasan Gate, a quick scout and strike mission. All newcomers to the Vaasan Gate were given such assignments, allowing them to get a feel for the tundra. When first the call had gone out for adventurers, there had been no guidance offered for their excursions into the wild. Many had struck right out from the gate and deep into Vaasa, never to be heard from again. But the Army of Bloodstone was offering more instruction and control, and offering it in a way more mandatory than suggestive.

Entreri wasn't fond of such rules, but neither did he hold much desire to strike out any distance from the gate. He did not wish to find his end seeking the bottom of a bottomless bog.

Jarlaxle turned slowly in a circle, seeming to sniff the air as he did. When he came full around, pointing again to the northeast, the general direction of the far-distant Great Glacier, he nodded and tipped his hat.

"This way, I think," the drow said.

Jarlaxle started off, and with a shrug, having no better option, Entreri started after him.

They stayed among the rocky foothills of the Galena Mountains, not wanting to try the muddy, flat ground. That course left them more vulnerable to goblin ambushes, but the pair were not particularly afraid of doing battle against such creatures.

"I thought there were monsters aplenty to be found and vanquished here," Entreri remarked after an hour of trudging around gray stones and across patches of cold standing water. "That is what the posted notices in Heliogabalus claimed, is it not?"

"Twenty gold pieces a day," Jarlaxle added. "And all for the pleasure of killing ten goblins. Yes, that was the sum of it, and perhaps the lucrative bounty proved quite effective. Could it be that all the lands about the gate have been cleared?"

"If we have to trek for miles across this wilderness, then my road is back to the south," said Entreri.

"Ever the optimist."

"Ever the obvious."

Jarlaxle laughed and adjusted his great hat. "Not for many more miles," he said. "Did you not notice the clear sign of adversaries?"

Entreri offered a skeptical stare.

"A print beside the last puddle," Jarlaxle explained.

"That could be days old."

"It is my understanding that such things are not so lasting here on the surface," the drow replied. "In the Underdark, a boot print in soft ground might be a millennium old, but up here. . . ."

Entreri shrugged.

"I thought you were famous for your ability to hunt down enemies."

"That comes from knowing the ways of folk, not the signs on the ground. I find my enemies through the information I glean from those who have seen them."

"Information gathered at the tip of your dagger, no doubt."

"Whatever works. But I do not normally hunt the wilderness in pursuit of monsters."

"Yet you are no stranger to the signs of such wild places," said the drow. "You know a print."

"I know that something made an impression near the puddle," Entreri clarified. "It might have been today, or it might have been several days ago—anytime since the last rain. And I know not what made it."

"We are in goblin lands," Jarlaxle interrupted. "The posted notices told me as much."

"We are in lands full of people pursuing goblins," Entreri reminded.

"Ever the obvious," the drow said.

Entreri scowled at him.

They walked for a few hours, then as storm clouds gathered in the north, they turned back to the Vaasan Gate. They made it soon after sunset, and after a bit of arguing with the new sentries, managed to convince them that they, including the dark elf, had left that same gate earlier in the day and should be re-admitted without such lengthy questioning.

Moving through the tight, well-constructed, dark brick corridors, past the eyes of many suspicious guards, Entreri turned for the main hall that would take them back to the Fugue and their tent.

"Not just yet," Jarlaxle bade him. "There are pleasures a'many to be found here, so I have been told."

"And goblins a'many to kill out there, so you've been told."

"It never ends, I see."

Entreri just stood at the end of the corridor, the reflection of distant campfires twinkling in Jarlaxle's eyes as he looked past his scowling friend.

"Have you no sense of adventure?" the drow asked.

"We've been over this too many times."

"And yet still you scowl, and you doubt, and you grump about."

"I have never been fond of spending my days walking across muddy trails."

"Those trails will lead us to great things," Jarlaxle said. "I promise."

"Perhaps when you tell me of them, my mood will improve," Entreri replied, and the dark elf smiled wide.

"These corridors might lead us to great things, as well," the drow answered. "And I think I need not tell you of those."

Entreri glanced back over his shoulder out at the campfires through the distant, opened doors. He chuckled quietly as he turned back to Jarlaxle, for he knew that resistance was hopeless against that one's unending stream of persuasion. He waved a hand, indicating that Jarlaxle should lead on, then moved along behind him.

There were many establishments—craftsmen, suppliers, but mostly taverns—in the Vaasan Gate. Merchants and entrepreneurs had been quick to the call of Gareth Dragonsbane, knowing that the hearty adventurers who went out from the wall would often be well-rewarded upon their return, given the substantial bounty on the ears of goblins, orcs, ogres and other monsters. So too had the ladies of the evening come, displaying their wares in every tavern, often congregating around the many gamblers who sought to take the recent earnings from foolish and prideful adventurers.

All the taverns were much the same, so the pair moved into the first in line. The sign on the wall beside the doorway read: "Muddy Boots and Bloody Blades," but someone had gouged a line across it and whittled in: "Muddy Blades and Bloody Boots" underneath, to reflect the frustrations of late in even finding monsters to kill.

Jarlaxle and Entreri moved through the crowded room, the drow drawing more than a few uncomfortable stares as he went. They split up as they came upon a table set with four chairs where only two men were sitting, with Jarlaxle approaching and Entreri melting back in to the crowd.

"May I join you?" the drow asked.

Looks both horrified and threatening came back at him. "We're waiting on two more," one man answered.

Jarlaxle pulled up a chair. "Very well, then," he said. "A place to rest my weary feet for just a moment then. When your friends arrive, I will take my leave."

The two men glanced at each other.

"Be gone now!" one snarled, coming forward in his chair, teeth bared as if he meant to bite the dark elf.

Next to him, his friend put on an equally threatening glower, and crossed his large arms over his strong chest, expression locked in a narrow-eyed gaze. His eyes widened quickly, though, and his arms slid out to either side—slow, unthreatening—when he felt the tip of a dagger against the small of his back.

The hard expression on the man who'd leaned toward Jarlaxle similarly melted, for under the table, the drow had drawn a tiny dagger, and though he couldn't reach across with that particular weapon, with no more than a thought, he had urged the enchanted dirk to elongate. Thus, while Jarlaxle hadn't even leaned forward in his chair, and while his arms had not come ahead in the least, the threatening rogue felt the blade tip quite clearly, prodding against his belly.

"I have changed my mind," Jarlaxle said, his voice cold. "When your friends arrive, they will need to find another place to repose."

"You smelly . . ."

"Hardly."

". . . stinking drow," the man went on. "Drawing a weapon in here is a crime against King Gareth."

"Does the penalty equate to that for gutting a fool?"

"Stinking drow," the man repeated. He glanced over at his friend then put on a quizzical expression.

"One at me back," said the other. "I'm not for helping ye."

The first man looked even more confused, and Jarlaxle nearly laughed aloud at the spectacle, for behind the other man stood the crowd of people that filled every aisle in Muddy Boots and Bloody Blades, but none appeared to be taking any note of him. Jarlaxle recognized the gray cloak of the nearest man and knew it to be Entreri.

"Are we done with this foolery?" Jarlaxle asked the first man.

The man glared at him and started to nod then shoved off the table, sliding his chair back.

"A weapon!" he cried, leaping to his feet and pointing at the drow. "He drew a weapon!"

A tumult began all around the table, with men spinning and leaping into defensive stances, many with hands going to their weapons, and some, like Entreri, using the moment to melt away into the crowd. Like all the taverns at the Vaasan Gate, however, Muddy Boots and Bloody Blades anticipated such trouble. Within the span of a couple of heartbeats—the time it took Jarlaxle to slide his own chair back and hold up his empty hands, for the sword had shrunken to nothingness at his bidding—a group of Bloodstone soldiers moved in to restore order.

"He poked me with a sword!" the man cried, jabbing his finger Jarlaxle's way.

The drow pasted on a puzzled look and held up his empty hands. Then he adjusted his cloak to show that he had no sword, no weapon at all, sheathed at his belt.

That didn't stop the nearest soldier from glowering at him, though. The man bent low and did a quick search under the table.

"So clever of you to use my heritage against me," Jarlaxle said to the protesting man. "A pity you didn't know I carry no weapon at all."

All eyes went to the accuser.

"He sticked me, I tell ye!"

"With?" Jarlaxle replied, holding his arms and cape wide. "You give me far too much credit, I fear, though I do hope the ladies are paying you close heed."

A titter of laughter came from one side then rumbled into a general outburst of mocking howls against the sputtering man. Worse for him, the guards seemed less than amused.

"Get on your way," one of the guards said to him, and the laughter only increased.

"And his friend put a dagger to me back!" the man's still-seated companion shouted, drawing all eyes to him. He leaped up and spun around.

"Who did?" the soldier asked.

The man looked around, though of course Entreri was already all the way to the other side of the room.

"Him!" the man said anyway, pointing to one nearby knave. "Had to be him."

A soldier moved immediately to inspect the accused, and indeed the man was wearing a long, slender dirk on his belt.

"What foolishness is this?" the accused protested. "You would believe that babbling idiot?"

"My word against yours!" the other man shouted, growing more confident that his guess had been accurate.

"Against *ours,* you mean," said another man.

More than a dozen, all companions of the newly accused man, came forward.

"I'm thinking that ye should take more care in who ye're pointing yer crooked fingers at," said another.

The accuser was stammering. He looked to his friend, who seemed even more ill at ease and helpless against the sudden turn of events.

"And I'm thinking that the two of you should be going," said the accused knave.

"And quick," added another of his rough-looking friends.

"Sir?" Jarlaxle asked the guard. "I was merely trying to take some repose from my travels in Vaasa."

The soldier eyed the drow suspiciously for a long, long while, then turned away and started off.

"You cause any more disturbances and I'll put you in chains," he warned the man.

"But . . ."

The protesting victim ended with a gasp as the soldier behind him kicked him in the behind, drawing another chorus of howls from the many onlookers.

"We're not for leaving!" the man's companion stubbornly decreed.

"Ye probably should be thinking that one over a bit more," warned one of the friends of the man he had accused, stealing his bluster.

It all quieted quickly, and Jarlaxle took a seat at the vacant table, waving a serving wench over to him.

"A glass of your finest wine and one of your finest ale," he said.

The woman hesitated, her dark eyes scanning him.

"No, he was not falsely accusing me," Jarlaxle confided with a wink.

The woman blushed and nearly fell over herself as she moved off to get the drinks.

"By this time, another table would have opened to us," said Entreri, taking a seat across from the drow, "without the dramatics."

"Without the *enjoyment,"* Jarlaxle corrected.

"The soldiers are watching us now."

"Precisely the point," explained the drow. "We want all at the Vaasan Gate to know of us. Reputation is exactly the point."

"Reputation earned in battle with common enemies, so I thought."

"In time, my friend," said Jarlaxle. His smile beamed at the young woman, who had already returned with the drinks. "In time," he repeated, and he gave the woman a piece of platinum—many times the price of the wine and ale.

"For tales of adventure and those we've yet to make," he said to her slyly, and she blushed again, her dark eyes sparkling as she considered the coin. Her smile was shy but not hard to see as she scampered off.

Jarlaxle turned and held his glass up to Entreri then repeated his last sentence as a toast.

Defeated yet again by the drow's undying optimism, Entreri tapped his glass with his own and took a long and welcomed drink.

CHAPTER

NOT SO MUCH AN ORC

4

Arrayan Faylin pulled herself out of her straw bed, dragging her single blanket along with her and wrapping it around her surprisingly delicate shoulders. That distinctly feminine softness was reflective of the many surprises people found when looking upon Arrayan and learning of her heritage.

She was a half-orc, like the vast majority of residents in the cold and windswept city of Palishchuk in the northeastern corner of Vaasa, a settlement in clear view of the towering ice river known as the Great Glacier.

Arrayan had human blood in her as well—and some elf, so her mother had told her—and certainly her features had combined the most attractive qualities of all her racial aspects. Her reddish-brown hair was long and so soft and flowing that it often seemed as if her face was framed by a soft red halo. She was short, like many orcs, but perhaps as a result of that reputed elf blood, she was anything but stocky. While her face was wide, like that of an orc, her other features—large emerald green eyes, thick lips, narrow angled eyebrows, and a button nose—were distinctly un-orclike, and that curious blend, in Arrayan's case, had a way of accenting the positives of the attributes from every viewing angle.

She stretched, yawned, shook her hair back from her face, and rubbed her eyes.

As the mental cobwebs of sleep melted away, Arrayan's excitement began to mount. She moved quickly across the room to her desk, her bare feet slapping the hard earth floor. Eagerly she grabbed her spellbook from a nearby shelf, used her other hand to brush clear the center area of the desk then slid into her chair, hooking her finger into the correct tab of the organized tome and flipping it open to the section entitled "Divination Magic."

As she considered the task ahead of her, her fingers began trembling so badly that she could hardly turn the page.

Arrayan fell back in her seat and forced herself to take a long, deep breath. She went over the mental disciplines she had learned several years before in a wizard's tower in distant Damara. If she could master control as a teenager, certainly in her mid-twenties she could calm her eagerness.

A moment later, she went back to her book. With a steady hand, the wizard examined her list of potential spells, discerned those she believed would be the most useful, including a battery of magical defenses and spells to dispel offensive wards before they were activated, and began the arduous task of committing them to memory.

A knock on her door interrupted her a few minutes later. The gentle nature of it, but with a sturdiness behind it to show that the light tap was deliberate, told her who it might be. She turned in her chair as the door pushed open, and a huge, grinning, tusky face poked in. The half-orc's wide eyes clued Arrayan in to the fact that she had let her blanket wrap slip a bit too far, and she quickly tightened it around her shoulders.

"Olgerkhan, well met," she said.

It didn't surprise her how bright her voice became whenever that particular half-orc appeared. Physically, the two seemed polar opposites, with Olgerkhan's features most definitely favoring his orc side. His lip was perpetually twisted due to his huge, uneven canines, and his thick forehead and singular bushy brow brought a dark shadow over his bloodshot, jaundiced eyes. His nose was flat and crooked, his face marked by small and uneven patches of hair, and his forehead sloped out to peak at that imposing brow. He wasn't overly tall, caught somewhere between five-and-a-half and six feet, but he appeared much larger, for his limbs were thick and strong and his chest would have fit appropriately on a man a foot taller than he.

The large half-orc licked his lips and started to move his mouth as if he meant to say something.

Arrayan pulled her blanket just a bit tighter around her. She really wasn't overly embarrassed; she just didn't give much thought to such things, though Olgerkhan obviously did.

"Are they here?" Arrayan asked.

Olgerkhan glanced around the room, seeming puzzled.

"The wagons," Arrayan clarified, and that brought a grin to the burly half-orc's face.

"Wingham," he said. "Outside the south gate. Twenty colored wagons."

Arrayan returned his smile and nodded, but the news did cause her a bit of trepidation. Wingham was her uncle, though she had never really seen him for long enough stretches to consider herself to be close to him and his traveling merchant band. In Palishchuk, they were known simply as "Wingham's Rascals," but to the wider region of the Bloodstone Lands, the band was called "Weird Wingham's Wacky Weapon Wielders."

"The show is everything," Wingham had once said to Arrayan, explaining the ridiculous name. "All the world loves the show." Arrayan smiled even wider as she considered his further advice that day when she was but a child, even before she had gone to Damara to train in arcane magic. Wingham had explained to her that the name, admittedly stupid, was a purposeful calling card, a way to confirm the prejudices of the humans, elves, dwarves, and other races. "Let them think us stupid," Wingham had told her with a great flourish, though Wingham always spoke with a great flourish. "Then let them come and bargain with us for our wares!"

Arrayan realized with a start that she had paused for a long while. She glanced back at Olgerkhan, who seemed not to have noticed.

"Any word?" she asked, barely able to get the question out.

Olgerkhan shook his thick head. "They dance and sing but little so far," he explained. "Those who have gone out to enjoy the circus have not yet returned."

Arrayan nodded and jumped up from her seat, moving swiftly across the room to her wardrobe. Hardly considering the action, she let her blanket fall—then caught it at the last moment and glanced back sheepishly to Olgerkhan.

He averted his eyes to the floor and crept back out of the room, pulling the door closed.

He was a good one, Arrayan realized, as she always tried to remind herself.

She dressed quickly, pulling on leather breeches and a vest, and a thin belt that held several pouches for spell components, as well as a set of writing materials. She started for the door but paused and pulled a blue robe of light material from the wardrobe, quickly removing the belt then donning the robe over her outfit. She rarely wore her wizard robes among her half-orc brethren, for they considered the flowing garment with its voluminous sleeves of little use, and the only fashion the males of Palishchuk seemed to appreciate came from her wearing less clothing, not more.

The robe was for Wingham, Arrayan told herself as she refitted the belt and rushed to the door.

Olgerkhan was waiting patiently for her, and she offered him her arm and hurried him along to the southern gate. A crowd had gathered there, flowing out of the city of nearly a thousand residents. Filtering her way through, pulling Olgerkhan along, Arrayan finally managed to get a glimpse of the source of the commotion, and like so many of her fellow Palishchukians, she grinned widely at the site of Weird Wingham's Wacky Weapon Wielders. Their wagon caravan had been circled, the bright colors of the canopies and awnings shining brilliantly in the glow of the late-summer sun. Music drifted along the breeze, carrying the rough-edged voice of one of Wingham's bards, singing a tale of the Galena Mountains and Hillsafar Hall.

Like all the rest swept up in the excitement, Arrayan and Olgerkhan found themselves walking more swiftly then even jogging across the ground, their steps buoyed by eagerness. Wingham's troupe came to Palishchuk only a few times each year, sometimes only once or twice, and they always brought with them exotic goods bartered in faraway lands, and wondrous tales of distant heroes and mighty villains. They entertained the children and adults alike with song and dance, and though they were known throughout the lands as difficult negotiators, any of the folk of Palishchuk who purchased an item from Weird Wingham knew that he was getting a fine bargain.

For Wingham had never forgotten his roots, had never looked back with anything but love on the community that had worked so hard to allow him and all the other half-orcs of his troupe to shake off the bonds of their heritage.

A pair of jugglers anchored the main opening into the wagon circle, tossing strange triple-bladed knives in an unbroken line back and forth to each other, the weapons spinning over the heads of nervous and delighted Palishchukians as they entered or departed. Just inside the ring, a pair of bards performed, one playing a curved, flutelike instrument while the other sang of the Galenas. Small kiosks and racks of weapons and clothing filled the area, and the aroma of a myriad of exotic perfumes and scented candles aptly blanketed the common smell of rot in the late summer tundra, where plants grew fast and died faster through the short mild period, and the frozen grip on the topsoil relinquished, releasing the fragrance of seasons past.

For a moment, a different and rarely felt aspect of Arrayan's character filtered through, and she had to pause in her step to bask in the vision of a grand ball in a distant city, full of dancing, finely dressed women and men. That small part of her composite didn't hold, though, when she noticed an old half-orc, bent by age, bald, limping, but with a sparkle in his bright eyes that could not help but catch the eye, however briefly, of any young woman locking stares with him.

"Mistress Maggotsweeper!" the old half-orc cried upon seeing her.

Arrayan winced at the correct recital of her surname, one she had long ago abandoned, preferring her Elvish middle name, Faylin. That didn't turn her look sour, though, for she knew that her Uncle Wingham had cried out with deep affection. He seemed to grow taller and straighter as she closed on him, and he wrapped her in a tight and powerful hug.

"Truly the most anticipated, enjoyable, lovely, wonderful, amazing, and most welcome sight in all of Palishchuk!" Wingham said, using the lyrical barker's voice he had so mastered in his decades with his traveling troupe. He pushed his niece back to arms' length. "Every time I near Palishchuk, I fear that I will arrive only to discover that you are off to Damara or somewhere other than here."

"But you know that I would return in a hurry if I learned that you were riding back into town," she assured him, and his eyes sparkled and his crooked smile widened.

"I have ridden back with some marvelous finds again, as always," Wingham promised her with an exaggerated wink.

"As always," she agreed, her tone leading.

"Playing coy?"

At Arrayan's side, Olgerkhan grunted disapprovingly, even threateningly, for "coy"—*koi* in the Orcish tongue—was the name of a very lewd game.

Wingham caught the hint in the overprotective warning and backed off a step, eyeing the brutish Olgerkhan without blinking. Wingham hadn't survived the harshness of Vaasa for so many years by being blind to any and every potential threat.

"Not *koi*," Arrayan quickly explained to her bristling companion. "He means sly, sneaky. My uncle is implying that I might know something more than I am telling him."

"Ah, the book," said Olgerkhan.

Arrayan sighed and Wingham laughed.

"Alas, I am discovered," said Arrayan.

"And I thought that your joy was merely at the sight of me," Wingham replied with feigned disappointment.

"It is!" Arrayan assured him. "Or would be. I mean . . . there is no . . . Uncle, you know . . ."

Though he was obviously enjoying the sputtering spectacle, Wingham mercifully held up a hand to calm the woman.

"You never come out to find me on the morning of the first day, dear niece. You know that I will be quite busy greeting the crowd. But I am not surprised to see you out here this day, this early. Word has preceded me concerning Zhengyi's writing."

"Is it truly?" Arrayan asked, hardly able to get the words out of her mouth.

She practically leaped forward as she spoke them, grabbing at her uncle's shoulders. Wingham cast a nervous glance around them.

"Not here, girl. Not now," he quietly warned. "Come tonight when the wagons' ring is closed and we shall speak."

"I cannot wait for—" Arrayan started to say, but Wingham put a finger over her lips to silence her.

"Not here. Not now.

"Now, dear lady and gentleman," Wingham said with his showman's flourish. "Do examine our exotic aromas, some created as far away as Calimshan, where the wind oft carries mountains of sand so thick that you cannot see your hand if you put it but an inch from your face!"

Several other Palishchukian half-orcs walked by as Wingham spoke, and Arrayan understood the diversion. She nodded at her uncle, though she was truly reluctant to leave, and pulled the confused Olgerkhan away. The couple browsed at the carnival for another hour or so then Arrayan took her leave and returned to her small house. She spent the entirety of the afternoon pacing and wringing her hands. Wingham had confirmed it: the book in question was Zhengyi's.

Zhengyi the Witch-King's own words!

Zhengyi, who had dominated dragons and spread his darkness across all the Bloodstone Lands. Zhengyi, who had mastered magic and death itself. Mighty beings such as the Witch-King did not pen tomes idly or carelessly. Arrayan knew that Wingham understood such things. The old barker was no stranger to items of magical power. The fact that Wingham wouldn't even discuss the book publicly told Arrayan much; he knew that it was a special item. She had to wait, and the sunset couldn't come fast enough for her.

When it arrived, when finally the bells began to signal the end of the day's market activity, Arrayan grabbed a wrap and rushed out her door. She wasn't surprised to find Olgerkhan waiting for her, and together they moved swiftly through the city, out the southern gate, and back to Wingham's circled wagons.

The guards were ushering out the last of the shoppers, but they greeted Arrayan with a nod and allowed her passage into the ring.

She found Wingham sitting at the small table set in his personal wagon, and at that moment he seemed very different from the carnival barker. Somber and quiet, he barely looked up from the table to acknowledge the arrival of his niece, and when she circled him and regarded what lay on the table before him, Arrayan understood why.

There sat a large, ancient tome, its rich black cover made of leather but of a type smoother and thicker than anything Arrayan had ever seen. It invited touching for its edges dipped softly over the pages they protected. Arrayan didn't dare, but she did lean in a bit closer, taking note of the various designs quietly and unobtrusively etched onto the spine and cover. She made out the forms of dragons, some curled in sleep, some rearing and others in graceful flight, and it occurred to her that the book's soft covering might be dragon hide.

She licked her dry lips and found that she was suddenly unsure of her course. Slowly and deliberately, the shaken woman took the seat opposite her uncle and motioned for Olgerkhan to stay back by the door.

A long while passed, and Wingham showed no signs of breaking the silence.

"Zhengyi's book?" Arrayan mustered the courage to ask, and she thought the question incredibly inane, given the weight of the tome.

Finally, Wingham looked up at her and gave a slight nod.

"A spellbook?"

"No."

Arrayan waited as patiently as she could for her uncle to elaborate, but again, he just sat there. The uncustomary behavior from the normally extroverted half-orc had her on the edge of her seat.

"Then what—?" she started to ask.

She was cut short by a sharp, "I don't know."

After yet another interminable pause, Arrayan dared to reach out for the tome. Wingham caught her hand and held it firmly, just an inch from the black cover.

"You have equipped yourself with spells of divination this day?" he asked.

"Of course," she answered.

"Then seek out the magical properties of the tome before you proceed."

Arrayan sat back as far as she could go, eyeing her uncle curiously. She had never seen him like this, and though the sight made her even more excited about the potential of the tome, it was more than a little unsettling.

"And," Wingham continued, holding fast her hand, "you have prepared spells of magical warding as well?"

"What is it, uncle?"

The old half-orc stared at her long and hard, his gray eyes flashing with intrigue and honest fear.

Finally he said, "A summoning."

Arrayan had to consciously remember to breathe.

"Or a sending," Wingham went on. "And no demon is involved, nor any other extra-planar creatures that I can discern."

"You have studied it closely?"

"As closely as I dared. I am not nearly proficient enough in the Art to be attempting such a tome as this. But I know how to recognize a demon's name, or a planar's, and there is nothing like that in this tome."

"A spell of divination told you as much?"

"Hundreds of such spells," Wingham replied. He reached down and produced a thin black metal wand from his belt, holding it up before him. "I have burned this empty—thrice—and still my clues are few. I am certain that Zhengyi used his magic to conceal something . . . something magnificent. And certain I am, too, that this tome is a key to unlocking that concealed item, whatever it might be."

Arrayan pulled her hand free of his grasp, started to reach for the book, but changed her mind and crossed both of her hands in her lap. She sat alternately staring at the tome and at her uncle.

"It will certainly be trapped," Wingham said. "Though I have been able to find none—and not for lack of trying!"

"I was told that you only recently found it," said Arrayan.

"Months ago," replied Wingham. "I spoke of it to no one until I had exhausted all of my personal resources on it. Also, I did not want the word of it to spread too wide. You know that many would be interested in such a tome as this, including more than a few powerful wizards of less than sterling reputation."

Arrayan let it all sink in for a moment, and she began to grin. Wingham had waited until he was nearing Palishchuk to let the word slip out of Zhengyi's tome because he had planned all along to give it to Arrayan, his powerful magic-using niece. His gift to her would be her own private time with the fascinating and valuable book.

"King Gareth will send investigators," Wingham explained, further confirming Arrayan's suspicions. "Or a group, perhaps, whose sole purpose will be to confiscate the tome and return it to Bloodstone Village or Heliogabalus, where more powerful wizards ply their craft. Few know of its existence—those who have heard the whispers here in Palishchuk and Mariabronne the Rover."

Arrayan perked up at the mention of Mariabronne, a tracker whose title was nearing legendary status in the wild land. Mariabronne had grown quite wealthy on the monster-ear bounty offered at the Vaasan Gate, so it was rumored. He knew almost everyone, and everyone knew him. Friendly and plain-spoken, cunning and clever, but disarmingly simple, the ranger had a way of putting people—even those well aware of his reputation—into a position of underestimating him. Arrayan had met him only twice, both times in Palishchuk, and had found herself laughing at his many tales, or sitting wide-eyed at his recounting of amazing adventures. He was a tracker by trade, a ranger in service to the ways of the wilderness, but by Arrayan's estimation, he was possessed of a bard's character. There was mischief behind his bright and curious eyes to be sure.

"Mariabronne will ferry word to Gareth's commanders at the Vaasan Gate," Wingham went on, and the sound of his voice broke Arrayan from her contemplations.

His smile as she looked up to regard him told the woman that she had betrayed quite a few of her feelings with her expressions, and she felt her cheeks grow warm.

"Why did you tell anyone?" she asked.

"This is too powerful a tome. Its powers are beyond me."

"And yet you will allow me to inspect it?"

"Your powers with such magic are beyond mine."

Arrayan considered the daunting task before her in light of the deadline Wingham's revelations to Mariabronne had no doubt put upon her.

"Fear not, dear niece, my words to Mariabronne were properly cryptic—more so even than the whispers I allowed to drift north to Palishchuk, where I knew they would find your ears. He likely remains in the region and nowhere near the Gate, and I fully expect to see him again before he goes to Gareth's commanders. You will have all the time you need with the tome."

He offered Arrayan a wink then motioned to the black-bound book.

The woman stared at it but did not move to turn over its cover.

"You have not prepared any magical wards," Wingham reasoned after a few long moments.

"I did not expect . . . it is too . . ."

Wingham held up his hand to stop her. Then he reached back behind his chair and pulled out a leather bag, handing it across to Arrayan.

"Shielded," he assured her as she took it. "No one watching you, even with a magical eye, will understand the power of the item contained within this protected satchel."

Arrayan could hardly believe the offer. Wingham meant to allow her to take the book with her! She could not hide her surprise as she continued to consider her uncle, as she replayed their long and intermittent history. Wingham didn't know her all that well, and yet he would willingly hand over what might prove to be the most precious item he had ever uncovered in his long history of unearthing precious artifacts? How could she ever prove herself worthy of that kind of trust?

"Go on, niece," Wingham bade her. "I am not so young and am in need of a good night's sleep. I trust you will keep your ever-curious uncle informed of your progress?"

Hardly even thinking of the movement, Arrayan lifted out of her chair and leaned forward, wrapping Wingham with her slender arms and planting a huge kiss on his cheek.

CHAPTER 5

BODY COUNT

Entreri came leaping down the mountainside, springing from stone to stone, never keeping his path straight. He was hardly aware of his movements, yet every step was perfect and in complete balance, for the assassin had fallen into a state of pure battle clarity. His movements came with fluid ease, his body reacting just below his level of consciousness perfectly in tune with what he instinctively determined he needed to do. Entreri moved at a full sprint as easily on the broken, jagged trail down the steep slope of the northern Galena foothills, a place where even careful hikers might turn an ankle or trip into a crevice, as if he was running across a grassy meadow.

He skipped down along a muddy trail as another spear flew over his head. He started around a boulder in his path, but went quickly up its side instead, then sprang off to the left of the boulder to the top of another large stone. A quick glance back showed him that the goblins were closing on his flank, moving down easier ground in an attempt to cut him off before he reached the main trail.

A thin smile showed on Entreri's face as he leaped from that second boulder back to the ground, rushing along and continuing to veer to the west, his left.

The crackle of a thunderbolt back the other way startled him for a moment, until he realized that Jarlaxle had engaged the monsters with a leading shot of magic.

Entreri brushed the thought away. Jarlaxle was far from him, leaving him on his own against his most immediate enemies.

On his own. Exactly the way Artemis Entreri liked it.

He came to a straight trail running north down the mountainside and picked up his pace into a full run, with goblins coming in from the side and hot on his heels. As he neared the bottom of the trail, he spun and swiped his magical sword in an arc behind him, releasing an opaque veil of dark ash from its enchanted, blood-red blade. As he came around to complete the spin, Entreri fell forward into a somersault, then turned his feet as he rolled back up, throwing his momentum to the side and cutting a sharp turn behind one boulder. He hooked his fingers as he skidded past and caught himself, then threw himself flat against the stone and held his breath.

A slight gasp told the assassin the exact position of his enemies. He drew his jeweled dagger, and as the first goblin flashed past, he struck, quick and hard, a jab that put the vicious blade through the monster's ribs.

The goblin yelped and staggered, lurching and stumbling, and Entreri let it go without further thought. He came out around the rock in a rush and dived to his knees right before the swirl of ash.

Goblin shins connected on his side, and the monster went tumbling. A third came close behind, tangling with the previous as they crashed down hard.

Entreri scrambled forward and rolled over, coming to his feet with his back to the remaining ash. Without even looking, he flipped his powerful sword in his hand and jabbed it out behind him, taking the fourth goblin in line right in the chest.

The assassin turned and retracted his long blade, snapping it across to pick off a thrusting spear as the remaining goblin pair composed themselves for a coordinated attack.

"Getsun innk's arr!" one goblin instructed the other, which Entreri understood as "Circle to his left!"

Entreri, dagger in his right hand, sword in his left, went down in a crouch, weapons out wide to defend against both.

"Beenurk!" the goblin cried. "Go more!"

The other goblin did as ordered and Entreri started to turn with it, trying to appear afraid. He wanted the bigger goblin to focus on his expression, and so it apparently did, for Entreri sneakily flipped the dagger over in his grip then snapped his hand up and out. He was still watching the circling goblin when he let fly at the other one, but he knew that he had hit the mark when the bigger goblin's next command came out as nothing more than a blood-filled gurgle.

The assassin slashed his sword across, creating another ash field, then leaped back as if meaning to retrieve his dagger. He stopped in mid-stride, though, and reversed momentum to charge back at the pursuing goblin. He rolled right over the goblin's thrusting sword, going out to the humanoid's right, a complete somersault that landed Entreri firmly back on his feet in a low crouch. As he went, he flipped Charon's Claw from his left hand to his right. He angled the blade perfectly so that when he stood, the blade came up right under the goblin's ribs.

His momentum driving him forward, Entreri lifted the goblin right from the ground at the tip of his fine sword, the creature thrashing as it slid down the blade.

Entreri snapped a retraction, then spun fast, bringing the blade across evenly at shoulder level, and when he came around, the fine sword crossed through the squealing goblin's neck so cleanly that its head remained attached only until the creature fell over sideways and hit the ground with a jolt.

The assassin leaped away, grabbing at the dagger hilt protruding from the throat of the kneeling, trembling goblin. He gave a sudden twist and turn as he yanked the weapon free, ensuring that he had taken the creature's throat out completely. By then, the two he had tripped were back up and coming in—though tentatively.

Entreri watched their eyes and noted that they were glancing more often to the side than at him. They wanted to run, he knew, or they were hoping for reinforcements.

And the latter was not a fleeting hope, for Entreri could hear goblins all across the mountainside. Jarlaxle's impetuousness had dropped them right into the middle of a tribe of the creatures. They had only seen three at the campfire, milling around a boiling kettle of wretched smelling stew. But behind that campfire was a concealed cave opening.

Jarlaxle hadn't heard Entreri's warning, or he hadn't cared, and their sudden assault had brought forth a stream of howling monsters.

He was outnumbered two to one, but Entreri had the higher ground, and he used it to facilitate a sudden, overpowering attack. He came forward stabbing with his sword then throwing it out across to the left, and back to the right. He heard the ring of metal on metal as the goblin off to his right parried the backhand with its own sword, but that hardly interrupted Entreri's flow.

He strode forward, sending Charon's Claw in a motion down behind him, then up over his shoulder. He came forward in a long-reaching downward swipe, one designed to cleave his enemy should the goblin leap back.

To its credit, it came forward again.

But that was exactly what Entreri had anticipated.

The goblin's sword stabbed out—and a jeweled dagger went against the weapon's side and turned it out, altering the angle just enough to cause a miss. His hand working in a sudden blur, Entreri sent his dagger up and over the blade, then down and around, twisting as he went to turn the sword out even more. He slashed Charon's Claw across to his right as he did, forcing the other goblin to stay back, and continued his forward rush, again rolling his dagger, turning the sword even farther. And yet again, he rolled his blade, walking it right up the goblin's sword. He finally disengaged with a flourish, pulling his dagger in close, then striking out three times in rapid succession, drawing a grunt with each successive hit.

Bright blood widening around the three punctures, the goblin staggered back.

Confident that it was defeated, Entreri had already turned

by that point, his sword working furiously to fend the suddenly ferocious attacks by the other goblin. He parried a low thrust, a second heading for his chest, and picked off a third coming in at the same angle.

The goblin screamed and pressed a fourth thrust.

Entreri flung his dagger.

The goblin moaned once then went silent. Its sword tip drifted toward the ground as its gaze, too, went down to consider the dagger hilt protruding from its chest.

It looked back at Entreri. Its sword fell to the ground.

"My guess is that it hurts," said the assassin.

The goblin fell over dead.

Entreri kicked the dead creature over onto its back then tugged his dagger free. He glanced up the mountainside to the continuing tumult, though he saw no new enemies there. Back down the mountain, he noted that the first goblin that had passed him, the one he had stung in the side, had moved off.

A flash of fire to the side caught his attention. He could only imagine what carnage Jarlaxle was executing.

Jarlaxle ran to the center of a clearing, goblins closing in all around him, spears flying at him from every direction.

His magical wards handled the missiles easily enough, and he was quite confident that the crude monsters possessed none of sufficient magical enhancement to get through the barriers and actually strike him. A dozen spears came out at him and were harmlessly deflected aside, but closely following, coming out from behind every rock surrounding the clearing, it seemed, came a goblin, weapon in hand, howling and charging.

Apparently, the reputation of the dark elves was lost on that particular group of savages.

As he had counted on their magical deficiencies to render their spears harmless, so did Jarlaxle count on the goblins' intellectual limitations. They swarmed in at him, and with a shrug Jarlaxle revealed a wand, pointed it at his own feet, and spoke a command word.

The ensuing fireball engulfed the drow, the goblins, and the whole of the clearing and the rocks surrounding it. Screams of terror accompanied the orange flames.

Except there were no flames.

Completely ignoring his own illusion, Jarlaxle watched with more than a little amusement as the goblins flailed and threw themselves to the ground. The creatures thrashed and slapped at flames, and soon their screams of terror became wails of agony. The dark elf noted some of the dozen enemies lying very still, for so consumed had they been by the illusion of the fireball that the magic had created through their own minds the same result actual flames from such a blast might have wrought.

Jarlaxle had killed nearly half the goblins with a single simple illusion.

Well, the drow mused, not a simple illusion. He had spent hours and hours, burning out this wand through a hundred recharges, to perfect the swirl of flames.

He didn't pat himself on the back for too long, though, for he still had half a dozen creatures to deal with. They were all distracted, however, and so the drow began to pump his arm, calling forth the magic of the bracer he wore on his right wrist to summon perfectly weighted daggers into his hand. They went out in a deadly stream as the drow turned a slow circle.

He had just completed the turn, putting daggers into all six of the thrashing goblins—and into three of the others, just to make sure—when he heard the howling approach of more creatures.

Jarlaxle needed no magical items. He reached inside himself, into the essence of his heritage, and called forth a globe of absolute darkness. Then he used his keen hearing to direct him out of the clearing off to the side, where he slipped from stone to stone away from the goblin approach.

"Will you just stop running?" Entreri asked under his breath as he continued his dogged pursuit of the last wounded goblin.

The blood trail was easy enough to follow and every so often he spotted the creature zigzagging along the broken trail below him. He had badly stung the creature, he believed, but the goblin showed no sign of slowing. Entreri knew that he should just let the creature bleed out, but frustration drove him on.

He came upon one sharp bend in the trail but didn't turn. He sprang atop the rock wall lining the ravine trail and sprinted over it, leaping across another crevice and barreling on straight down the mountainside. He saw the winding trail below him, caught a flash of the running goblin, and veered appropriately, his legs moving on pure instinct to keep him charging forward and in balance along stones and over dark holes that threatened to swallow him up. He tripped more than once, skinning a knee and twisting an ankle, but never was it a catastrophic fall. Hardly slowing with each slight stumble, Entreri growled through the pain and focused on his prey.

He crossed the snaking path and resisted the good sense to turn and follow its course, again cutting across it to the open, rocky mountainside. He crossed the path again, and a few moments later came up on the fourth bend.

Certain he was ahead of his foe, he paused and caught his breath, adjusted his clothing, and wiped the blood from his kneecap.

The terrified, wounded goblin rounded a bend, coming into view. So intent on the trail behind it, the wretch never even saw Entreri as it ran along.

"You could have made this so much easier," Entreri said, drawing his weapons and calmly approaching.

The assassin's voice hit the goblin's sensibilities as solidly as a stone wall would have smacked its running form. The creature squealed and skidded to an abrupt stop, whined pitifully, and fell to its knees.

"Pleases, mister. Pleases," it begged, using the common tongue.

"Oh, shut up," the killer replied.

"Surely you'll not kill a creature that so eloquently begs for its life," came a third voice, one that only surprised Entreri momentarily—until he recognized the speaker.

He had no idea how Jarlaxle might have gotten down that quickly, but he knew better than to be surprised at anything Jarlaxle did. Entreri sheathed his sword and grabbed the goblin by a patch of its scraggly hair, yanking its head back violently. He let his jeweled dagger slide teasingly across the creature's throat, then moved it to the side of the goblin's head.

"Shall I just take its ears, then?" he asked Jarlaxle, his tone showing that he meant to do no such thing and to show no such mercy.

"Always you think in terms of the immediate," the drow replied, and he moved up to the pair. "In those terms, by the way, we should be fast about our business, for a hundred of this one's companions are even now swarming down the mountainside."

Entreri moved as if to strike the killing blow, but Jarlaxle called out and stopped him.

"Look to the long term," the drow bade him.

Entreri cast a cynical look Jarlaxle's way.

"We are competing with a hundred trackers for every ear," the drow explained. "How much better will our progress become with a scout to guide us?"

"A scout?" Entreri looked down at the sniveling, trembling goblin.

"Why of course," said Jarlaxle, and he walked over and calmly moved Entreri's dagger away from the goblin's head. Then he took hold of Entreri's other hand and gently urged it from its grip on the goblin's hair. He pushed Entreri back a step then bent low before the creature.

"What do you say to that?" he asked.

The dumbfounded goblin stared at him.

"What is your name?"

"Gools."

"Gools? A fine name. What do you say, Gools? Would you care to enter into a partnership with my friend and me?"

The goblin's expression did not change.

"Your job will be quite simple, I assure you," said the drow. "Show us the way to monsters—you know, your friends and such—then get out of our way. We will meet you each day—" he paused and looked around—"right here. It seems a fine spot for our discussions."

The goblin seemed to be catching on, finally. Jarlaxle tossed him a shiny piece of gold.

"And many more for Gools where that came from. Interested?"

The goblin stared wide-eyed at the coin for a long while then looked up to Jarlaxle and slowly nodded.

"Very well then," said the drow.

He came forward, reaching into a belt pouch, and brought forth his hand, which was covered in a fine light blue chalky substance. The dark elf reached for the goblin's forehead.

Gools lurched back at that, but Jarlaxle issued a stern warning, bringing forth a sword in his other hand and putting on an expression that promised a painful death.

The drow reached for the goblin's forehead again and began drawing there with the chalk, all the while uttering some arcane incantation—a babbling that any third-year magic student would have known to be incoherent blather.

Entreri, who understood the drow language, was also quite certain that it was gibberish.

When he finished, Jarlaxle cupped poor Gools's chin and forced the creature to look him right in the eye. He spoke in the goblin tongue, so there could be no misunderstanding.

"I have cast a curse upon you," he said. *"If you know anything of my people, the drow, then you understand well that this curse will be the most vicious of all. It is quite simple, Gools. If you stay loyal to me, to us, then nothing will happen to you. But if you betray us, either by running away or by leading us to an ambush, the magic*

of the curse will take effect. Your brains will turn to water and run out your ear, and it will happen slowly, so slowly! You will feel every burn, every sting, every twist. You will know agony that no sword blade could ever approach. You will whine and cry and plea for mercy, but nothing will help you. And even in death will this curse torment you, for its magic will send your spirit to the altar of the Spider Queen Lolth, the Demon Goddess of Chaos. Do you know of her?"

Gools trembled so badly he could hardly shake his head.

"You know spiders?" Jarlaxle asked, and he walked his free hand over the goblin's sweaty cheek. *"Crawly spiders."*

Gools shuddered.

"They are the tools of Lolth. They will devour you for eternity. They will bite"—he pinched the goblin sharply—*"you a million million times. There will be no release from the burning of their poison."*

He glanced back at Entreri, then looked the terrified goblin in the eye once more.

"Do you understand me, Gools?"

The goblin nodded so quickly that its teeth chattered with the movement.

"Work with us, and earn gold," said the drow, still in the guttural language of the savage goblins. He flipped another gold piece at the creature. Gools didn't even move for it, though, and the coin hit him in the chest and fell to the dirt. *"Betray us and know unending torture."*

Jarlaxle stepped back, and the goblin slumped. Gools did manage to retain enough of his wits to reach down and gather the second gold piece.

"Tomorrow, at this time," Jarlaxle instructed. Then, in Common, he began, "Do you think—?"

He stopped and glanced back up the mountainside at the sudden sound of renewed battle.

Entreri and Gools, too, looked up the hill, caught by surprise. Horns began to blow, and goblins squealed and howled, and the ring of metal on metal echoed on the wind.

"Tomorrow!" Jarlaxle said to the goblin, poking a finger his way. "Now be off, you idiot."

Gools scrambled away on all fours, finally put his feet under him, and ran off.

"You really think we'll see that one ever again?" Entreri asked.

"I care little," said the drow.

"Ears?" reminded Entreri.

"You may wish to earn your reputation one ear at a time, my friend, but I never choose to do things the hard way."

Entreri started to respond, but Jarlaxle held up a hand to silence him. The drow motioned up the mountainside to the left and started off to see what the commotion was all about.

"Now I know that I have walked into a bad dream," Entreri remarked.

He and Jarlaxle leaned flat against a rock wall, overlooking a field of rounded stone. Down below, goblins ran every which way, scrambling in complete disarray, for halflings charged among them—dozens of halflings riding armored war pigs.

The diminutive warriors swung flails, blew horns, and threw darts, veering their mounts in zigzagging lines that must have seemed perfectly chaotic to the poor, confused goblins.

From their higher vantage point, however, Entreri and Jarlaxle could see the precision of the halflings' movements, a flowing procession of destruction so calculated that it seemed as if the mounted little warriors had all blended to form just a few singular, snakelike creatures.

"In Menzoberranzan, House Baenre sometimes parades its forces about the streets to show off their discipline and power," Jarlaxle remarked. "These little ones are no less precise in their movements."

Entreri had not witnessed such a parade in his short time in the dark elf city, but in watching the weaving slaughter machine of the halfling riders, he easily understood his companion's point.

It was easy, too, for the pair to determine the timeline of the one-sided battle, and so they began making their way down the slope, Jarlaxle leading Entreri onto the stony field as the last of the goblins was cut down.

"Kneebreakers!" the halflings cried in unison, as they lined their war pigs up in perfect ranks. A few had been injured, but only one seemed at all seriously hurt, and halfling priests were already hard at work attending to him.

The halflings' self-congratulatory cheering stopped short, though, when several of them loudly noted the approach of two figures, one a drow elf.

Weapons raised in the blink of an eye, and shouts of warning told the newcomers to hold their ground.

"Inurree waflonk," Jarlaxle said in a language that Entreri did not understand.

As he considered the curious expressions of the halflings, however, and remembered his old friend back in Calimport, Dwahvel Tiggerwillies, and some of her linguistic idiosyncrasies, he figured out that his friend was speaking the halfling tongue—and, apparently, quite fluently. Entreri was not surprised.

"Well fought," Jarlaxle translated, offering a wink to Entreri. "We watched you from on high and saw that the unorganized goblins hadn't a chance."

"You do realize that you're a dark elf, correct?" asked one of the halflings, a burly little fellow with a brown mustache that curled in circles over his cheeks.

Jarlaxle feigned a look of surprise as he held one of his hands up before his sparkling red eyes.

"Why, indeed, 'tis true!" he exclaimed.

"You do realize that we're the Kneebreakers, correct?"

"So I heard you proclaim."

"You do realize that we Kneebreakers have a reputation for killing vermin, correct?"

"If you did not, and after witnessing that display, I would spread the word myself, I assure you."

"And you do realize that dark elves fall into that category, of course."

"Truly? Why, I had come to believe that the civilized races, which some say include halflings—though others insist that halflings can only be thought of as civilized when there is not food to be found—claim superiority because of their willingness to judge others based on their actions and not their heritage. Is that not one of the primary determining factors of civility?"

"He's got a point," another halfling mumbled.

"I'll give him a point," said yet another, that one holding a long (relatively speaking), nasty-tipped spear.

"You might also have noticed that many of the goblins were already dead as you arrived on the scene," Jarlaxle added. "It wasn't infighting that slew them, I assure you."

"You two were battling the fiends?" asked the first, the apparent leader.

"Battling? Slaughtering would be a better term. I do believe that you and your little army here have stolen our kills." He did a quick scan and poked his finger repeatedly, as if counting the dead. "Forty or fifty lost gold pieces, at least."

The halflings began to murmur among themselves.

"But it is nothing that my friend and I cannot forgive and forget, for truly watching your fine force in such brilliant maneuvering was worthy of so reasonable an admission price," Jarlaxle added.

He swept one of his trademark low bows, removing his hat and brushing the gigantic diatryma feather across the stones.

That seemed to settle the halfling ranks a bit.

"Your friend, he does not speak much?" asked the halfling leader.

"He provides the blades," Jarlaxle replied.

"And you the brains, I presume."

"I, or the demon prince now standing behind you."

The halfling blanched and spun around, along with all the others, weapons turning to bear. Of course, there was no monster to be seen, so the whole troupe spun back on a very amused Jarlaxle.

"You really must get past your fear of my dark-skinned heritage," Jarlaxle explained with a laugh. "How else might we enjoy our meal together?"

"You want us to feed you?"

"Quite the contrary," said the drow. He pulled off his traveling pack and brought forth a wand and a small wineskin. He glanced around, noting a small tumble of boulders, including a few low enough to serve as tables. Motioning that way, he said, "Shall we?"

The halflings stared at him dubiously and did not move.

With a great sigh, Jarlaxle reached into his pack again and pulled forth a tablecloth and spread it on the ground before him, taking care to find a bare spot that was not stained by goblin blood. He stepped back, pointed his wand at the cloth, and spoke a command word. Immediately, the center area of the tablecloth bulged up from the ground. Grinning, Jarlaxle moved to the cloth, grabbed its edge, and pulled it back, revealing a veritable feast of sweet breads, fruits, berries, and even a rack of lamb, dripping with juices.

A row of halfling eyes went so wide they seemed as if they would fall out and bounce along the ground together.

"Being halflings, and civilized ones at that, I assume you have brought a fair share of eating utensils, plates, and drinking flagons, correct?" said the drow, aptly mimicking the halfling leader's manner of speaking.

Some of the halflings edged their war pigs forward, but the stubborn leader held up his hand and eyed the drow with suspicion.

"Oh, come now," said Jarlaxle. "Could you envision a better token of my friendship?"

"You came from the wall?"

"From the Vaasan Gate, of course," Jarlaxle answered. "Sent out to scout by Commander Ellery Tranth Dopray Kierney Dragonsbane Peidopare herself."

Entreri tried hard not to wince at the mention of the woman's name, for he thought his friend was playing a dangerous game.

"I know her well," said the halfling leader.

"Do you?" said the drow, and he brightened suddenly as if it all had just fallen in place for him. "Could it be that you are the renowned Hobart Bracegirdle himself?" he gasped.

The halfling straightened and puffed out his chest with pride, all the answer the companions needed.

"Then you must dine with us," said Jarlaxle. "You must! I . . ." He paused and gave Entreri a hard look. "We," he corrected, "insist."

Again the hard look, and from that prodding, he did manage to pry a simple "Indeed" out of the assassin.

Hobart looked around at his companions, most of them openly salivating.

"Always could use a good meal after a battle," he remarked.

"Or before," said another of the troupe.

"Or during," came a deadpan from Jarlaxle's side, and the drow's face erupted with a smile as he regarded Entreri.

"Charm is a learned skill," Jarlaxle whispered through his grin.

"So is murder," the human whispered back.

Entreri wasn't exactly comfortable sitting in a camp with dozens of drunken halflings. He couldn't deny that the ale was good, though, and few races in all the Realms could put out a better selection of tasty meats than the halflings, though the food from their packs hardly matched the feast Jarlaxle had magically summoned. Entreri remained silent throughout the meal, enjoying the fine food and wine, and taking the measure of his hosts. His companion, though, was not so quiet, prodding Hobart and the others for tales of adventure and battle.

The halflings were more than willing to comply. They spoke of their rise to fame, when King Gareth first claimed the throne and the Bloodstone Lands were even wilder than their present state.

"It is unusual, is it not, for members of your race to prefer the road and battle to comfortable homes?" Jarlaxle asked.

"That's the reputation," Hobart admitted.

"And we're knowing well the reputation of dark elves," said another of the troupe, and all of the diminutive warriors laughed, several raising flagons in toast.

"Aye," said Hobart, "and if we're to believe that reputation, we should have killed you out on the slopes, yes?"

"To warrior halfling adventurers," Jarlaxle offered, lifting his flagon of pale ale.

Hobart grinned. "Aye, and to all those who rise above the limitations of their ancestors."

"Huzzah!" all the other halflings cheered.

They drank and toasted some more, and some more, and just when Entreri thought the meal complete, the main chef, a chubby fellow named Rockney Hamsukker called out that the lamb was done.

That brought more cheers and more toasts, and more—much more—food.

The sun was long gone and still they ate, and Jarlaxle began to prod Hobart again about their exploits. Story after story of goblins and orcs falling to the Kneebreakers ensued, with Hobart even revealing the variations on the "swarm," the "weave," and the "front-on wallop," as he named the Kneebreaker battle tactics.

"Bah," Jarlaxle snorted. "With goblins and orcs, are tactics even necessary? Hardly worthy opponents."

The camp went silent, and a scowl spread over Hobart's face. Behind him, another Kneebreaker stood and dangled his missile weapon, a pair of iron balls fastened to a length of cord for the outsiders to clearly see.

Entreri stopped his eating and stared hard at that threatening halfling, quickly surmising his optimum route of attack to inflict the greatest possible damage on the largest number of enemies.

"In numbers, of course," Jarlaxle clarified. "For most groups, numbers of goblinkin could prove troublesome. But I have watched you in battle, you forget?"

Hobart's large brown eyes narrowed.

"After your display on the stony field, good sir Hobart, you will have a difficult time of convincing me that any but a great number of goblinkin could prove of consequence to the Kneebreakers. Did those last goblins even manage a single strike against your riders?"

"We had some wounded," Hobart reminded him.

"More by chance than purpose."

"The ground favored our tactics," Hobart explained.

"True enough," Jarlaxle conceded. "But am I to believe that a troupe so precise as your own could not easily adapt to nearly any terrain?"

"I work very hard to remind my soldiers that we live on the precipice of disaster," Hobart declared. "We are one mistake from utter ruin."

"The warrior's edge, indeed," said the drow. "I do not underestimate your victories, of course, but I know there is more."

Hobart hooked his thick thumbs into the sides of his shining plate mail breastplate.

"We've been out a long stretch," he explained. " 'Twas our goal to return to the Vaasan Gate with enough ears to empty Commander Ellery's coffers."

"Bah, but you're just looking to empty Ellery from her breeches!" another halfling said, and many chortled with amusement.

Hobart looked around, grinning, at his companions, who murmured and nodded.

"And so we shall—the coffers, I mean."

The halfling leader snapped his stubby fingers in the air and a nervous, skinny fellow at Jarlaxle and Entreri's right scrambled about, finally producing a large bag. He looked at Hobart, returned the leader's continuing smile, then overturned the bag, dumping a hundred ears, ranging in size from the human-sized goblins' ears, several that belonged to creatures as large as ogres, and a pair so enormous Jarlaxle could have worn either as a hat.

Hobart launched back into his tales, telling of a confrontation with a trio of ogres and another ogre pair in the company of some hobgoblins. He raised his voice, almost as a bard might sing the tale, when he reached the climactic events, and the Kneebreakers all around him began to cheer wildly. One halfling pair stood up and re-enacted the battle scene, the giant imposter leaping up on a rock to tower over his foes.

Despite himself, Artemis Entreri could not help but smile. The movements of the halflings, the passion, the food, the drink, all of it, reminded him so much of some of his closest friends back in Calimport, of Dwahvel Tiggerwillies and fat Dondon.

The giant died in Hobart's tale—and the halfling giant died on the rock with great dramatic flourish—and the entire troupe took up the chant of, "Kneebreakers! Kneebreakers!"

They danced, they sang, they cheered, they ate, and they drank. On it went, long into the night.

Artemis Entreri had perfected the art of sleeping light many years before. The man could not be caught by surprise, even when he was apparently sound asleep. Thus, the stirring of his partner had him wide awake in moments, still some time before the dawn. All around them, the Kneebreakers snored and grumbled in their dreams, and the few who had been posted as sentries showed no more signs of awareness.

Jarlaxle looked at Entreri and winked, and the assassin nodded curiously. He followed the drow to the sleeping halfling with the bag of ears, which was set amid several other bags of equal or larger size next to the halfling that served as the pack mule for the Kneebreakers. With a flick of his long, dexterous fingers, Jarlaxle untied the bag of ears. He slid it out slowly then moved silently out of camp, the equally quiet Entreri close behind. Getting past the guards without being noticed was no more difficult than passing a pile of stones without having them shout out.

The pair came to a clearing under the light of the waning moon. Jarlaxle popped a button off of his fine waistcoat, grinning at Entreri all the while. He pinched it between his fingers, then snapped his wrist three times in rapid succession.

Entreri was hardly surprised when the button elongated and

widened, and its bottom dropped nearly to the ground, so that it looked as if Jarlaxle was holding a stovepipe hat that would fit a mountain giant.

With a nod from Jarlaxle, Entreri overturned the bag of ears and began scooping them into Jarlaxle's magical button bag. The drow stopped him a couple of times, indicating that he should leave a few, including one of the giant ears.

A snap of Jarlaxle's wrist then returned his magical bag to its inauspicious button form, and he put it on the waistcoat in its proper place and tapped it hard, its magic re-securing it to the material. He motioned for Entreri to move away with him then produced, out of thin air of course, a dust broom. He brushed away their tracks.

Entreri started back toward the halfling encampment, but Jarlaxle grabbed him by the shoulder to stop him. The drow offered a knowing wink and drew a slender wand from an inside pocket of his great traveling cloak. He pointed the wand at the discarded bag and the few ears, then spoke a command word.

A soft popping sound ensued, accompanied by a puff of smoke, and when it cleared, standing in place of the smoke was a small wolf.

"Enjoy your meal," Jarlaxle instructed the canine, and he turned and headed back to camp, Entreri right behind. The assassin glanced back often, to see the summoned wolf tearing at the ears, then picking up the bag and shaking it all about, shredding it.

Jarlaxle kept going, but Entreri paused a bit longer. The wolf scrambled around, seeming very annoyed at being deprived of a further meal, Entreri reasoned, for it began to disintegrate, its temporary magic expended, reducing it to a cloud of drifting smoke.

The assassin could only stare in wonder.

They had barely settled back into their blankets when the first rays of dawn peeked over the eastern horizon. Still, many hours were to pass before the halflings truly stirred, and Entreri found some more much-needed sleep.

The sudden tumult in camp awakened him around highsun. He groggily lifted up on his elbows, glancing around in amusement at the frantic halflings scrambling to and fro. They lifted stones and kicked remnants of the night's fire aside. They peeked under the pant legs of comrades, and often got kicked for their foolishness.

"There is a problem, I presume," Entreri remarked to Jarlaxle, who sat up and stretched the weariness from his body.

"I do believe our little friends have misplaced something. And with all the unorganized commotion, I suspect they'll be long in finding it."

"Because a bag of ears would hear them coming," said Entreri, his voice as dry as ever.

Jarlaxle laughed heartily. "I do believe that you are beginning to figure it all out, my friend, this journey we call life."

"That is what frightens me most of all."

The two went silent when they noted Hobart and a trio of very serious looking fellows staring hard at them. In procession, with the three others falling respectfully two steps behind the Knee-breaker commander, the group approached.

"Suspicion falls upon us," Jarlaxle remarked. "Ah, the intrigue!"

"A fine and good morning to you, masters Jarlaxle and Entreri," Hobart greeted, and there was nothing jovial about his tone. "You slept well, I presume."

"You would be presuming much, then," said Entreri.

"My friend here, he does not much enjoy discomfort," explained Jarlaxle. "You would not know it from his looks or his reputation, but he is, I fear, a bit of a fop."

"Every insult duly noted," Entreri said under his breath.

Jarlaxle winked at him.

"An extra twist of the blade, you see," Entreri promised.

"Am I interrupting something?" Hobart asked.

"Nothing you would not be interrupting in any case if you ever deign to speak to us," said Entreri.

The halfling nodded then looked at Entreri curiously, then similarly at Jarlaxle, then turned to regard his friends. All four shrugged in unison.

"Did you sleep the night through?" Hobart asked.

"And most of the morning, it would seem," Jarlaxle answered.

"Bah, 'tis still early."

"Good sir halfling, I do believe the sun is at its zenith," said the drow.

"As I said," Hobart remarked. "Goblin hunting's best done at twilight. Ugly little things get confident when the sun wanes, of course. Not that they ever have any reason to be confident."

"Not with your great skill against them, to be sure."

Hobart eyed the drow with clear suspicion. "We're missing something," he explained. "Something you'd be interested in."

Jarlaxle glanced Entreri's way, his expression not quite innocent and wide-eyed, but more curious than anything else—the exact look one would expect from someone intrigued but fully ignorant of the theft. Entreri had to fight hard to keep his own disinterested look about him, for he was quite amused at how perfectly Jarlaxle could play the liars' game.

"Our bag of ears," said Hobart.

Jarlaxle blew a long sigh. "That is troubling."

"And you will understand why we have to search you?"

"And our bedrolls, of course," said the drow, and he stepped back and held his cloak out wide to either side.

"We'd see it if it was on you," said Hobart, "unless it was magically stored or disguised." He motioned to one of the halflings behind him, a studious looking fellow with wide eyes, which he blinked continually, and thin brown hair sharply parted and pushed to one side. Seeming more a scholar than a warrior, the little one drew out a long blue wand.

"To detect magic, I presume," Jarlaxle remarked.

Hobart nodded. "Step apart, please."

Entreri glanced at Jarlaxle then back to the halfling. With a shrug he took a wide step to the side.

The halfling pointed his wand, whispered a command, and a glow engulfed Entreri for just a moment then was gone.

The halfling stood there studying the assassin, and his wide eyes kept going to Entreri's belt, to the jeweled dagger on one hip then to the sword, powerfully enchanted, on the other. The halfling's face twisted and contorted, and he trembled.

"You would not want either blade to strike you, of course," said Jarlaxle, catching on to the silent exchange where the wand was clueing the little wizard in to just how potent the human's weapons truly were.

"You all right?" Hobart asked, and though the wand-wielder could hardly draw a breath, he nodded.

"Turn around, then," Hobart bid Entreri, and the assassin did as he was asked, even lifting his cloak so the prying little scholar could get a complete picture.

A few moments later, the wand-wielder looked at Hobart and shook his head.

Hobart held his hand out toward Jarlaxle, and the other halfling lifted his wand. He spoke the command once more and the soft glow settled over a grinning Jarlaxle.

The wand-wielder squealed and fell back, shading his eyes.

"What?" Hobart asked.

The other one stammered and sputtered, his lips flapping, and kept his free hand up before him.

Entreri chuckled. He could only imagine the blinding glow of magic that one saw upon the person of Jarlaxle!

"It's not . . . there's . . . I mean . . . never before . . . not in King Gareth's own . . ."

"What?" Hobart demanded.

The other shook his head so rapidly that he nearly knocked himself over.

"Concentrate!" demanded the Kneebreaker commander. "You know what you're looking for!"

"But . . . but . . . but . . ." the halfling managed to say through his flapping lips.

Jarlaxle lifted his cloak and slowly turned, and the poor halfling shielded his eyes even more.

"On his belt!" the little one squealed as he fell away with a gasp. His two companions caught him before he tumbled, and steadied him, straightening him and brushing him off. "He has an item of holding on his belt," the halfling told Hobart when he'd finally regained his composure. "And another in his hat."

Hobart turned a wary eye on Jarlaxle.

The drow, grinning with confidence, unfastened his belt—with a command word, not through any mundane buckle—and slid the large pouch free, holding it up before him.

"This is your point of reference, yes?" he asked the wand-wielder, who nodded.

"I am found out, then," Jarlaxle said dramatically, and he sighed.

Hobart scowled.

"A simple pouch of holding," the drow explained, and tossed it to Hobart. "But take care, for within lies my precious Cormyrean brandy. I know, I know, I should have shared it with you, but you are so many, and I feared its potent effect on ones so little."

Hobart pulled the bottle from the pouch and held it up to read the label. His expression one of great approval, he slid it back into the pouch. Then he rummaged through the rest of the magical container, nearly climbing in at one point.

"We share the brandy, you and I, a bit later?" Jarlaxle proposed when Hobart was done with the pouch.

"Or if that hat of yours is holding my ears, I take it for my own, drink just enough to quench my thirst and use the rest as an aid in lighting your funeral pyre."

Jarlaxle laughed aloud. "I do so love that you speak directly, good Sir Bracegirdle!" he said.

He bowed and removed his hat, brushing it across the ground, then spun it to Hobart.

The halfling started to fiddle with it, but Jarlaxle stopped him with a sharp warning.

"Return my pouch first," he said, and the four halflings looked at him hard. "You do not wish to be tinkering with two items of extra-dimensional nature."

"Rift. Astral. Bad," Entreri explained.

Hobart stared at him then at the amused drow and tossed the pouch back to Jarlaxle. The Kneebreaker commander began inspecting the great, wide-brimmed hat, and after a moment, discovered that he could peel back the underside of its peak.

"A false compartment?" he asked.

"In a sense," Jarlaxle admitted, and Hobart's expression grew curious as the flap of cloth came out fully in his hand, leaving the underside of the peak intact, with no compartment revealed. The halfling then held up the piece of black cloth, a circular swatch perhaps half a foot in diameter.

Hobart looked at it, looked around, casually shrugged, and shook his head. He tossed the seemingly benign thing over his shoulder.

"No!" Jarlaxle cried, but too late, for the spinning cloth disk elongate in the air and fell at the feet of Hobart's three companions, widening and opening into a ten foot hole.

All three squealed and tumbled in.

Jarlaxle put his hands to his face.

"What?" Hobart asked. "What in the six hundred and sixty-six layers of the Abyss?"

Jarlaxle slipped his belt off and whispered into its end, which swelled and took on the shape of a snake's head. The whole belt began to grow and come alive.

"They are all right?" the drow casually asked of Hobart, who was at the edge of the hole on his knees, shouting down to his companions. Other Kneebreakers had come over as well, staring into the pit or scrambling around in search of a rope or a branch to use as a ladder.

Jarlaxle's snake-belt slithered over the edge.

Hobart screamed and drew his weapon, a beautifully designed short sword with a wicked serrated edge.

"What are you doing?" he cried and seemed about to cleave the snake.

Jarlaxle held up his hand, bidding patience. Even that small delay was enough, for the fast-moving and still growing snake was completely in the pit by then, except for the tip of its tail, which fastened itself securely around a nearby root.

"A rope of climbing," the drow explained. Hobart surveyed the scene. "Have one take hold and the rope will aid him in getting out of the pit."

It took a few moments and another use of the wand to confirm the claim, but soon the three shaken but hardly injured halflings were back out of the hole. Jarlaxle walked over and calmly lifted one edge of the extra-dimensional pocket. With a flick of his wrist and a spoken command, it fast reverted to a cloth disk that would fit perfectly inside the drow's great hat. At the same time, the snake-rope slithered up Jarlaxle's leg and crawled around his waist, obediently winding itself inside the belt loops of his fine trousers. When it came fully around, the "head" bit the end of the tail and commenced swallowing it until the belt was snugly about the drow's waist.

"Well . . ." the obviously flustered Hobart started to say, staring at the wand-wielder. "You think . . " Hobart tried to go on. "I mean, is there . . . ?"

"I should have killed you in Calimport," Entreri said to Jarlaxle.

"For the sake of a flustered halfling, of course," the drow replied.

"For the sake of my own sanity."

"Truer than you might realize."

"A-anything else you need to look at on that one?" Hobart finally managed to sputter.

The wand-wielder shook his head so forcefully that his lips made popping and smacking noises.

"Consider my toys," Jarlaxle said to Hobart. "Do you really believe that your ears are of such value to me that I would risk alienating so many entertaining and impressive newfound friends in acquiring them?"

"He's got a point," said the halfling standing next to Hobart.

"All the best to you in your search, good Sir Bracegirdle," said Jarlaxle, taking his hat back and replacing the magical cloth. "My offer for brandy remains."

"I expect you would favor a drink right now," Entreri remarked.

"Though not as much as that one," he added, indicating the flabbergasted, terrified, and stupefied wand-wielder.

"Medicinal purposes," Jarlaxle added, looking at the trembling little halfling.

"He's lucky you didn't strike him blind," added Entreri.

"Would not be the first time."

"Stunning."

CHAPTER
IN WATERS TOO DEEP
6

Black spots circled and danced before her eyes and a cold sweat was general about her body, glistening, it seemed, from every pore.

Arrayan tried to stand straight and hold fast to her concentration, but those spots! She put one foot in front of the other, barely inching her way to the door across the common room of her tiny home.

Three strides will take me to it, she thought, a sorry attempt at willing herself to shake her state of disorientation and vertigo and just take the quick steps.

The knocking continued even more insistently.

Arrayan smiled despite her condition. From the tempo and frantic urgency of the rapping, she knew it was Olgerkhan. It was always Olgerkhan, caring far too much about her.

The recognition of her dear old friend emboldened Arrayan enough for her to fight through the swirling black dots of dizziness for just a moment and get to the door. She cracked it open, leaning on it but painting an expression that tried hard to deny her weariness.

"Well met," she greeted the large half-orc.

A flash of concern crossed Olgerkhan's face as he regarded her, and it took him a long moment to reply, "And to you."

"It is far too early for a visit," Arrayan said, trying to cover, though she could tell by the position of the sun, a brighter spot in the typically gray Palishchuk sky, that it was well past mid-morning.

"Early?" Olgerkhan looked around. "We will go to Wingham's, yes? As we agreed?"

Arrayan had to pause a moment to suppress a wave of nausea and dizziness that nearly toppled her from the door.

"Yes, of course," she said, "but not now. I need more sleep. It's too early."

"It's later than we agreed."

"I didn't sleep well last night," she said. The effort of merely standing there was starting to take its toll. Arrayan's teeth began to chatter. "You understand, I'm sure."

The large half-orc nodded, glanced around again, and stepped back.

Arrayan moved her hand and the weight of her leaning on the door shut it hard. She turned, knowing she had to get back to her bed, and took a shaky step away, then another. The inching along wouldn't get her there in time, she knew, so she tried a quick charge across the room.

She got one step farther before the floor seemed to reach up and swallow her. She lay there for a long moment, trying to catch her breath, trying with sheer determination to stop the room from spinning. She would have to crawl, she knew, and she fought hard to get to her hands and knees to do just that.

"Arrayan!" came a shout from behind her, and it sounded like it was a hundred miles away.

"Oh my, Arrayan," the voice said in her ear a moment later, cracking with every word. Arrayan hardly registered the voice and barely felt powerful Olgerkhan sweep her into his arms to carry her gently to her bed.

He continued to whisper to her as he pulled a blanket up over her, but she was already far, far away.

"Knellict will not be pleased if we fail in this," Canthan Dolittle said to Athrogate upon the dwarf's return to their small corner table in Muddy Boots and Bloody Blades.

"How many times ye meaning to tell me that, ye dolt?" asked the black-bearded dwarf.

"As many as it takes for you to truly appreciate that—"

Canthan sucked in his breath and held his tongue as Athrogate rose up over the edge of the table, planting both of his calloused hands firmly on the polished wood. The dwarf kept coming forward, leaning over so near to the studious man that the long braids of his beard and the gem-studded ties settled in Canthan's lap. Canthan could feel the heat and smell the stench of the dwarf's breath in his face.

"Knellict is—" Canthan started again.

"A mean son of a pig's arse," Athrogate finished for him. "Yeah, I'm knowin' it all too well, ye skinny dolt. Been the times when I've felt the sting of his crackling fingers, don't ye doubt."

"Then we must not forget."

"Forget?" Athrogate roared in his face.

Canthan blanched as all conversation around their table stopped. The dwarf, too, caught on to the volume of his complaint, and he glanced back over his shoulder to see several sets of curious eyes focusing on him.

"Bah, what're ye lookin' at, lest it be yer doom?" he barked at them. Athrogate held no small reputation for ferocity at the Vaasan Gate, having dominated the hunt for bounty ears for so many months, and having engaged in more than a dozen tavern brawls, all of which had left his opponents far more battered than he. The dwarf narrowed his eyes, accentuating his bushy eyebrows all the more, and gradually sank back into his chair. When the onlookers finally turned their attention elsewhere, Athrogate wheeled back on his partner. "I ain't for forgetting nothing," he assured Canthan.

"Forgive my petulance," said Canthan. "But please, my short and stout friend, never again forget that you are here as my subordinate."

The dwarf glowered at him.

"And I am Knellict's underling," Canthan went on, and this mention of the powerful, merciless archmage did calm Athrogate somewhat.

Canthan was indeed Knellict's man, and if Athrogate moved on Canthan, he'd be facing a very angry and very potent wizard in a short amount of time. Knellict had left the Fugue and gone back to the Citadel of Assassins, but Knellict could move as quickly as he could unexpectedly.

"We ain't to fail in this," the dwarf grumbled, coming back to the original point. "Been watching them two closely."

"They go out into Vaasa almost every day. Do you follow?"

The dwarf snorted and shook his head. "I ain't for meeting no stinking drow elf out there in the wilds," he explained. "I been watching them on their return. That's enough."

"And if they don't return?"

"Then they're dead in the bogs and all the better for us," Athrogate replied.

"They are making quite a reputation in short order," said Canthan. "Every day they come in with ears for bounty. They are outperforming much larger groups, by all reports, and indeed have long since surpassed the amount of coin handed out at the Vaasan Gate for bounty in so short a time—a performance until very recently pinnacled by yourself, I believe."

Athrogate grumbled under his breath.

"Very well, then, though I would have hoped that you would trail them through all their daily routines," said Canthan.

"Ye thinking they got contacts in the wastelands?"

"It remains a possibility. Perhaps the drow elves have risen from their Underdark holes to find a spot in Vaasa—they have been known to seize similar opportunities."

"Well, if that Jarlaxle fellow's got drow friends in Vaasa, then I'm not for going there." He fixed Canthan's surprised expression with a fierce scowl. "I'm tougher'n any drow elf alone," he growled, "but I'm not for fighting a bevy o' the damned tricksters!"

"Indeed."

Athrogate paused for a long time, letting that "indeed" sink in, trying to gauge if there was any sarcasm in the word or if it was honest acceptance and agreement.

"Besides," he said at length, "Hobart's boys been seeing them often, as've others. Rumors're sayin' that Jarlaxle's got himself a goblin scout what's leadin' him to good hunting grounds."

"That cannot sit well with Hobart," Canthan reasoned. "The Kneebreakers view goblins as vermin to be killed and nothing more."

"A lot o' them pair's not sitting well with Hobart of late, so I'm hearin'," Athrogate agreed. "Seems some o' them halflings're grumbling about the ears Entreri and Jarlaxle're bringing in. Seems them halflings lost a bunch o' their own earned ears."

"A pair of thieves? Interesting."

"It'd be a lot more interestin' and a lot easier to figure it all out if yer friends would get us some history on them two. They're a powerful pair—it can't be that they just up and started slaughterin' things. Got to be a trail."

"Knellict is fast on the trail of that information, do not doubt," said Canthan. "He is scouring the planes of existence themselves in search of answers to the dilemma of Artemis Entreri and this strange drow, Jarlaxle. We will have our answers."

"Be good to know how nasty we should make their deaths," grumbled the dwarf.

Canthan just clucked and let it go. Indeed, he suspected that Knellict would send him a message to do just that and be rid of the dangerous pair.

So be it.

Olgerkhan grunted and sucked in his breath as poor Arrayan tried to eat the soup he'd brought. Her hand shook so badly she spilled most of the steaming liquid back into the bowl long before the large spoon had come up level with her mouth. Again and again she tried, but by the time the spoon reached her mouth and she sipped, she could barely wet her lips.

Finally Olgerkhan stepped forward and took Arrayan's shaking hand.

"Let me help you," he offered.

"No, no," Arrayan said. She tried to pull her hand away but didn't have much strength behind it. Olgerkhan easily held on. "It is quite . . ."

"I am your friend," the large half-orc reminded her.

Arrayan started to argue, as the prideful woman almost always did when someone fretted over her, but she looked into Olgerkhan's eyes and her words were lost in her throat. Olgerkhan was not a handsome creature by any standards. He favored his orc heritage more than his human, with a mouth that sported twisted tusks and splotchy hair sprouting all over his head and face. He stood crooked, his right shoulder lower than his left, and farther forward. While his muscled, knotted limbs exuded strength, there was nothing supple or typically attractive about them.

But his eyes were a different matter, to Arrayan at least. She saw tenderness in those huge brown orbs, and a level of understanding well beyond Olgerkhan's rather limited intelligence. Olgerkhan might not be able to decipher mystical runes or solve complex equations, but he was not unwise and never unsympathetic.

Arrayan saw all of that, staring at her friend—and he truly was the best friend she had ever known.

Olgerkhan's huge hand slid down her forearm to her wrist and hand, and she let him ease the spoon from her. As much for her friend's benefit as for her own, Arrayan swallowed her pride and allowed Olgerkhan to feed her.

She felt better when he at last tipped the bowl to her mouth, letting her drink the last of its contents, but she was still very weak and overwhelmed. She tried to stand and surely would have fallen had not her friend grabbed her and secured her. Then he scooped her into his powerful arms and walked her to her bed, where he gently lay her down.

As soon as her head hit her soft pillow, Arrayan felt her consciousness slipping away. She noted a flash of alarm on her half-orc friend's face, and as blackness closed over her, she felt him shake her, gently but insistently, several times.

A moment later, she heard a *thump,* and somewhere deep inside she understood it to be her door closing. But that hardly mattered to Arrayan as the darkness enveloped her, taking her far, far away from the land of waking.

Olgerkhan's arms flailed wildly as he scrambled down the roads of Palishchuk, heading to one door then another, changing direction with every other step. Palishchuk was not a close-knit community; folk kept to themselves except in times of celebration or times of common danger. Olgerkhan didn't have many friends, and all but Arrayan, he realized, were out hunting that late-summer day.

He gyrated along, gradually making his way south. He banged on a couple more doors but no one answered, and it wasn't until he was halfway across town that he realized the reason. The sound of the carnival came to his ears. Wingham had opened for business.

Olgerkhan sprinted for the southern gate and to the wagon ring. He heard Wingham barking out the various attractions to be found and charged in the direction of his voice. Pushing through the crowd he inadvertently bumped into and nearly ran over poor Wingham. The only thing that kept the barker up was Olgerkhan's grasping hands.

Large guards moved for the pair, but Wingham, as his senses returned, waved them away.

"Tell me," he implored Olgerkhan.

"Arrayan," Olgerkhan gasped.

As he paused to catch his breath, the half-orc noticed the approach of a human—he knew at first glance that it was a full human, not a half-orc favoring the race. The man looked to be about forty, with fairly long brown hair that covered his ears and tickled his neck. He was lean but finely muscled and dressed in weathered, dirty garb that showed him to be no stranger to the Vaasan wilderness. His bright brown eyes, so striking against his ruddy complexion and thick dark hair, gave him away. Though Olgerkhan had not seen him in more than two years, he recognized the human.

Mariabronne, he was called, a ranger of great reputation in the Bloodstone Lands. In addition to his work at the Vaasan Gate, Mariabronne had spent the years since Gareth's rise and the fall of Zhengyi patrolling the Vaasan wilds and serving Palishchuk as a courier to the great gates and as a guide for the half-orc city's hunting parties.

"Arrayan?" Wingham pressed. He grabbed Olgerkhan's face and forced the gasping half-orc to look back at him.

"She's in bed," Olgerkhan explained. "She's sick."

"Sick?"

"Weak . . . shaking," the large half-orc explained.

"Sick, or exhausted?" Wingham asked and began to nod.

Olgerkhan stared at him, confused, not knowing how to answer.

"She tried the magic," Mariabronne whispered at Wingham's side.

"She is not without magical protections," said Wingham.

"But this is Zhengyi's magic we are speaking of," said the ranger, and Wingham conceded the point with a nod.

"Bring us to her, Olgerkhan," Wingham said. "You did well in coming to us."

He shouted some orders at his compatriots, telling them to take over his barker's spot, and he, Mariabronne, and Olgerkhan rushed out from the wagon ring and back into Palishchuk.

CHAPTER
DREAMERS
7

Entreri rocked his chair up on two legs and leaned back against the wall. He sipped his wine as he watched the interaction between Jarlaxle and Commander Ellery. The woman had sought the drow out specifically, Entreri knew from her movements, though it was obvious to him that she was trying to appear as if she had not. She wasn't dressed in her armor, nor in any uniform of the Army of Bloodstone, and seemed quite the lady in her pink dress, subtly striped with silvery thread that shimmered with every step. A padded light gray vest completed the outfit, cut and tightly fitted to enhance her womanly charms. She carried no weapon—openly, at least—and it had taken Entreri a few minutes to even recognize her when first he'd spotted her among the milling crowd. Even on the field when she had arrived in full armor, dirty from the road, Entreri had thought her attractive, but now he could hardly pull his eyes from her.

When he realized the truth of his feelings it bothered him more than a little. When had he ever before been distracted by such things?

He studied her movements as she spoke to Jarlaxle, the way she leaned forward, the way her eyes widened, sparkling with interest. A smile, resigned and helpless, spread across the assassin's face and he briefly held out his glass in a secret toast to his dark elf companion.

"This chair and that chair free o' bums?" a gruff voice asked, and Entreri looked to the side to see a pair of dirty dwarves staring back at him.

"Well?" the other one asked, indicating one of the three empty chairs.

"Have the whole table," Entreri bade them.

He finished his drink with a gulp then slipped from his seat and moved away along the back wall. He took a roundabout route so as to not interrupt Jarlaxle's conversation.

"Well met to you, Comman—*Lady* Ellery," Jarlaxle said, and he tipped his glass of wine to her.

"And now you will claim that you didn't even recognize me, I expect."

"You underestimate the unique aspect of your eyes, good lady," said the drow. "In a full-face helm, I expect I would not miss that singular beauty."

Ellery started to respond but rocked back on her heels for just an instant.

Jarlaxle did well to mask his grin.

"There are questions I would ask of you," Ellery began, and her voice gained urgency when the drow turned away.

He spun right back, though, holding a second glass of wine he had apparently found waiting on the bar. He held it out to the woman, and she narrowed her eyes and glanced around suspiciously. How was it that the second glass of wine had been waiting there?

Yes, I knew you would come to me, Jarlaxle's smile clearly revealed when Ellery accepted the drink.

"Questions?" the drow prompted the obviously flabbergasted woman a few moments later.

Ellery tried to play it calm and collected, but she managed to dribble a bit of wine from the corner of her mouth and thought herself quite the clod while wiping it.

"I have never met a dark elf before, though I have seen a pair from afar and have heard tales of a half-drow making a reputation for herself in Damara."

"We do have a way of doing that, for good or for ill."

"I have heard many tales, though," Ellery blurted.

"Ah, and you are intrigued by the reputation of my dark race?"

She studied him carefully, her eyes roaming from his head to his feet and back up again. "You do not appear so formidable."

"Perhaps that is the greatest advantage of all."

"Are you a warrior or a wizard?"

"Of course," the drow said as he took another sip.

The woman's face crinkled for a brief moment. "It is said that drow are masters of the arts martial," she said after she recovered. "It is said that only the finest elf warriors could do individual battle against the likes of a drow."

"I expect that no elves who sought to prove such a theory are alive to confirm or deny."

Ellery's quick smile in response clued Jarlaxle in to the fact that she was catching on to his wit—a manner that was always a bit too dry and unrelenting for most surface dwellers.

"Is that a confirmation or a boast?" she asked.

"It just is."

A wicked smile grew on the woman's face. "Then I say again, you do not look so formidable."

"Is that an honest observation or a challenge?"

"It just is."

Jarlaxle held out his glass and Ellery tapped hers against it. "Some day, perhaps, you will happen upon me in Vaasa and have your answer," Jarlaxle said. "My friend and I have found some success in our hunts out there."

"I have noted your trophies," she said, and again her eyes scanned the drow head to toe.

Jarlaxle laughed aloud. He quieted quickly, though, under the intensity of Ellery's stare, her bright eyes boring into his.

"Questions?" he asked.

"Many," she answered, "but not here. Do you think that your friend will be well enough without you?"

As she asked, both she and Jarlaxle turned to the table in the back corner, where the drow had left Entreri, only to find that he was gone.

When they looked back at each other, Jarlaxle shrugged and said, "Answers."

They left the bustle of Muddy Boots and Bloody Blades behind, Jarlaxle following the woman as she easily navigated the myriad corridors and hallways of the wall complex. They moved down one side passage and crossed through the room where monster ears were exchanged for bounty. Moving toward the door at the rear of the chamber gave the drow an angle to see behind the desks, and he spotted a small chest.

He made a note of that one.

The door led the pair into another corridor. A right turn at a four-way intersection led them to another door.

Ellery casually fished a key out of a small belt pouch, and Jarlaxle watched her curiously, his senses more acutely attuning to his surroundings. Had the warrior woman planned their encounter from the beginning?

"A long way to walk for the answers to a few questions," he remarked, but Ellery just glanced back at him, smiling.

She grabbed a nearby torch and took it with her into the next chamber, moving along the wall to light several others.

Jarlaxle's smile widened along with his curiosity as he came to recognize the purpose of the room. Dummies stood silently around the perimeter and archery targets lined the far wall. Several racks were set here and there, all sporting wooden replicas of various weapons.

Ellery moved to one such rack and drew forth a wooden long sword. She studied it for a moment then tossed it to Jarlaxle, who caught it in one hand and sent it into an easy swing.

Ellery drew out a second blade and lifted a wooden shield.

"No such shield for me?" the drow asked.

With a giggle, Ellery tossed the second sword his way. "I have heard that your race favors a two-bladed fighting style."

Jarlaxle caught the tossed blade with the edge of the first wooden sword, breaking its fall, balancing it, then sending it into a controlled spin.

"Some do," he replied. "Some are quite adept with long blades of equal length."

A flick of his wrist sent the second sword spinning skyward, and the drow immediately disregarded it, looking over at Ellery, placing his remaining sword tip down on the floor, tucking one foot behind his other ankle and assuming a casual pose on the planted blade.

"Myself, I prefer variety," he added with more than a little suggestion in his tone.

As he finished, he caught the dropping second blade in his free hand.

Ellery eyed him cautiously, then led his gaze to the weapons' rack. "Is there another you'd prefer?"

"Prefer? For?"

The woman's eyes narrowed. She strapped the shield onto her left arm, then reached over and drew a wooden battle-axe from the rack.

"My dear Lady Ellery," said Jarlaxle, "are you challenging me?"

"I have heard so many tales of the battle prowess of your race," she replied. "I will know."

Jarlaxle laughed aloud. "Ah yes, answers."

"Answers," Ellery echoed.

"You presume much," said the drow, and he stepped back and lifted the two blades before him, testing their weight and balance. He sent them into a quick routine, spinning one blade over the other, then quick-thrusting the second. He retracted the blades immediately, bringing them to rest at his side. "What interest would I have in doing battle with you?"

Ellery let the axe swing easily at the end of her arm. "Are you not curious?" she asked.

"About what? I have already seen far too many human warriors, male and female." He sent one of the wooden swords in a spin again, then paused and offered a coy glance at Ellery. "And I am not impressed."

"Perhaps I can change your mind."

"Doubtful."

"Do you fear to know the truth?"

"Fear has nothing to do with it. You brought me here to satisfy your curiosity, not mine. You ask of me that I reveal something of myself to you, for your sake. You will reveal your battle prowess at the reward of satisfying your curiosity. For me, there is . . . ?"

Ellery straightened and stared at him sourly.

"The chance to win," she said a moment later.

"Winning means little," said the drow. "Pride is a weakness, don't you know?"

"Jarlaxle does not like to win?"

"Jarlaxle likes to survive," the drow replied without hesitation. "That is not so subtle a difference."

"Then what?" Ellery asked, impatience settling into her tone.

"What?"

"What is your price?" she demanded.

"Are you so desperate to know?"

She stared at him hard.

"A lady of your obvious charms should not have to ask such a question," the drow said.

Ellery didn't flinch. "Only if you win."

Jarlaxle cocked his head to the side and let his eyes roam the woman's body. "When I win, you will take me to your bedchamber?"

"You will not win."

"But if I do?"

"If that is your price."

Jarlaxle chuckled. "Pride is a weakness, my lady, but curiosity . . ."

Ellery stopped him by banging the axe hard against her shield.

"You talk too much," she said as she strode forward.

She lifted her axe back over her shoulder, and when Jarlaxle settled into a defensive stance, she charged in.

She pumped her arm as if to strike but stepped ahead more forcefully with her opposite foot and shield-rushed instead, battering at the drow's weapons left to right. She started to step in behind that momentum, the usual move, but then pivoted instead, spinning around backward and dropping low. She let her weapon arm out wide, axe level and low as she came around.

Had he expected the move, Jarlaxle could have easily stepped in behind the shield and stabbed her.

But he hadn't expected it, and he knew as Ellery came around, forcing him to leap the sailing axe, that the woman had judged his posture perfectly. He had underestimated her, and she knew it.

Jarlaxle fell back as Ellery came up fast and pressed the attack, chopping her axe in a more straightforward manner. He tried to counter, thrusting his right sword out first, then his left, but the woman easily blocked the first with her shield and deftly parried the second out wide on one downswing with her axe.

Jarlaxle snapped his right hand across, however, batting the side of that axe hard, then rolled his left hand in and over, again smacking the same side of the axe. He did a quick drum roll on the weapon, nearly tearing it from Ellery's hand and forcing it out wider with every beat.

But Ellery reacted properly, rolling her shield shoulder in tight and bulling ahead to force too much of a clench for Jarlaxle to disarm her.

"If I win, I will have you," the drow said.

Ellery growled and shoved out hard with her shield, driving him away.

"And what will Ellery claim if she wins?" Jarlaxle asked.

That stopped the woman even as she began to charge in once more. She settled back on her heels and peered at the drow from over the top of her shield.

"If I win," she began and paused for effect then added, *"I will have you."*

Jarlaxle's jaw might have hit the floor, except that Ellery's shield would surely have caught it, for the woman used the moment of distraction to launch another aggressive charge, barreling in, shield butting and axe slashing. It took every bit of Jarlaxle's speed and agility for him to keep away from that axe, and he only managed it by rolling to the side and allowing Ellery to connect with the shield rush. The drow used the momentum to get away, throwing himself back and into a roll. He came lightly to his feet and side-stepped fast, twisting as he went to avoid a wild slash by the woman.

"Ah, but you cheat!" he cried and he kept backing, putting considerable ground between the two. "My good lady, you steal all of my incentive. Should I not just drop my weapons and surrender?"

"Then if I win, I deny you!" she cried, and she charged.

Jarlaxle shrugged, and whispered, "Then you will not win."

The drow dodged left, then fast back to the right as Ellery tried to compensate, and though she tried to maintain her initiative, she found herself suddenly barraged by a dizzying array of thrusts, slashes, and quick, short stabs. At one point, Jarlaxle even somehow moved his feet out in front and dropped to the floor, sweeping her legs out. She didn't fall directly but stumbled, twisting and turning.

It was futile, though, for she went down to the floor.

Her agility served her well then, as she rolled to the side and got up to one knee in time to intercept the drow's expected charge. She parried and blocked the first wave of attacks, and even managed to work her way back to a standing position.

Jarlaxle pressed the attack, his blades coming at her from a dizzying array of angles. She worked her arms furiously, positioning her shield, turning her axe, and she dodged and backed, twisting to avoid those cunning strikes that managed to slip through her defenses. On a couple of occasions, the woman saw an opening and could have pressed the attack back the other way.

But she didn't.

She played pure defense and showed the drow a series of apparent openings, only to close them fast as Jarlaxle tried to press in. At one point, her defense was so quick that the drow overbalanced and his great hat slipped down over his eyes. For just a moment, though, for he swept one hand up, pulled the hat from his head and tossed it aside. Beads of perspiration marked his bald head.

He laughed and came on hard again, pressing the attack until he had Ellery in full flight away from him.

"You are young, but you fight like a drow veteran," Jarlaxle congratulated after yet another unsuccessful attack routine.

"I am not so young."

"You have not seen thirty winters," the drow protested.

The grin that creased Ellery's wide face made her look even younger. "I spent my childhood under the shadow of the Witch-King," she explained. "Bloodstone Village knew war continually from the Vaasan hordes. No child there was a stranger to the blade."

"You were taught well," Jarlaxle said.

He straightened and brought one sword up in salute.

Not ready to let such an obvious opening pass, Ellery leaped ahead, axe swinging wildly.

Halfway into that swing, she realized that she had been baited, and so she laughed helplessly as she saw her target easily spinning to the side. Her laugh became a yelp when the flat of Jarlaxle's wooden sword slapped hard against her rump.

She started to whirl around to face him, but he was too quick, and she got slapped hard again, and a third time before the drow finally disengaged and leaped back.

"By all measures, that should be scored as a victory," Jarlaxle argued. "For if my blades were real, I could have hamstrung you thrice over."

"Your blows were a bit high for that."

"Only because I did not wish to sting your legs," he answered, and he arched his eyebrow suggestively.

"You have plans for them?"

"Of course."

"If you are so eager then you should let me win. I promise, you would find it more enjoyable."

"You said you would deny me."

"I have changed my mind."

Jarlaxle straightened at that, his swords coming down to his sides. He looked at her, smiled, shrugged, and dropped his blades.

Ellery howled and leaped forward.

But the drow had planned his disarmament carefully and precisely, dropping the swords from on low so that they fell perfectly across his feet. A quick hop and leg tuck sent both swords flying back to his hands, and he landed in a spin, blades swiping across to slap hard at Ellery's axe. Jarlaxle rolled in right behind the stumbling woman's outstretched arms, and right behind the stumbling woman, catching her from behind and with one arm wrapped around, his sword tight against her throat.

"I prefer to lead," he whispered into her ear.

The drow could feel her shivering under the heat of his breath, and he had a marvelous view of her breasts heaving from the exertion of the fight.

Ellery slumped, her axe falling to the floor. She reached across, unstrapped her shield, and tossed it aside.

Jarlaxle inhaled deeply, taking in her scent.

She turned and grabbed at him hard, pressing her lips against his. She would only let him lead so far, it seemed.

Jarlaxle wasn't about to complain.

Entreri didn't know if he was supposed to be walking so freely through the corridors of the Vaasan Gate, but no guards presented themselves to block his progress. He had no destination in mind; he simply needed to walk off his restlessness. He was tired, but no bed could lure him in, for he knew that no bed of late had offered him any real rest.

So he walked, and the minutes rolled on and on. When he found a side alcove set with a tall ladder, he let his curiosity guide him and climbed. More corridors, empty rooms, and stairwells greeted him above and he kept on his meandering way through the dark halls of this massive fortress. Another ladder took him to a small landing and a door, loose-fitting and facing east, with light glowing around its edges. Curious, Entreri pushed it open.

He felt the wind on his face as he stared into the first rays of dawn, reaching out from the Vaasan plain and crawling over the valleys and peaks of the Galenas, lighting brilliant reflections on the mountain snow.

The sun stung Entreri's tired eyes as he walked out and along the parapet of the Vaasan Gate. He paused often, stood and stared, and cared not for the passage of time. The wall top was more than twenty feet wide at its narrowest points and swelled to more than twice that width in some spots, and from there Entreri truly came to appreciate the scope of the enormous construction. Several towers dotted the length of the wall stretching out before the assassin to the east, and he noted the occasional sentry, leaning or sitting. Still with no indication that he should not be there, he walked out of the landing and along the top of the great wall, some forty or fifty feet above the wasteland stretching out to the north. His eyes remained in that direction primarily, rarely glancing south to the long valley running between the majestic Galenas. He could see the tents of the Fugue, even his own, and he wondered if Jarlaxle had gone back there but thought it more likely that Ellery had offered him a more comfortable setting.

The curious couple did not remain in his thoughts any more than did the southland. The north held his attention and his eyes, where Vaasa stretched out before him like a flattened, rotting corpse. He veered that way in his stroll, moving nearer to the waist-high wall along the edge so that he could better take in the view of Vaasa awakening to the dawn's light.

There was a beauty there, Entreri saw, primal and cold: hard-edged stones, sharp-tipped skeletons of long dead trees, and the soft, sucking bogs. Blasted by war, torn by the march of armies, scalded by the fires of wizard spells and dragon breath, the land itself, the soul of Vaasa, had survived. It had taken all the hits and blasts and stomping boots and had come out much as it had been before.

So many of those who had lived there had perished, but Vaasa had survived.

Entreri passed a sentry, sitting half asleep and with his back against the northern wall. The man looked at him with mild curiosity then nodded as the assassin strode past him.

Some distance away, Entreri stopped his walk and turned fully to survey the north, resting his hands on the waist-high wall that ran the length of the gate. He looked upon Vaasa with a mixture of affection and self-loathing—as if he was looking into a mirror.

"They think you dead," he whispered, "because they do not see the life that teems beneath your bogs and stones, and in every cave, crack, and hollow log. They think they know you, but they do not."

"Talking to the land?" came a familiar voice, and Entreri found his moment of contemplation stolen away by the approach of Jarlaxle. "Do you think it hears you?"

Entreri considered his friend for a moment, the bounce in his gait, the bit of moisture just below the brim of his great hat, the look of quiet serenity behind his typically animated expression. Something more was out of place, Entreri realized, before it even fully registered to him that Jarlaxle's eye patch had been over the other eye back in the tavern.

Entreri could guess easily enough the route that had at last taken Jarlaxle to the wall top, and only then did the assassin truly appreciate that several hours had passed since he had left his friend in Muddy Boots and Bloody Blades.

"I think there are some who would do well to hear me less," he answered, and turned his eyes back to Vaasa.

Jarlaxle laughed and moved right beside him on the wall, leaning on the rail with his back to the northern land.

"Please do not let my arrival here disturb your conversation," said the drow.

Entreri didn't reply, didn't even look at him.

"Embarrassed?"

That did elicit a dismissive glance.

"You have not slept," Jarlaxle remarked.

"My sleep is not your concern."

"Sleep?" came the sarcastic response. "Is that what you would call your hours of restlessness each night?"

"My sleep is not your concern," Entreri said again.

"Your lack of sleep is," the drow corrected. "If the reflexes slow. . . ."

"Would you like a demonstration?"

Jarlaxle yawned, drawing another less-than-friendly glare. The drow returned it with a smile—one that was lost on Entreri, who again stared out over the muddy Vaasan plane. Jarlaxle, too, turned and leaned to the north, taking in the preternatural scene. The morning fog swirled in gray eddies in some places, and lifted up like a waking giant in others.

Indeed, Vaasa did seem as if a remnant of the time before the reasoning races inhabited the world. It seemed a remnant of a time, perhaps, before any creatures walked the lands at all, as if the rest of the world had moved along without carrying Vaasa with her.

"A forgotten land," Jarlaxle remarked, glancing at Entreri.

The assassin returned that look, even nodded a bit, and the drow was surprised to realize that Entreri had understood his reference exactly.

"What do you see when you look out there?" Jarlaxle asked. "Wasted potential? Barrenness where there should be fertility? Death where there should be life?"

"Reality," Artemis Entreri answered with cold finality.

He turned and offered one stern look to the drow then walked past him.

Jarlaxle heard the uncertainty in Entreri's voice, sensed that the man was off-balance. And he knew the source of that imbalance, for he had played no small part in ensuring that Idalia's flute had found its way into Artemis Entreri's hand.

He stayed at the rail for some time, soaking in the scene before him, remembering the night just passed, and considering his always dour friend.

Most of all, the dark elf wondered what he might do to dominate the first, recreate the second, and alter the third.

Always wondering, always thinking.

CHAPTER
THE RIDE OF MARIABRONNE
8

Arrayan had to pause and consider the question for a long while before answering. Where had she left the book? The woman felt the fool, to be sure. How could she have let something that powerful out of her sight? How could she not even remember where she'd placed it? Her mind traced back to the previous night, when she had dared start reading the tome. She remembered casting every defensive spell she knew, creating intricate wards and protections against the potentially devastating magic Zhengyi had placed on the book.

She looked back at the table in the center of the room, and she knew that she had cracked open the book right there.

A sense of vastness flooded her memories, a feeling of size, of magic, and a physical construct too large to be contained within.

"I took it out," she said, turning back to Wingham and Mariabronne. "Out of here."

"You left it somewhere beyond your control?" Wingham scolded, his voice incredulous. He leaped up from his seat, as if his body was simply too agitated to be contained in a chair. "An item of that power?"

Mariabronne put a hand on Wingham's arm to try to calm him. "The book is out of the house," he said to Arrayan. "Somewhere in Palishchuk?"

Arrayan considered the question, trying desperately to scour her memories. She glanced over at Olgerkhan, needing his always rock-solid support.

"No," she answered, but it was more a feeling than a certainty. "Out of the city. The city was . . . too small."

Wingham slipped back into his seat and for a moment seemed to be gasping for breath. "Too small? What did you create?"

Arrayan could only stare at him. She remembered leaving the house with the book tucked under her arm, but only vaguely, as if she were walking within a dream. Had it been a dream?

"Have you left the house since your return from your journey with the book?" Mariabronne asked.

The woman shook her head.

"Any sense of where you went?" the ranger pressed. "North? South near Wingham's caravan?"

"Not to Uncle Wingham," Arrayan replied without pause.

Wingham and Mariabronne looked at each other.

"Palishchuk only has two gates open most of the time," Mariabronne said. "South and north."

"If not south, then. . . ." said Wingham.

Mariabronne was first to stand, motioning for the others to follow. Olgerkhan moved immediately to Arrayan's side, offering her a shawl to protect her from the chilly wind in her weakened form.

"How could I have been so foolish?" the woman whispered to the large half-orc, but Olgerkhan could only smile at her, having no practical answers.

"The book's magic was beyond your control, perhaps," Mariabronne replied. "I have heard of such things before. Even the great Kane, for all his discipline and strength of will, was nearly destroyed by the Wand of Orcus."

"The wand was a god's artifact," Arrayan reminded him.

"Do not underestimate the power of Zhengyi," said Mariabronne. "No god was he, perhaps, but certainly no mortal either." He paused and looked into the troubled woman's eyes. "Fear not," he said. "We'll find the book and all will be put right."

The city was quiet that late afternoon, with most of the folk still off in the south at Wingham's circus. The quartet saw almost no one as they made their way to the north gate. Once there, Mariabronne bent low before Arrayan and bade her to lift one foot. He inspected her boot then studied the print she'd just made. He motioned for the others to hold and went to the gate then began poking around, studying the tracks on the muddy ground.

"You left and returned along the same path," he informed Arrayan. The ranger pointed to the northeast, toward the nearest shadows of the Great Glacier, the towering frozen river that loomed before them. "Few others have come through this gate in the last couple of days. It should not be difficult to follow your trail."

Indeed it wasn't, for just outside the area of the gate, Arrayan's footprints, both sets, stood out alone on the summer-melted tundra. What was surprising for Mariabronne and all the others, though, was how far from the city Arrayan's trail took them. The Great Glacier loomed larger and larger before them as they trudged to the northeast, and more directly north. The city receded behind them and night descended, bringing with it a colder bite to the wind. The air promised that the summer, like all the summers before it so far north, would be a short one, soon to end. An abrupt change in the weather would freeze the ground in a matter of days. After that, the earth would be held solid for three quarters of the year or more. It was not unknown for the summer thaw to last less than a single month.

"It's no wonder you were so weary," Wingham said to Arrayan some time later, the miles behind them.

The woman could only look back at him, helpless. She had no idea she'd been so far from the city and could only barely remember leaving her house.

The foursome came up on a ridge, looking down on a wide vale, a copse of trees at its low point down the hill before them and a grouping of several large stones off to the right.

Arrayan gasped, "There!"

She pointed, indicating the stones, the memory of the place flooding back to her.

Mariabronne, using a torch so he could see the tracks, was about to indicate the same direction.

"No one else has come out," the ranger confirmed. "Let us go and collect the book that I might bring it to King Gareth."

Arrayan and Olgerkhan caught the quick flash of shock on Wingham's face at that proclamation, but to his credit, the shrewd merchant didn't press the issue just then.

Mariabronne, torch in hand, was first to move around the closest, large boulder. The others nearly walked into his back when they, too, moved around the corner only to discover that the ranger had stopped. As they shuffled to his side to take in the view before him, they quickly came to understand.

For there was Zhengyi's book, suspended in the air at about waist height by a pair of stone-gray tentacles that rolled out from its sides and down to, and into, the ground. The book was open, with only a few pages turned. The foursome watched in blank amazement as red images of various magical runes floated up from the open page and dissipated in the shimmering air above the book.

"What have you done?" Wingham asked.

Mariabronne cautiously approached.

"The book is reading itself," Olgerkhan observed, and while the statement sounded ridiculous as it was uttered, another glance at the book seemed to back up the simple half-orc's plain-spoken observation.

"What is that?" Wingham asked as Mariabronne's torchlight extended farther back behind the book, revealing a line of squared gray stone poking through the tundra.

"Foundation stones," Arrayan answered.

The four exchanged nervous glances, then jumped as a spectral hand appeared in mid-air above the opened book and slowly turned a single page.

"The book is excising its own dweomers," Arrayan said. "It is enacting the magic Zhengyi placed within its pages."

"You were but a catalyst," Wingham added, nodding his head as if it was all starting to make sense to him. "It took from you a bit of your life-force and now it is using that to facilitate Zhengyi's plans."

"What plans?" asked Olgerkhan.

"The magic was in the school of creation," Arrayan replied.

"And it is creating a structure," said Mariabronne as he moved the length of the foundation stones. "Something large and formidable."

"Castle Perilous," muttered Wingham, and all three looked at him with great alarm, for that was a name not yet far enough removed from the consciousness of the region for any to comfortably hear.

"We do not yet know anything of the sort," Mariabronne reminded him. "Only that the book is creating a structure. Such artifacts are not unknown. You have heard of the work of Doern, of course?"

Arrayan nodded. The legendary wizard Doern had long ago perfected a method of creating minor extra-dimensional towers adventurers could summon to shield them from the dangers and hardships of the open road.

"It is possible that Zhengyi created this tome, perhaps with others like it, so that his commanders could construct defensible fortresses without the need of muscle, tools, supplies, and time," Mariabronne reasoned, edging ever closer to the fascinating book. "It could be, Wingham, that your niece Arrayan has done nothing more than build herself a new and impressive home."

Wingham, too, moved to the book, and from up close the rising, dissipating runes showed all the more clearly. Individual, recognizable characters became visible. Wingham started to wave his hand over the field of power above the opened book.

What little hair the old half-orc had stood on end and he gave a yelp then went flying back and to the ground. The other three were there in a moment, Arrayan helping him to sit up.

"It seems that Zhengyi's book will protect itself," Mariabronne remarked.

"Protect itself while it does what?" Wingham asked, his teeth chattering from the jolt.

All four exchanged concerned glances.

"I think it is time for me to ride to the Vaasan Gate," Mariabronne said.

"Past time," Arrayan agreed.

Mariabronne and Wingham dropped Arrayan and Olgerkhan at the woman's house then went to the south gate of Palishchuk and to Wingham's wagons beyond.

"My horse is stabled in the city," Mariabronne protested repeatedly, but Wingham kept waving the thought and the words away.

"Just follow," he instructed. "To all our benefit."

When they arrived at Wingham's wagon, the old half-orc rushed inside, returning almost immediately with a small pouch.

"An obsidian steed," he explained, reaching into the leather bag and pulling forth a small obsidian figurine depicting an almost skeletal horse with wide, flaring nostrils. "It summons a nightmare that will run tirelessly—well, at least until the magic runs out, but that should be long after the beast has taken you to the Vaasan Gate."

"A nightmare?" came the cautious response. "A creature of the lower planes?"

"Yes, yes, of course, but one controlled by the magic of the stone. You will be safe enough, mighty ranger."

Mariabronne gingerly took the stone and cradled it in his hands.

"Just say 'Blackfire,' " Wingham told him.

"Blackfi—" Mariabronne started to reply, but Wingham cut him short by placing a finger over his lips.

"Speak it not while you hold the stone, unless you are ready to be ridden yourself," the half-orc said with a chuckle. "And please, do not summon the hellish mount here in my camp. I do so hate when it chases the buyers away."

"And eats more than a few, I am sure."

"Temperamental beast," Wingham confirmed.

Mariabronne tapped his brow in salute and started away, but Wingham grabbed him by the arm.

"Discretion, I beg," the old half-orc pleaded.

Mariabronne stared at him for a long while. "To diminish Arrayan's involvement?"

"She began it," Wingham said, and he glanced back toward the city as if Arrayan was still in sight. "Perhaps she is feeding it with her very life-force. The good of all might weigh darkly on the poor girl, and she is without fault in this."

Again Mariabronne paused a bit to study his friend. "The easy win, at the cost of her life?" he asked, and before Wingham could answer, he added, "Zhengyi's trials have often proved a moral dilemma to us all. Mayhaps we could defeat this construct, and easily so, but at the cost of an innocent."

"And the cost of our own souls for making that sacrifice," said Wingham.

Mariabronne offered a comforting smile and nodded his agreement. "I will return quickly," he promised.

Wingham glanced back to the north again, as if expecting to see a gigantic castle looming over the northern wall of the city.

"That would be wise," he whispered.

Just south of Wingham's wagon circle, Mariabronne lifted the obsidian steed in both his cupped hands. "Blackfire," he whispered as he placed the figurine on the ground, and he nearly shouted as the stone erupted in dancing black and purple flames. Before he could react enough to fall back from the flames, though, he realized that they weren't burning his flesh.

The flames flared higher. Mariabronne watched, mesmerized.

They leaped to greater proportions, whipping about in the evening breeze, and gradually taking the form of a horse, a life-sized replica of the figurine. Then the fires blew away, lifting into the air in a great ball that puffed out to nothingness, leaving behind what seemed to be a smoking horse. The indistinct edges of wispy smoke dissipated, and a more solid creature stood before the ranger, its red eyes glaring at him with hate, puffs of acrid smoke erupting from its flared nostrils, and gouts of black flame exploding from its hooves as it pawed at the ground.

"Blackfire," Mariabronne said with a deep exhale, and he worked very hard to calm himself.

He reminded himself of the urgency of his mission, and he moved slowly and deliberately, fully on guard and with his hand on the pommel of Bayurel, his renowned bastard sword, a solid, thick blade enchanted with a special hatred for giantkin.

Mariabronne swallowed hard when he came astride the nightmare. He gingerly reached up for the creature's mane, which itself seemed as if it was nothing more than living black fire. He grabbed tightly when he felt its solidity, and with one fluid move, launched himself upon the nightmare's back. Blackfire wasted no time in rearing and snorting fire, but Mariabronne was no novice to riding, and he held firm his seat.

Soon he was galloping the fiery steed hard to the south, the shadows of the Galenas bordering him on his left, the city of Palishchuk and the Great Glacier fast receding behind him. It was normally a five-day journey, but the nightmare didn't need to rest, didn't let up galloping at all. Miles rolled out behind the ranger. He took no heed of threats off to the side of the trail—a goblin campfire or the rumble of a tundra yeti—but just put his head down and let the nightmare speed him past.

After several hours, Mariabronne's arms and legs ached from the strain, but all he had to do was conjure an image of that magical book and the structure it was growing, all he had to do was imagine the danger that creation of the Witch-King might present, to push past his pain and hold fast his seat.

He found that Wingham's estimation was a bit optimistic, however, for he felt the weakening of the magic in his mount as the eastern sky began to brighten with the onset of dawn. No stranger to the wilderness, Mariabronne pulled up in his ride and scanned the area about him, quickly discerning some promising spots for him to set a camp. Almost as soon as he dismounted, the nightmare became a wavering black flame then disappeared entirely.

Mariabronne took the obsidian figurine from the ground and felt its weight in his hand. It seemed lighter to him, drained of substance, but even as he stood there pondering it, he felt a slight shift as the weight increased and its magic began to gather. In that way the figurine would tell him when he could call upon its powers again.

The ranger reconnoitered the area, enjoyed a meal of dried bread and salted meat then settled in for some much needed sleep.

He awoke soon after mid-day and immediately went to the figurine. It was not yet fully recovered, he recognized, but he understood implicitly that he could indeed summon the nightmare if he so desired. He stepped back and surveyed the area more carefully under the full light of day. He glanced both north and south, measuring his progress. He had covered nearly half the ground to the Vaasan gate in a single night's ride—thrice the distance he could have expected with a living horse on the difficult broken ground, even if he had been riding during the daylight hours.

Mariabronne nodded, glanced at the figurine, and replaced it in his pouch. He resisted the stubborn resolve to begin hiking toward the Vaasan Gate and instead forced himself to rest some more, to take a second meal, and to go through a regimen of gently stretching and preparing his muscles for another night's long ride. Before the last rays of day disappeared behind the Vaasan plain in the west, the ranger was back upon the hellish steed, charging hard to the south.

He made the great fortress, again without incident, just before the next dawn.

Recognized and always applauded by the guards of the Army of Bloodstone, Mariabronne found himself sharing breakfast with the Honorable General Dannaway Bridgestone Tranth, brother of the great Baron Tranth who had stood beside Gareth in the war with the Witch-King. Rising more on his family's reputation than through any deed, Dannaway served as both military commander and mayor of the eclectic community of the Vaasan Gate and the Fugue.

Normally haughty and superior-minded, Dannaway carried no such pretensions in his conversations with Mariabronne the Rover. The ranger's fame had more than made him worthy to eat breakfast with the Honorable General, so Dannaway believed, and that was a place of honor that Dannaway reserved for very few people.

For his part, and though he never understood the need of more than a single eating utensil, Mariabronne knew how to play the game of royalty. The renowned warrior, often called the Tamer of Vaasa, had oft dined with King Gareth and Lady Christine at their grand Court in Bloodstone Village and at the second palace in Heliogabalus. He had never been fond of the pretension and the elevation of class, but he understood the practicality, even necessity, of such stratification in a region so long battered by conflict.

He also understood that his exploits had put him in position to continue to better the region, as with this very moment, as he recounted the happenings in Palishchuk to the plump and aging Honorable General. Soon after he had begun offering the details, Dannaway summoned his niece, Commander Ellery, to join them.

Dannaway gave a great, resigned sigh, a dramatic flourish, as Mariabronne finished his tale.

"The curse of Zhengyi will linger on throughout my lifetime and those of my children, and those of their children, I do fear," he said. "These annoyances are not uncommon, it seems."

"Let us pray that it is no more than an annoyance," said Mariabronne.

"We have trod this path many times before," Dannaway reminded him, and if the general was at all concerned, he did not show it. "Need I remind you of the grand dragon statue that grew to enormous proportions in the bog north of Darmshall, and . . . what? Sank into the bog, I believe.

"And let us not forget the gem-studded belt discovered by that poor young man on the northern slopes of the Galenas," Dannaway went on. "Yes, how was he to know that the plain gray stone he found the belt wrapped around, and carelessly threw aside after strapping on the belt, was actually the magical trigger for the twenty-five fireball-enchanted rubies set into the belt? Were it not for the witnesses—his fellow adventurers watching him from a nearby ridge—we might never have known the truth of that Zhengyian relic. There really wasn't enough left of the poor man to identify."

"There really wasn't anything left of the man at all," Ellery added.

A mixture of emotions engulfed Mariabronne as he listened to Dannaway's recounting. He didn't want to minimize the potential danger growing just north of Palishchuk, but on the other hand he was somewhat relieved to recall these other incidents of Zhengyian leftovers, tragic though several had been. For none of the many incidents had foretold doom on any great scale, a return of Zhengyi or the darkness that had covered the Bloodstone Lands until only eleven years ago.

"This is no minor enchantment, nor is it anything that will long remain unnoticed, I fear. King Gareth must react, and quickly," the ranger said.

Dannaway heaved another overly dramatic sigh, cast a plaintive look at Ellery, and said, "Assemble a company to ride with Mariabronne back to Palishchuk."

"Soldiers alone?" the woman replied, not a hint of fear or doubt in her strong, steady voice.

"As you wish," the general said.

Ellery nodded and looked across at the ranger with undisguised curiosity. "Perhaps I will accompany you personally," she said, drawing a look of surprise from her uncle. "It has been far too long since I have looked upon Palishchuk, in any case, nor have I visited Wingham's troupe in more than a year."

"I would welcome your company, Commander," Mariabronne replied, "but I would ask for more support."

Dannaway cut in, "You do not believe I would allow the Commander of the Vaasan Gate Militia to travel to the shadows of the Great Glacier alone, do you?"

Mariabronne fell back as if wounded, though of course it was all a game.

"The Rover," Dannaway said slyly. "It is not a title easily earned, and you have earned it ten times over by all accounts."

"Honorable General, Mariabronne's reputation . . ." Ellery started to intervene, apparently not catching on to the joke.

Dannaway stopped her with an upraised hand. "The Rover," he said again. "It is the title of a rake, though an honorable one. But that is not my concern, my dear Ellery. I do not fear for you in Mariabronne's bed, nor in the bed of any man. You are a Paladin of Bloodstone, after all.

"Nay, the Rover is also a remark on the nature of this adventurer," Dannaway went on, obviously missing Ellery's sour expression. "Mariabronne is the scout who walks into a dragon's lair to satisfy his curiosity. King Gareth would have used young Mariabronne to seek out Zhengyi, no doubt, except that the fool would have strolled right up to Zhengyi and asked him his name for confirmation. Fearless to the point of foolish, Mariabronne?"

"Lack of confidence is not a trait I favor."

Dannaway laughed raucously at that then turned to Ellery. "Bring a small but powerful contingent with you, I beg. There are many dragon lairs rumored in the Palishchuk region."

Ellery looked at him long and hard for a time, as if trying to make sense of it all.

"I have several in mind, soldiers and otherwise," she said, and Mariabronne nodded his satisfaction.

With another grin and bow to Dannaway, he took his leave so that he could rest up for the ride back to the north. He settled in to the complimentary room that was always waiting for him off the hallway that housed the garrison's commanders. He fell asleep hoping that Dannaway's casual attitude toward the construct was well-warranted.

He slept uneasily though, for in his heart, Mariabronne suspected that this time the remnant of Zhengyi might be something more.

You are a Paladin of Bloodstone, after all.

Ellery couldn't prevent a wince from tightening her features at that remark, for it was not yet true—and might never be, she knew, though many others, like Dannaway, apparently did not. Many in her family and among the nobles awaited the day when she would demonstrate her first miracle, laying on hands to heal the wounded, perhaps. None of them doubted it would happen soon, for the woman held a sterling reputation and was descended from a long line of such holy warriors.

Ellery's other friends, of course, knew better.

Well away from the general, she moved from foot to foot, betraying her nervousness.

"I can defeat him if need be," she told the thin man standing in the shadow of the wall's angular jag. "I have taken the measure of his skill and he is as formidable as you feared."

"Yet you believe you can kill him?"

"Have you not trained me in exactly that art?" the woman replied. "One strike, fatal? One move, unstoppable?"

"He is superior," came the thin voice of the thin man, a scratching and wheezing sound, but strangely solid in its confident and deathly even tone.

Ellery nodded and admitted, "Few would stand against him for long, true."

"But Ellery is among those few?"

"I do not make that claim," she replied, trying hard to not sound shaken. Then she added the reminder, as if to herself and not to the thin man, "My axe has served me well, served King Gareth well, and served you well."

That brought a laugh, again wheezy and thin, but again full of confidence—well-earned confidence, Ellery knew.

"An unlikely continuum of service," he observed. She could see the man's smirk, stretching half out of the shadows. "You do not agree?" asked the thin man, and Ellery, too, smirked and found humor in the irony.

Few would see the logic of her last statement, she realized, because few understood the nuance of politics and practicality in Damara and Vaasa.

"Speak it plainly," the thin man bade her. "If the need arises, you are confident that you can defeat the drow elf, Jarlaxle?"

The woman straightened at the recriminating tone. She didn't glance around nervously any longer, but stared hard at her counterpart.

"He has a weakness," she said. "I have seen it. I can exploit it. Yes. He will not be able to defeat that which you have trained me to execute."

The thin man replied, "Ever were you the fine student."

Emboldened, Ellery bowed at the compliment.

"Let us hope it will not come to that," the thin man went on. "But they are a hard pair to read, this drow and his human companion."

"They travel together and fight side by side, yet the human seems to hold the black-skinned one in contempt," Ellery agreed. "But I see no weakness there that we might exploit," she quickly added, as her counterpart's countenance seemed to brighten with possibility. "A blow against one is a blow against both."

The thin man paused and absorbed that reasoning for a short while, and she was far from certain he agreed.

"The ranger is an excitable one," he said, shifting the subject. "Even after twenty years of hunting the Vaasan wilderness, Mariabronne is easily agitated."

"This is a relic of Zhengyi he has discovered. Many would consider that reason to become agitated."

"You believe that?"

"Wingham believes that, so says Mariabronne, and not for the purposes of making a deal, obviously, or the half-orc opportunist would have quietly sold the artifact."

That had the thin man leaning back more deeply into the shadows, the darkness swallowing almost all of his fragile form. He brought his hands up before him, slender fingertips tap-tapping together.

"Wingham is no fool," the shadowy figure warned.

"He knows magic, if nothing else," Ellery replied. "I would trust his judgment on this."

"So Zhengyi left a book," muttered the thin man, "a book of power."

"A book of creation, so says Mariabronne."

"You will go to Palishchuk?"

"I will."

"With an appointed escort of your choosing?"

"Of course. Mariabronne will lead a small group in the morning."

"You know whom to choose?"

Ellery didn't even try to hide her surprise when she said, "You wish a place on the caravan?"

The thin man tapped his fingers together a few more times, and in the shadows, Ellery could see him nodding.

"Your exploits have not gone unnoticed," Ellery said to Jarlaxle that night, back in Muddy Boots and Bloody Blades.

"If they had, I would be deeply wounded," the drow replied, tipping his glass and offering a lewd wink.

Ellery blushed despite herself, and Jarlaxle thought her red hair only accentuated the sudden color in her cheeks.

"I travel to Palishchuk tomorrow," she said, composing herself.

"I have heard of this place, Palishchuk—half-orcs, correct?"

"Indeed, but quite civilized."

"We should celebrate your departure."

"Our departure."

That caught the drow off his guard, but of course, he didn't show it.

"I am assembling a troupe to make the journey," she explained. "Your exploits have not gone unnoticed."

"Nor have they been accomplished alone."

"Your friend is invited as well."

As she spoke of Entreri, the pair of them turned together to regard the man who stood beside the bar, a mug of ale growing warm on the counter before him, and his typical background sneer hidden just behind his distanced expression. He wore his gray cloak back over one shoulder, showing the fine white shirt that Ilnezhara had given him before the journey to the Vaasan Gate and also revealing the jeweled hilt of his fabulous dagger, sheathed on his hip. It did not escape the attention of Jarlaxle and Ellery that those around Entreri were keeping a respectful step back, were affording him more personal space than anyone else in the bar.

"He has that quality," Jarlaxle mused aloud.

He continued to admire Entreri even as Ellery looked at him for an explanation. But the drow didn't bother to voice his observation. Entreri was far from the largest man in the tavern and had made no aggressive moves toward anyone, yet it was obvious that those around him could sense his strength, his competence. It had to be his eyes, Jarlaxle presumed, for the set of his stare spoke of supreme concentration—perhaps the best attribute of a true warrior.

"Will he go?" the drow heard Ellery ask, and from her tone, it was apparent to him that it was not the first time she had posed the question.

"He is my friend," Jarlaxle replied, as if that description settled everything. "He would not let me walk into danger alone."

"Then you agree?"

Jarlaxle turned to her and grinned wickedly. "Only if you promise me that I will not be cold in the night wind."

Ellery returned his smile then placed her drink down on the table beside them.

"At dawn," she instructed, and she started away.

Jarlaxle grabbed her arm and said, "But I am cold."

"We are not yet on the road," she said.

Ellery danced from his grasp and moved across the floor and out of the tavern.

Jarlaxle continued to grin as he considered her curves from that most advantageous angle. The moment she was out of sight, he snapped his gaze back at Entreri and sighed, knowing the man would resist his persuasion, as always.

It was going to be a long night.

Looking splendid in her shining armor, shield strapped across her back and axe set at her side, Ellery sat upon a large roan mare at the head of the two wagon caravan. Mariabronne rode beside her on a bay. A pair of mounted soldiers complimented them at the back of the line, two large and angry looking men. One of them was the bounty clerk, Davis Eng, the other an older man with gray hair.

The two women driving the first wagon were not of the Army of Bloodstone, but fellow mercenaries from the local taverns. One Jarlaxle knew as Parissus of Impiltur, large-boned, round-faced, and with her light-colored hair cropped short. Often had he and Entreri heard the woman boasting of her exploits, and she did seem to take great pleasure in herself.

The other was one that Jarlaxle couldn't help but know, for her name sat atop the board listing bounty payouts. She called herself Calihye and was a half-elf with long black hair and a beautiful, angular face—except for that angry-looking scar running from one cheek through the edge of her thin lips and to the middle of her chin. When she called out to Commander Ellery that she was ready to go, Jarlaxle and his human companion—surprised to find themselves assigned to driving the second wagon—heard a distinct lisp, undoubtedly caused by the scar across her lips.

"Bah!" came a grumble from the side. "Hold them horses, ye dolts be durned. I'm huffin' and puffin' and me blood's but to burn!"

All watched as a dwarf rambled across the short expanse from the gate, his muscled arms bare and pumping in cadence with his determined strides, his black beard wound into two long braids. He had a pair of odd-looking morning stars strapped in an **X** across his back, their handles reaching up and wide beyond the back of his bushy head. Each ended in a spiked metal ball, the pair bouncing and rolling at the end of their respective chains in similar cadence to the pumping movements. While that was normal enough, the material of the weapons gleamed a dullish and almost translucent gray. Glassteel, they were, a magical construct of rare and powerful properties.

"Ye ask me to go, and so I'm for going, but then ye're not for waiting, so what're ye knowin'? Bah!"

"Your pardon, good Athrogate," said Commander Ellery. "I thought that perhaps you had changed your mind."

"Bah!" Athrogate snorted back.

He walked to the back of the open wagon, pulled a bag from his belt and tossed it inside—which made a second dwarf already in the wagon dodge aside—then grabbed on with both his hands and flipped himself up and over to take a seat beside a thin, fragile-looking man.

Jarlaxle noted that with some curiosity, thinking that a dwarf would normally have chosen the seat beside the other dwarf, which remained open. There were only three in the back of the wagon, which could have held six rather easily.

"They know each other," the drow remarked to Entreri, indicating the dwarf and the man.

"You find that interesting?" came the sarcastic remark.

Jarlaxle just gave a "Hmm," and turned his attention back to the reins and the horses.

Entreri glanced at him curiously, then considered the obnoxious dwarf and the frail-looking man again. Earlier, Jarlaxle had reasoned that the man must be a sage, a scholar brought on to help decipher the mystery of whatever it was that they were going to see in this northern city of Palishchuk.

But that dwarf was no scholarly type, nor did he seem overly curious about matters cerebral. If he and the man knew each other, as Jarlaxle had reasoned, then might there be more to the man than they had presumed?

"He is a wizard," Entreri said quietly.

Jarlaxle looked over at the assassin, who seemed unaware of the movement as he clenched and unclenched his right hand, upon which he had not long ago worn the enchanted gauntlet that accompanied his sword. The magic-defeating gauntlet was lost to him, and it likely occurred to Entreri, in considering the wizard, that he might wish he was wearing it before their journey was over. Though the man had done nothing to indicate any threat toward Entreri, the assassin had never been, and never would be, comfortable around wizards.

He didn't understand them.

He didn't want to understand them.

Usually, he just wanted to kill them.

Ellery motioned to them all and she and Mariabronne began walking their horses out to the north, the wagons rolling right behind, the other two soldiers falling in to flank Entreri and Jarlaxle's supply wagon.

Jarlaxle began to talk, of course, noting the landscape and telling tales of similar places he had visited now and again. And Entreri tuned him out, of course, preferring to keep his focus on the other nine journeying beside him and the drow.

For most of his life, Artemis Entreri had been a solitary adventurer, a paid killer who relied only upon himself and his own instincts. He felt a distinct discomfort with the company, and surely wondered how the drow had ever convinced him to go along.

Perhaps he wondered why Jarlaxle had wanted to go in the first place.

PART 2

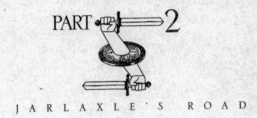

JARLAXLE'S ROAD

Jarlaxle left Ilnezhara and Tazmikella excitedly discussing the possibilities of Zhengyi's library a short while after the fall of the lich's tower. As soon as he had exited the dragon's abode, the drow veered from the main road that would take him back to Heliogabalus proper. He wandered far into the wilderness, to a grove of dark oaks, and did a quick scan of the area to ensure that no one was about. He leaned back against a tree and closed his eyes, and replayed in his thoughts the conversation, seeing again the sisters' expressions as they rambled on about Zhengyi.

They were excited, of course, and who could blame them? But there was something else in the look of Ilnezhara when first she had spoken to him about the crumbled tower. A bit of fear, he thought again.

Jarlaxle smiled. The sisters knew more about Zhengyi's potential treasures than they were letting on, and they feared the resurfacing artifacts.

Why would a dragon fear anything?

The wince on Ilnezhara's face when he told her that the book had been destroyed flashed in his thoughts, and he realized that he'd do well to keep his treasure—the tiny skull gem—safely hidden for a long, long time. Ilnezhara hadn't completely believed him, he suspected, and that was never a good thing when dealing with a dragon. He knew without doubt that the dragon sisters would try to confirm that he was speaking the truth. Of course, as was their hoarding nature, the dragons would desire such a tome as the one that had constructed the tower, but that expression on Ilnezhara's face spoke to something beyond so simple and obvious a desire.

Despite his better instincts the drow produced the tiny glowing skull, just for a moment. He clutched it tightly in his hand and let his thoughts flow into the magic, accepting whatever road the skull laid out before him. Kimmuriel, the psionicist dark elf Jarlaxle had left to command his mercenary band, Bregan D'aerthe, had long ago taught him a way of getting some sense of the purpose of a magical item. Of course Jarlaxle already knew a portion of the skull's properties, for it had no doubt been a large part of creating the tower. He understood logically that the skull had been the conduit between the life-force of that fool Herminicle and the creation power of the tome itself.

All hints of color faded from Jarlaxle's vision. Even in the dark of night he recognized that he was moving into a sort of alternate visual realm. He recoiled at first, fearing that the skull was taking his life-force, was draining him of living energy and moving him closer to death.

He fast realized that such was not the case, however. Rather, the power of the skull was allowing his sensibilities to enter the nether realm.

He sensed the bones of a dead squirrel right below his feet, and those of many other creatures who had died in that place. He felt no pull to them, however, just a recognition, an understanding that they were there.

But he did feel a pull, clearly so, and he turned and walked out of the grove, letting the skull guide him.

Soon he stood in the remains of an ancient, forgotten cemetery. A couple of stones might have been markers, or perhaps they were not, but Jarlaxle knew with certainty that it was a cemetery, where any other wanderer who happened upon the place might not guess.

Jarlaxle felt the long-buried corpses, buried in neat rows. They were calling to him, he thought . . .

No, he realized, and he opened his eyes wide and looked down at the skull. They weren't calling to him, they were waiting for him to call to them.

The drow took a deep and steadying breath. He noted the remains of a dwarf and a halfling, but when he concentrated on them, he understood that they were not connected in any way but by the ground in which they rested and were connected in no way to the dark elf.

This skull was focused in its power. It held strength over humans—alive and dead, so it would seem.

"Interesting," Jarlaxle whispered to the chilly night air, and he subconsciously glanced back in the direction of Ilnezhara's tower.

Jarlaxle held the glowing item up before his twinkling eyes.

"If I had initially found the tome and had enacted the creation power with my life-force, would the skull that grew within the pages have been that of a drow?" he asked. "Could a dragon have made a skull that would find its connection to long-dead dragons?"

He shook his head as he spoke the words aloud, for they just didn't sound correct to him. The disposition of the skull predated the construction of the tower and had been embedded within the book before the foolish human Herminicle had found it. The book was predetermined to that end result, he believed.

Yes, that sounded better to the aged and magically-literate dark elf. Zhengyi held great power over humans and had also commanded an army of the dead, so the tales said. The skull was surely one of his artifacts to affect that end.

Jarlaxle glanced back again in the direction of the distant tower.

It was no secret that Zhengyi had also commanded flights of dragons—disparate wyrms, somehow brought together under a singular purpose and under his control.

The drow's smile widened and he realized that a journey to Vaasa was indeed in his future.

Happily so.

CHAPTER

THE WIND ON THE ROAD

9

"We'll keep close to the foothills," Ellery said to Jarlaxle, pulling her horse up beside the bouncing wagon. "There have been many reports of monsters in the region and Mariabronne has confirmed that they're about. We'll stay in the shadows away from the open plain."

"Might our enemies not be hiding in wait in those same shadows?" Jarlaxle asked.

"Mariabronne is with us," Ellery remarked. "We will not be caught by surprise." She smiled with easy confidence and turned her horse aside.

Jarlaxle set his doubting expression upon Entreri.

"Yes," the assassin assured him, "almost everyone I've killed uttered similar last words."

"Then I am glad once again that you are on my side."

"They've often said that, too."

Jarlaxle laughed aloud.

Entreri didn't.

The going was slower on the more uneven ground under the shadows of the Galenas, but Ellery insisted and she was, after all, in command. As the sun began its lazy slide down the western sky, the commander ordered the wagons up into a sheltered lea between mounds of tumbled stones and delegated the various duties of setting the camp and defenses. Predictably, Mariabronne went out to scout and the pair of soldiers set watch-points—though curiously, Entreri thought, under the guidance of the dwarf with the twin morning stars. Even more curious, the thin sage sat in contemplation off to the side of the main encampment, his legs crossed before him, his hands resting on his knees. It was more than simple meditation, Entreri knew. The man was preparing spells they might need for nighttime defense.

Similarly, the other dwarf, who had introduced himself as Prattcus Bristlebeard, built a small altar to Moradin and began calling upon his god for blessing. Ellery had covered both the arcane and the divine.

And probably a little of both with Jarlaxle, Entreri thought with a wry grin.

The assassin went out from the main camp soon after, climbing higher into the foothills and finally settling on a wide boulder that afforded him a superb view of the Vaasan lowlands stretching out to the west.

He sat quietly and stared at the setting sun, long rays slanting across the great muddy bog, bright lines of wetness shining brilliantly. Dazzling distortions turned the light into shimmering pools of brilliance, demanding his attention and drawing him into a deeper state of contemplation. Hardly aware of the movement, Entreri reached to his belt and drew forth a small, rather ordinary-looking flute, a gift of the dragon sisters Ilnezhara and Tazmikella.

He glanced around quickly, ensuring that he was alone, then lifted the flute to his lips and blew a simple note. He let that whistle hang in the air then blew again, holding it a little longer. His delicate but strong fingers worked over the instrument's holes and he played a simple song, one he had taught himself or one the flute had taught to him; he couldn't be certain of which. He continued for a short while, letting the sound gather in the air around him, bidding it to take his thoughts far, far away.

The flute had done that to him before. Perhaps it was magic or perhaps just the simple pleasure of perfect timbre, but under the spell of his playing, Artemis Entreri had several times managed to clear his thoughts of all the normal clutter.

A short while later, the sun much lower in the sky, the assassin lowered the flute and stared at it. Somehow, the instrument didn't sound as fine as on those other occasions he'd tested it, nor did he find himself being drawn into the flute as he had before.

"Perhaps the wind is countering the puff of your foul breath," Jarlaxle said from behind him.

The drow couldn't see the scowl that crossed Entreri's face—was there ever to be a time when he could be away from that pestering dark elf?

Entreri laid the flute across his lap and stared off to the west and the lowering sun, the bottom rim just touching the distant horizon and setting off a line of fires across the dark teeth of the distant hills. Above the sun, a row of clouds took on a fiery orange hue.

"It promises to be a beautiful sunset," Jarlaxle remarked, easily scaling the boulder and taking a seat close beside the assassin.

Entreri glanced at him as if he hardly cared.

"Perhaps it is because of my background," the drow continued. "I have gone centuries, my friend, without ever witnessing the cycles of the sun. Perhaps the absence of this daily event only heightens my appreciation for it now."

Entreri still showed no hint of any response.

"Perhaps after a few decades on the surface I will become as bored with it as you seem to be."

"Did I say that?"

"Do you ever say anything?" Jarlaxle replied. "Or does it amuse you to let all of those around you simply extrapolate your words from your continuing scowls and grimaces?"

Entreri chortled and looked back to the west. The sun was lower still, half of it gone. Above the remaining semicircle of fire, the clouds glowed even more fiercely, like a line of fire churning in the deepening blue of the sky.

"Do you ever dream, my friend?" Jarlaxle asked.

"Everyone dreams," Entreri replied. "Or so I am told. I expect that I do, though I hardly care to remember them."

"Not night dreams," the drow explained. "Everyone dreams, indeed, at night. Even the elves in our Reverie find dream states and visions. But there are two types of dreamers, my friend, those who dream at night and those who dream in the day."

He had Entreri's attention.

"Those night-dreamers," Jarlaxle went on, "they do not overly concern me. Nighttime dreams are for release, say some, a purging of the worries or a fanciful flight to no end. Those who dream in the night alone are doomed to mundanity, don't you see?"

"Mundanity?"

"The ordinary. The mediocre. Night-dreamers do not overly concern me because there is nowhere for them to rise. But those who dream by day . . . those, my friend, are the troublesome ones."

"Would Jarlaxle not consider himself among that lot?"

"Would I hold any credibility at all if I did not admit my troublesome nature?"

"Not with me."

"There you have it, then," said the drow.

He paused and looked to the west, and Entreri did too, watching the sun slip lower.

"I know another secret about daydreamers," Jarlaxle said at length.

"Pray tell," came the assassin's less-than-enthusiastic reply.

"Daydreamers alone are truly alive," Jarlaxle explained. He looked back at Entreri, who matched his stare. "For daydreamers alone find perspective in existence and seek ways to rise above the course of simple survival."

Entreri didn't blink.

"You do daydream," Jarlaxle decided. "But only on those rare occasions your dedication to . . . to what, I often wonder? . . . allows you outside your perfect discipline."

"Perhaps that dedication to perfect discipline is my dream."

"No," the drow replied without hesitation. "No. Control is not the facilitation of fancy, my friend, it is the fear of fancy."

"You equate dreaming and fancy then?"

"Of course! Dreams are made in the heart and filtered through the rational mind. Without the heart . . ."

"Control?"

"And only that. A pity, I say."

"I do not ask for your pity, Jarlaxle."

"The daydreamers aspire to mastery of all they survey, of course."

"As I do."

"No. You master yourself and nothing more, because you do not dare to dream. You do not dare allow your heart a voice in the process of living."

Entreri's stare became a scowl.

"It is an observation, not a criticism," said Jarlaxle. He rose and brushed off his pants. "And perhaps it is a suggestion. You, who have so achieved discipline, might yet find greatness beyond a feared reputation."

"You assume that I want more."

"I know that you need more, as any man needs more," said the drow. He turned and started down the back side of the boulder. "To live and not merely to survive—that secret is in your heart, Artemis Entreri, if only you are wise enough to look."

He paused and glanced back at Entreri, who sat staring at him hard, and tossed the assassin a flute, seemingly an exact replica of the one Entreri held across his lap.

"Use the real one," Jarlaxle bade him. "The one Ilnezhara gave to you. The one Idalia fashioned those centuries ago."

Idalia put a key inside this flute to unlock any heart, Jarlaxle thought but did not speak, as he turned and walked away.

Entreri looked at the flute in his hands and at the one on his belt. He wasn't really surprised that Jarlaxle had stolen the valuable item and had apparently created an exact copy—no, not exact, Entreri understood as he considered the emptiness of the notes he had blown that day. Physically, the two flutes looked exactly alike, and he marveled at the drow's work as he compared them side by side. But there was more to the real creation of Idalia.

A piece of the craftsman's heart?

Entreri rolled the flute over in his hands, his fingers sliding along the smooth wood, feeling the strength within the apparent delicateness. He lifted the copy in one hand, the original in the other, and closed his eyes. He couldn't tell the difference.

Only when he blew through the flutes could he tell, in the way the music of the real creation washed over him and through him, taking him away with it into what seemed like an alternate reality.

"Wise advice," a voice to the side of the trail greeted Jarlaxle as he moved away from his friend.

Not caught by surprise, Jarlaxle offered Mariabronne a tip of his great hat and said, "You listened in on our private conversation?"

Mariabronne shrugged. "Guilty as charged, I fear. I was moving along the trail when I heard your voice. I meant to keep going, but your words caught me. I have heard such words before, you see, when I was young and learning the ways of the wider world."

"Did your advisor also explain to you the dangers of eavesdropping?"

Mariabronne laughed—or started to, but then cleared his throat instead. "I find you a curiosity, dark elf. Certainly you are different from anyone I have known, in appearance at least. I would know if that is the depth of the variation, or if you are truly a unique being."

"Unique among the lesser races, such as humans, you mean."

This time, Mariabronne did allow himself to laugh.

"I know about the incident with the Kneebreakers," he said.

"I am certain that I do not know of what you speak."

"I am certain that you do," the ranger insisted. "Summoning the wolf was a cunning turn of magic, as returning enough of the ears to Hobart to ingratiate yourself, while keeping enough to build your legend was a cunning turn of diplomacy."

"You presume much."

"The signs were all too easily read, Jarlaxle. This is not presumption but deduction."

"You make it a point to study my every move, of course."

Mariabronne dipped a bow. "I and others."

The drow did well to keep the flicker of alarm from his delicate features.

"We know what you did, but be at ease, for we pass no judgment on that particular action. You have much to overcome concerning the reputation of your heritage, and your little trick did well in elevating you to a position of respectability. I cannot deny any man, or drow, such a climb."

"It is the end of that climb you fear?" Jarlaxle flashed a wide smile, one that enveloped the whole spectrum from sinister to disarming, a perfectly non-readable expression. "To what end?"

The ranger shrugged as if it didn't really matter—not then, at least. "I judge a person by his actions alone. I have known halflings who would cut the throat of an innocent human child and half-orcs who would give their lives in defense of the same. Your antics with the Kneebreakers brought no harm, for the Kneebreakers are an amusing lot whose reputation is well solidified, and they live for adventure and not reputation, in any case. Hobart has certainly forgiven you. He even lifted his mug in toast to your cleverness when it was all revealed to him."

The drow's eyes flared for just a moment—a lapse of control. Jarlaxle was unused to such wheels spinning outside his control, and he didn't like the feeling. For a moment, he almost felt as if he was dealing with the late Matron Baenre, that most devious of dark elves, who always seemed to be pacing ahead of him or even with him. He quickly replayed in his mind all the events of his encounters with the Kneebreakers, recalling Hobart's posture and attitude to see if he could get a fix upon the point when the halfling had discovered the ruse.

He brought a hand up to stroke his chin, staring at Mariabronne all the while and mentally noting that he would do well not to underestimate the man again. It was a difficult thing for a dark elf to take humans and other surface races seriously. All his life Jarlaxle had been told of their inferiority, after all.

But he knew better than that. He'd survived—and thrived—by rising above the limitations of his own prejudices. He affirmed that again, taking the poignant reminder in stride.

"The area is secure?" he asked the ranger.

"We are safe enough."

The drow nodded and started back for the camp.

"Your words to Artėmis Entreri were well spoken," Mariabronne said after him, halting him in his tracks. "The man moves with the grace of a true warrior and with the confidence of an emperor. But only in a martial sense. He is one and alone in every other sense. A pity, I think."

"I am not sure that Artemis Entreri would appreciate your pity."

"It is not for him that I express it but for those around him."

Jarlaxle considered the subtle difference for just a moment then smiled and tipped his hat.

Yes, he thought, Entreri would take that as a great compliment.

More's the pity.

The ground was uneven, sometimes soft, sometimes hard, and full of rocks and mud, withered roots and deep puddles. The drivers and riders in the wagons bounced along, rocking in the uneven sway of the slow ride, heads lolling as they let the jolts play out. Because of the continual jarring, it took Entreri a few moments to detect the sudden vibration beneath his cart, sudden tremors building in momentum under the moving wheels. He looked to Jarlaxle, who seemed similarly awakening to the abrupt change.

Beside the wagon, Ellery's horse pawed the ground. Across and to the front, the horse of one guard reared and whinnied, hooves slashing at the air.

Mariabronne locked his horse under tight control and spurred the creature forward, past Ellery and Entreri's wagon then past the lead wagon.

"Ride through it and ride hard!" the ranger shouted. "Forward, I say! With all speed!"

He cracked his reigns over one side of his horse's neck then the other, spurring the animal on.

Entreri reached for the whip, as did the woman driving the front wagon. Jarlaxle braced himself and stood up, looking around them, as Ellery regained control of her steed and chased off after Mariabronne.

"What is it?" Entreri bade his companion.

"I'm feeling a bump and a bit of a shake," yelled Athrogate from the back of the wagon in front. "I'm thinkin' to find a few monsters to break!"

Entreri watched the dwarf bring forth both his morning stars with a blazing, fluid movement, the balls immediately set to spinning before him.

Athrogate lost all concentration and rhythm a split second later, however, as the ground between the wagons erupted and several snakelike creatures sprang up into the air. They unfurled little wings as they lifted, hovering in place, little fanged mouths smiling in hungry anticipation.

The horse reared again and the poor rider could hardly hold on. Up leaped a snake-creature, right before his terror-wide eyes. He instinctively threw his hands before his face as the serpent spat a stream of acid into his eyes.

Down he tumbled, his weapon still sheathed aside his terrified, leaping horse, and all around him more winged snakes sprang from holes and lifted into the air.

Streams of spittle assaulted the man, setting his cloak smoldering with a dozen wisps of gray smoke. He screamed and rolled as more and more acid struck him, blistering his skin.

His horse leaped and bucked and thundered away, a group of snakes flying in close and hungry pursuit.

Beside the gray-haired man, Davis Eng kept his horse under control and crowded in to try to shield his fallen comrade, but more and more winged snakes came forth from the ground, rising up to intercede. Out came Davis Eng's broadsword, and a quick slash folded one of the hovering snakes around the blade and sent it flying away as he finished through with his great swing.

But another snake was right there, spitting into the soldier's face, blinding him with its acid. He swept his blade back furiously, whipping it about in a futile effort to keep the nasty little creatures at bay.

More venom hit the man and his mount. Another pair of snakes dived in from behind and bit hard at the horse, causing it to rear and shriek in pain. The soldier held on but lost all thoughts of helping his prostrated companion. That prone man continued to squirm under a barrage of acidic streams. He clawed at the ground, trying to get some traction so that he could propel himself away.

But a snake dived onto his neck, wrapping its body around him and driving its acid-dripping fangs into his throat. He grabbed at it frantically with both hands, but other snakes dived in fast and hard, spitting and biting.

Entreri shouted out, and the horses snorted and bucked in terror and swerved to the right, moving up along the uneven and rising foothill.

"Hold them!" Jarlaxle cried, grabbing at the reigns.

The wagon jolted hard, its rear wheel clipping a stone and diving into a deep rut. The horse team broke free, pulling the harness from the frame and taking both Jarlaxle and Entreri with them—for the moment at least. Both kept their sensibilities enough to let go as they came forward from the jolt and tug, and neither was foolish enough to try to resist the sudden momentum. They hit the ground side by side, Entreri in a roll and the drow landing lightly on his feet and running along to absorb the shock.

Entreri came up to his feet in a flash, sword and dagger in hand and already working. He set opaque veils of ash in the air around him, visually shielding himself from the growing throng of winged snakes.

Streams of acidic spittle popped through the sheets of black ash, but the assassin was not caught unaware. Already turning and shifting to avoid the assault, he burst through hard, catching the snakes by surprise as they had tried to catch him. A slash of Charon's Claw took down a pair, and a stab of his jeweled dagger stuck hard into the torso of a third. That snake snapped its head forward to bite at the assassin's wrist, but Entreri was a flash ahead of it, twisting his hand down and flicking the blade to send the creature flying away.

Before the creature had even cleared from the blade, the assassin was on the defensive again, slashing his sword to fend a trio of diving serpents and to deflect three lines of acid.

More came at him from the other side, and he knew he could never defeat them all. He surrendered his ground, leaping back down the hill toward the two dwarves and the thin man, who had formed a triangular defensive posture in the back of the rolling wagon.

Athrogate's twin morning stars moved in a blur, spiked metal balls spinning fast at the end of their respective chains. He worked them out and around with tremendous precision, never interrupting their flow, but cunningly altering their angles to clip and send spinning any snakes that ventured too close. Athrogate let out a series of rhyming curses as he fought, for lines of acidic spittle assaulted him, sending wisps of smoke from his beard and tunic.

Pratcus stood behind him, deep in prayer, and every now and then he called out to Moradin then gently touched his wild bodyguard, using healing magic to help repair some of his many wounds.

To the side of the cleric, the thin man waggled his fingers, sending forth bolts of energy that drove back the nearest creatures.

Entreri knew he had to catch that wagon.

"Make way!" he cried, cutting fast to the side, coming up even with the back of the wagon as he leaped atop a rock.

Athrogate turned fast, giving him safe passage onto the bed. Before the dwarf could yell, "Hold the flank!" Entreri went right past him, between the other dwarf and the thin man. He scrambled over the bench rail to take a seat between the two drivers, both of whom were ducking and screaming in pain.

Entreri threw the hood of his cloak up over his head and grabbed the reins from Calihye. The half-elf woman was obviously blinded and almost senseless.

"Keep them away from me!" he shouted to the trio behind.

He bent low in the seat, urging the horses on faster.

Parissus, sitting to Entreri's right, mumbled something and slumped in hard against him, causing him to twist and inadvertently tug the reins and slow the team. With a growl, Entreri shoved back, not quite realizing that the woman had lost all consciousness. She tumbled back the other way and kept going, right over the side. Entreri grabbed at her but couldn't hold her and hold the team in its run.

He chose the wagon.

The woman rolled off, falling under the front wheel with a grunt, then a second grunt as the back wheel bounced over her.

Calihye cried out and grabbed at Entreri's arm, yelling at him to stop the wagon.

He turned to glower at her, to let her know in no uncertain terms that if she didn't immediately let go of him, he'd toss her off the other side.

She fell back in fear and pain then screamed again as another stream of acidic venom hit her in the face, blistering one cheek.

Hold on! Hold on!

That was all the poor, confused Davis Eng could think as the assault continued. Gone were his hopes for aiding his fallen friend, for he rode on the very edge of doom, disoriented, lost in a sea of hovering, biting, spitting serpents. Lines of blood ran down his arms and along the flanks of his horse, and angry blisters covered half his face.

"Abominations of Zhengyi!" he heard his beloved commander yell from somewhere far, far away—too distant to aid him, he knew.

He had to find a direction and bolt his horse away, but how could he begin to do anything but hold on for all his life?

His horse reared, whinnied, and spun on its hind legs. Then something hit it hard from the side, stopping the turn, and the soldier lurched over and could not hold on.

But a hand grabbed him hard and yanked him upright, then slid past him and grabbed at his reigns, straightening him and his horse out and leading them on.

So great was Mariabronne's control of his mount that the horse accepted the stinging hits from the abominations, accepted the collision with Davis Eng's horse, and carried on exactly as the ranger demanded, finding a line out of there and galloping away.

On the ground behind Mariabronne, the fallen soldier kept squirming and rolling, but he was obviously beyond help. It pained Mariabronne greatly to abandon him, but there was clearly no choice, for dozens of snake creatures slithered around him, biting him repeatedly, filling his veins with their venom.

The horses could outrun the creatures, Mariabronne knew, and that was this other soldier's—and his own—only hope.

The warrior woman cried out, bending low and slashing her axe through the air as her horse thundered on toward the soon-to-be-overwhelmed drow. He worked his arms frantically—and magnificently, Ellery had to admit—sending a stream of spinning daggers at the nearby snakes. He spun continually as well, his cloak flying wide and offering more than nominal protection against the barrage of acidic venom flying his way. Still, he got hit more than once and grimaced in pain, and Ellery was certain that he couldn't possibly keep up the seemingly endless supply of missiles.

She bent lower, winced, and nearly fell from her seat as a stream of caustic fluid struck the side of her jaw, just under the bottom edge of her great helm. She kept her wits about her enough to send her axe swiping forward to tear the wing from another of the snakes, but a second got in over the blade and dived hard onto her wrist and hand. Hooked fangs came forth and jabbed hard through Ellery's gauntlet.

The knight howled and dropped her axe then furiously shook her hand, sending both the gauntlet and the serpent tumbling away. She shouted to the drow and drove her steed on toward him, reaching out her free hand for his.

Jarlaxle caught her grip, his second hand working fast down low with a dagger, and Ellery's surprise was complete when she found herself sliding back from her seat rather than tugging the drow along. Some magic had gripped the dark elf, she realized, for his strength was magnified many times over and he did not yield a step as her horse galloped by.

She was on the ground in a flash, stunned and stumbling, but Jarlaxle held her up on her feet.

"What . . . ?" she started to ask.

The drow jerked her in place in front of him, and Ellery noted faint sparkles in the air around them both, a globe of some sort.

"Do not pull away!" he warned.

He lifted his other hand to show her a black, ruby-tipped wand in his delicate fingers.

The woman's eyes went wide with fear as she glanced over Jarlaxle's shoulder to see a swarm of snakes flying at them.

Jarlaxle didn't show the slightest fear. He just pointed his wand at the ground and uttered a command that dropped a tiny ball of fire from its end.

Ellery instinctively recoiled, but the drow held her fast in his magically-enhanced iron grip.

She recoiled even more when the fireball erupted all around her, angry flames searing the air. She felt her breath sucked out of her lungs, felt the sudden press of blazing heat, and all around her and the drow, the globe sparked and glowed in angry response.

But it held. The killing flames could not get through. Outside that space, though, for a score of feet all around, the fires ate hungrily.

Serpents fell flaming to the ground, charred to a crisp before they landed. Off to the side, the wagon Entreri and Jarlaxle had unceremoniously abandoned flared, the corn in the supply bags already popping in the grip of the great flames. Across the other way, the body of the fallen soldier crackled and charred, as did the dozen serpents that squirmed atop it.

A puff of black smoke billowed into the air above the warrior and the drow. The wagon continued to burn, sending a stream up as well, its timbers crackling in protest.

But other than that, the air around them grew still, preternaturally serene, as if Jarlaxle's fireball had cleansed the air itself.

A wave of heat flashed past Entreri—the hot winds of Jarlaxle's fireball. He heard the thin man in the wagon behind him yell out in the surprise, followed by Athrogate's appreciative, "Good with the boom for clearin' the room!"

If the assassin had any intention of slowing and looking back, though, it was quickly dismissed by the *plop* of acidic spittle on the hood of his cloak and the flapping of serpent wings beside his ear.

Before he could even move to address that situation, he heard a thrumming sound followed by a loud *whack* and the sight of the blasted serpent spiraling out to the side. The thrumming continued and Entreri recognized it as Athrogate's morning stars, the dwarf working them with deadly precision.

"I got yer back, I got yer head," came the dwarf's cry. "Them snakes attack ye, they wind up dead!"

"Just shut up and kill them," Entreri muttered under his breath—or so he thought. A roar of laughter from Athrogate clued him in that he had said it a bit too loudly.

Another serpent went flying away, right past his head, and Entreri heard a quick series of impacts, each accompanied by a dwarf's roar. Entreri did manage to glance to the side to see the remaining woman, fast slipping from consciousness, beginning to roll off the side of the wagon. With a less-than-amused grimace, Entreri grabbed her and tugged her back into place beside him.

Entreri then glanced back and saw Athrogate running around in a fury. His morning stars hummed and flew, splattering snakes and tossing them far aside, launching them up into the air or dropping them straight down to smack hard into the ground.

Behind the two dwarves the thin man stood at the back of the wagon, facing the way they had come and waggling his fingers. A cloud of green fog spewed forth from his hands, trailing the fast-moving wagon.

The serpents in close pursuit pulled up and began to writhe and spasm when they came in contact with the fog. A moment later, they began falling dead to the ground.

"Aye!" the other dwarf cried.

"Poison the air, ye clever wizard?" said Athrogate. "Choking them stinkin', spittin' liza—"

"Don't say it!" Entreri shouted at him.

"What?" the dwarf replied.

"Just shut up," said the assassin.

Athrogate shrugged, his morning stars finally losing momentum and dropping down at the end of their respective chains.

"Ain't nothing left to hit," he remarked.

Entreri glared at him, as if daring him to find a rhyming line.

"Ease up the team," the thin man said. "The pursuit is no more."

Entreri tugged the reigns just a bit and coaxed the horses to slow. He turned the wagon to the side and noted the approach of Mariabronne and the wounded soldier, the ranger still handling both their mounts. Entreri moved around a bit more onto the flat plain, allowing himself a view of the escape route. The wizard's killing cloud of green fog began to dissipate, and the distant burning wagon came more clearly into sight, a pillar of black smoke rising into the air.

Beside him, Calihye coughed and groaned.

Mariabronne handed the soldier's horse over to the care of Athrogate then turned his own horse around and galloped back to the body of the other fallen woman. Looking past him, Entreri noted that the other soldier was dead, for the man's charred corpse was clearly in sight.

From the sight of the fallen woman, all twisted, bloody, and unmoving, the assassin gathered that they had lost two in the encounter.

At least two, he realized, and to his own surprise, a quiver of alarm came over him and he glanced around, calming almost immediately when he noted Jarlaxle off to the other side, up in the foothills, calmly walking toward them. He noted Ellery, too, a bit behind the drow, moving after her scared and riderless mount.

The wounded woman on the ground groaned and Entreri turned to see Mariabronne cradling her head. The ranger gently lifted her battered form from the mud and set her over his horse's back then slowly led the mount back to the wagon.

"Parissus?" Calihye asked. She crawled back into a sitting position, widened her eyes, and called again for her friend, more loudly. "Parissus!"

The look on Mariabronne's face was not promising. Nor was the lifeless movement of Parissus, limply bouncing along.

"Parissus?" the woman beside Entreri cried again, even more urgently as her senses returned. She started past the assassin but stopped short. "You did this to her!" she cried, moving her twisted face right up to Entreri's.

Or trying to, for when the final word escaped her lips, it came forth with a gurgle. Entreri's strong hand clamped against her throat, fingers perfectly positioned to crush her windpipe. She grabbed at the hold with both hands then dropped one low—to retrieve a weapon, Entreri knew.

He wasn't overly concerned, however, for she stopped short when the tip of the assassin's jeweled dagger poked in hard under her chin.

"Would you care to utter another accusation?" Entreri asked.

"Be easy, boy," said Athrogate.

Beside him, the other dwarf began to quietly chant.

"If that is a spell aimed at me, then you would be wise to reconsider," said Entreri.

The dwarf cleric did stop—but only when a drow hand grabbed him by the shoulder.

"There is no need for animosity," Jarlaxle said to them all. "A difficult foe, but one vanquished."

"Because you decided to burn them, and your companion," accused the shaken, shivering half-elf soldier.

"Your friend was dead long before I initiated the fireball," said the drow. "And if I had not, then I and Commander Ellery would have suffered a similar fate."

"You do not know that!"

Jarlaxle shrugged as if it did not matter. "I saved myself and Commander Ellery. I could not have saved your friend, nor could you, in any case."

"Abominations of Zhengyi," said Mariabronne, drawing close to the others. "More may be about. We have no time for this foolishness."

Entreri looked at the ranger, then at Jarlaxle, who nodded for him to let the half-elf go. He did just that, offering her one last warning glare.

Calihye gagged a bit and fell back from him, but recovered quickly. She scrambled from the wagon bench and over to her fallen companion. Mariabronne let her pass by, but looked to the others and shook his head.

"I got some spells," the dwarf cleric said.

Mariabronne walked away from the horse, leaving the woman with her fallen friend. "Then use them," he told the dwarf. "But I doubt they will be of help. She is full of poison and the fall broke her spine."

The dwarf nodded grimly and ambled past him. He grabbed at the smaller Calihye, who was sobbing uncontrollably, and seemed as if she would melt into the ground beside the horse.

"Parissus . . ." she whispered over and over.

"A stream of drats for being her," Athrogate muttered.

"At least," said Jarlaxle.

The sound of an approaching horse turned them all to regard Ellery.

"Mariabronne, with me," the commander instructed. "We will go back and see what we can salvage. I need to retrieve my battle-axe and we have another horse running free. I'll not leave it behind." She glanced at the fallen woman, as Pratcus and Calihye were easing her down from the horse. "What of her?"

"No," Mariabronne said, his voice quiet and respectful.

"Put her in the wagon then, and get it moving along," Ellery instructed.

Her callous tone drew a grin from Entreri. He could tell that she was agitated under that calm facade.

"I am Canthan," he heard the thin man tell Jarlaxle. "I witnessed your blast. Most impressive. I did not realize that you dabbled in the Art."

"I am a drow of many talents."

Canthan bowed and seemed impressed.

"And many items," Entreri had to put in.

Jarlaxle tipped his great hat and smiled.

Entreri didn't return his smile, though, for the assassin had caught the gaze of Calihye. He saw a clear threat in her blue-gray eyes. Yes, she blamed him for her friend's fall.

"Come along, ye dolts, and load the wagon!" Athrogate roared as Mariabronne and Ellery started off. "Be quick afore Zhengyi attacks with a dragon! *Bwahaha!*"

"It will be an interesting ride," Jarlaxle said to Entreri as he climbed up onto the bench beside the assassin.

"'Interesting' is a good word," Entreri replied.

CHAPTER

WITH OPEN HEART

10

At ease, my large friend," Wingham said, patting his hands in the air to calm the half-orc.

But Olgerkhan would not be calmed. "She's dying! I tried to help, but I cannot."

"We don't know that she's dying."

"She's sick again, and worse now than before," Olgerkhan continued. "The castle grows and its shadow makes Arrayan sick."

Wingham started to respond again but paused and considered what Olgerkhan had said. No doubt the somewhat dim warrior was making only a passing connection, using the castle to illustrate his fears for Arrayan, but in that simple statement Wingham heard a hint of truth. Arrayan had opened the book, after all. Was it possible that in doing so, she had created a magical bond between herself and the tome? Wingham had suspected that she'd served as a catalyst, but might it be more than that?

"Old Nyungy, is he still in town?" the merchant asked.

"Nyungy?" echoed Olgerkhan. "The talespinner?"

"Yes, the same."

Olgerkhan shrugged and said, "I haven't seen him in some time, but I know his house."

"Take me to it, at once."

"But Arrayan . . ."

"To help Arrayan," Wingham explained.

The moment the words left his mouth, Olgerkhan grabbed his hands and pulled him away from the wagon, tugging him to the north and the city. They moved at full speed, which meant the poor old merchant was half-running and half-flying behind the tugging warrior.

In short order, they stood before the dilapidated door of an old, three-story house, its exterior in terrible disrepair, dead vines climbing halfway up the structure, new growth sprouting all over it with roots cracking into the foundation stones.

Without the slightest pause, Olgerkhan rapped hard on the door, which shook and shifted as if the heavy knocks would dislodge it from its precarious perch.

"Easy, friend," Wingham said. "Nyungy is very old. Give him time to answer."

"Nyungy!" Olgerkhan yelled out.

He thumped the house beside the door so hard the whole of the building trembled. Then he moved his large fist back in line with the door and cocked his arm.

He stopped when the door pulled in, revealing a bald, wrinkled old man, more human than orc in appearance, save teeth too long to fit in his mouth. Brown spots covered his bald pate, and a tuft of gray hair sprouted from a large mole on the side of his thick nose. He trembled as he stood there, as if he might just fall over, but in his blue eyes, both Olgerkhan and Wingham saw clarity that defied his age.

"Oh, please do not strike me, large and impetuous child," he said in a wheezing, whistling voice. "I doubt you'd find much sport in laying me low. Wait a few moments and save yourself the trouble, for my old legs won't hold me upright for very long!" He ended with a laugh that fast transformed into a cough.

Olgerkhan lowered his arm and shrugged, quite embarrassed.

Wingham put a hand on Olgerkhan's shoulder and gently eased him aside then stepped forward to face old Nyungy.

"Wingham?" the man asked. "Wingham, are you back again?"

"Every year, old friend," answered the merchant, "but I have not seen you in a decade or more. You so used to love the flavors of my carnival . . ."

"I still would, young fool," Nyungy replied, "but it is far too great a walk for me."

Wingham bowed low. "Then my apologies for not seeking you out these past years."

"But you are here now. Come in. Come in. Bring your large friend, but please do not let him punch my walls anymore."

Wingham chuckled and glanced at the mortified Olgerkhan. Nyungy began to fade back into the shadows of the house, but Wingham bade him to stop.

"Another time, certainly," the merchant explained. "But we have not come for idle chatter. There is an event occurring near to Palishchuk that needs your knowledge and wisdom."

"I long ago gave up the road, the song, and the sword."

"It is not far to travel," Wingham pressed, "and I assure you that I would not bother you if there was any other way. But there is a great construct in process—a relic of Zhengyi's, I suspect."

"Speak not that foul name!"

"I agree," Wingham said with another bow. "And I would not, if there was another way to prompt you to action."

Nyungy rocked back a bit and considered the words. "A construct, you say?"

"I am certain that if you climbed to your highest room and looked out your north window, you could see it from here."

Nyungy glanced back into the room behind him, and the rickety staircase ascending the right-hand wall.

"I do not much leave the lowest floor. I doubt I could climb those stairs." He was grinning when he turned back to Wingham, then kept turning to eye Olgerkhan. "But perhaps your large friend here might assist me—might assist us both, if your legs are as old as my own."

Wingham didn't need the help of Olgerkhan to climb the stairs, though the wooden railing was fragile and wobbly, with many balusters missing or leaning out or in, no longer attached to the rail. The old merchant led the way, with Olgerkhan carrying Nyungy close behind and occasionally putting his hand out to steady Wingham.

The staircase rose about fifteen feet, opening onto a balcony that ran the breadth of the wide foyer and back again. Across the way, a second staircase climbed to the third story. That one seemed more solid, with the balusters all in place, but it hadn't been used in years, obviously, and Wingham had to brush away cobwebs to continue. As the stairs spilled out on the south side of the house, Wingham had to follow the balcony all the way back around the other side to the north room's door. He glanced back when he got there, for Nyungy was walking again and had lost ground with his pronounced limp. Nyungy waved for him to go on, and so he pressed through the door, crossing to the far window where he pulled aside the drape.

Staring out to the north, Wingham nearly fell over, for though he had expected to view the growing castle, he didn't expect how dominant the structure would be from so far away. Only a few days had passed since Wingham had ventured to the magical book and the structure growing behind it, and the castle was many times the size it had been. Wingham couldn't see the book from so great a distance, obviously, but the circular stone keep that grew behind it was clearly visible, rising high above the Vaasan plain. More startling was the fact that the keep was far to the back of the structure, centering a back wall anchored by two smaller round towers at its corners. From those, the walls moved south, toward Palishchuk, and Wingham could see the signs of a growing central gatehouse at what he knew would be the front wall of the upper bailey.

Several other structures were growing before the gatehouse as well, an outer bailey and a lower wall already climbed up from the ground.

"By the gods, what did he do?" old Nyungy asked, coming up beside Wingham.

"He left us some presents, so it would seem," Wingham answered.

"It seems almost a replica of Castle Perilous, curse the name," Nyungy remarked.

Wingham looked over at the old bard, knowing well that

Nyungy was one of the few still alive who had glimpsed that terrible place during the height of Zhengyi's power.

"A wizard did this," Nyungy said.

"Zhengyi, as I explained."

"No, my old friend Wingham, I mean now. A wizard did this. A wizard served as catalyst to bring life to the old power of the Witch-King. Now."

"Some curses are without end," Wingham replied, but he held back the rest of his thoughts concerning Arrayan and his own foolishness in handing her the book. He had thought it an instruction manual for necromancy or golem creation or a history, perhaps. He could never have imagined the truth of it.

"Please come out with me, Nyungy," Wingham bade.

"To there?" the old man said with a horrified look. "My adventuring days are long behind me, I fear. I have no strength to do battle with—"

"Not there," Wingham explained. "To the house of a friend: my niece, who is in need of your wisdom at this darkening hour."

Nyungy looked at Wingham with unveiled curiosity and asked, "The wizard?"

Wingham's grim expression was all the answer the older half-orc needed.

Wingham soon found that Olgerkhan had not been exaggerating in his insistence that the old merchant go quickly to Arrayan. The woman appeared many times worse than before. Her skin was pallid and seemed bereft of fluid, like gray, dry paper. She tried to rise up from the bed, where Olgerkhan had propped her almost to a sitting position with pillows, but Wingham could see that the strain was too great and he quickly waved her back to her more comfortable repose.

Arrayan looked past Wingham and Olgerkhan to the hunched, elderly half-orc. Her expression fast shifted from inviting to suspicious.

"Do you know my friend Nyungy?" Wingham asked her.

Arrayan continued to carefully scrutinize the old half-orc, some spark of distant recognition showing in her tired eyes.

"Nyungy is well-versed in the properties of magic," Wingham explained. "He will help us help you."

"Magic?" Arrayan asked, her voice weak.

Nyungy came forward and leaned over her. "Little Arrayan Maggotsweeper?" he said. The woman winced at the sound of her name. "Always a curious sort, you were, when you were young. I am not surprised to learn that you are a wizard—and a mighty one, if that castle is any indication."

Arrayan absorbed the compliment just long enough to recognize the implication behind it then her face screwed up with horror.

"I did not create the castle," she said.

Nyungy started to respond, but he stopped short, as if he had just caught on to her claim.

"Pardon my mistake," he said at last.

The old half-orc bent lower to look into her eyes. He bade Olgerkhan to go and fetch her some water or some soup, spent a few more moments scrutinizing her, then backed off as the larger half-orc returned. With a nod, Nyungy motioned for Wingham to escort him back into the house's front room.

"She is not ill," the old bard explained when they had moved out of Arrayan's chamber.

"Not sick, you mean?"

Nyungy nodded. "I knew it before we arrived, but in looking at her, I am certain beyond doubt. That is no poison or disease. She was healthy just a few days ago, correct?"

"Dancing lightly on her pretty feet when she first came to greet me upon my arrival."

"It is the magic," Nyungy reasoned. "Zhengyi has done this before."

"How?"

"The book is a trap. It is not a tome of creation, but one of *self*-creation. Once one of suitable magical power begins to read it, it entraps that person's life essence. As the castle grows, it does so at the price of Arrayan's life-force, intellect, and magical prowess. She is creating the castle, subconsciously."

"For how long?" Wingham asked, and he stepped over and glanced with concern into the bedroom.

"Until she is dead, I would guess," said Nyungy. "Consumed by the creation. I doubt that the merciless Zhengyi would stop short of such an eventuality out of compassion for his unwitting victim."

"How can we stop this?" Wingham asked.

Nyungy glanced past him with concern then painted a look of grim dread on his face when he again met Wingham's stare.

"No, you cannot," Wingham said with sudden understanding.

"That castle is a threat—growing, and growing stronger," reasoned Nyungy. "Your niece is lost, I fear. There is nothing I can do, certainly, nor can anyone else in Palishchuk, to slow the progression that will surely kill her."

"We have healers."

"Who will be powerless, at best," answered the older half-orc. "Or, if they are not, and offer Arrayan some relief, then that might only add to the energy being channeled into the growth of Zhengyi's monstrosity. I understand your hesitance here, my friend. She is your relation—beloved, I can see from your eyes when you look upon her. But do you not remember the misery of Zhengyi? Would you, in your false compassion, help foster a return to that?"

Wingham glanced back into the room once more and said, "You cannot know all this for sure. There is much presumption here."

"I know, Wingham. This is not mere coincidence. And you know, too." As he finished, Nyungy moved to the counter and found a long kitchen knife. "I will be quick about it. She will not see the strike coming. Let us pray it is not too late to save her soul and to diminish the evil she has unwittingly wrought."

Wingham could hardly breathe, could hardly stand. He tried to digest Nyungy's words and reasoning, looking for some flaw, for some sliver of hope. He instinctively put his arm out to block the old half-orc, but Nyungy moved with a purpose that he had not known in many, many years. He brushed by Wingham and into the bedroom and bade Olgerkhan to stand aside.

The large half-orc did just that, leaving the way open to Arrayan, who was resting back with her eyes closed and her breathing shallow.

Nyungy knew much of the world around Palishchuk. He had spent his decades adventuring, touring the countryside as a wandering minstrel, a collector of information and song alike. He had traveled extensively with Wingham for years as well, studying magic and magical items. He had served in Zhengyi's army in the early days of the Witch-King's rise, before the awful truth about the horrible creature was fully realized. Nyungy didn't doubt his guess about the insidious bond that had been created between the book and the reader, nor did he question the need for him to do his awful deed before the castle's completion.

His mind was still sharp; he knew much.

What he did not comprehend was the depth of the bond between Arrayan and Olgerkhan. He didn't think to hide his intent as he brandished that long knife and moved toward the helpless woman.

Something in his eyes betrayed him to Olgerkhan. Something in his forward, eager posture told the young half-orc warrior that the old half-orc was about no healing exercise—at least, not in any manner Olgerkhan's sensibilities would allow.

Nyungy lurched for Arrayan's throat and was stopped cold by a powerful hand latching onto his forearm. He struggled to pull away, but he might as well have been trying to stop a running horse.

"Let me go, you oaf!" he scolded, and Arrayan opened her eyes to regard the two of them standing before her.

Olgerkhan turned his wrist over, easily forcing Nyungy's knife-hand up into the air, and the old half-orc grimaced in pain.

"I must . . . You do not understand!" Nyungy argued.

Olgerkhan looked from Nyungy to Wingham, who stood in the doorway.

"It is for her own good," Nyungy protested. "Like bloodletting for poison, you see?"

Olgerkhan continued to look to Wingham for answers.

Nyungy went on struggling then froze in place when he heard Wingham say, "He means to kill her, Olgerkhan."

Nyungy's eyes went wide and wider still when the young, strong half-orc's fist came soaring in to smack him in the face, launching him backward and to the floor, where he knew no more.

CHAPTER
PALISHCHUK'S SHADOW
11

Hurry!" Calihye shouted at Entreri. "Drive them harder!"

Entreri grunted in reply but did not put the whip to the team. He understood her desperation, but it was hardly his problem. Across a wide expanse of rocky ground with patches of mud, far up ahead, loomed the low skyline of Palishchuk. They were still some time away from the city, Entreri knew, and if he drove the team any harder, the horses would likely collapse before they reached the gates.

Jarlaxle sat beside him on the bench, with Athrogate next to him, far to Entreri's left. Pratcus sat in the back, along with Calihye and the two wounded, the soldier Davis Eng and Calihye's broken companion, Parissus.

"Harder, I say, on your life!" Calihye screamed from behind.

Entreri resisted the urge to pull the team up. Jarlaxle put a hand on his forearm, and when he glanced at the drow, Jarlaxle motioned for him to not respond.

In truth, Entreri wasn't thinking of shouting back at the desperate woman, though the thought of drawing his dagger, leaping back, and cutting out her wagging tongue occurred to him more than once.

A second hand landed on the assassin's other shoulder, and he snapped his cold and threatening glare back the other way, face-to-face with Pratcus.

"The lady Parissus is sure to be dying," the dwarf explained. "She's got moments and no more."

"I cannot drive them faster than—" Entreri started to reply, but the dwarf cut him short with an upraised hand and a look that showed no explanation was needed.

"I'm only telling ye so ye don't go back and shut the poor girl up," Pratcus explained. "Them half-elves are a bit on the lamenting side, if ye get me meaning."

"There is nothing you can do for the woman?" Jarlaxle asked.

"I got all I can handle in keeping Davis Eng alive," Pratcus explained. "And he weren't hurt much at all in comparison, except a bit o' acid burns. It's the damn bites she got. So many of 'em. Poisoned they were, and a nasty bit o' the stuff. And Parissus, she'd be dying without the poison, though I'm sure there's enough to kill us all running through her veins."

"Then have Athrogate smash her skull," Entreri said. "Be done with it, and done with her pain."

"She's far beyond any pain, I'm thinking."

"More's the pity," said Entreri.

"He gets like that when he's frustrated," Jarlaxle quipped.

He received a perfectly vicious look from Entreri and of course, the drow responded with a disarming grin.

"That soldier gonna live, then?" asked Athrogate, but Pratcus could only shrug.

Behind them all, Calihye cried out.

"Saved me a swat," Athrogate remarked, understanding, as did they all from the hollow and helpless timbre of the shriek that death had at last come for Parissus.

Calihye continued to wail, even after Pratcus joined her and tried to comfort her.

"Might be needing a swat, anyway," Athrogate muttered after a few moments of the keening.

Ellery pulled her horse us beside the rolling wagon, inquiring of the cleric for Parissus and her soldier.

"Nasty bit o' poison," Entreri and Jarlaxle heard the dwarf remark.

"We're not even to the city, and two are down," Entreri said to the drow.

"Two less to split the treasures that no doubt await us at the end of our road."

Entreri didn't bother to reply.

A short while later, the Palishchuk skyline much clearer before them, the troupe noted the circle of brightly colored wagons set before the city's southern wall. At that point, Mariabronne galloped past the wagon, moving far ahead.

"Wingham the merchant and his troupe," Ellery explained, coming up beside Entreri.

"I do not know of him," Jarlaxle said to her.

"Wingham," Athrogate answered slyly, and all eyes went to him, to see him holding one of his matched glassteel morning stars out before him, letting the spiked head sway and bounce at the end of its chain with the rhythm of the moving wagon.

"Wingham is known for trading in rare items, particularly weapons," Ellery explained. "He would have more than a passing interest in your sword," she added to Entreri.

Entreri grinned despite himself. He could imagine handing the weapon over to an inquiring "Wingham," whoever or whatever a "Wingham" might be. Without the protective gauntlet, an unwitting or weaker individual trying to hold Charon's Claw would find himself overmatched and devoured by the powerful, sentient item.

"A fine set of morning stars," Jarlaxle congratulated the dwarf.

"Finer than ye're knowing," Athrogate replied with a grotesque wink. "Putting foes to flying farther than ye're throwing!"

Entreri chortled.

"Fine weapons," Jarlaxle agreed.

"Enchanted mightily," said Ellery.

Jarlaxle looked from the rocking morning star back to the commander and said, "I will have to pay this Wingham a visit, I see."

"Bring a sack o' gold!" the dwarf hollered. "And a notion to part with it!"

"Wingham is known as a fierce trader," Ellery explained.

"Then I really will have to pay him a visit," said the drow.

Pratcus waddled back up to lean between Entreri and the drow. "She's gone," he confirmed. "Better for her that it went quick, I'm thinking, for she weren't to be using her arms or legs e'er again."

That did make Entreri wince a bit, recalling the bumps as the wagon had bounced over poor Parissus.

"What of Davis Eng?" Ellery asked.

"He's a sick one, but I'm thinking he'll get back to his feet. A few tendays in the bed'll get him up."

"A month?" Ellery replied. She did not seem pleased with that information.

"Three gone," Entreri mumbled to the drow, who didn't really seem to care.

Ellery obviously did, however. "Keep him alive, at all cost," she instructed then she turned her horse aside and drove her heels into its flanks, launching it away.

Accompanied by the continuing sobs of Calihye, Entreri took the wagon the rest of the way to Palishchuk. On Ellery's orders, he rolled the cart past Wingham's circus and to the city's southern gate, where they were given passage without interference—no doubt arranged by Mariabronne, who had long ago entered the city.

They pulled up beside a guardhouse, just inside the southern gate, and stable hands and attendants came to greet them.

"I promise you that I will not forget what you did," Calihye whispered to Entreri as she moved past him to climb down from the wagon.

Jarlaxle again put a hand on the assassin's forearm, but Entreri wasn't about to respond to that open threat—with words anyway.

Entreri rarely if ever responded to threats with words. In his thoughts, he understood that Calihye would soon again stand beside Parissus.

A trio of city guards hustled out to collect Davis Eng, bidding

Pratcus to go with them. Another couple came out to retrieve the body of Parissus.

"We have rooms secured inside, though we'll not be here long," Ellery explained to the others. "Make yourself at ease; take your rest as you can."

"You are leaving us?" the drow asked.

"Mariabronne has left word that I am to meet him at Wingham's circus," she explained. "I will return presently with word of our course."

"Your course," Calihye corrected, drawing all eyes her way. "I'm through with you, then."

"You knew the dangers when you joined my quest," Ellery scolded, but not too angrily, "as did Parissus."

"I'm to be no part of a team with that one," Calihye retorted, tipping her chin in Entreri's direction. "He'll throw any of us to our doom to save himself. A wonder it is that even one other than him and that drow survived the road."

Ellery looked at the assassin, who merely shrugged.

"Bah! But yer friend fell and flees to the Hells," Athrogate cut in. "We're all for dyin', whate'er we're tryin', so quit yer cryin'! *Bwahaha!*"

Calihye glowered at him, which made him laugh all the more. He waddled away toward the guardhouse, seeming totally unconcerned.

"He is one to be wary of," Jarlaxle whispered to Entreri, and the assassin didn't disagree.

"You agreed to see this through," Ellery said to Calihye. She moved over as she spoke, and forcibly turned the woman to face her. "Parissus is gone and there's naught I, or you, can do about it. We've a duty here."

"Your own duty, and mine no more."

Ellery leveled a hard stare at her.

"Will I be finding myself an outlaw in King Gareth's lands, then, because I refuse to travel with a troupe of unreliables?"

Ellery's look softened. "No, of course not. I will ask of you only that you stay and look over Davis Eng. It seems that he'll be journeying with us no farther as well. When we are done with Palishchuk, we will return you to the Vaasan Gate—with Parissus's body, if that is your choice."

"And my share is still secure?" the woman dared ask. "And Parissus's, which she willed to me before your very eyes?"

To the surprise of both Entreri and Jarlaxle, Ellery didn't hesitate in agreeing.

"An angry little creature," Jarlaxle whispered to his friend.

"A source of trouble?" Entreri mused.

"Mariabronne has returned," Wingham informed Olgerkhan when he found the large half-orc back at Nyungy's house. "He has brought a commander from the Vaasan Gate, along with several other mercenaries, to inspect the castle. They will find a way, Olgerkhan. Arrayan will be saved."

The warrior looked at him with undisguised skepticism.

"You will join them in their journey," Wingham went on, "to help them in finding a way to defeat the curse of Zhengyi."

"And you will care for Arrayan?" Olgerkhan asked with that same evident doubt. He glanced to the side of the wide foyer, to a door that led to a small closet. "You will protect her from him?"

Wingham glanced that way, as well. "You put the great Nyungy in a closet?"

Olgerkhan shrugged, and Wingham started that way.

"Leave him in there!" Olgerkhan demanded.

Wingham spun back on him, stunned that the normally docile—or controllable, at least—warrior had so commanded him.

"Leave him in there," Olgerkhan reiterated. "I beg of you. He can breathe. He is not dangerously bound."

The two stared at each other for a long while, and it seemed to Olgerkhan as if Wingham was fighting an internal struggle over some decision. The old merchant started to speak a couple of times, but kept stopping short and finally just assumed a pensive pose.

"I will not care for Arrayan," Wingham said decided at last.

"Then I will not leave her."

Wingham stepped toward Olgerkhan, reaching into his coat pocket as he did. Olgerkhan leaned back, defensive, but calmed when he noted the objects Wingham had produced: a pair of rings, gold bands with a clear gemstone set in each.

"Where is she?" Wingham asked. "Back at her house?"

Olgerkhan stared at him a bit longer, then shook his head. He glanced up the stairs then led the way to the first balcony. In a small bedroom, they came upon Arrayan, lying very still but breathing with a smooth rhythm.

"She felt better, a bit," Olgerkhan explained.

"Does she know of Nyungy?"

"I told her that he was with you, looking for some answers."

Wingham nodded, then moved to his niece. He sat on the bed beside her, blocking much of Olgerkhan's view. He bent low for a moment then moved aside.

Olgerkhan's gaze was drawn to the woman and to the ring Wingham had placed on her finger. The clear gem sparkled for a brief moment then it went gray, as if smoke had somehow filtered into the gemstone. It continued to darken as Olgerkhan moved closer, and by the time he gently lifted Arrayan's hand for a closer inspection, the gem was as inky black as onyx.

The warrior looked at Wingham, who stood with his hand out toward Olgerkhan, holding the other ring.

"Are you strong enough to share her burden?" Wingham asked.

Olgerkhan looked at him, not quite understanding. Wingham held up the other ring.

"These are Rings of Arbitration," the old merchant explained. "Both a blessing and a curse, created long ago by magic long lost to the world. Only a few pairs existed, items crafted for iovers who were bound body and soul."

"Arrayan and I are not—"

"I know, but it does not matter. What matters is what's in your heart. Are you strong enough to share her burden, and are you willing to die for her, or beside her, should it come to that?"

"I am. Of course," Olgerkhan answered without the slightest hesitation.

He reached for Wingham and took the offered ring. With but a fleeting glance at Arrayan, he slid the ring on his finger. Before he even had it in place, a profound weariness came over him. His vision swam and his head throbbed with a sharp pain. His stomach churned from the waves of dizziness and his legs wobbled as if they would simply fold beneath him. He felt as if a taloned hand had materialized within him and had begun to tug at his very life-force, twanging that thin line of energy so sharply and insistently that Olgerkhan feared it would just shatter, explode into a scattering of energy.

He felt Wingham's hand on him, steadying him, and he used the tangible grip as a guide back to the external world. Through his bleary vision he spotted Arrayan, lying still but with her eyes open. She moved one arm up to brush back her thick hair, and even through the haze it was apparent to Olgerkhan that the color had returned to her face.

He understood it all then, so clearly. Wingham had asked him to "share her burden."

That thought in mind, the half-orc growled and forced the dizziness aside, then straightened his posture, grabbed Wingham's hand with his own, and pointedly moved it away. He looked to the old merchant and nodded. Then he glanced down at his ring and watched as a blood-red mist flowed into it and swirled in the facets of the cut stone. The mist turned gray, but a light gray, not the blackness he had seen upon poor Arrayan's finger.

He glanced back at the woman, at her ring, and saw that it, too, was no longer onyx black.

"Through the power of the rings, the burden is shared," Wingham whispered to him. "I can only hope that I have not just given a greater source of power to the growing construct."

"I will not fail in this," Olgerkhan assured him, though neither of them really knew what "this" might actually mean.

Wingham moved over and studied Arrayan, who was resting more comfortably, obviously, though she had again closed her eyes.

"It is a temporary reprieve," the merchant said. "The tower will continue to draw from her, and as she weakens, so too will you. This is our last chance—our only chance—to save her. Both of you will go with Mariabronne and Gareth's emissary. Defeat the power that has grown dark on our land, but if you cannot, Olgerkhan, then there is something else you must do for me."

The large half-orc stood attentively, staring hard at old Wingham.

"You must not let the castle have her," Wingham explained.

"Have her?"

"Consume her," came the reply. "I cannot truly comprehend what that even means, but Nyungy, who is wiser than I, was insistent on this point. The castle grows through the life-force of Arrayan, and the castle has made great gains because we did not know what we battle. Even now, we cannot understand how to defeat it, but defeat it you must, and quickly. And if you cannot, Olgerkhan, I will have your word that you will not let the castle consume my dear Arrayan!"

Olgerkhan's gaze went to Arrayan again as he tried to sort through the words, and as Wingham's meaning finally began to dawn on him, his soft appearance took on a much harder edge. "You ask me to kill her?"

"I ask for your mercy and demand of you your strength."

Olgerkhan seemed as if he would stride over and tear Wingham's head from his shoulders.

"If you cannot do this for me then . . ." Wingham began, and he lifted Arrayan's limp arm and grabbed at the ring.

"Do not!"

"Then I will have your word," said the merchant. "Olgerkhan, there is no choice before us. Go and do battle, if battle is to be found. Mariabronne is wise in the ways of the world, and he has brought an interesting troupe with him, including a dark elf and a wizened sage from Damara. But if the battle cannot be won, or won in time, then you must not allow the castle to take Arrayan. You must find the strength to be merciful."

Olgerkhan was breathing in rough pants by then, and he felt his heart tearing apart as he looked at his dear Arrayan lying on the bed.

"Put her hand down," Olgerkhan said at length. "I understand and will not fail in this. The castle will not have Arrayan, but if she dies at my hand, know that I will fast follow her to the next world."

Wingham slowly nodded.

"Better this than to enter the castle beside that troublesome dwarf," said Davis Eng, his voice weak with poison.

Herbalists had come to him, and Pratcus had worked more spells over him. He would survive, they all agreed, but it would be some time before he even had the strength to return to the Vaasan Gate, and it would likely be tendays before he could lift his sword again.

"Athrogate?" Calihye asked.

"A filthy little wretch."

"If he heard you say that, he'd crush your skull," the woman replied. "The finest fighter at the wall, so it was said, and there's more than a little magic in those morning stars he swings so cleverly."

"Strength of arm is one thing. Strength of heart another. Has one so fine ever thought to enlist in the Army of Bloodstone?"

"By serving at the wall, he serves the designs of King Gareth," Calihye reminded.

Flat on his back, Davis Eng lifted a trembling hand and waved that notion away.

Calihye persisted. "How many monster ears has he delivered to your Commander Ellery, then? And those of giants, too. Not many can lay claim to felling a giant in single combat, but it's one that Athrogate all too easily brandishes."

"And how do you know he was alone? He's got that skinny friend of his—more trouble than the dwarf!"

"And more dangerous," said Calihye. "Speak not ill of Canthan in my presence."

Davis Eng lifted his head enough to glower at her.

"And be particularly wise to do as I say as you lie there helplessly," the woman added, and that made the man lay his head back down.

"I didn't know you were friends."

"Me and Canthan?" The woman snorted. "The more ground's between us, the calmer beats my heart. But like your dwarf, that one is better on my side than my opponent's." She paused and moved across the small room to the fire pit, where a kettle of stew simmered. "You want more?"

The man waved and shook his head. It already seemed as though he was falling far, far away from the conscious world.

"Better to be out here, indeed," Calihye said—to herself, for Davis Eng had lapsed into unconsciousness. "They're for going into that castle, so I'm hearing, and that's no place I'm wanting to be, Athrogate and Canthan beside me or not."

"But did you not just say that the dwarf was a fine warrior?" came a different voice behind her, and the woman froze in place. "And the skinny one even more dangerous?"

Calihye didn't dare turn about; she knew from the proximity of the voice that the newcomer could take her down efficiently if she threatened him. How had he gotten so near? How had he even gotten into the room?

"Might I even know who's addressing me?" she dared ask.

A hand grabbed her shoulder and guided her around to look into the dark eyes of Artemis Entreri. Anger flared in Calihye's eyes, and she had to fight the urge to leap upon the man who had allowed her friend to fall beneath the wagon wheels.

Wisdom overcame the temptation, though, for in looking at the man, standing so at ease, his hands relaxed and ready to bring forth one of his ornamented weapons in the blink of an eye, she knew that she had no chance.

Not now. Not with her own weapons across the way next to Davis Eng's bed.

Entreri smiled at her, and she knew that her glance at the sleeping soldier had betrayed her.

"What do you want?" she asked.

"I wanted you to keep on speaking, that I could hear what I needed to hear and be on my way," Entreri replied. "Since that is not an option, apparently, I decided to bid you continue."

"Continue what?"

"Your appraisal of Athrogate and Canthan, to start," said the assassin. "And any information you might offer on the others."

"Why should I offer anyth—"

She bit off the last word, and nearly the tip of her tongue as faster than her eye could even follow, the assassin had his jeweled dagger in his hand and tip-in against the underside of her chin.

"Because I do not like you," Entreri explained. "And unless you make me like you in the next few minutes, I will make your death unbearable."

He pressed in just a bit harder, forcing Calihye up on her tip-toes.

"I can offer gold," she said through her gritted teeth.

"I will take whatever gold of yours I want," he assured her.

"Please," she begged. "By what right—"

"Did you not threaten me out on the road?" he said. "I do not let such chatter pass me by. I do not leave enemies alive in my wake."

"I am not your enemy," she rasped. "Please, if you let me show you."

She lifted one hand as if to gently stroke him, but he only grinned and pressed that awful dagger in more tightly, breaking the skin just a bit.

"I don't find you charming," Entreri said. "I don't find you alluring. It annoys me that you are still alive. You have very little time left."

He let the dagger draw a bit of the half-elf's life-force into its vampiric embrace. Calihye's eyes widened in an expression so full of horror that the assassin knew he had her undivided attention.

He reached up with his other hand, planted it on her chest, and retracted the dagger as he unceremoniously shoved her back and to the side of the cooking pit.

"What would you ask of me?" Calihye gasped, one hand clutching her chin as if she believed she had to contain her life's essence.

"What more is there to know of Athrogate and Canthan?"

The woman held up her hands as if she didn't understand.

"You battle monsters for your living, yet you fear Canthan," said Entreri. "Why?"

"He has dangerous friends."

"What friends?"

The woman swallowed hard.

"Two beats of your fast-beating heart," said Entreri.

"They say he is associated with the citadel."

"What citadel? And do understand that I grow weary of prying each word from your mouth one at a time."

"The Citadel of Assassins."

Entreri nodded his understanding, for he had indeed heard whispers of the shadowy band, living on after the fall of Zhengyi, digging out their kingdom in the shadows created by the brilliance of King Gareth's shining light. They were not so different than the pashas Entreri had served for so long on the streets of Calimport.

"And the dwarf?"

"I know not," said Calihye. "Dangerous, of course, and mighty in battle. That he even speaks to Canthan frightens me. That is all."

"And the others?"

Again the woman held up her hand as if she did not understand. "The other dwarf?"

"I know nothing of him."

"Ellery?" he asked, but he shook his head even as the name left his lips, doubting there was anything the half-elf might tell him of the red-haired commander. "Mariabronne?"

"You have not heard of Mariabronne the Rover?"

A glare from Entreri reminded her that it really wasn't her place to ask the questions.

"He is the most renowned traveler in Vaasa, a man of legend," Calihye explained. "It is said that he could track a swift-flying bird over mountains of empty stone. He is fine with the blade and finer with his wits, and always he seems in the middle of momentous events. Every child in Damara can tell you tales of Mariabronne the Rover."

"Wonderful," the assassin muttered under his breath. He moved across the room to Calihye's sword belt, hooked it with his foot and sent it flying to her waiting grasp.

"Well enough," he said to her. "Is there anything more you wish to add?"

She looked from the sword to the assassin and said, "I cannot travel with you—I am charged with guarding Davis Eng."

"Travel? Milady, you'll not leave this room. But your words satisfied me. I believe you. And I assure you, that is no small thing."

"Then what?"

"You have earned the right to defend yourself."

"Against you?"

"While I suspect you would rather fight him,"—he gave a quick glance at the unconscious Davis Eng—"I do not believe he is up to the task."

"And if I refuse?"

"I will make it hurt more."

Calihye's look moved from one of uncertainty to that primal and determined expression Entreri had seen so many times before, the look that a fighter gets in her eye when she knows there is no escape from the battle at hand. Without blinking, without taking her gaze from him for one second, Calihye drew her sword from its scabbard and presented it defensively before her.

"There is no need for this," she remarked. "But if you must die now, then so be it."

"I do not leave enemies in my wake," Entreri said again, and out came Charon's Claw.

He felt a slight tug at his consciousness from the sentient weapon but put the intrusion down with a thought. Then he came on, a sudden and brutal flurry of movement that sent his dagger out ahead and his sword sweeping down.

Calihye snapped her blade up to block, but Entreri shifted the angle at the last minute, making the sword flash by untouched—until, that is, he reversed the flow and slapped it hard against the underside of her sword, bringing forth a yelp of surprise to accompany the loud ringing of metal.

Entreri hit her sword again as she tried to bring it to bear, then retreated a step.

The woman slipped back behind the fire pit and glanced at Entreri from above the glow. Her gaze went down to the cooking pot, just briefly.

Enough for Entreri.

Charon's Claw came across vertically as Calihye broke for the pot, launching it and the tripod on which it stood forward to send hot stew flying. She followed with a howl, one that turned to surprise as she saw the wall of black ash Entreri's sword had created.

Still, she could not halt her momentum as she leaped the small fire pit, and she followed the pot through the ash wall, bursting out with a wild slashing of her sword to drive the no-doubt retreating intruder back even farther.

Except that he was not there.

"How?" Calihye managed to say even as she felt the explosion of pain in her kidney.

Fire burned through her and before she regained her sensibilities she was on her knees. She tried to turn her shoulders and send her sword flashing back behind her, but a boot stopped her elbow short, painfully extending her arm, and the sword flew from her hand.

She felt the heavy blade settle onto her collarbone, its evil edge against the side of her neck.

Entreri knew he should just be done with her then and there. Her hatred on the road had sounded as a clear warning bell to him that she might one day repay him for the perceived wrong.

But something washed over him in that moment, strong and insistent. He saw Calihye in a different light, softer and vulnerable, one that made him reconsider his earlier words to her—almost. He looked past the scar on her face and saw the beauty that was there beneath. What had driven a woman such as her to so hard a road, he wondered?

He retracted the sword, but instead of bringing it in to take his enemy's head, he leaned in very close to her, his breath hot in her ear.

Disturbed by his emotions, Entreri roughly shook them away.

"Remember how easily you were beaten," he whispered. "Remember that I did not kill you, nor did I kill your friend. Her death was an unfortunate accident, and would that I could go back to that frantic moment and catch her before she fell, but I cannot. If you cannot accept that truth then remember this."

The assassin brought the tip of his awful dagger up against her cheek, and the woman shuddered with revulsion.

"I will make it hurt, Calihye. I will make you beg me to be done with it, but. . . ."

It took Calihye a few moments to realize that the cold metal of the demonic blade was no longer against her skin. She slowly dared to open her eyes then even more slowly dared to turn back.

The room was empty save for Davis Eng, who lay with his eyes wide and terror-filled, obviously having witnessed the last moments of the one-sided fight.

CHAPTER
THE LOOK IN HER EYE
12

By the time Entreri caught up to Jarlaxle and the others, they were camped on a hillock beyond Palishchuk's northern wall. From that vantage point, the growing black castle was all too clear to see.

"When I left here last it was no more than foundation stones, and seemingly for a structure much smaller than this," Mariabronne informed them in hushed tones. "Wingham named it a replica of Castle Perilous, and I fear now that he was correct."

"And you once glanced upon that awful place," Ellery said.

"Well, if none are in there, then we'll make it our halls!" roared Athrogate. "Got me some friends to be guardin' our walls!"

"Got you a habit to bring on your fall," Jarlaxle muttered under his breath, but loud enough for Athrogate to hear, which of course only brought a burst of howling laughter from the wild-eyed dwarf.

"Good grief," said the drow.

"Only kind I'm likin'!" Athrogate said without missing a beat.

"I doubt it is uninhabited or's to stay that way for long," Pratcus put in. "I can feel the evilness emanating from the thing—a beacon call, I'm guessing, for every monster in this corner o' Vaasa."

Entreri looked over at Jarlaxle and the pair exchanged knowing glances. The strange castle, as with the similar tower they'd previously encountered, likely needed no garrison from without. That tower had nearly killed them both, had destroyed perhaps his greatest artifact in the battle. Entreri wondered how much more formidable might the castle be, for it was many times the size of that single tower.

"Whatever your feeling, good dwarf, and whatever our fears, it is of course incumbent upon us to investigate more closely," Canthan put in. "That is our course, is it not, Commander Ellery?"

Entreri caught something in the undertones of Canthan's words. A familiarity?

"Indeed, our duty seems clear to that very course," Ellery replied.

It seemed to Entreri that she was being a bit too formal with the thin wizard, a bit too standoffish.

"In the morning then," Mariabronne said. "Wingham said he would meet us here this night and he is not one to break his word."

"And so he has not," came a voice from down the hill, and the troupe turned as one to regard the old half-orc trudging up the side of the hillock, arm-in-arm with a woman whose other arm was locked with that of another half-orc, a large and hulking specimen.

Normally, Entreri would have focused on the largest of the group, for he carried himself like a warrior and was large enough to suggest that he presented a potential threat. But the assassin was not looking at that one, not at all, his eyes riveted to the woman in the middle. She seemed to drift into the light of their campfire like some apparition from a dream. Though arm-in-arm with both men flanking her, she seemed apart from them, almost ethereal. There was something familiar about her wide, flat face, about the sparkle in her eyes and the tilt of her mouth as she smiled, just a bit nervously. There was something warm about her, Entreri sensed somewhere deep inside, as if the mere sight of her had elicited memories long forgotten and still not quite grasped of a better time and a better place.

She glanced his way and was locked by his gaze. For a long moment, there seemed a tangible aura growing in the air between them.

"As promised, Mariabronne, I have brought my niece Arrayan Faylin and her escort Olgerkhan," Wingham said, breaking the momentary enchantment.

Arrayan blinked, cleared her throat, and pulled her gaze away.

"The book was lost to us for a time," Mariabronne explained to the others. "It was Arrayan who discovered it and the growth about it north of the city. It was she who first recognized this dark power and alerted the rest of us."

Entreri looked from the woman to Jarlaxle, trying hard to keep the panic out of his expression. Memories of the tower outside of Heliogabalus buried those of that distant and unreachable warmth, and the fact that the woman was somehow connected to that evil construct of the Witch-King's stung Entreri's sensibilities.

He paused and considered that sensation.

Why should he care?

The look Entreri gave to Arrayan when Wingham introduced her was not lost upon Jarlaxle.

Nor had it been lost on the large escort at Arrayan's other side, the drow noted.

Jarlaxle, too, had been caught a bit off guard when first he glanced Wingham's niece, for the attractive woman was hardly what he had expected of a half-orc. She clearly favored her human heritage far more than her orc parent or grandparent, and more than that, Jarlaxle saw a similarity in Arrayan to another woman he had known—not a human, but a halfling.

If Dwahvel Tiggerwillies had a human cousin, Jarlaxle mused, she would look much like Arrayan Faylin.

Perhaps that had helped to spark Entreri's obvious interest.

Jarlaxle thought the whole twist perfectly entertaining. A bit dangerous, perhaps, given the size of Arrayan's escort, but then again, Artemis Entreri could certainly take care of himself.

The drow moved to join his companion as the others settled

in around the northern edge of the hilltop. Entreri was on the far side, keeping watch over the southern reaches, the short expanse of ground between the encampment and the city wall.

"A castle," Entreri muttered as Jarlaxle moved to crouch beside him. "A damned castle. Ilnezhara told you of this."

"Of course not," the drow replied.

Entreri turned his head and glared at him. "We came north to Vaasa and just happened to stumble upon something so similar to that which we had just left in Damara? An amazing coincidence, wouldn't you agree?"

"I told you that our benefactors believed there might be treasures to find," the drow innocently replied. He moved closer and lowered his voice as he added, "The appearance of the tower in the south indicated that other treasures might soon be unearthed, yes, but I told you of this."

"Treasures?" came the skeptical echo. "That is what you would call this castle?"

"Potentially . . ."

"You've already forgotten what we faced in that tower?"

"We won."

"We barely escaped with our lives," Entreri argued. He followed Jarlaxle's concerned glance back to the north and realized that he had to keep his voice down. "And for what gain?"

"The skull."

"For my gauntlet? Hardly a fair trade. And how do you propose we do battle with this construct now that the gauntlet is no more? Has Ilnezhara given you some item that I do not know about, or some insight?"

Jarlaxle fought very hard to keep his expression blank. The last thing he wanted to do at that moment, given the nature of Entreri's glance at Arrayan, was explain to him the connection between Herminicle the wizard, Herminicle the lich, and the tower itself.

"A sense of adventure, my friend," was all Jarlaxle said. "A grand Zhengyian artifact, a tome, perhaps, or perhaps some other clue, awaits us inside. How can we not explore that possibility?"

"A dragon's lair often contains great treasures, artifacts even, and by all reasoning such a hunt would constitute the greatest of adventures," Entreri countered with understated sarcasm. "When we are done here, perhaps our 'benefactors' will hand us maps to their distant kin. One adventurous road after another."

"It is a thought."

Entreri just shook his head slowly and turned to gaze back at the southland and the distant wall of Palishchuk.

Jarlaxle laughed and patted him on the shoulder then rose and started away.

"There are connections among our companions that we do not yet fully understand," Entreri said, causing the dark elf to pause for just a moment.

Jarlaxle was glad that his companion remained as astute and alert as ever.

"What's it about, ye skinny old lout?" Athrogate roared as he approached Canthan on the far western side of the hillock, where the wizard had set up his tent—an ordinary inverted **V**-shaped affair suitable for one, or perhaps for two, if they were as thin as the wizard.

"Be silent, you oaf," Canthan whispered from inside the tent. "Come in here."

Athrogate glanced around. The others seemed perfectly content and busy with their own affairs. Pratcus and Ellery worked at the fire, cooking something that smelled good, but in truth, there was no food that didn't smell good to Athrogate. On the northern end of the flat-topped hill, Arrayan and Olgerkhan sat staring off into the darkness, while across the way to the south, that damned dark elf had gone to join his swarthy friend. Mariabronne was off somewhere in the night, Athrogate knew, along with the odd half-orc Wingham.

With a shrug, the black-bearded dwarf dropped to his knees and crawled into Canthan's tent. There was no light in there, other than the distant glow of the campfire, but Athrogate needed no more than that to realize he was alone in the tent. But where had Canthan's voice come from?

"What're ye about?" Athrogate asked.

"Be silent, fool, and come up here."

"Up?" As he moved toward the voice, Athrogate's face brushed into a rope hanging down from the apex of the tent. "Up?"

"Climb the rope," came a harsh whisper from above.

It seemed silly to the dwarf, for if he had stood up, his head would have lifted the tent from the ground. He had been around Canthan long enough to understand the wizard's weird ways, however, and so, with another shrug, he grasped the rope and started to climb. As soon as his bent legs lifted off the ground, Athrogate felt as if he had left the confines of the tent. Grinning mischievously, the dwarf pumped his powerful arms more urgently, hand-walking up the rope. Where he should have bumped into the solid barrier of the tent roof, he found instead a strange foggy area, a magical rift between the dimensions. He charged through and ran out of rope—it simply ended in mid-air!

Athrogate threw himself into a forward roll, landing on a soft rug. He tumbled to a sitting position and found himself in a fairly large room, perhaps a dozen feet square, and well-furnished with many plush rugs, a couple of hardwood chairs, and a small pedestal atop which sat a crystal ball. Canthan peered into the orb.

"Well," said Athrogate, "if ye was to bring such goodies as these, then why'd ye make a tent fit for a dwarf on his knees?"

Canthan waved at him with impatience, and the dwarf sighed at the dismissal of his hard-earned cleverness. He shrugged it away, stood, and walked across the soft carpet to take a seat opposite the skinny wizard.

"Naked halflings?" he asked with a lewd wink.

"Our answers, from Knellict, no less," Canthan said, once again invoking the name of the imposing wizard to steal the grin from Athrogate's smug expression.

The dwarf moved his face up to the crystal ball, staring in. His wildly distorted face filled the globe and brought a yelp from Canthan, who fell back and glowered at him.

"Ain't seein' nothing, except yerself," said Athrogate. "And ye're skinnier than e'er!"

"A wizard might look into the ball. A dwarf can only look through it."

"Then why'd ye call me up here?" Athrogate asked, settling back in the chair. He glanced around the room again, and noted a blazing hearth across the way with a pot set in it. "Got anything good for eating?"

"The citadel's spies have searched far and wide for answers," Canthan explained. "All the way to Calimport."

"Never heard of it. That a place?"

"On Faerûn's far southwestern shores." Canthan said, though Athrogate was not at all impressed. "That is where our friends—and they haven't even changed their names—originated from. Well, the drow came from Menzoberranzan."

"Never heard of it, either."

"It does not matter," the wizard replied. "The two of them were in Calimport not so long ago, accompanied by many other dark elves from the Underdark."

"Heard o' that, and yep, that'd be where them dark elves come from."

"Shut up."

The dwarf sighed and shrugged.

"They tried to conquer the back streets of the city," Canthan said.

"Streets wouldn't give up, would they?"

Again, the wizard narrowed his eyes and glared at the dwarf. "They went against the thieves' guilds, which are much like our own citadel. This Jarlaxle person sought to control the cutpurses and killers of Calimport."

Athrogate considered that for a few moments, then took on a more serious expression. "Ye think they come here wanting the same thing?"

"There is no indication that they brought any allies with them, from all we've seen," explained the wizard. "Perhaps they have been humbled and understand their place among us. Perhaps not, and if not. . . ."

"Yeah, I know, we kill 'em to death in battle," the dwarf said, seeming almost bored.

"Ellery is ready to deal with the drow."

"Bah, I can swat 'em both and be done with it."

Canthan came forward in a rush, his eyes wide, his expression wild. "Do not underestimate them!" he warned. "This is no ordinary duo. They have traveled the breadth of Toril, and for a drow to do so openly is no small matter."

"Yeah, yeah, yeah," Athrogate agreed, patting his gnarled hand in the air to calm the volatile wizard. "Take care and caution and all that. Always that."

"Unlike your typical methods."

"Ones that got me where I am." He paused and hopped up, then did a quick inspection of himself, even seeming to count his fingers. "With all me pieces intact, and what do ye know about that?"

"Shut up."

"Keep saying it."

"You forget why we came out here? Knellict sent us with a purpose."

"Yeah, yeah, yeah."

"You just be ready," said Canthan. "If it comes to blows, then we can hope that Ellery will finish the drow. The other one is your task."

Athrogate snapped his fingers in the air.

Even with Athrogate still sitting there, Canthan started to go on, to work through a secondary plan, just in case. But he stopped short, realizing from the dwarf's smug expression that powerful Athrogate really didn't think it necessary.

In truth, and in considering the many enemies he had watched Athrogate easily dispatch, neither did Canthan.

Commander Ellery ran to the eastern edge of the hillock. To her left loomed the growing replica of Castle Perilous, Palishchuk to her right seeming diminished by the sheer grandiosity of the new construction. Before her rose the northeastern peaks of the Galenas, running north to collide with the gigantic floe of the Great Glacier. Ellery squinted and ducked lower, trying to alter the angle of the black horizon, for she caught a movement down there in the near pitch blackness.

"What was it, then?" asked Pratcus the dwarf, hustling up beside her.

Ellery shook her head and slowly pulled the axe from her the harness on her back.

Across the way, Entreri and Jarlaxle took note, too, as did Olgerkhan and Arrayan.

A form blacker than the shadows soared up at the commander, flying fast on batlike wings.

Ellery fell back with a yelp, as did Pratcus, but then, acting purely on instinct, the woman retracted her axe arm, took up the handle in both hands, and flung the weapon end-over-end at her approaching assailant.

The axe hit with a dull thud and crackle, and the winged creature lurched higher into the air. Ellery ducked low as it came over her.

"Demons!" Pratcus howled when he saw the beast in the glow of their campfire, light glistening off its clawed hands and feet, and its horned, hideous head. It was humanoid with wide wings. Taller than Pratcus, but shorter than Ellery, the creature was both solid and sinewy.

"Gargoyles," Jarlaxle corrected from across the way.

The obsidian beast clawed at Ellery's axe, which she had

embedded deep into its chest, dark blood flowing from either side of the sharp gash. It remained outstretched horizontally for a bit longer, but then tumbled head down and crashed and rolled across the hilltop.

Ellery was on it in a flash.

"More coming!" she yelled.

She skidded down to her knees beside the fallen gargoyle, grasped her axe in both hands, and tore it free.

Behind her, Pratcus was already spellcasting, calling on the magic of Dumathoin, the dwarf god, the Keeper of Secrets under the mountain. He finished with a great flourish, lifting his arms high and wide, and as he spoke the last syllable of the spell, a burst of brilliant light filled the air around him, as if the sun itself had risen.

And in that light, the dwarf and the others saw that Ellery's words were on the mark, for dark shapes fluttered this way and that at the edges of the glowing magic.

"So the fun begins," Entreri said to Jarlaxle.

He drew his sword and dagger and charged forward into the fray, veering as he went, though he was hardly aware of it, to move closer to the woman Arrayan.

"Form defenses!" Ellery yelled. A call from Mariabronne somewhere down the hill turned her and the others. "Tight formations!" she cried as she sprinted off to the lip of the rise, then disappeared into the night.

Entreri dipped forward into a roll as a gargoyle dived for him, the creature's hind claws slashing at the air above the assassin. He came up with a slash and clipped the gargoyle's foot before it rushed out of range.

Entreri couldn't follow, for a second was upon him, arms slapping wildly. The creature tried to come forward to bite or gore with its horn, but Entreri's sword came up and around, forcing it back and bringing both of its arms over to the assassin's left.

Entreri stepped forward and right, feinting with his dagger as he went by. The gargoyle turned to roll behind him, but the assassin switched weapons, sword to his left, dagger to his right and with a reverse grip. He stepped forward with his left foot, but dug it in and stopped short, reversing his momentum, turning back into the closing gargoyle.

A claw raked his shoulder, but it was not a serious wound. The assassin willingly traded that blow with his own, burying his dagger on a powerful backhand deep into the center of the gargoyle's chest.

For good measure, Entreri drew some of the gargoyle's life-force through his vampiric blade, and he felt the soothing warmth as his wound fast mended.

As he withdrew and turned again, Entreri let fly a backhand with his sword as well, creasing the creature's face and sending it crashing to the ground. He completed the spin, bringing his hands together, and when he righted himself, he had his weapons back in their more comfortable positions, Charon's Claw in his right, jeweled dagger in his left.

Entreri glanced right to see Arrayan, Olgerkhan, and the dwarf Pratcus formed into a solid defensive triangle, then back to the left where Jarlaxle crouched and pumped his arm, sending a stream of daggers at a gargoyle as it flew past. The creature pulled up, wings wide to catch the air. It hovered for a second, accepting another stinging hit, then pivoted in mid-air and dived hard at the drow.

Jarlaxle met Entreri's glance for just a second, offered an exaggerated wink, then created a globe of darkness, completely obscuring his form and the area around him.

Entreri couldn't help but wince as the gargoyle dived into it full speed.

Any thoughts he had of going to his friend were short-lived, though, and he instinctively dropped and rolled, slashing his sword to fend another of the horned creatures.

Still another was on the ground and charging at him, its limp telling him that it was the same one he had earlier slashed.

Entreri bent his knees and lifted his hips from the ground, arching his back. With a snap of his finely-toned muscles, he flipped himself up to his feet, and met the charge with a sidelong swipe that forced the gargoyle to pull up short.

The second dropped behind him, but the assassin was not caught off guard. He turned as the creature landed, dagger thrusting—not with any chance to hit, but merely to keep the gargoyle back a stride.

Over and around went his sword, right to left, then back left to right, and in that second roll, he had the gargoyle's eyes and arms following the blade. Back went the sword the other way again, and the gargoyle had to twist even more off balance.

Entreri let the blade go all the way over until its tip was straight down. He turned with it and under it, lifting it and the gargoyle's arms high. Again the creature tried to twist away, but Entreri's movement had leaned him in at the creature. He let himself fall at the gargoyle, thrusting his dagger into the creature's side as he went.

The assassin easily regained his balance, using the weight of the gargoyle to steady his fall. He tore his dagger free as he spun back to face the second, pursuing gargoyle.

Across came the sword, and the gargoyle leaped high, wings beating, to get above it. Entreri let the sword's opaque black ash flow and he went forward as the gargoyle passed over him. He ducked low under the ash wall and waved the sword back behind him to create a second one.

Even as the gargoyles turned together to consider the puzzle, Entreri burst forth through the veil, sword stabbing right, dagger thrusting left. He cut fast to the right, where he had scored a hit, and came in with a dagger stab to the creature's gut, followed by a half-turn that allowed him to bash the howling gargoyle's face with the pommel of Charon's Claw. He reversed his grip on the dagger as he pulled it free then jabbed it back once, twice, thrice, into the wounded beast.

He leaped forward as if to meet the second gargoyle, his ruse forcing the creature to break its momentum, but Entreri stopped short and whirled, his sword coming across at shoulder level to take the head from the wounded beast.

Entreri let himself fall over backward, timing it perfectly with the renewed approach of the second, which leaped above him as it charged past.

Up he stabbed with his sword, gashing the gargoyle beside the knee, and he rolled back, coming up to his feet behind the creature as it struggled to turn around.

Too slow.

Entreri took the thing in its kidney with his dagger, and the gargoyle howled and leaped away, spinning as it went.

But the assassin was right there with it, Charon's Claw coming across low-to-high. The gargoyle tried to block and lost an arm for the effort.

It hardly noticed that, however, for the assassin pressed in, his dagger scoring a hit on the gargoyle's hip. Entreri hooked and tugged as he fast retracted, dropping his left foot far back and pulling the gargoyle forward just a bit.

Close enough for Charon's Claw. Across came the assassin's right hand, the mighty sword creasing the gargoyle from face to wounded hip.

It shrieked, an unearthly sound indeed, and stumbled back a step, then another. It tried to beat its wings to lift away, but it was too late for that, and with a confused look at the assassin, it fell over dead.

Bolts of luminescent green flared from Arrayan's fingers, burning into a charging gargoyle. One after another, her magically-created missiles reached out and seared the creature, and with each, its steps toward her became more unsteady.

Still, watching the woman, Pratcus feared that the gargoyle would rush over her. He shook the sight away—she would have to hold!—and continued his magical casting, leaping toward Olgerkhan as he did battle with two of the creatures, his heavy club smashing at their reaching, clawed hands. Bluish magic flowed from Pratcus and into the large half-orc. Healing energy stemmed the flow of blood from a wound the half-orc had suffered in the first exchange.

A shout from the side turned the dwarf on his heel, just in time to see the gargoyle collide with Arrayan, both going down in a heap. The dwarf leaped in and slugged the gargoyle in the back of its horned head with his mailed fist. He knew even as he connected that Arrayan's missiles had already finished the job, though. He grabbed the dead thing's shoulders and yanked it off the woman, then took Arrayan's hand and tugged her to her feet.

Blood ran freely from Arrayan's broken nose, but the dwarf had no time for that at the moment. He turned and began his spellcasting, and Arrayan did, too, though her arcane chant was slurred by the blood in her mouth.

Her missiles fired first, reaching out and swerving to either side of Olgerkhan to alternately slam the creatures he was frantically battling.

"Close your eyes!" Pratcus yelled an instant before his spell went off.

A burst of brilliant light filled the area around the battle, and Olgerkhan and both gargoyles recoiled in horrified surprise. Before the large half-orc or Arrayan could question the dwarf's tactic, however, the purpose became apparent, for the gargoyle to Olgerkhan's left began flailing helplessly at the air, obviously blinded.

Olgerkhan went for the one on the right instead. He swiped his heavy club across in front of him. As it went out far to the left, he let go with his trailing hand. He rolled the club under his left arm as he continued his swing, bringing it in behind his back, where he caught it again with his right. He rolled the weapon over so that its butt was sticking out before him, recaptured it closer to the leading edge with his left hand, and thrust if forward into the midsection of the leaping gargoyle as he, too, strode ahead.

The devastating impact doubled the gargoyle over, and Olgerkhan stepped away fast and slid his club back so that both his hands were on its handle again. With a roar, the brutish half-orc brought it in a great overhand swipe that cracked against the back of the gargoyle's head and drove it face down to the ground.

Olgerkhan went for the second gargoyle, and Pratcus was already casting another healing spell for the warrior, when Arrayan yelped and flew forward, hit hard by the head butt of yet another diving creature.

Pratcus turned his attention to the gargoyle standing at his side, of course, but not before noting that Olgerkhan, too, arched his back in sudden pain, though nothing had hit him there. With no time to sort through the puzzle, the dwarf launched a sidelong swipe with his small mace.

The gargoyle caught it by the handle, just under the spiked head, but that was exactly what the dwarf had expected. Pratcus's muscled legs uncoiled, launching him into the creature, and he let fly a left jab that crunched the gargoyle squarely in the face. That, not the mace, was Pratcus's preferred method of attack, for he wore heavy metal gauntlets powerfully enchanted for battle.

The dwarf continued to bore in, pressing his face into the gargoyle's chest. He let go of his mace and began driving his fists one after another into the gargoyle's midsection, each heavy blow bringing forth a gasping growl and lifting the gargoyle from the ground.

Beside him, Arrayan re-oriented herself to the battle.

A heavy thump brought her attention to Olgerkhan, his club sending the blind gargoyle into a sidelong spin, so brutal was the blow.

Arrayan caught movement out of the corner of her eye and grabbed at her pouch where she kept her spellcasting ingredients. She waved her hand and called forth her magic, and the air above and to the side of Olgerkhan filled with stringy, weblike strands. Arrayan had nothing upon which to set her web, so it didn't stop the descent of the gargoyle, but by the time the creature hit the ground between her and Olgerkhan, it was all tangled and fighting furiously to pull free of the sticky filaments.

Its predicament only worsened when a second gargoyle flew past Arrayan, tumbling down at the entangled one's feet and tripping it up. Right behind that battered form came Pratcus, howling his battle cry.

And Olgerkhan was there, too, driving his club down with heavy chops that shattered gargoyle bone.

Those chops quickly diminished, though, and Pratcus turned to question the large half-orc. The words stuck in the dwarf's mouth, however, when he realized that Olgerkhan was gasping for breath, exhausted and struggling.

The dwarf eyed him with curiosity, not quite understanding. The warrior had suffered no serious hits, and the fight had barely begun.

Shaking his head, Pratcus could only turn and look for something else to hit.

Entreri wondered why he even bothered to stand up again after yet another roll beneath the reaching claws of a diving gargoyle. He also wondered why in the Nine Hells the warrior dwarf and the thin wizard hadn't yet joined the fray. He figured that would soon enough be remedied, in any case, as a gargoyle swept down into the wizard's small tent, tearing through the fabric with abandon.

But the two were not in there.

Entreri's eyes narrowed as the tent fell away, leaving the gargoyle standing confused before a rope hanging in mid-air. The gargoyle tugged then climbed. Its head and shoulders disappeared into an extra-dimensional pocket.

There was a brilliant flash of flame, and the decapitated body of the gargoyle tumbled to the ground. Out of thin air leaped Athrogate, one of his morning stars smoking.

"Give me the boys and yerself fights the girls," he roared. "For everyone knows there's claws in them curls! *Bwahaha!*"

Entreri prayed that a dozen gargoyles would throttle the little beast.

A pair seemed as if they would do exactly that, soaring down fast, but the dwarf's spinning morning stars kept them at bay, and a searing bolt of lightning flashed out from the extra-dimensional pocket.

From across the way, Entreri marked that lightning blast clearly, for so intense was the power that the gargoyles were incinerated and thrown away. He saw Canthan's face peeking out above the rope, and he knew then that the frail-looking wizard was not one to be taken lightly.

A third gargoyle, on the ground, charged at the dwarf, who howled and charged right back. The creature came in and snapped its head forward to gore with its horn, but Athrogate leaped and similarly head-butted, forcing an impact with the creature's forehead before it could bring the horn in line.

Dwarf and gargoyle bounced back, both standing staring at each other, and seeming as if on shaky legs.

Athrogate yelled, *"Bwahaha!"* again, snorted and launched a wad of spit into the gargoyle's face.

"Mark ye with spit so I know where to hit!" he cried.

The dwarf went into a sudden spin, coming around with a leading morning star that crunched against the stunned gargoyle's face. The creature's head snapped back. Its arms out wide, the gargoyle arched its back and stared up at the dark sky.

Athrogate twisted his torso as he continued his spin so that his arms were on the diagonal, and his second morning star's spiked head came in on the gargoyle descending from on high.

The creature jolted down and seemed to bounce, and it appeared as if it would just fall over.

The dwarf was taking no chances, though, or was just enjoying it all too much. He put the weapons in tighter alternating spins above his head, slamming the gargoyle several times, driving it back, back, until he finally just let the dead thing fall to the ground.

"Bwahaha!" the dwarf yelled as he charged in the direction of Pratcus and the two half-orcs.

He cut back suddenly, though, his heavy boots digging ruts in the ground.

Entreri shook his head and started the same way, but he pulled up as the dwarf halted and turned around. He knew what had gotten Athrogate's attention, and a lump appeared in his throat as he watched a quartet of gargoyles diving at the drow's globe of darkness.

"Jarlaxle!" he cried.

The assassin winced as the gargoyles disappeared into the impenetrable shadow.

Howls and screams, shrieks of pain and bloodthirsty hunger, erupted from within.

Entreri found it hard to breathe.

"Get there, dwarf," he heard himself whispering.

CHAPTER
THE LIVING CASTLE
13

Pratcus could tell that the half-orcs beside him were faltering, and he frantically cheered them on with both words and prayers. He called upon his god to bless his allies and sent waves of healing magic into them, sealing their wounds.

But still they floundered. Arrayan threw out bursts of destructive magical energy, but her repertoire fast diminished, and many of her magical attacks were no more than cantrips, minor spells that inconvenienced an enemy more than they truly hurt it. No one could question the determination and bravery of Olgerkhan, standing strong as rock against the current of the gargoyle river—at least at first. Eventually the large half-orc seemed more a mound of sand, cracking and weakening, his very solidity seeming to lessen.

Something was wrong, Pratcus knew. Either the pair was not nearly as formidable as they had initially seemed, or their strength was draining far too quickly.

The gargoyles seemed to sense it, too. They came on more furiously and more directly, and Pratcus fell back as one crossed over Olgerkhan, the half-orc's sluggish swing not coming close to intercepting it, and dived at the cleric.

Pratcus threw his hands up defensively, expecting to be overwhelmed, but he noticed the gargoyle jerk awkwardly, then again. As the dwarf dodged aside, the creature didn't react but just kept its current course, slamming face-first into the ground.

Pratcus's eyes widened as he noted two feathered arrows protruding from the dead gargoyle's side. The dwarf scrambled to the northern lip of the hillock and saw his two missing companions battling furiously. Ellery guarded Mariabronne's flank, her mighty axe cutting great sweeps through the air, taking the reaching limbs from any gargoyles who ventured too near. With the warrior-woman protecting him, Mariabronne, the legendary Rover of Vaasa, put his great bow to deadly use, sending lines of arrows soaring into the night sky, almost every one finding its mark in the hide of a hovering gargoyle.

"I need ye!" Pratcus yelled down, and the two heroes heeded the call and immediately charged the dwarf's way. Even that movement was perfectly coordinated, with Ellery circling around Mariabronne, protecting his rear and both flanks, while the ranger's bow *twanged* in rapid order, clearing any enemies from before them.

They joined Pratcus not a moment too soon, for Olgerkhan was near to collapse. The half-orc, down on one knee, barely managed to defend himself against a gargoyle that would have soon killed him had not Mariabronne's arrow taken the thing in the throat.

Beside the large half-orc, Arrayan, her spells depleted, stood with dagger in hand. She slashed wildly, her every movement off-balance and exaggerated, her every cut leaving openings in her defenses that any novice warrior could easily exploit.

Ellery leaped to Arrayan's side as the gargoyle bore down on the half-orc woman, its arms out wide to wrap her in its deadly embrace.

That momentum halted when an overhand chop put the warrior-woman's axe head deep into the gargoyle's chest.

Arrayan fell back with a squeal, tripping to the ground. Ellery noted a second creature's approach and tried desperately to tear her axe free, but it got hooked on one of the dead creature's ribs. Ellery reached across with her shield to fend it off but knew she was vulnerable.

The gargoyle's shriek was not one of hungry victory, however, but of pain and surprise, as a pair of arrows knifed into its chest.

Ellery managed to glance back and offer an appreciative nod to Mariabronne.

The ranger didn't notice, for he was already sighting his next target, bow drawn and arrow ready to fly.

Beside him, Pratcus breathed a sigh of relief.

Athrogate could not get to the globe in time, and Entreri watched helplessly as the four gargoyles disappeared into the darkness. Howls and shrieks erupted immediately, a flurry of claws slapping at flesh and a cacophony of opposing screeches, blending and melding into a macabre song of death.

"Jarlaxle," Entreri whispered, and he knew again that he was alone.

"They do make a mess of it," remarked a familiar voice, and Entreri nearly jumped out of his boots when he noted the dark elf standing next to him.

Jarlaxle held a thin metallic wand tipped with a ruby. He reached out and spoke a command word, and a tiny pill of fire arched out at the globe of darkness.

Noting the angle of the fiery pea and the approach of Athrogate, it seemed to Entreri almost as if the drow was tossing it to the roaring dwarf. Entreri thought to yell out a warning to Athrogate, but he knew that his call could do nothing to deter the committed warrior.

The pea disappeared into the darkness.

So did the dwarf.

A burst of flame lit the night, erupting from the globe, and when it was done, the darkness was gone and six gargoyles lay smoldering on the ground.

Athrogate ran out the other side, trailing wisps of smoke and a stream of colorful curses.

"Tough little fellow," Jarlaxle remarked.

"More's the pity," said Entreri.

Across the way, Canthan poked his head out of his extra-dimensional pocket and watched the goings-on with great amusement. He saw Ellery and Mariabronne charge to the aid of the dwarf cleric and the two half-orcs and was distracted by the roar of Athrogate—that one was always roaring!—as the dwarf bounded toward a globe of darkness.

It was a drow's globe, Canthan knew, and if the dark elf was inside it, the wizard could only hope the gargoyles would make fast work of him.

A familiar sight, usually one leaving his own hands, crossed into his field of vision, right to left, and he backtracked it quickly to see the dark elf standing beside Entreri, wand in hand.

A glance back made Canthan wince for his gruff ally, but it was one of instinct and reaction, certainly not of sympathy for the dwarf.

Athrogate came through the fireball, of course, smoking and cursing.

Canthan hardly paid him any heed, for his gaze went back to Jarlaxle. Who was this drow elf? And who was that deadly sidekick of his, standing amidst the inedible carrion of dead gargoyles? The wizard didn't lie to himself and insist that he wasn't impressed. Canthan had served Knellict for many years, and in the hierarchy of the Citadel of Assassins, survival meant never underestimating either your friends or your foes.

"Why are you here, drow?" Canthan whispered into the night air.

At that moment, Jarlaxle happened to turn his way and obviously spotted him, for the drow gave a tip of his great plumed hat.

Canthan chewed his lip and silently cursed himself for the error.

He should have cast an enchantment of invisibility before poking his head out.

But the drow would have seen him anyway, he suspected.

He gave a helpless sigh and grabbed the rope, rolling out so that he landed on his feet. A glance around told him that the fight was over, the gargoyles destroyed, and so with a snap of his fingers, he dismissed his extra-dimensional pocket.

"The castle is alive," Olgerkhan said.

He was bent over at the waist, huffing and puffing, and it seemed to the others that it was all he could do to hold his footing and not sink down to his knees. At his side, Arrayan put a hand on his shoulder, though she seemed equally drained.

"And already more gargoyles are . . . growing," said old Wingham, coming up the northern side of the hill. "On the battlements, I mean. Even as that force flew off into the night, more began to take shape in their vacated places."

"Well now, there is a lovely twist," Canthan remarked.

"We must tear down the castle," declared Pratcus. "By the will o' Moradin, no such an abomination as that will stand! Though I'm guessing that Dumathoin'd be wanting to find out how the magic o' the place is doing such a thing."

"A high wall of iron and stone," Mariabronne said. "Tear it down? Has Palishchuk the capability to begin such a venture as that?" From his tone, it was clear that the ranger's question was a rhetorical one.

"We are fortunate that this group flew our way," said Wingham. "What havoc might they have wrought upon the unsuspecting folk of Palishchuk?"

"Unsuspecting no more, then," the ranger agreed. "We will set the defenses."

"Or prepare the runnin'," put in a snickering Athrogate.

"King Gareth will send an army if need be," said Ellery. "Pratcus is correct. This abomination will not stand."

"Ah, but would we not all be the fools to attack an armored turtle through its shell?" said Jarlaxle, turning all eyes, particularly those of Entreri, his way.

"Ye got a better idea?" Athrogate asked.

"I have some experience with these Zhengyian constructs," the drow admitted. "My friend and I defeated a tower not unlike this one, though much smaller of course, back on the outskirts of Heliogabalus."

Athrogate raised an eyebrow at that. "Ye were part o' that? A few days afore ye—*we* left on the caravan to Bloodstone Pass? That big rumble in the east?"

"Aye, good dwarf," Jarlaxle replied. " 'Twas myself and good Entreri here who laid low the tower and its evil minions."

"Bwahaha!"

Entreri just shook his head as Jarlaxle dipped a low bow.

"The way to win," the drow said as he straightened, "is from the inside. Crawl in through the hard shell to the soft underbelly."

"Soft? Now there's a word," remarked an obviously flustered and suspicious Entreri, and when Jarlaxle glanced his way, he saw that his friend was none too happy. And none too trusting, his dark eyes throwing darts at the drow.

"We're listening, good drow," Mariabronne prompted.

"The castle has a king—a life-force holding it together," Jarlaxle explained, though of course he had no idea if he was on target or not.

Certainly the tower back in Heliogabalus had crumbled when the gem had been plucked from the book, and the sisters told him that killing the lich would have served the same purpose, but in truth, he had no more than a guess concerning the much grander structure—and if the structure was so much bigger, then what of its "king"?

"If we destroy this life-force, the tower—the castle—will unbind," the drow went on. "All that will be left will be a pile of stone and metal for the blacksmiths and stonemasons to forage through." He noted as he finished that both Arrayan and Olgerkhan shifted uneasily.

That told him a lot.

"Perhaps it would be better to alert King Gareth," a doubting Mariabronne replied.

"Master Wingham can send runners from Palishchuk to that end," Commander Ellery declared. "For now, our course is clear—through the shell then and to the soft insides."

"So says yerself," blustered Athrogate.

"So I do, good dwarf," said Ellery. "I will enter the castle at dawn." She paused and glanced at each of them in turn. "I brought you out here for just an eventuality such as this. Now the enemy is clear before us. Palishchuk cannot wait for word to get to Bloodstone Village and for an army to be assembled. And so I go in. I will not command any of you to follow, but—"

"Of course you will not have to," Jarlaxle interrupted, and when all eyes turned his way again, he dipped another bow. "We ventured forth for just an eventuality such as this, and so by your side, we stand." By *his* side, Jarlaxle could feel Entreri's gaze boring into him.

"Bwahaha!" Athrogate bellowed again.

"Yes, of course we must investigate this further," said Canthan.

"By Dumathoin!" said Pratcus.

"All of you, then," Wingham remarked, "with Arrayan and Olgerkhan, you will vanquish this menace. Of that I am sure."

"Them two?" Athrogate asked with a great *"Harrumph."*

"They represent the finest of Palishchuk," Wingham replied.

"Then get the whole damn town running now, and save yerself the trouble!"

"Easy, good dwarf," said Canthan.

"We'll be spending more time dragging them two about than hunting the enemy," Athrogate grumbled. "I ain't for—"

"Enough, good dwarf," said Canthan.

Arrayan moved from Olgerkhan's side to face the furious dwarf.

"We will not fail in this," she said.

"Bah!" Athrogate snorted, and he turned away.

"Two replacements for us," Entreri whispered to Jarlaxle as they moved back across the hilltop to their respective bedrolls.

"You would not wish to miss this grand adventure, of course."

"You knew about it all along," the assassin accused. "The sisters sent us up here for precisely this."

"We have already been through this," replied the drow. "A library has been opened, obviously, and so the adventure unwinds."

"The tower we defeated wouldn't serve as a guardhouse for this structure," Entreri warned. "And that lich was beyond us."

"The lich is destroyed."

"So is my glove."

Jarlaxle stopped walking and stared at his friend for a few moments.

"A fine point," he conceded finally, "but worry not, for we'll find a way."

"That is the best answer you can find?"

"We always do find a way."

"And we always shall, I suppose?"

"Of course."

"Until the last time. There will be only one last time."

Jarlaxle considered that for a few moments.

Then he shrugged.

"First time them two fall down will only be giving me a softer place to put me boot," Athrogate grumbled, sitting on the torn fabric that used to be Canthan's tent.

He rambled on with his unceasing complaints, but the wizard wasn't listening. Canthan's eyes were focused across the way, where Wingham was sitting with Arrayan and Olgerkhan.

Something wasn't right with those two.

"What? What?" the dwarf asked him, apparently taking heed of the fact that he wasn't being listened to and not much enjoying it.

Canthan began to cast a quick spell, and a translucent shape, somewhat like an ear, appeared floating in mid-air before him. He puffed on it and it drifted away, gliding toward the conversation on the northern side of the encampment. The female, Arrayan, moved off, leaving Wingham alone with the brutish Olgerkhan.

And with Canthan, though of course Wingham didn't know that.

"You know our deal," the old half-orc said, his tone grave.

"I know."

"It must not get too far gone," Wingham said. "There can be no delay, no staying of your hand if the killing blow is needed."

"I know!" the larger half-orc growled.

"Olgerkhan, I am as wounded by this possibility as are you," Wingham said. "This is neither my choice nor my desire. We follow the only road possible, or all is already lost."

His voice trailed off and Olgerkhan held his response as Arrayan moved back to them.

"Interesting," mumbled Canthan.

"What? *What?*" bellowed Athrogate.

"Nothing, perhaps," said the wizard, turning to face his friend. He glanced back across the way as he added, "Or perhaps everything."

Face down, his arms bound behind him, his head hooded, Nyungy had all but given up hope. Resigned to his doom, he wasn't even crying out anymore.

But then a hand grabbed his hood and gently pulled it back, and the old sage found himself staring into the face of his friend.

"How many days?" he gasped through his dry, cracked lips.

"Only two," Wingham replied. "I tried to get to you earlier, but Olgerkhan . . ." He finished with a sigh and held up his wrists, cut cord still hanging from them.

"Your young friend has gone mad!"

"He protects the girl."

"Your niece." There was no missing the accusation in that tone.

Wingham looked at Nyungy hard, but only for a moment, then moved around and began to untie him. "To simply murder—"

"It is not murder, as she brought it on herself."

"Unwittingly."

"Irrelevant. You would see the city endangered for the sake of one girl?" asked the sage. Again Wingham held up his wrists, but Nyungy was too sly to fall for that ruse. "You play a dangerous game here, Wingham."

Wingham offered a sigh and said, "The game was begun before ever I knew the dangers, and once set in motion, there was no other course before us."

"You could have killed the girl and been done with it."

Wingham paused for just a moment. "Come," he bade his old friend. "We must prepare the city."

"Where is the girl?"

"Heroes have come from the Vaasan Gate."

"Where is the girl?"

"She went into the castle."

Nyungy's eyes widened and he seemed as if he might simply fall over.

"With Commander Ellery, niece of Gareth Dragonsbane," Wingham explained, "and with Mariabronne the Rover."

Nyungy continued to stare, then nodded and asked, "Olgerkhan is with her?"

"With instructions to not allow the structure to take her. At all costs."

The old sage considered it all for some time. "Too dangerous," he decided with a shake of his head, and he started walking past Wingham.

"Where are you going?"

"Didn't you just say that we had to go and prepare the city? But prepare it for what? To defend, or to run?"

"A little of both, I fear," Wingham conceded.

PART 3

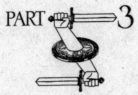

SECRETS WITHIN
SECRETS WITHOUT

Many times during his journey back to the apartment he shared with Entreri, Jarlaxle fished the violet-glowing gem out of his pocket. Many times he held it up before his eyes, pondering the possibilities hidden inside its skull-like facets as he vividly recalled the sensations at the graveyard. It was a power, necromancy, of which Jarlaxle knew little, and one that piqued his curiosity. What gains might he realize from that purple gem?

The book that had hidden it had been destroyed. Gone too was the tower it had created from feeding on the life-force of Herminicle. All that remained was rubble and scraps. But the gem survived, and it thrummed with power. It was the real prize. The book had been the icing, as sweet as anything Piter spread on his creations, but the gem, that violet skull, was the cake itself. If its powers could be harnessed and utilized. . . .

To build another tower, perhaps?

To find a better connection to the dead? For information?

To find allies among the dead?

The dark elf could hardly contain his grin. He so loved new magical toys to examine, and his near-disastrous companionship with the infamous artifact Crenshinibon, the Crystal Shard, had done little to dampen his insatiable curiosity. He wished that Kimmuriel was available to him, for the drow psionicist could unravel the deepest of magical mysteries with ease. If only Jarlaxle had found the skull gem before his last meeting with his lieutenant.

But he would have to wait tendays for their next appointed rendezvous.

"What can you do for me?" he whispered to the skull gem, and perhaps it was his imagination, but the item seem to flare with eagerness.

And that Zhengyian artifact was of little consequence, comparatively speaking, if the fear in Ilnezhara's eyes was any indication. What other treasures lay up there in wait for him and Entreri? What other toys had Zhengyi left scattered about to bring mischief to his vanquishers?

Power to topple a king, perhaps?

Or power to create a king?

That last thought hung in the air, waiting for the drow to grab it and examine it.

He considered the road he and Entreri had traveled to get to Heliogabalus in the still untamed Bloodstone Lands. Wandering adventurers they were, profiteers in heroes' clothing. Living free and running free, turning their backs to the wind, whichever way that wind was blowing. No purpose led them, save the drow's desire for a new experience, some excitement different from that which had surrounded him for so many centuries. For Entreri, the same?

No, Jarlaxle thought. It wasn't the lure of new experiences that guided Entreri, but some other need that the assassin likely didn't even understand himself. Entreri didn't know why he stayed by Jarlaxle's side along their meandering road.

But Jarlaxle knew, and he knew, too, that Entreri would stay with him as that road led them farther to the north to the wilds of Vaasa and the promise of greater treasure than even the skull gem.

How might Entreri react if Jarlaxle decided they should stay for some time—forever, perhaps, as measured in the life of a human? If Zhengyian artifacts fell into their hands, the power to tear down a kingdom or to build one, would Entreri willingly participate?

"One journey at a time," Jarlaxle decided, even as he came upon the wooden staircase that led to the balcony of their second story apartment. The sun was up by then, burning through the heavy mist of the eastern sky.

Jarlaxle paused there to consider the parting words of the two dragon sisters:

"The secrets of Zhengyi were greater than Zhengyi. The folk of Damara, King Gareth most of all, pray that those secrets died with the Witch-King," Ilnezhara had said with certainty.

"But now we know that they did not," Tazmikella had added. "Some of them, at least, have survived."

Jarlaxle remembered the words and recalled even more vividly the timbre with which they were spoken, the reverence and even fear. He recalled the look in their respective eyes, sparkling with eagerness, intrigue, and terror.

"With all due respect, King Gareth," Jarlaxle said to the misty morning air, "let us hope that little was destroyed."

He glanced down the street to the little shop where he had set up Piter the baker. Its doors weren't open yet, but Jarlaxle knew that his portly friend would not refuse him admittance.

A short while later, he started up the staircase, knowing that the first battle along his new road, that of convincing the sour, still-hurting Entreri, lay behind his multi-trapped door.

CHAPTER 14
ZHENGYI'S ALTERNATE WORLD

So complete was the castle construction that by the time the nine companions approached the front gates the next morning, they found a fanciful and well-designed flagstone walkway leading to them. On the walls to either side of the closed portcullis, half-formed gargoyles leered at the approaching troupe, and in the few moments it took them to reach the portcullis, those statues grew into an even more defined form.

"They will be ready to launch into the sky again this night," Mariabronne noted. "Wingham would do well to force Palishchuk into a strong defensive posture."

"For all the good that'll do 'em," Athrogate grumbled.

"Then let us be quick about our task," Ellery replied.

"We heroes," Entreri muttered under his breath, so that only Jarlaxle, standing right beside him at the back of the line, could hear.

The drow was about to respond, but he felt a sudden tug at his sensibilities. Not sure what that might mean, Jarlaxle put a hand over the magical button on his waistcoat, wherein he had stored the skull gem. A look of concern flashed over his angular face. Could it be that the magical gems could call to each other? Had he erred in bringing his skull gem near to the new construct?

Mariabronne was first to the portcullis, its iron spikes as thick as his arms. He peered through the bars at the castle's lower bailey.

"It appears empty," he reported as the others came up beside him.

"I can get a grapnel over the wall, perhaps, and locate the hoist."

"No need," Canthan said, and the thin wizard nodded at Athrogate.

"Bah!" the dwarf snorted and he moved up and gently nudged Mariabronne aside. "Gonna pop out me guts, ye stupid mage."

"We all have our uses," Canthan replied to him. "Some of us attend to them without so much blather, however."

"Some of ye sit back and wiggle yer fingers while some of us stop clubs with our faces."

"Good that there's not much beauty to steal then."

"Bah!"

The other seven listened with some amusement, but the banter struck Entreri and Jarlaxle more poignantly.

"Those two sound a bit familiar," Entreri lamented.

"Though not as witty, of course, and therein lies the rub," said the drow.

Athrogate spat in his hands and grabbed at the portcullis, knees bent. He grunted and tried to straighten, to no effect, so he gave another roar, spat in his hands again, and reset his grip.

"A little help, if ye might," he said.

Mariabronne grabbed the portcullis on one side of the dwarf, while both Pratcus and Olgerkhan positioned themselves on the other side.

"Not yerselves, ye bunch o' dolts," the dwarf grumbled.

Behind them, Canthan completed the words of a spell and a wave of energy rolled out from the wizard's hands to encompass the dwarf. Muscles bulged and bones crackled as they grew, and Athrogate swelled to the size of a large man, and continued to grow.

"And again!" the dwarf demanded, his voice even more resonant.

Canthan uttered a second enchantment, and soon Athrogate was the size of an ogre, his already muscular arms as thick as old trees.

"Bah!" he growled in his booming bass voice, and with a roar of defiance, he began to straighten his legs.

The portcullis groaned in protest, but the dwarf pressed on, bringing it up from the ground.

"Get ye going!" he howled, but even as he said it, even as Entreri and Ellery both made to dive under, Athrogate growled and began to bend, and the other three couldn't begin to slow the descent of the huge barrier.

Entreri, the quicker by far to the ground, was also the quicker to halt his movement and spin back, and he managed to grab the diving Ellery as he went and deflect her enough so that she did not get pinned under the heavy spiked gate as it crashed back to earth. The commander cried out, as did Arrayan and Pratcus, but Canthan merely chuckled and Jarlaxle, caught up in the curious sensations of the skull gem, hadn't even heard the call or noticed the lifting of the portcullis, let alone the near loss of one of their companions. When he looked at Athrogate, suddenly so much larger than before, his eyes widened and he fell back several steps.

"Oh, ye son of a bar whore!" Athrogate cursed, and it did not miss Jarlaxle's notice that Entreri shot the dwarf a quick glance that would have curdled milk. Because of the gate's swift descent, the drow wondered? Or was it those few words? Very rarely did Jarlaxle glimpse into the depths of the puzzle that was Artemis Entreri, for the disciplined assassin rarely wore his emotions in his expression.

Every now and then, though. . . .

Athrogate stormed about, rubbing his calloused hands together and repeatedly tightening his belt, a great and decorated girdle with a silver buckle set with crossed lightning bolts.

"By the gods, dwarf," Mariabronne said to Athrogate. "I do believe that you were lifting that practically by yourself, and that our helping hands were of little or no consequence. When you bent, I felt as if a mountain was descending upon me."

"Wizard's spell," Athrogate grumbled, though he hardly sounded convinced.

"Then I pray you cast the enchantment on us others," Mariabronne bade Canthan. "This gate will rise with ease in that case."

"My spells are exhausted," the wizard said, as unconvincingly as the dwarf.

Jarlaxle looked from Canthan to Athrogate, sizing them up. No doubt the spell of enlargement had played some role, but that was not the source of the dwarf's incredible strength. Again Athrogate went to his belt, tightening it yet another notch, and the drow smiled. There were girdles said to imbue their wearer with the strength of a giant, the greatest of which were the storm giants that threw lightning bolts across mountain peaks. Jarlaxle focused on Athrogate's belt buckle and the lightning bolts it displayed.

Athrogate went back to stand in front of the portcullis, hands on hips and staring at it as if it were a betraying wife. Once or twice he started to reach out and touch the thick bars, but always he retracted his hands and grumbled.

"I ain't about to lift it," he finally admitted.

The dwarf grumbled again and nodded as the first of Canthan's enlargement dweomers wore off, reducing him to the size of a large man. By the time Athrogate sighed and turned about, he was a dwarf again. Intimidating, to be sure, but still a dwarf.

"Over the wall, then," said Mariabronne.

"Nah," the dwarf corrected.

He pulled his twin morning stars off of his back and set them to twirling, glassteel gleaming dully in the soft morning light. He brought the handle of the one in his left hand up before his face and whispered something. A reddish-gray liquid began to ooze from the small nubs on the striking ball, coating the whole of the business end of the weapon. Then he brought up the right-hand weapon and similarly whispered, and the liquid oozed forth on that one too, only the gooey stuff was blue-gray instead of red.

"Get back, ye dolt," he said when Ellery moved near to investigate. "Ye're not for wanting to get any o' this on that splendid silver armor o' yers. *Haha!*"

His laugh became a growl and he put his morning stars up in whistling spins above his head. Then he turned a complete circuit, gathering momentum, and launched the red-covered weapon head in a mighty swing against one of the portcullis's vertical bars. He followed with a smash from the other weapon, one that created an explosion that shook the ground beneath the feet of all the stunned onlookers. Another spin became a second thunderous retort, the dwarf striking—one, two, and always with the red-colored morning star leading—a perpendicular bar.

Another hit took that crossing, horizontal bar again. To the amazement of all save Canthan, who stood watching with a sour expression, the thick cross bar broke in half, midway between two vertical spikes. Athrogate back went to work on his initial target, one of those spikes.

The red-colored weapon head clanged against it, about eye level with the furious, wildly-dancing dwarf, followed by a strike with the bluish one a bit lower down.

The spike bent outward. Athrogate hit it again in the same place, once, twice, and the spike fell away, leaving enough room for the companions to squeeze through and into the castle bailey.

Athrogate came to a sudden stop, his morning star heads bouncing around him. He planted his hands on his hips and inspected his handiwork then gave a nod of acceptance.

"For a bit of a kick is why ye got me hired. Anything else ye're wantin' blasting while I got 'em fired?"

Seven stunned expressions and the look of one bored wizard came back at him, eliciting a roaring, *"Bwahaha!"*

"Would that he slips with both and hits himself repeatedly in the face," Entreri muttered to Jarlaxle.

"So then when he's gone, my friend Entreri can take his place?" the drow quipped back.

"Shut up."

"He is a powerful ally."

"And a mighty enemy."

"Watch him closely, then."

"From behind," Entreri agreed.

Entreri did just that, staring hard at the dwarf, who stood with hands on hips, gazing through the gap he had hammered in the portcullis. The power of those swings, magic and muscle, were noteworthy, the assassin knew, as was the ease with which Athrogate handled his weapons. Entreri didn't particularly like the dwarf and wanted to throttle him with every stupid rhyme, but the assassin respected the dwarf's martial prowess. He suspected that he would soon come to blows with Athrogate, and he was not looking forward to the appointment.

Before the group, beyond the corridor cutting between the two small gatehouses, the castle's lower bailey opened wide. To either side of the gatehouse corridor they could see openings: stairwells leading to the wall top, with perhaps inner tunnels snaking through the wide walls.

"Left, right, or center?" Athrogate asked. "Best we quickly enter."

"Will you stop that?" Entreri demanded, and he got a typical, *"Bwahaha!"* in reply.

"The book is straight back, yes?" Mariabronne asked Arrayan, who was standing at his side.

The woman paused for a moment and tried to get her bearings. Her eyes fixed upon the central keep, the largest structure in the castle, which loomed beyond the inner bailey wall.

"Yes," she said, "straight back. I think."

"Do better than that," Canthan bade her, but Arrayan had only a weak and apologetic expression in response.

"Then straight ahead," Ellery told the dwarf.

Entreri noticed that Jarlaxle moved as if to say something in protest. The drow stayed silent, though, and noted the look the assassin was offering his way.

"Be ready," Jarlaxle quietly warned.

"What do you know?"

Jarlaxle only shrugged, but Entreri had been around the drow long enough to understand that he would not have said anything if he wasn't quite sure that trouble was looming. In looking at the castle, the dark stones and hard iron, Entreri had the same feeling.

They moved through the gates and halted on the muddy courtyard, Athrogate at the lead, Pratcus and Ellery close behind. Jarlaxle paused as soon as he slipped through the portcullis, and swayed with a sudden weakness. An overwhelming feeling of power seemed to focus its sentient attention on him. He looked at Arrayan and knew immediately that it was not her. The castle had progressed far beyond her.

The drow's eyes went to the ground ahead, and in his mind he looked down, down, past the skeletons buried in the old graveyard, for that is what the place once had been. He visualized tunnels and a great chamber. He knew that something down there was waiting for him.

The others took no note of Jarlaxle's delay, for they were more concerned with what lay ahead. A few stone buildings dotted the open bailey: a stable against the left-hand wall immediately inside, a blacksmith's workshop situated in the same place on the right, and a pair of long, low-ceilinged barracks stretching back from both side walls to the base of the taller wall that blocked the inner bailey. The only free-standing structure was a round, two-story, squat tower, set two-thirds of the way across the courtyard before the gates of the inner wall.

Mariabronne moved up beside Ellery and motioned to the tower. The commander nodded her agreement and waved for Athrogate to lead the way.

"I would not . . ." Jarlaxle started to say, but his words were buried by Athrogate's sudden shout.

All eyes turned to the dwarf as he leaped back—or tried to, for a skeletal hand had thrust up through the soft summer tundra dirt to hold fast his ankle. Athrogate twisted, yelped, and went tumbling to the ground. He was back to his feet almost as soon as he landed, though, leaping up and shouting out again, but in rage, not surprise.

The skeletal hand clawed higher into the air, a bony arm coming out to the elbow.

Athrogate's morning star smashed it to dust.

But the skeleton's other hand prodded through the soil to the side, and as the dwarf moved to smash that one he cried, *"Hunnerds!"*

Perhaps it was an exaggeration borne of shock, or perhaps it was an accurate assessment, for all across soft ground of the outer bailey, the skeletal hands of long-dead humanoids clawed up through the hard soil.

Athrogate finished the skeleton's second hand and charged ahead, roaring, "Skinny bones to grind to dust!"

And Pratcus leaped up right beside him. Presenting his anvil-shaped holy symbol, the priest swore, "By the wisdom of Moradin, the grace of Dumathoin and the strength of Clangeddin, I damn thee foul beasts to dust!"

One skeleton, half out of its hole, vibrated under waves of unseen energy, its bony frame rattling loudly. But the others, all across the way, continued to claw their way free of the turf.

Black spots danced before Jarlaxle's eyes, and his head thrummed with a rhythmic chanting, an arcane and evil-sounding cant, calling to the skeletons. The skull-shaped gem in his button seemed to gain weight and substance then, and he felt it vibrating on his chest. Through its power the drow keenly sensed the awakening around him, and understood the depth of the undead parade. From the sheer strength of the call, he expected that the place had served as a burial ground for the Palishchuk half-orcs, or their orc ancestors, for centuries.

Hundreds of skeletal teeth rattled in the drow's thoughts. Hundreds of long-dead voices awakened once more in a communal chanted song. And there remained that one, deeper, larger force, overwhelming with its strength.

He felt a squeeze on his biceps and cried out, then spun and used the magic of his bracer to drop a dagger into his hand. He started to strike but felt his wrist grabbed suddenly, brutally. Jarlaxle opened his eyes as if awakening from a bad dream, and there stood a confused and none-too-happy Artemis Entreri, holding him arm and wrist, and staring at him dumbfounded.

"No, it is all right," the dark elf assured him as he shook his head and pulled away.

"What are you seeing?" Entreri asked. "What do you know?"

"That we are in trouble," the drow answered, and together, the pair turned to face the rising onslaught.

"Cleave with your sword, don't stab," the drow informed Entreri.

"Good to have you looking out for me," Entreri sarcastically replied before he leaped forward and slashed across at an approaching skeleton.

Charon's Claw cut through the reaching monster's ribs to slam hard against its backbone. Entreri expected the blow to cut the skinny undead monstrosity in half, but the skeleton staggered a couple of steps to the side and came on again.

And again Entreri hit it, even harder.

Then again as the stubborn creature relentlessly moved in.

The assassin fell back a step, then dived sidelong as a brilliant bolt of lightning flashed before him, blasting through the skeleton.

The bony monster staggered several steps with that hit, and a pair of ribs fell away, along with one arm. But still it came on, heading toward the disbelieving Jarlaxle and the slender wand the drow held.

Entreri waded in and cracked the skeleton's skull with a two-handed downward chop.

Finally, the undead creature fell to the ground, its bony frame folding up into a neat pile.

"Not your ordinary animations," Jarlaxle remarked.

"We are in trouble," Entreri agreed.

Pratcus stared at his anvil-shaped silver holy symbol as if it had deceived him. The dwarf's lip quivered and he whispered the name of his gods, one after another, the trembling in his voice begging them for an explanation.

"Blunt weapons!" he heard Mariabronne cry. "Shatter their bones!"

But the dwarf priest stood there, shaking his head in disbelief.

A bony hand came out of the ground and grabbed him by the ankle, but Pratcus, still muttering, easily managed to yank his foot away. A second hand clawed forth from the ground and in the torn turf between them, the top of a skull appeared.

Pratcus howled, and he held the screaming note, leaped into the air, and dropped straight down, his metal-shod fist leading in a pile-driving punch atop the skull. He felt the bone crackle beneath him, but the angry dwarf, far from satisfied, put his feet under him again. He leaped up and bashed the skull again, smashing his hand right through it.

The reaching fingers on the skeletal hands shivered and bent over, becoming very still.

"Good enough for ye, ye devils," the confused and angry dwarf remarked then he slugged the skull yet again.

Mariabronne didn't draw his long sword but instead brought forth a small mace. Relying more on speed and skill than on brute force, the ranger whirled, slapping repeatedly at a pair of skeletons coming in at him. None of the blows was heavy in nature, but chip after chip fell away as Mariabronne, seeming almost like a king's drummer, rattled off dozens of strikes.

Beside him, Ellery didn't bother changing weapons, as her heavy-bladed axe was equally devastating to bone as to flesh. Fragments of rib or arm or leg splintered under her devastating chops. But still the skeletons came on, undeterred and unafraid, and for every one that Ellery or Mariabronne broke apart, two more took its place.

Behind them Olgerkhan worked his club frantically and

Arrayan fired off a series of minor magic spells, glowing missiles of pure energy, mostly. But neither were overly effective, and both half-orcs were obviously tiring quickly again.

Olgerkhan shielded Arrayan with his sizeable bulk and grunted more in pain than battle rage as bony fingers raked at his flesh. Then he howled in terror as one skeleton slipped past him. It had an open path to Arrayan.

The large half-orc tried to turn and catch up but was surprised to learn that he didn't have to, for the animated undead monster did not approach the woman.

Olgerkhan believed he knew why. He closed on the skeleton and smashed it with all his strength anyway, not wanting the others to take note of its aversion to Arrayan.

Of all the companions, none was better equipped to deal with such creatures than was Athrogate. His spinning morning stars, though he hadn't placed any of the enchantments upon them, devastated the skeletal ranks, each strike reducing bone to dust or launching a skull from its perch atop a bony spine. The dwarf truly seemed to be enjoying himself as he leaped ahead of the others into the midst of the skeletal swarm. His weapons worked in a devastating blur, and white powder filled the air around him, every explosive hit accompanied by his howling laughter.

Canthan stayed close to his diminutive companion the whole time. The wizard enacted only one more spell, summoning a huge, disembodied, semi-translucent hand that floated in mid-air before him.

A skeleton rushed in at him and the five-fingered guardian grasped it, wrapping huge digits around its bony frame. With a grin and a thought, Canthan commanded the hand to squeeze, and the skeleton shattered beneath the power of its grip.

The hand, closed into a fist, darted across as a second skeleton approached the wizard. The spell effect slugged the creature hard and sent it flying away.

"Press on," Mariabronne ordered. "The keep is our goal—our only goal!"

But the ranger's words were lost to the wind a moment later, when Olgerkhan faltered and cried out. Mariabronne turned to see the large half-orc slump to one knee, his half-hearted swings barely fending the clawing skeletons.

"Dwarves, to him!" the ranger cried.

Pratcus took up the charge, throwing himself at the skeletons crushing in around Olgerkhan, but Athrogate was too far away and too wildly engaged to begin to extract himself.

Similarly, Jarlaxle had lagged behind back by the wall. The drow showed no eagerness to wade out into the mounting throng of undead, despite the fact that his companion, though his weapons were ill-suited for battling skeletons, had moved toward the half-orcs before the ranger had even cried out.

Canthan, too, did not go for Olgerkhan and Arrayan, but instead slipped to one side as the ranger and Ellery turned and went for the half-orcs. Canthan retreated to the position held clear by Jarlaxle. With a thought, the wizard sent his enchanted hand back out behind him, gigantic fingers flicking aside skeletons. It reached Athrogate, who looked at it with some curiosity. Then it grabbed the dwarf and lifted him from his feet. The hand sped him in fast pursuit of its wizard master.

Mariabronne, Ellery, and Pratcus formed a defensive triangle around Olgerkhan, beating back the skeletons' assault. Entreri, meanwhile, grabbed Arrayan by the arm and started to pull her away, slashing aside any undead interference.

"Come along," he ordered the woman, but he felt her lagging

behind, and when he glanced at her, he understood why.

Arrayan collapsed to the ground.

Entreri sheathed his weapons, slipped his arm around her shoulders, then slid his other arm under her knees and hoisted her. Slipping in and out of consciousness, Arrayan still managed to put her arms around Entreri's neck to help secure the hold.

The assassin ran off, zigzagging past the skeletons.

Behind Entreri, when a break finally presented itself, Mariabronne grabbed Olgerkhan and ushered him to his feet. Still, when the ranger let him go, the half-orc nearly fell over again.

"I do so enjoy baby-sitting," Canthan muttered as Entreri carried the nearly unconscious Arrayan beside him.

Entreri scowled, and for a moment both Jarlaxle and Canthan thought he might lash out at the insulting wizard.

"Is she wounded?" the drow asked.

Entreri shrugged as he considered the shaky woman, for he saw no obvious signs of injury.

"Yes, pray tell us why our friend Arrayan needs to be carried around when there is not a drop of her blood spilled on the field," Canthan put in.

Again Entreri scowled at him. "Tend to your friend, wizard," he said, a clear warning, as the disembodied hand floated in and deposited a very angry Athrogate on the ground before them.

"Join up and battle to the keep!" Mariabronne called to the group.

"Too many," Jarlaxle shouted back. "We cannot fight them on the open field. Our only hope is through the wall tunnels."

Mariabronne didn't immediately answer, but one look across the field showed him and the three with him that the drow's observations were on target. For dozens of skeletons were up and approaching and more clawing skeletal hands were tearing through practically every inch of turf across the outer bailey.

"Clear a path for them," Canthan ordered Athrogate.

The dwarf gave a great snort and set his morning stars to spinning again. Canthan's huge magical hand worked beside him, and soon the pair had cleared the way for Mariabronne and the other three to rejoin those at the wall.

Jarlaxle disappeared into the left-hand gatehouse, then came back out a few moments later and motioned for them all to follow. Shielded by Canthan's magical hand, holding back the undead horde, all nine slipped into the gatehouse and into the tunnel beyond. A heavy door was set at the end of that tunnel, which Mariabronne closed and secured not a moment too soon, for before the ranger had even turned around to regard the other eight, the clawing of skeletal fingers sounded on the portal.

"An auspicious beginning, I would say," said Canthan.

"The castle protects itself," Jarlaxle agreed.

"It protects many things, so it would seem," Canthan replied, and he managed a sly glance Arrayan's way.

"We cannot continue like this," Mariabronne scolded. "We are fighting in pockets, protective of our immediate companions and not of the group as a whole."

"Might be that we didn't think some'd be needin' so much damn protecting," Athrogate muttered, his steely-eyed gaze locked on the two half-orcs.

"It is what it is, good dwarf," said the ranger. "This group must find harmony and unity if we are to reach the keep and find our answers. We are here together, nine as one."

"Bah!"

"Therein lies our only hope," said Mariabronne.

To the apparent surprise of Athrogate, Canthan agreed. "True enough," the wizard said, cutting the dwarf's next grunt short. "Nine as one and working toward a single goal."

The timbre of his voice was less than convincing, and it didn't pass the notice of both Entreri and Jarlaxle that Canthan had cast a glance Arrayan's way as he spoke.

CHAPTER

SPITTING MONSTERS

15

The tunnel through the wall was narrow and short, forcing everyone other than Athrogate and Pratcus to stoop low. Poor Olgerkhan had to bend nearly in half to navigate the corridor, and many places were so narrow that the broad-shouldered half-orc had to turn sideways to slip through. They came to a wider area, a small circular chamber with the corridor continuing as before out the other side.

"Stealth," Jarlaxle whispered. "We do not want to get into a fight in these quarters."

"Bah!" Athrogate snorted, quite loudly.

"Thank you for volunteering to take the lead," Entreri said, but if that was supposed to be any kind of negative remark to the boisterous and fearsome dwarf, it clearly missed the mark.

"On we go, then!" Athrogate roared and he rambled out of the room and along the corridor, his morning stars in his hands and bouncing along. The weapons often clanged against the stone walls and every time one did, the others all held their breath. Athrogate, of course, only howled with laughter.

"If we kill him correctly, he will block the corridor enough for us to escape," said Entreri, who was third in line, just behind the dwarves and just ahead of Jarlaxle.

"There is nothing waiting for us behind," Pratcus reminded.

"Leaving without that one would constitute a victory," said

Entreri, and Athrogate laughed all the louder.

"On we go then!" he roared again. "Hearty dwarves and feeble men. Now's the time for kind and kin, together banded for the win! *Bwahaha!*"

"Enough," Entreri growled, and just then they came upon a wider and higher spot in the uneven corridor, and the assassin set off. A stride, spring, and tuck sent him right over Pratcus's head, and Athrogate let out a yelp and spun as if he expected Entreri to set upon him with his weapons.

As Athrogate turned, however, Entreri went by, and by the time the confused dwarves stopped hopping about and focused ahead once more, the assassin was nowhere to be found.

"Now what was that all about?" Athrogate asked of Jarlaxle.

"He is not my charge, good dwarf."

"He's running out ahead, but for what?" the dwarf demanded. "To tell our enemies we're here?"

"I expect that you have done a fine enough job of that without Artemis Entreri's help, good dwarf," the drow replied.

"Enough of this," said Mariabronne from behind Ellery, who was right behind the drow. "We have not the time nor the luxury of fighting amongst ourselves. The castle teems with enemies as it is."

"Well, where'd he go, then?" asked the dwarf. "He scouting or killing? Or a bit of both?"

"Probably more than a bit," Jarlaxle replied. "Go on, I pray you, and with all speed and with all the stealth you might muster. We will find adversity this day at every corner—I pray you don't invite more than we will happen upon without your . . . enthusiasm."

"Bah!" snorted Athrogate.

He spun around and stomped off—or started to, for barely had he gone two strides, coming up fast on a sharp bend in the corridor, when a form stepped out to block his way.

It was humanoid and fleshy, as tall as a man, but stocky like a dwarf, with massive fleshy arms and twisted, thick fingers. Its head sat square and thick on a short stump of a neck, its pate completely hairless, and no light of life shone in its cold eyes. It came right at

Athrogate without hesitation, the biggest clue of all that the creature wasn't truly alive.

"What're ye about?" the dwarf started to ask, indicating that he, unlike Pratcus and Jarlaxle behind him, didn't quite comprehend the nature of the animated barrier. "What?" the dwarf asked again as the creature fast approached.

"Golem!" Jarlaxle cried.

That broke all hesitation from Athrogate, and he gave a howl and leaped ahead, eager to meet the charge. A quick overhand flip of the morning stars, one after the other, got them past the slow-moving creature's defenses.

Both slapped hard against the thick bare flesh, and both jolted the golem.

But neither really seemed to hurt the creature nor slow it more than momentarily.

Pratcus fell back for fear of getting his head crushed on a backswing as Athrogate launched himself into a furious series of arm-pumping, shoulder-spinning attacks. His morning stars hummed and struck home, once then again.

And still the golem pressed in, slapping at him, grabbing at him.

The dwarf dodged a crossing punch, but the move put him too close to the left hand wall, and the ball head of his weapon rang loudly off the stone, halting its rhythmic spin. Immediately, the golem grabbed the morning star's chain.

Athrogate's other arm pumped fast, and he scored a hit with his second weapon across the golem's cheek and jaw. Bone cracked and flesh tore, and when the ball bounced away, it left the golem's face weirdly distorted, jaw hanging open and torn.

Again, though, the golem seemed to feel no pain and was not deterred. It tugged back, and stubborn Athrogate refused to let go of his weapon and was lifted from his feet and pulled in.

A small crossbow quarrel whipped past him as he flew, striking the golem in the eye.

That brought a groan, and a pool of mucus popped out of the exploded orb, but the golem did not relent, yanking the dwarf right in to its chest and enwrapping Athrogate in its mighty arms.

The dwarf let out a yelp of pain, not for the crushing force as yet, but because he felt a point ramming into his armor, as if the golem was wearing a spiked shield across its chest.

Then the stabbing pain was gone and the golem began to squeeze. For all of his strength, Athrogate thought in an instant that he would surely be crushed to death. Then he got stabbed again, and he cried out.

Pratcus was fast to him, calling to Moradin and throwing waves of magical healing energy into the tough warrior. Behind the cleric, Jarlaxle reloaded and let fly another bolt, scoring a hit in the golem's other eye to blind the creature entirely.

The drow pressed himself flat against the corridor wall as he shot, allowing Mariabronne an angle to shoot past him with his great bow. A heavier, more deadly arrow knifed into the golem's shoulder.

Athrogate yelped as he was prodded again and again. He didn't understand; what weapon was this strange creature employing?

And why did the golem suddenly let him go?

He hit the floor and hopped backward, bowling Pratcus over in the process.

Then the dwarf understood, as the stabbing blade popped forth from the golem's chest yet again.

Athrogate recognized that red steel sword tip. The dwarf gave a laugh and started back at the golem but stopped abruptly and put his hands on his hips, watching with great amusement as the sword prodded through yet again.

Then it retracted and the golem collapsed in a heap.

Artemis Entreri reached down and wiped his sword on the fleshy pile.

"Ye could've warned us," Athrogate said.

"I yelled out, but you were too loud to hear," the assassin replied.

"The way is clear to the keep at the wall's corner," Entreri explained. "But once we go through that door, onto the building's second story balcony, we'll be immediately pressed."

"By?" asked Mariabronne.

"Gargoyles. A pair of them." He kicked at the destroyed golem and added, "More, if any are in wait behind the tower's northern door that will take us along the castle's eastern wall."

"We should lead with magic and arrows," Mariabronne remarked, and he looked alternately at Canthan and Jarlaxle.

"Just move along, then," said the thin wizard. "The longer we tarry, the more fighting we will find, I expect. The castle is creating defenses as we stand and chatter—spitting monsters."

"And regenerating them, if the gargoyles are any indication," said Mariabronne.

"Looking like a good place for training young dwarf warriors, then," Athrogate chimed in. "Pour a bit o' the gutbuster down their throats and set 'em to fighting and fighting and fighting. Something to be said for never running out o' monster faces to crush."

"When we're done with it, you can have it, then," Jarlaxle assured the brutish little warrior. "For your children."

"Haha! All thirty of them are already out and fighting, don't ye doubt!"

"A sight I'll have to one day witness, I'm sure."

"Haha!"

"May we go on and be done with this?" asked Canthan, and he motioned to Entreri. "Lead us to the room and clear the door for me."

Entreri gave one last glance at the annoying dwarf then started off along the corridor. It widened a bit, and ramped up slightly, ending in a heavy wooden, iron-banded door. Entreri glanced back at the group, nodded to confirm that it was the correct room, then turned around and pushed through the door.

Immediately following him, almost brushing his back, came a fiery pea. It arced into the open tower room, over the balcony. Just as it dropped from sight below the railing, it exploded, filling the entire tower area with a great burst of searing flame.

Howls came from within and from without. Athrogate rubbed his boots on the stone for traction and went tearing through the door, morning stars already spinning. He was met by a gargoyle, its wings flaming, lines of smoke rising from the top of its head. The creature clawed at him, but half-heartedly, for it was still dazed from the fireball.

Athrogate easily ducked that grasp, spun, and walloped the gargoyle in the chest with his morning star.

Over the railing it went, and with a second gargoyle fast following as Athrogate rambled along.

Into the room went Pratcus, Jarlaxle—wearing a concerned expression—close behind, with Ellery and Mariabronne pressing him.

Canthan came next, chuckling under his breath and glancing this way and that. As he crossed to the threshold, though, a hand shot out from the side, grabbing him roughly by the collar.

There stood Artemis Entreri, somehow hidden completely from sight until his sudden movement.

"You thought I went into the room," he said.

Canthan eyed him, his expression going from surprise to a hint of fear to a sudden superior frown. "Remove your hand."

"Or your throat?" Entreri countered. "You thought I went into the room, yet you launched your fireball without warning."

"I expected that you would be wise enough not to get in the way of a battle mage," Canthan retorted, a double-edged timbre to his voice to match the double edge of his words.

The mounting sound of battle inside rolled out at the pair, along with Olgerkhan's insistence that they get out of the way.

Neither Entreri nor Canthan bothered to look the half-orc's way. They held their pose, staring hard at each other for a few moments.

"I know," Canthan teased. "Next time, you will not wait to ask questions."

Entreri stole his grin and his comfort, obviously, when he replied, "There will be no next time."

He let go of the mage, giving him a rough shove as he did. With a single movement, leaping into the room, he brought forth both his dagger and sword. His first thought as he came up on his battling companions was to get out of Canthan's line of fire.

Over the railing he went, landing nimbly on the lip of the balcony beyond. Up on one foot, he pointed the toe of the other and slid it into the gap between the bottom of the railing and the floor.

He rolled forward off the ledge. As he swung down to the lowest point, he tightened his leg to somewhat break the momentum, then pulled his locked foot free and tucked as he spun over completely, dropping the last eight feet to the tower floor. Immediately a trio of gargoyles and a flesh golem descended upon him, but they were all grievously damaged from the fireball. None of the gargoyles had working wings, and one couldn't lift its charred arms up to strike.

That one led the way to Entreri, ducking its head and charging in with surprising ferocity.

Charon's Claw halted that charge, creasing the creature's skull and sending it hopping back and down to a sitting position on the floor. It managed to cast one last hateful glance at Entreri before it rolled over dead.

The look only brought a grin to the assassin's face, but he didn't, couldn't, dwell on it. He went into a furious leaping spin, dagger stabbing and sword slashing. The creatures were limping, slow, and Entreri just stayed ahead of them, darting left and right, continually turning them so that they bumped and tangled each other. And all the while his dagger struck at them, and his sword slashed at them.

The balcony above was quickly secured as well, with Athrogate and his mighty swipes launching yet another gargoyle into the air. That one almost hit Entreri as it crashed down, but he managed to get back behind the falling creature. It hit the floor right in front of him, and the flesh golem, closing in, tripped over it.

Charon's Claw cleaved the lunging golem's head in half.

Entreri darted out to the right, staying under the balcony. He saw Mariabronne and Ellery on the stone stairway that lined the tower's eastern, outer wall, driving a battered and dying gargoyle before them.

The gargoyles saw them too, and one rushed their way.

Entreri made short work of the other, taking off its one working arm with a brutal sword parry, then rushing in close and driving his dagger deep into the creature's chest. He twisted and turned the blade as he slid off to the side, then brought Charon's Claw across the gargoyle's throat for good measure.

The creature went into a frenzy, thrashing and flailing, blood flying. It had no direction for its attacks, though, and Entreri simply danced away as it wound itself to the floor, where it continued its death spasms.

Entreri came up behind the second gargoyle, which was already engaged with the ranger, and drove his sword through its spine.

"Well fought," said Mariabronne.

"By all," Ellery quickly added, and Entreri got the distinct impression that the woman did not appreciate the ranger apparently singling him out above her.

She didn't look so beautiful to Entreri in that moment, and not just because she had taken a garish hit on one shoulder, the blood flowing freely down her right arm.

Pratcus hustled down next, muttering with every step as he closed on the wounded woman. "Sure'n me gods're getting sick o' hearing me call," he cried. "How long can we keep this up, then?"

"Bah!" Athrogate answered. "Forever and ever!"

To accentuate his point, the wild dwarf leaped over to one broken gargoyle, the creature pitifully belly-crawling on the floor, its wings and most of its torso ravaged by the flames of Canthan's fireball. The gargoyle noted his approach and with hate-filled eyes tried to pull itself up on its elbows, lifting its head so that it could spit at Athrogate.

The dwarf howled all the louder and more gleefully, and brought his morning stars in rapid order crunching down on the gargoyle's head, flattening it to the floor.

"Forever and ever," Athrogate said again.

Entreri cast a sour look in Jarlaxle's direction as if to say, "He'll get us all killed."

The drow merely shrugged and seemed more amused with the dwarf than concerned, and that worried Entreri all the more.

And frustrated him. For some reason, the assassin felt vulnerable, as if he could be wounded or killed. As he realized the truth of his emotions, he understood too that never before had he harbored such feelings. In all the battles and deadly struggles of the past three decades of his life, Artemis Entreri had never felt as if his next fight might be his last.

Or at least, he had never cared.

But suddenly he did care, and he could not deny it. He glanced at Jarlaxle again, wondering if the drow had found some new enchantment to throw over him to so put him off-balance. Then he looked past Jarlaxle to the two Palishchuk half-orcs. They stood against the outer southern wall, obviously trying to stay small and out of the way. Entreri focused his gaze on Arrayan, and he had to resist the urge to go over to her and assure her that they would get through this.

He winced as the feeling passed, and he dropped his hand to Charon's Claw and lifted the blade a few inches from its scabbard. He sent his thoughts into the sword, demanding its fealty, and it predictably responded by assailing him with a wall of curses and demands of its own, telling him that he was inferior, assuring him that one day he would slip up and the sword would dominate him wholly and melt the flesh from his bones as it consumed his soul.

Entreri smiled and slid the sword away, his moment of empathy and shared fear thrown behind.

"If the castle's resources are unlimited, ours are not," Canthan was saying as Entreri tuned back into the conversation. From the way the mage muttered the words and glanced at Athrogate, Entreri knew that the dwarf was still proclaiming that they could fight on until the end of time.

"But neither can we wait and recuperate," Ellery said. "The castle's defenses will simply continue to regenerate and come against us."

"Ye have a better plan, do ye?" asked Pratcus. "Not many more spells to be coming from me lips. I bringed a pair o' scrolls, but them two're of minor healing powers, and I got a potion to get yer blood flowing straight but just the one. I used more magic in the wagon run from the flying snakes and more magic in the fight on the hill than I got left in me heart and gut. I'll be needing rest and prayers to get any more."

"How long?" asked Ellery.

"Half a night's sleep."

Ellery, Mariabronne, and Canthan were all shaking their heads.

"We don't have that," the commander replied.

"On we go," Athrogate declared.

"You sound as if you know our course," said Ellery.

Athrogate poked his hand Arrayan's way. "She said she found that book out here, over by where that main keep now stands," he reasoned. "We were going for that, if I'm remembering right."

"We were indeed," said Mariabronne. "But that is only a starting place. We don't truly know what the book is, nor do we know if it's still there."

"Bah!" Athrogate snorted.

"It is still there," replied a quiet voice from the side, and the group turned as one to regard Arrayan, who seemed very, very small at that moment.

"What d'ye know?" Athrogate barked at her.

"The book is still there," Arrayan said. She stood up a bit straighter and glanced over at Olgerkhan for support. "Uncle Wingham didn't tell you everything."

"Then perhaps you should," Canthan replied.

"The tower . . . all of this, was created by the book," Arrayan explained.

"That was our guess," Mariabronne cut in, an attempt to put her at ease, but one that she pushed aside, holding her hand up to quiet the ranger.

"The book is part of the castle, rooted to it through tendrils of magic," Arrayan went on. "It sits open." She held her palms up, as if she was cradling a great tome. "Its pages turn of their own accord, as if some reader stands above it, summoning a magical breeze to blow across the next sheaf."

As Canthan suspiciously asked Arrayan how she might know all of this, Entreri and Jarlaxle glanced at each other, neither surprised, of course.

Entreri swallowed hard, but that did not relieve the lump in his throat. He turned to Arrayan and tried to think of something to say to interrupt the conversation, for he knew what was coming and knew that she should not admit . . .

"It was I who first opened Zhengyi's book," she said, and Entreri sucked in his breath. "Uncle Wingham bade me to inspect it while Mariabronne rode to the Vaasan Gate. We hoped to give you a more complete report when you arrived in Palishchuk."

Olgerkhan shifted nervously at her side, a movement not lost on any of the others.

"And?" Canthan pressed when Arrayan did not continue.

Arrayan stuttered a couple of times then replied, "I do not know."

"You do not know what?" Canthan snapped back at her, and he took a stride her way, seeming so much more imposing and powerful than his skinny frame could possibly allow. "You opened the book and began to read. What happened next?"

"I . . ." Arrayan's voice trailed off.

"We've no time for your cryptic games, foolish girl," Canthan scolded.

Entreri realized that he had his hands on his weapons and realized too that he truly wanted to leap over and cut Canthan's throat out at that moment.

Or rush over and support Arrayan.

"I started to read it," Arrayan admitted. "I do not remember anything it said—I don't think it *said* anything—just syllables, guttural and rhyming."

"Good!" Athrogate interrupted, but no one paid him any heed.

"I remember none . . . just that the words, if they were words, found a flow in my throat that I did not wish to halt."

"The book used you as its instrument," Mariabronne reasoned.

"I do not know," Arrayan said again. "I woke up back at my house in Palishchuk."

"And she was sick," Olgerkhan piped in, stepping in front of the woman as if daring anyone to make so much as an accusation against her. "The book cursed her and makes her ill."

"And so Palishchuk curses us by making us take you along?" Canthan said, and his voice did not reveal whether he was speaking with complete sarcasm or logical reasoning.

"You can all run from it, but she cannot," Olgerkhan finished.

"You are certain that it is at the main keep?" Mariabronne asked, and though he was trying to be understanding and gentle, there was no missing the sharp edge at the back of his voice.

"And why did you not speak up earlier?" demanded Canthan. "You would have us fighting gargoyles and fiends forever? To what end?"

"No!" Arrayan pleaded. "I did not know—"

"For one who practices the magical arts, you seem to know very little," the older wizard scolded. "A most dangerous and foolhardy combination."

"Enough!" said Mariabronne. "We will get nowhere constructive with this bickering. What is past is past. We have new information now and new hope. Our enemy is identified beyond these animates it uses as shields. Let us find a path to the keep and to the book, for there we will find our answers, I am certain."

"Huzzah your optimism, ranger," Canthan spat at him. "Would you wave King Gareth's banner before us and hire trumpeters to herald our journey?"

That sudden flash of anger and sarcasm, naming the beloved king no less, set everyone on their heels. Mariabronne furrowed his brow and glared at the mage, but what proved more compelling to Jarlaxle and Entreri was the reaction of Ellery.

Far from the noble and heroic commander, she seemed small and afraid, as if she was caught between two forces far beyond her.

"Relation of Dragonsbane," Jarlaxle whispered to his companion, a further warning that something wasn't quite what it seemed.

"The keep will prove a long and difficult run," Pratcus intervened. "We gotta be gathering our strength and wits about us, and tighten our belts'n'bandages. We know where we're going, so where we're going's where we're goin'."

"Ye said that right!" Athrogate congratulated.

"A long run and our only run," Mariabronne agreed. "There we will find our answers. Pray you secure that door above, good Athrogate. I will scout the northern corridor. Recover your breath and your heart. Partake of food and drink if you so need it, and yes, tighten your bandages."

"I do believe that our sadly poetic friend just told us to take a break," Jarlaxle said to Entreri, but the assassin wasn't even listening.

He was thinking of Herminicle and the tower outside of Heliogabalus.

He was looking at Arrayan.

Jarlaxle looked that way too, and he stared at Entreri until he at last caught the assassin's attention. He offered a helpless shrug and glanced back at the woman.

"Don't even think it," Entreri warned in no ambiguous voice. He turned away from Jarlaxle and strode to the woman and her brutish bodyguard.

An amused Jarlaxle watched him every step of the way.

"A fine flute you crafted, Idalia the monk," he whispered under his breath.

He wondered if Entreri would agree with that assessment or if the assassin would kill him in his sleep for playing a role in the grand manipulation.

"I would have a moment with you," Entreri said to Arrayan as he approached.

Olgerkhan eyed him with suspicion and even took a step closer to the woman.

"Go and speak with Commander Ellery or one of the dwarves," Entreri said to him, but that only made the brutish half-orc widen his stance and cross his arms over his massive chest, scowling at Entreri from under his pronounced brow.

"Olgerkhan is my friend," Arrayan said. "What you must say to me, you can say to him."

"Perhaps I wish to listen more than speak," said Entreri. "And I would prefer if it were just we two. Go away," he said to Olgerkhan. "If I wanted to harm Arrayan, she would already be dead."

Olgerkhan bristled, his eyes flaring with anger.

"And so would you," Entreri went on, not missing a beat. "I have seen you in battle—both of you—and I know that your magical repertoire is all but exhausted, Lady Arrayan. Forgive me for saying, but I am not impressed."

Olgerkhan strained forward and seemed as if he would leap atop Entreri.

"The book is draining you, stealing your life," the assassin said, after glancing around to make sure no others were close enough to hear. "You began a process from which you cannot easily escape."

Both of the half-orcs rocked off-balance at the words, confirming Entreri's guess. "Now, will you speak with me alone, or will you not?"

Arrayan gazed at him plaintively, then turned to Olgerkhan and bade him to go off for a few minutes. The large half-orc glowered at Entreri for a moment, but he could not resist the demands of Arrayan. Staring at the assassin every step of the way, he moved off.

"You opened the book and you started reading, then found that you could not stop," Entreri said to Arrayan. "Correct?"

"I . . . I think so, but it is all blurry to me," she replied. "Dreamlike. I thought that I had constructed enough wards to fend the residual curses of Zhengyi, but I was wrong. All I know is that I was sick soon after back in my house. Olgerkhan brought Wingham and Mariabronne, and another, Nyungy the old bard."

"Wingham insisted that you come into the castle with us."

"There was no other choice."

"To destroy the book before it consumes you," Entreri reasoned, and Arrayan did not argue the point.

"You were sickly, so you said."

"I could not get out of my bed, nor could I eat."

"But you are not so sickly now, and your friend . . ." He glanced back at Olgerkhan. "He cannot last through a single fight, and each swing of his war club is less crisp and powerful."

Arrayan shrugged and shook her head, lifting her hands up wide.

Entreri noticed her ring, a replica of the one Olgerkhan wore, and he noted too that the single gemstone set on that band was a different hue, darker, than it had been before.

From the side, Olgerkhan saw the woman's movement and began stalking back across the room.

"Take care how much you admit to our companions," Entreri warned before the larger half-orc arrived. "If the book is draining you of life, then it is feeding and growing stronger because of you. We will—we must—find a way to defeat that feeding magic, but one way seems obvious, and it is not one I would expect you or your large friend to enjoy."

"Is that a threat?" Arrayan asked, and Olgerkhan apparently heard, for he rushed the rest of the way to her side.

"It is free advice," Entreri answered. "For your own sake, good lady, take care your words."

He gave only a cursory glance at the imposing Olgerkhan as he turned and walked away. Given his experience with the lich Herminicle in the tower outside of Heliogabalus, and the words of the dragon sisters, the answer to all of this seemed quite obvious to

Artemis Entreri. Kill Arrayan and defeat the Zhengyian construct at its heart. He blew a sigh as he realized that not so long ago, he would not have been so repulsed by the idea, and not hesitant in the least. The man he had been would have long ago left Arrayan dead in a pool of her own blood.

But now he saw the challenge differently, and his task seemed infinitely more complicated.

"She read the book," he informed Jarlaxle. "She is this castle's Herminicle. Killing her would be the easy way to be done with this."

Jarlaxle shook his head through every word. "Not this time."

"You said that destroying the lich would have defeated the tower."

"So Ilnezhara and Tazmikella told me, and with certainty."

"Arrayan is this construct's lich—or soon to be," Entreri replied, and though he was arguing the point, he had no intention, if proven right, of allowing the very course he was even then championing.

But still Jarlaxle shook his head. "Partly, perhaps."

"She read the book."

"Then left it."

"Its magic released."

"Its call unleashed," Jarlaxle countered, and Entreri looked at him curiously.

"What do you know?" asked the assassin.

"Little—as little as you, I fear," the drow admitted. "But this . . ." He looked up and swept his arms to indicate the vastness of the castle. "Do you really believe that such a novice mage, that young woman, could be the life-force creating all of this?"

"Zhengyi's book?"

But still Jarlaxle shook his head, apparently convinced that there was something more at work. The drow remained determined, for the sake of purse and power alone, to find out what it was.

CHAPTER 16
IMPROVISING

With Entreri moving off ahead of them, the group passed swiftly out of the corner tower and along the corridors of the interior eastern wall. They didn't find any guardian creatures awaiting them, though they came upon a pair of dead gargoyles and a decapitated flesh golem, all three with deep stab wounds in the back.

"He is efficient," Jarlaxle remarked more than once of his missing friend.

They came to an ascending stair, ending in a door that stood slightly ajar to allow daylight to enter from beyond it. As they started up, the door opened and Artemis Entreri came through.

"We are at the joined point of the outer wall and the interior wall that separates the baileys of the castle," he explained.

"Stay along the outer wall to the back and the turn will take us to the main keep," Mariabronne replied, but Entreri shook his head with every word.

"When the gargoyles came upon us last night, they were not the castle's full contingent," the assassin explained. "From this point back, the outer wall is lined with the filthy creatures and crossing close to them will likely awaken them and have us fighting every step of the way."

"The inner wall to the center, then?" asked Ellery. "Where we debark it and spring across the courtyard to the keep's front door?"

"A door likely locked," Mariabronne reasoned.

"And locked before a graveyard courtyard that will present us with scores of undead to battle," Jarlaxle assured them in a voice that none questioned.

"Either way we're for fighting," Athrogate chimed in. "Choose the bony ones who're smaller in the biting!" He giggled then continued, "So lead on and be quick for it's soundin' exciting." The dwarf howled with laughter, but he was alone in his mirth.

"How far?" Mariabronne asked.

Entreri shrugged and said, "Seventy feet of ground from the inner gatehouse to the door of the keep."

"And likely a locked door to hold us out," added Ellery. "We'll be swarmed by the undead." She looked to Pratcus.

"I got me powers against them bony things," he said, though he appeared unconvinced. "But I found the first time that they didn't much heed me commands."

"Because they are being controlled by a greater power, likely," Jarlaxle said, and all eyes settled on him. He shrugged, showing them that it was just a guess. Then he quickly straightened, his red eyes sparkling, and looked to Entreri. "How far are we now to that keep?"

Entreri seemed perplexed for just a moment then said, "A hundred feet?"

"And how much higher is its top above the wall's apex here?"

Entreri looked back behind him, out the open door. Then he leaned back and glanced to the northeast, the direction of the circular keep.

"It's not very high," the assassin said. "Perhaps fifteen feet above us at its highest point."

"Lead on to the wall top," Jarlaxle instructed.

"What do ye know?" asked Athrogate.

"I know that I have already grown weary of fighting."

"Bah!" the dwarf snorted. "I heared ye drow elfs were all for the battle."

"When we must."

"Bah!"

Jarlaxle offered a smile to the dwarf as he squeezed past, moving up the stairs to follow Entreri to the outside landing. By the time the others caught up to him, he was nodding and insisting, "It will work."

"Pray share your plan," Mariabronne requested.

"That one's always tellin' folks to pray," Athrogate snorted to Pratcus. "Ye should get him to join yer church!"

"We drow are possessed of certain . . . tricks," Jarlaxle replied.

"He can levitate," said Entreri.

"Levitation is not flying," Canthan said.

"But if I can get close enough and high enough, I can set a grapnel on that tower top," Jarlaxle explained.

"That is a long climb, particularly on an incline," remarked the ranger, his head turning back and forth as he considered the two anchor points for any rope.

"Better than fighting all the way," said Jarlaxle.

As he spoke, he took off his hat and reached under the silken band, producing a fine cord. He extracted it, and it seemed to go on and on forever. The drow looped its other end on the ground at his feet as he pulled it from the hat and by the time he had finished, he had a fair-sized coil looped up almost to the height of his knees.

"A hundred and twenty feet," he explained to Entreri, who was not surprised by the appearance of the magical cord.

Jarlaxle then took off a jeweled earring, brought it close to his mouth and whispered to it. It grew as he moved it away, and by the time he had it near to the top end of the cord, it was the size of a small grappling hook.

Jarlaxle tied it off and began looping the cord loosely in one hand, while Entreri took the other end and tied it off on one of the crenellations along the tower wall.

"The biggest danger is that our movements will attract gargoyles," Jarlaxle said to the others. "It would not be wise to join in battle while we are crawling along the rope."

"Bah!" came Athrogate's predictable snort.

"Sort out a crossing order," Jarlaxle bade the ranger. "My friend, of course, will go first after I have set the rope, but we should get another warrior over to that tower top as quickly as possible. And she will need help," he added, nodding toward Arrayan. "I can do that with my levitation, and my friend might have something to assist . . . ?"

He looked at Entreri, who frowned, but did begin fishing in his large belt pouch. He pulled out a contraption of straps and hooks, which looked somewhat like a bridle for a very large horse, and he casually tossed it to the drow.

Jarlaxle sorted it out quickly and held it up before him, showing the others that it was a harness of sorts, known as a "housebreaker" to anyone familiar with the ways of city thieves.

"Enough banter," Ellery bade him, and she nodded to the north and the line of gargoyles hanging on the outside of the wall.

"A strong shove, good dwarf," Jarlaxle said to Athrogate, who rushed at him, arms outstretched.

"As I pass you," Jarlaxle quickly explained, before the dwarf could launch him from the wall—and probably the wrong way, at that! He positioned Athrogate at the inside lip of the tower top, then walked at a direct angle away from the distant keep. "Be quick," he bade Entreri.

"Set it well," the assassin replied.

Jarlaxle nodded and broke into a quick run. He leaped and called upon the power of his enchanted emblem, an insignia that resembled that of House Baenre, to bring forth magical levitation, lifting him higher from the ground. Athrogate caught him by the belt and launched him out toward the tower, and with the dwarf's uncanny strength propelling him, Jarlaxle found himself soaring away from the others.

Jarlaxle continued to rise as he went out from the wall. Halfway to the keep, he was up higher than its highest point. He was still approaching, but greatly slowing. The levitation power could make him go vertical only, so as the momentum of his short run and Athrogate's throw wore off, he was still twenty feet or so from the keep's wall. But he was up above it, and he began to swing the grapnel at the end of one arm.

"Gargoyles about the top," he called back to Entreri, who was ready to scramble at the other end of the rope. "They are not reacting to my presence, nor will they to yours, likely, until you step onto the stone."

"Wonderful," Entreri muttered under his breath.

He kept his visage determined and stoic, and his breath steady, but was assailed with images of the gargoyles walking over and tearing out the grapnel, then just letting him drop halfway across into the middle of the courtyard. Or perhaps they would swarm him while he hung helpless from the rope.

"Take in the slack quickly," Entreri said to Athrogate as Jarlaxle let fly the grapnel.

Even as it hit behind the keep's similarly crenellated wall, the dwarf began yanking in the slack, tightening the cord, which he stretched and tightly looped over the wall stone.

Off went Entreri, leaping from the wall to the cord. He hooked his ankles as he caught on, his arms pumping with fluid and furious motion. He hand-walked the cord, coiling his body, then unwinding in perfect synchrony, and so fast was he moving that it seemed to the others as if he was sliding down instead of crawling up.

In short order, he neared the roof of the keep. As he did, he let go with his feet and turned as he swung his legs down, gathering momentum. He rolled his backbone to gather momentum as he went around and back up, and he let go at the perfect angle and trajectory. Turning a half flip as he flew, drawing his weapons as he went, he landed perfectly on his feet on the wall top—just as a gargoyle rushed out to meet him.

The creature caught a sword slash across the face, followed by a quick dagger thrust to the throat, and Entreri followed the falling creature down, leaping from the wall to the roof in time to meet the charge of a second gargoyle.

"Come on, half-ugly," Athrogate, who was already in the house-breaker harness, said to Olgerkhan.

Before the half-orc warrior could respond, the dwarf leaped up to the top of the wall, grabbed him by the back of his belt, and swung out, hooking the harness to the cord as he went. With amazing strength, Athrogate held Olgerkhan easily with one arm while his other grabbed and tugged, grabbed and tugged, propelling him across the gap.

Olgerkhan protested and squirmed, trying to grab at the dwarf's arm for support.

"Ye hold still and save yer strength, ye dolt," Athrogate scolded. "I'm leaving ye there, and ye best be ready to hold a fight until I get back!"

At that, Olgerkhan calmed, and the rope bounced. The half-orc managed to glance back, as did Athrogate, to see Mariabronne scrambling onto the cord. The ranger moved almost as fluidly as had Entreri, and he gained steadily on the dwarf as they neared the growing sounds of battle.

Up above them, Jarlaxle lifted a bit higher, gaining a better angle from which to begin loosing his missiles, magical from a wand and poison-tipped from his small crossbow.

"Go next," Commander Ellery bade Pratcus. "They will need your magic."

She leaned on the wall, straining to see the fighting across the way. Every so often a gargoyle raised up from the keep's roof, its great leathery wings flapping, and Ellery could only pray that the creature didn't notice the rope and the helpless men scrambling across.

Pratcus hesitated and Ellery turned a sharp glare at him.

The dwarf grabbed at the rope and shook his head. "Won't be holding another," he explained.

Ellery slapped her hand on the stone wall top and turned to Canthan. "Have you anything to assist?"

The wizard shook his head. Then he launched so suddenly into spellcasting that Ellery fell back a step and gave a yelp. She turned as Canthan cast, firing off a lightning bolt that caught one gargoyle as it dived at Athrogate and Olgerkhan.

"Nothing to assist in the climbing, if that is what you meant," the wizard clarified.

"Whatever you can do," Ellery replied, her tone equally dry.

Entreri learned the hard way that his location atop the keep's roof had put him in close proximity to many of the gargoyles. He'd taken down three of them, but as four more of the beasts leaped and fluttered around him, the assassin began moving more defensively rather than trying to score any killing blows.

From up above, Jarlaxle took down one, launching a glob of greenish goo from a wand. It struck a gargoyle on its wings and drove it down, where it stuck fast, hopelessly adhered to the stone. A second of the gargoyles broke off from Entreri and soared out at the levitating drow, but before the assassin could begin to get his feet properly under him and go on the attack against the remaining two, another pair came up over the wall at him.

Muttering under his breath, the assassin continued his wild dance, using Charon's Claw to set up walls of opaque ash to aid him in his constant retreat. He glanced quickly at the rope line to note Athrogate's progress and had to admit to himself that he was glad to see the dwarf fast approaching—an admission he thought he'd never make where that one was concerned.

Entreri worked more deliberately then, trying not only to stay away from the claws and horns of the leaping and soaring foursome but to turn them appropriately so that his reinforcements could gain a quick advantage.

He started left, then cut back to the right, toward the center of the rooftop. He fell fast to one knee and thrust his sword straight up, gashing a dropping gargoyle that fast beat its wings to lift back out of reach. Entreri started to come back up to his feet, but a clawing hand slashed just above his head, so he threw himself forward into a roll instead. He came up quickly, spinning as he did, sword arm extended, to fend off the furious attacks. With their ability to fly and leap upon him, the beasts should have had him—would have had any typical human warrior—but Artemis Entreri was too quick for them and managed to sway the angle of his whipping blade to defend against attacks from above as well.

Hanging by the harness under the rope, Athrogate came right up to the keep's stone wall.

"Get up there and get ye fighting!" he roared at Olgerkhan.

With still just one arm, the dwarf hauled the large half-orc up over the lip of the stone wall. Olgerkhan clipped his foot as he went over, and that sent him into a headlong tumble onto the roof.

The dwarf howled with laughter.

"Go, good dwarf!" Mariabronne called from right behind him on the rope.

"Going back for the girl," Athrogate explained. "Climb over me, ye treehugger, and get into the fightin'!"

Not needing to be asked twice, Mariabronne scrambled over Athrogate. The ranger seemed to be trying to be gentle, or at least tried not to stomp on the dwarf's face. But Athrogate, both his hands free again, grabbed the ranger by the ankles and heaved him up and over to land crashing on the roof beside Entreri and Olgerkhan. Athrogate couldn't see any of that, since he was hanging under the rope, but he heard the commotion enough to bubble up another great burst of laughter.

As soon as the rope stopped bouncing, the dwarf released a secondary hook on the harness and a few quick pumps of his powerful arms had him zipping back down the decline toward the others. He clamped onto the rope though, bringing himself to an abrupt halt when he saw Pratcus climbing out toward him. Unlike Entreri and Mariabronne, the dwarf had not hooked his ankles over the rope but was simply hanging by his hands. He let go with the trailing hand and rotated his hips so that when he grabbed the rope again, that hand was in front. And on he went, rocking fast and hand-walking the rope.

Athrogate nodded and grinned as he watched the priest's progress. Pratcus wore a sleeveless studded leather vest, and the muscles in his arms bulged with the work—and with something else, Athrogate knew.

"Put a bit of an enchantment on yerself, eh?" Athrogate said as Pratcus approached. Athrogate turned himself around so that his head was down toward the other dwarf, and reached out to take Pratcus's hand.

"Strength o' the bull," Pratcus confirmed, and he grabbed hard at Athrogate's offered hand.

A spin and swing had Pratcus back up high beyond the hanging dwarf, where he easily caught the rope again and continued along his way.

Athrogate howled with laughter and resumed his descent to the tower wall.

"Who's next?" he asked the remaining trio.

Ellery glanced at Canthan. "Take Arrayan," she decided, "then Canthan, and I will go last."

"We've not the time for that, I fear," came a voice from above, and they all turned to regard Jarlaxle.

The drow tossed a second cord to Athrogate, and the dwarf reeled him in.

"The castle is awakening to our presence," Jarlaxle explained as he descended.

He motioned down toward the ground, some twenty feet below.

Athrogate started to argue but lost his voice when he followed Jarlaxle's lead to look down. For there was the undead horde again, clawing through the soil and moving out under the long rope.

"Oh, lovely," said Canthan.

"They're coming into the wall tunnels, too," Jarlaxle informed him.

"Ye think they're smart enough to cut the rope behind us?" Athrogate roared.

"Oh, lovely," said Canthan.

Jarlaxle nodded to Ellery.

"Go," he bade her. "Quickly."

Ellery strapped her axe and shield over her back and scrambled out onto the rope over the hanging Athrogate.

"Be quick or ye're to get me hairy head up yer bum," Athrogate barked at her.

She didn't look back and moved out as quickly as she could.

Take the half-orc girl and drop her to the horde, sounded a voice in Athrogate's head.

The dwarf assumed a puzzled look for just a moment, then cast a glance Canthan's way.

Our victory will be near complete when she is dead, the wizard explained.

"Come on, girl," the obedient Athrogate said to Arrayan.

Jarlaxle alit on the wall top beside the woman and grabbed her arm as she started for the dwarf. "I'll take her," he said to the dwarf, and to Canthan, he added, "You go with him."

Canthan tried not to betray his surprise and anger—and suspicion, for had the drow somehow intercepted his magical message to the dwarf? Or had Athrogate's glance his way somehow tipped off the perceptive Jarlaxle to his designs for Arrayan? Canthan used his customary sarcasm to shield those telling emotions.

"You can fly now?" the mage said.

"Levitate," Jarlaxle corrected.

"Straight up and down."

"Weightlessly," the drow explained, and he took the end of his second cord from Athrogate and looped it around the lead of the housebreaker harness. "We will be no drag on you at all, good dwarf."

Athrogate figured it all out and howled all the louder. Canthan was tentatively edging out toward him by then, so the dwarf reached up and grabbed the wizard by the belt, roughly pulling him out.

"Got me a drow elf kite!" Athrogate declared with a hearty guffaw.

"Hook your arms through the harness and hold on," Jarlaxle bade the wizard. "Free up the dwarf's arms, I beg, else this castle will catch us before we reach the other side."

Canthan continued to stare at the surprising drow, and he saw clearly in Jarlaxle's returned gaze that the dark elf's instructions had emanated from more than mere prudence. A line was being drawn between them, Canthan knew.

But the time to cross over that line and dare Jarlaxle to defy him had not yet come. He had kept plenty of spells handy and was far from exhausted, but trouble just then could cost him dearly against the castle's hordes, whatever the outcome of his personal battle with the drow.

Still staring at Jarlaxle, the wizard moved to the lip of the wall and tentatively bent over to find a handhold on Athrogate's harness. He yelped with surprise when the dwarf grabbed him again and yanked him over, holding him in place until he could wrap his thin arms securely through some of the straps. Then he yelped again as Athrogate planted his heavy boots against the stone wall, pushed off, and began hand-walking the rope.

Jarlaxle took up the slack quickly and moved to the lip with Arrayan.

"Do hold on," the dark elf bade her, and to her obvious shock, he just stepped off.

Perhaps to ease the grasping woman's nerves, the drow used his power of levitation to rise up a bit higher, putting more room between them and the undead monsters. Canthan had heard tell that all drow were possessed of the ability to levitate, but he suspected that Jarlaxle was in fact using some enchanted item—perhaps a ring or other piece of jewelry. He was well aware that the mysterious drow had more than a few magic items in his possession, and not knowing precisely what they were made the wizard all the more reluctant to let things go much farther between them.

"We're coming fast, Ellery!" Athrogate called to the woman up ahead. "Ye're gonna get yerself a dwarf head! *Bwahaha!*"

Ellery, no fool, seemed to pick up a bit of speed at that proclamation.

The rooftop was clear, but the fight was still on at the keep, for the undead had begun scaling the tower—or trying to, at least—and more gargoyles were awakening to the intrusion and flying to the central structure.

Mariabronne worked his bow furiously, running from wall to wall, shooting gargoyles above and skeletons scrambling up from below. Olgerkhan, too, moved about the rooftop, though sluggishly. He carried many wounds from the initial fight after Athrogate had unceremoniously tossed him over the wall, most of them received because the large warrior, so bone-weary by then, had simply been too slow to react. Still, he tried to help out, using gargoyle corpses as bombs to rain down on the climbing undead.

Artemis Entreri tried to block it all out. He had moved about eight feet down the small staircase along the back wall to a landing with a heavy iron door. The door was locked, he soon discovered, and cleverly so. A quick inspection had also shown him more than one trap set around the portal, another clear reminder that the Zhengyian construct knew how to protect itself. He was in no hurry, anyway—he didn't intend to open the door until the others had arrived—so he carefully and deliberately went over the details of the jamb, the latch, potential pressure plates set on the floor. . . .

"We've got to get in quickly!" Mariabronne cried out to him, and the ranger accentuated his warning with the twang of his great bow.

"Just keep the beasts off me," Entreri countered.

As if on cue, Olgerkhan cried out in pain.

"Breach!" Mariabronne shouted.

Cursing under his breath, Entreri turned from the door and rushed back up the stairs, to see Mariabronne ferociously battling a pair of gargoyles over to his right, near where the rope had been set. A third creature was fast approaching.

Behind the ranger, Olgerkhan slumped against the waist-high wall stones.

"Help me over!" the dwarf priest called from beyond the wall.

Olgerkhan struggled to get up, but managed to get his hand over.

Entreri hit the back of one gargoyle just as Pratcus gained the roof. The dwarf moved for Olgerkhan first, but just put on a disgusted look and walked past him as he began to cast his healing spell, aiming not for the more wounded half-orc, but for Mariabronne, who was beginning to show signs of battle wear, as claws slipped through his defenses and tore at him.

"We have it," the ranger cried to Entreri, and as the dwarf's healing washed over him, Mariabronne stood straighter and fought with renewed energy. "The door! Breach the door!"

Entreri paused long enough to glance past the trio to see Ellery's painfully slow progress on the rope and the other four working toward him in a strange formation, with Jarlaxle and Arrayan floating behind Athrogate and the hanging wizard.

He shook his head and ran back to the keep's uppermost door. He considered the time remaining before the rest arrived, and checked yet again for any more traps.

As usual, the assassin's timing was near perfect, and he clicked open the lock just as the others piled onto the stairwell behind him. Entreri swung the door in and stepped back, and Athrogate moved right past him.

Entreri grabbed him by the shoulder, stopping him.

"Eh?" the dwarf asked, and he meant to argue more, but Entreri had already put a finger over his pursed lips.

The assassin stepped past Athrogate and bent low. After a cursory inspection of the stones beyond the threshold, Entreri reached into a pouch and pulled forth some chalk dust. He tossed it out to cover a certain section of the stones.

"Pressure plate," he explained, stepping back and motioning for Athrogate to go on.

"Got yer uses," the dwarf grumbled.

Entreri waited for Jarlaxle, who brought up the rear of the line. The drow looked at him and grinned knowingly, then purposely stepped right atop the assassin's chalk.

"Make them believe you are more useful than you are," Jarlaxle congratulated, and Entreri merely shrugged.

"I do believe you are beginning to understand it all," Jarlaxle added. "Should I be worried?"

"Yes."

The simplicity of the answer brought yet another grin to Jarlaxle's coal-black face.

CHAPTER

CANTHAN'S CONFIRMATION

17

The door opened into a circular room that encompassed the whole of one floor of the keep. A basalt altar stood out from the northern edge of the room directly across from them. Red veins shot through the rock, accentuating the decorated covering of bas relief images of dragons. Behind the altar, between a pair of burning braziers, sat a huge egg, large enough for a man Entreri's size to curl up inside it.

"This looks like a place for fighting," Athrogate muttered, and he didn't seem the least dismayed by that probability.

Given the scene outside with the undead, the dwarf's words rang true, for all around the room, set equidistant to each other, stood sarcophagi of polished stone and decorated gold. The facings of the ornate caskets indicated a standing humanoid creature, arms in tight to its sides, with long feet and a long, canine snout.

"Gnolls?" Jarlaxle asked. Behind him, Entreri secured the door, expertly resetting the lock.

"Let us not tarry to find out," said Mariabronne, indicating the one other exit in the room: another descending stairwell over to their right. It was bordered by a waist-high railing, with the entry all the way on the other side of the room. The ranger, his eyes locked on the nearest sarcophagus, one hand ready on his sheathed sword, stepped out toward the center of the room. He felt a rumble, as if from a movement within that nearest sarcophagus, and he started to call out.

But they didn't need the warning, for they all felt it, and Entreri broke into motion, darting past the others to the railing. He grabbed onto it and rolled right over, dropping nimbly to the stairs below. Hardly slowing, he was at the second door in an instant, working his fingers around its edges, his eyes darting all about.

He took a deep breath. Though he saw no traps, the assassin knew he should inspect the door in greater detail, but he simply didn't have the time. Behind him, he heard his friends scrambling on the stairs, followed by the creaking sounds as the undead monsters within the sarcophagi pushed open their coffins.

He went for the lock.

But before he could begin, the door popped open.

Entreri fell back, drawing his weapons. Nothing came through, though, and the assassin calmed when he noted a smug-looking Canthan on the stairs behind him.

"Magical spell of opening?" Entreri asked.

"We haven't the time for your inspection," replied the mage. "I thought it prudent."

Of course you did, so long as I was close enough to catch the brunt of any traps or monsters lying in wait, Entreri thought but did not say—though his expression certainly told the others the gist of it.

"They're coming out," Commander Ellery warned from up in the room.

"Mummified gnolls," Jarlaxle said. "Interesting."

Entreri was not so interested and had no desire to see the strange creatures. He spun away from Canthan, drawing his weapons as he went, and charged through the door.

He was surprised, as were all the others as they came through, to find that he was not on the keep's lowest level. From the outside, the structure hadn't seemed tall enough to hold three stories, but sure enough, Entreri found himself on a balcony that ran around the circumference of the keep, opening to a sweeping stone stair on the northernmost wall. Moving to the waist-high iron railing, its balusters shaped to resemble twisting dragons with wings spread wide, Entreri figured out the puzzle. For the floor level below him was partially below ground—the circular section of it, at least. On the southernmost side of that bottom floor, a short set of stairs led up to a rectangular alcove that held the tower's main doors, so that the profile of that lowest level reminded the assassin of a keyhole, but one snubbed short.

And there, just at the top of those stairs, set in the rectangular alcove opposite the doors, sat the book of Zhengyi, the tome of creation, suspended on tendrils that looked all too familiar to Artemis Entreri. The assassin eventually pulled his eyes away from the enticing target and completed his scan of the floor below. He heard the door behind him close, followed immediately by some heavy pounding and Jarlaxle saying, with his typical penchant for understatement, "We should move quickly."

But Entreri wasn't in any hurry to go down the stairs or over the railing. He noted a pair of iron statues set east and west in the room below, and vividly recalled his encounter in Herminicle's tower. Even worse than the possibility of a pair of iron golems, the room below was not sealed, for every few feet around the perimeter presented an opening to a tunnel of worked and fitted stones, burrowing down into the ground. Might the horde of undead be approaching through those routes even then?

A sharp ring behind him turned Entreri around. Athrogate stood at the closed iron door, the locking bar and supports already rattling from the pounding of the mummified gnolls.

The dwarf methodically went to work, dropping his backpack to the ground and fishing out one piton after another. He set them strategically around the door and drove them deep into the stone with a single crack of his morning star—the one enchanted with oil of impact.

A moment later, he hopped back and dropped his hands on his hips, surveying his work. "Yeah, it'll hold them back for a bit."

"They're the least of our worries," Entreri said.

By that point, several of the others were at the rail, looking over the room and coming up with the same grim assessment as had

Entreri. Not so for Arrayan and Olgerkhan, though. The woman slumped against the back wall, as if merely being there, in such close proximity to the magical book, was rendering her helpless. Her larger partner didn't seem much better off.

"There are our answers," Canthan said, nodding toward the book. "Get me to it."

"Those statues will likely animate," Jarlaxle said. "Iron golems are no easy foe."

Athrogate roared with laughter as he walked up beside the drow. "Ain't ye seen nothing yet from Cracker and Whacker?" As he named the weapons, he presented them before the dark elf.

"Cracker and Whacker?" the drow replied.

Athrogate guffawed again as he glanced over the railing, looking down directly atop one of the iron statues. "Meet ye below!" he called and with that he whispered to each of his weapons, bidding them to pour forth their enchanted fluids. With another wild laugh, he hopped up atop the railing and dropped.

"Cracker and Whacker?" Jarlaxle asked again.

"He used to call them Rotter and Slaughter," Ellery replied, and Entreri noted that for the first time since he had met Jarlaxle, the drow seemed to have no answer whatsoever.

But as there was no denying Athrogate's inanity, nor was there any way to deny his effectiveness. He landed in a sitting position on the statue's iron shoulders, his legs wrapping around its head. The golem began to animate, as predicted, but before it could even reach up at the dwarf, Cracker slapped down atop its head. The black iron of the construct's skull turned reddish-brown, its integrity stolen by the secretions of a rust monster. When Whacker, gleaming with oil of impact, hit the same spot iron dust flew and the top of the golem's head caved in.

Still the creature flailed, but Athrogate had too great an advantage, whipping his weapons with precision, defeating the integrity of his opponent's natural armor with one morning star, then blasting away with the other. An iron limb went flying, and though the other hand managed to grab the dwarf and throw him hard to the floor, the tough and strong Athrogate bounced up and hit the golem with a one-two, one-two combination that had one leg flying free. Then he caved in the side of its chest for good measure.

But the other golem charged in, and other noises echoed from the tunnels.

Mariabronne and Ellery, Pratcus in tow, charged around to the stairwell while Entreri slipped over the railing and dropped the fifteen feet to the floor, absorbing his landing with a sidelong roll.

Canthan, too, went over the railing, dropping the end of a rope while its other end magically anchored in mid-air. He slid down off to the side of the fray with no intention of joining in. For the wizard, the goal was in sight, sitting there for the taking.

He wasn't pleased when Jarlaxle floated down beside him and paced him toward the front alcove.

"Just keep them off of me," Canthan ordered the drow.

"Them?" Jarlaxle asked.

Canthan wasn't listening. He paused with every step and began casting a series of spells, weaving wards around himself to fend off the defensive magic that no doubt protected the tome.

"Jarlaxle!" called Ellery. "To me!"

The drow turned and glanced at the woman. The situation in the room was under control for the time being, he could see, mostly owing to Athrogate's abilities and effectiveness against iron golems. One was down, thrashing helplessly, and the second was already lilting and wavering as blast after blast wracked it, with the dwarf rushing all around it and pounding away with abandon.

"Jarlaxle!" Ellery cried again.

The drow regarded her and shrugged.

"To me!" she insisted.

Jarlaxle glanced back at Canthan, who stood before the book, then turned his gaze back at Ellery. She meant to keep him away from it and for no other reason than to allow Canthan to examine it first. Ellery stared at him, her look showing him in no uncertain terms that if he disobeyed her, the fight would be on.

He glanced back at Canthan again and grew confident that he

still had time to play things through, for the wizard was moving with great caution and seemed thoroughly perplexed.

Jarlaxle started across the room toward Ellery. He paused and nodded to the stairs, where Olgerkhan and Arrayan were making their way down, the large half-orc practically carrying the bone-weary woman.

"Secure the perimeter," Ellery instructed them all, and she waved for the half-orcs to return to the balcony. "We must give Canthan time to unravel the mystery of this place." To Mariabronne and Entreri, she added, "Scout the tunnels to first door or thirty feet."

Entreri was only peripherally listening, for he was already scanning the tunnels. All of them seemed to take the same course: a downward-sloping, eight-foot wide corridor bending to the left after about a dozen feet. Torches were set on the walls, left and right, but they were unlit. Even in the darkness, though, the skilled Entreri understood that the floors were not as solid as they appeared.

"Not yet," the assassin said as Mariabronne started down one tunnel.

The ranger stopped and waited as Entreri moved back from the tunnel entrance and retrieved the head of a destroyed iron golem. He moved in front of one tunnel and bade the others to back up.

He rolled the head down, jumping aside as if expecting an explosion, and as he suspected, the item bounced across a pressure plate set in the floor. Fires blossomed, but not the killing flames of a fireball trap. Rather, the torches flared to life, and as the head rolled along to the bend, it hit a second pressure plate, lighting the opposing torches set there as well.

"How convenient," Ellery remarked.

"Are they all like that?" asked Mariabronne.

"Pressure plates in all," Entreri replied. "What they do, I cannot tell."

"Ye just showed us, ye dolt," said Athrogate.

Entreri didn't answer, other than with a wry grin. The first rule of creating effective traps was to present a situation that put intruders at ease. He looked Athrogate over and decided he didn't need to tell the dwarf that bit of common sense.

Strange that she should choose this moment to think herself a leader, the wizard mused when he heard Ellery barking commands in the distance. To Canthan, after all, Ellery would never be more than a pawn. He could not deny her effectiveness in her present role, though. The others didn't dare go against her, particularly with the fool Mariabronne nodding and flapping his lips at her every word.

A cursory glance told Canthan that Ellery was performing her responsibilities well. She had them all busy, moving tentatively down the different tunnels, with Olgerkhan and Arrayan back upstairs guarding the door. Pratcus anchored the arms of Ellery's scouting mission, the dwarf staying in the circular room and hopping about to regard each dark opening as Ellery, Entreri, Jarlaxle, Mariabronne, and Athrogate explored the passages.

Canthan caught a glimpse of Ellery as she came out one tunnel and turned into another, her shield on one arm, axe ready in the other.

"I have taught you well," Canthan whispered under his breath. He caught himself as he finished and silently scolded himself for allowing the distraction—any distraction—at that all-important moment. He took a deep breath and turned back to the book.

His confidence grew as he read on, for he felt the empathetic intrusions of the living tome and came to believe that his wards would suffice in fending them off.

Quickly did the learned mage begin to decipher the ways of the book. The runes appearing in the air above it and falling into it were translations of life energy, drawn from an outside source. That energy had fueled the construction, served as the living source of power animating the undead, caused the gargoyles to regenerate on their perches, and brought life to the golems.

Canthan could hardly draw a breath. The sheer power of the translation overwhelmed him. For some two decades, the wizards of the Bloodstone Lands considered Zhengyi's lichdom, his cheating of death itself, to be his greatest accomplishment, but the book . . .

The book rivaled even that.

The wizard devoured another page and eagerly turned to the next. In no time, he had come to the point where the lettering ended and watched in amazement as runes appeared in the air and drifted to the pages, writing as they went. The process had been vampiric at first, Canthan recognized, with the tome taking from the living force, but it had become more symbiotic, a joining of purpose and will.

The source of energy? Canthan mused. He considered Arrayan, her weakness and that of her partner. She had found the missing book, Mariabronne and Wingham had told them.

No, the wizard decided. That wasn't the whole of it. Arrayan was far more entwined in all of it than just having been drained of her life energies.

Canthan smiled when he finally understood the power of the tome and knew how to defeat it.

And not just defeat it, he hoped, but possess it.

He tore his gaze away from the page and glanced up the staircase to see Arrayan leaning back against a wall, watching Olgerkhan. She looked his way desperately, plaintively. Too much so, Canthan knew. There was more at stake for the young woman than merely whether or not they could find their way out of the castle. For her, it was much more personal than the safety of Palishchuk.

Entreri had shown them how to test each pressure plate safely, but Mariabronne needed no such instructions. The ranger had played through similar scenarios many times, and had the know-how and the equipment to work his way quickly down the tunnel he had chosen.

It had continued to bend around to the left for many feet, with pressure plates set between wall-set torches every dozen feet or so. Mariabronne lit the first by tapping the plate with a long telescoping pole, but he did not trigger the next, or the next after that, preferring to walk in near darkness.

Then, convinced all was clear, the ranger rushed back to the second set of torches and triggered the plate. He repeated the process, always lighting the torches two sets back.

After about fifty feet, the tunnel became a staircase, moving straight down for many, many steps.

Mariabronne glanced back the way he had come. Ellery had told them to inspect the tunnels just to thirty feet or so. The ranger had always been that advanced and independent scout, though, and he trusted his instincts. Down he went, testing the stairs and the walls. Slowly and steadily, he put three dozen steps behind him before it simply became too dark for him to continue. Not willing to mark his position clearly by lighting a candle or torch of his own, Mariabronne sighed and turned back.

But then a light appeared below him, behind the slightly ajar door of a chamber at the bottom of the stairs. Mariabronne eyed it for a long while, the hairs on the back of his neck tingling and standing on end. Such were the moments he lived for, the precipice of disaster, the taunt of the unknown.

Smiling despite himself, Mariabronne crept down to the door. He listened for a short while and dared to peek in. Every castle must have a treasure room was his first thought, and he figured he was looking in on one of the antechambers to just that. Two decorated sarcophagi were set against the opposite wall, framing a closed iron door. Before them, in the center of the room, a brazier burned brightly, a thin line of black smoke snaking up to the high ceiling above. Centering that ceiling was a circular depression set with some sort of bas relief that Mariabronne could not make out—though it looked to him as if there were egglike stones set into it.

Stone tables covered in decorated silver candelabra and assorted trinkets lined the side walls, and the ranger made out some silver bells, a gem-topped scepter, and a golden censer. Religious items, mostly, it seemed to him. A single cloth hung from one table, stitched with a scene of gnolls dancing around a rearing black dragon.

"Lovely combination," he whispered.

Mariabronne glanced back up the ascending corridor behind him. Perhaps he shouldn't press on. He could guess easily enough what those sarcophagi might hold.

The ranger grinned. Such had been the story of his life: always pushing ahead farther than he should. He recalled the scolding King Gareth had given to him upon his first official scouting expedition in eastern Vaasa. Gareth had bade him to map the region along the Galenas for five miles.

Mariabronne had gone all the way to Palishchuk.

That was who he was and how he played: always on the edge and always just skilled enough or lucky enough to sneak out of whatever trouble his adventurous character had found.

So it was still, and he couldn't resist. The Honorable General Dannaway of the Vaasan Gate had been wise indeed not to entrust Ellery to Mariabronne's care alone.

The ranger pushed open the door and slipped into the room. Gold and silver reflected in his brown eyes, gleaming in the light of the brazier. Mariabronne tried hard not to become distracted, though, and set himself in line with the coffins.

As he had expected, their dog-faced, decorated lids swung open.

As one gnoll mummy strode forth from its coffin, Mariabronne was there, a smile on his face, his sword deftly slashing and stabbing. He hit the creature several times before it had even cleared the coffin, and when it reached for him with one arm, lumbering forward, Mariabronne gladly took that arm off at the elbow.

The second was on him by then, and the ranger hopped back. He went into a quick spin, coming around fast, blade level, and the enchanted sword creased the gnoll's abdominal area, tearing filthy gray bandages aside and opening up a gash across the belly of the dried-out husk of the undead creature. The gnoll mummy groaned and slowed its pursuit. Mariabronne smiled all the wider, knowing that his weapon could indeed hurt the thing.

And the two undead creatures simply weren't fast enough to present a serious threat to the skilled warrior. Mariabronne's blade worked brilliantly and with lightning speed and pinpoint accuracy, finding every opening in the mummies' defenses, taking what was offered and never asking for more. He fought with no sense of urgency, as was his trademark, and it was rooted in the confidence that whatever came along, he would have the skills to defeat it.

A rattle from above tested that confidence. Both mummies were ragged things by then, much more so than they had been when first they had emerged from their coffins, with rag wrappings hanging free and deep gashes oozing foul odors and the occasional drip of ichor all around them both. One had only half an arm, a gray-black bony spur protruding from the stump. The other barely moved, its gut hanging open, its legs torn. The ranger led them to the near side of the room, back to the door through which he'd entered, then he disengaged and dashed back to find the time to glance up at the rattle.

He noted one of the egg shapes rocking back and forth above the brazier. It broke free of the ceiling and dropped to the flaming bowl. Mariabronne's eyes widened with curiosity as he watched it fall. He came to realize that it was not an egg-shaped stone but an actual egg of some sort. It hit the flaming stones in the bowl and cracked open, and a line of blacker smoke rushed out of it, widening as it rose.

Hoping it was no poison, Mariabronne darted back at the mummies, thinking to slash through them and get in position for a fast exit. He hit the nearest again in the gut, extending the already deep wound so thoroughly that the creature buckled over, folded in half, and fell into a heap. The other swung at Mariabronne, but the ranger was too fast. He ducked the lumbering blow and quick-stepped past, nearly to the door.

"You shall not run!" came a booming voice in his ears, and the ranger felt a shiver course his spine. Accompanying that voice was a sudden, sharp gust of wind that whipped the ranger's cloak up over his back.

Worse for Mariabronne, though, the wind slammed the door.

He rolled and turned as he came around, so that he faced the room with his back to the door. His jaw dropped as he followed the billowing column of black smoke up and up to where it had formed into the torso and horned head of a gigantic, powerful demonic creature that radiated an aura of pure evil. Its head and facial features resembled that of a snub-nosed bulldog, with huge canines and a pair of inward-hooking horns at the sides of its wide head. Its arms and hands seemed formed of smoke, great grasping black hands with fingers narrowing to sharp points.

"Well met, human," the demon creature said. "You came here seeking adventure and a test of your skills, no doubt. Would you leave when you have at last found it?"

"I will send you back to the Abyss, demon!" Mariabronne promised.

He started forward but realized his error immediately, for in his fascination with the more formidable beast, he had taken his eye off the mummy. It came forward with a lumbering swing. The ranger twisted and ducked the blow. But that second, cropped arm stabbed in, the sheared, sharpened bone gashing Mariabronne's neck. Again Mariabronne's speed extracted him before the mummy could follow through, but he felt the warmth of his own blood dribbling down his neck.

Before he could even consider that, however, he was leaping aside once more.

The smoky creature blew forth a cone of fiery breath.

"D*ae*mon," the beast corrected. "And my home is the plane of Gehenna, where I will gladly return. But not until I feast upon your bones."

Flames danced up from Mariabronne's cloak and he spun, pulling it free as he turned. He noted then that the pursuing mummy had not been so fortunate, catching the daemon fire full force. It thrashed about, flames dancing all over it, one arm waving frantically, futilely.

Mariabronne threw his cloak upon it for good measure.

Then he leaped forward and the daemon came forth, smoke forming into powerful legs as it stepped free of the brazier. It raked with its shadowy hands and its head snapped forward to bite at Mariabronne, but again the ranger realized at once that he was the superior fighter and that his sword could indeed inflict damage upon the otherworldly creature.

"Gehenna, then," he cried. "But you will go there hungry!"

"Fool, I am always hungry!"

Its last word sounded more as a gurgle, as the ranger's fine sword creased its face. In his howl of triumph, though, Mariabronne didn't hear the second egg drop.

Or the third.

CHAPTER 18

THE RANGER'S JOURNEY

The sound of battle echoed up the corridor and into the main room of the tower. Canthan snarled at the noise but refused to turn away from the tome. He felt certain there were more secrets buried within that book. Energy made his skin tingle and hummed in the air around it. The book was magical, the runes were magical, and he had a much better understanding of how the castle had come about, about the source of energy that had facilitated the construction, but there was more. Something remained hidden just below the surface. The magical runes even then appearing on the page might prove to be a clue.

The ring of steel distracted him. He turned back to see an agitated Pratcus hopping from one foot to the other in the middle of the room. Ellery came out of one tunnel, and cut to the side from where the sound emanated. She looked at Pratcus as Athrogate emerged from a tunnel opposite. Up on the balcony, Olgerkhan and Arrayan leaned over the railing, looking down with concern.

"Who?" Ellery asked.

"Gotta be the ranger," Pratcus answered.

Ellery ran toward the sound. "Which tunnel?" she asked, for the torches in all had gone dark again, and the echoes of the sounds confused her.

All eyes went to the dwarf, but Pratcus just shrugged.

Then from above, Olgerkhan cried out, "Breach!"

The fight had come.

"Just keep them off me!" Canthan growled, and he forced his attention back to the open book.

Another egg fell and broke open, and that made five.

Mariabronne finished the first with a two-handed overhead chop, but he was too busy leaping away from fiery daemon breath to applaud himself for the kill.

He went into a frenzy, spinning, rolling, and slashing, scoring hit after hit, and he came to realize that the creatures could only breathe their fire on him from a distance. So he ran, alternately closing on each. He took a few hits and gave a few more, and his confidence only heightened when, upon hearing more rattling from above, he leaped over and shouldered the brazier to the floor.

The rattling stopped.

There would be no more than the four standing against him. All he had to do was hold out until his companions arrived.

He sprang forward and charged but skidded to a stop and cut to the side. He used the sarcophagi as shields and kept the clawing, smoky hands at bay.

His smile appeared once more, that confidence reminiscent of the young Mariabronne who had rightly earned the nickname "the Rover" and had also earned a rakish reputation with ladies all across Damara. His sense of adventure overwhelmed him. He never felt more alive, more on the edge of disaster, of freedom and doom, than he was in times of greatest danger.

"Are all of Gehenna so slow?" he tried to say, to taunt the daemons, but halfway through the sentence he coughed up blood.

The ranger froze. He brought his free hand up to his neck to feel the blood still pumping. A wave of dizziness nearly dropped him.

He had to dive aside as two of the daemons loosed cones of fire at him, and so weak did he feel that he almost didn't get back to his feet—and when he did, he overbalanced so badly that he nearly staggered headlong into a third of the beasts.

"Priest, I need you!" Mariabronne the Rover shouted through the blood, and all at once he wasn't so confident and exuberant. "Priest! Dwarf, I need you!"

Entreri and Jarlaxle rushed into the room to join the others. Sounds of fighting from above assailed them, and both Entreri and Athrogate started that way.

Then came the desperate call from Mariabronne, "Priest, I need you!"

"Athrogate, hold the balcony!" Ellery ordered. "The rest with me!"

Entreri heard Arrayan's cry and ignored the commander's order. In his thoughts, he pictured the doom of Dwahvel, his dear halfling friend, and so overwhelming was that sensation that he never paused long enough to consider it. He sprinted past the dwarf and hit the stairs running, taking them three at a time. He cut to the right, though the door and his companions were on the balcony to the left.

Then he cut back sharply to the left and leaped up to the slanted stairway railing in a dead run. His lead foot hit and started to slide, but the assassin stamped his right foot hard on the railing and leaped away, spinning as he went so that when he lifted up near the floor of the balcony, his back was to the railing. He threw his hands up and caught the balusters, and with the others on the floor below looking at him with mouths hanging open, Entreri's taut muscles flexed and tugged. He curled as he rose, throwing his feet up over his head. Not only was his backward flip over the railing perfectly executed, not only did he land lightly and in perfect balance, but on the way over he managed to draw both dagger and sword.

He spun as he landed and threw himself into the nearest gnoll mummy, his blades working in a scything whirlwind. Gray wrappings exploded into the air, flying all around him.

Down below, Jarlaxle looked to Ellery and said, "Consider the room secured."

Ellery managed one quick look the drow's way as she sprinted toward the tunnel entrances.

"Which one?" she asked again of Pratcus, who ran beside her.

"Yerself to the right, meself to the left!" the dwarf replied, and they split into the two possible openings.

Jarlaxle followed right behind them, but paused there. Athrogate rambled back from the stairs, trying to catch up.

Torches flared to life as Ellery ran through. A split second later, Pratcus's heavy strides similarly lit the first pair in his descending corridor.

"Which one, then?" Athrogate asked Jarlaxle.

"Here!" Ellery cried before the drow could answer, and both Jarlaxle and Athrogate took up the chase of the woman warrior.

In the other tunnel, Pratcus, too, heard the call, just as he passed the second set of torches, which flared to life. The dwarf instinctively slowed but shook his head. Perhaps his tunnel would intersect with the other and he wouldn't have to lose all the time backtracking, he thought, and he decided to light up one more set of torches.

He hit the next pressure plate, turning sidelong so that he could quickly spin around if the light didn't reveal an intersection.

But the torches didn't ignite.

Instead came a sudden clanging sound, and Pratcus just happened to be looking the right way to see the iron spike slide out of the wall.

He thought to throw himself aside but only managed to cry out. The spike moved too fast. It hit him in the gut and drove him back hard against the far corridor wall. It kept going, plunging right through the dwarf and ringing hard against the stone behind him.

With trembling hands, Pratcus grabbed at the stake. He tried to gather his wits, to call upon his gods for some magical healing.

But the dwarf knew that he'd need more than that.

Flames licked at Mariabronne from every angle. He drove his sword through a daemon's head, tore it free and decapitated another as he swung wildly. All the room was spinning, though, and he was staggering more than charging as he went for the last pair of daemons.

His consciousness flitted away; he felt the rake of claws. He lifted an arm to defend himself and a monstrous maw clamped down upon it.

Black spots became a general darkness. He felt cold . . . so cold.

Mariabronne the Rover summoned all of his strength and went into a sudden and violent frenzy, slashing wildly, punching and kicking.

Then the ranger's journey was before him, the only road he ever rightly expected while following his adventurous spirit.

He was at peace.

Blackness engulfed Arrayan as the mummy's strong hands closed around her throat. She couldn't begin to concentrate enough to throw one of her few remaining spells, and she knew that her magic had not the strength to defeat or even deter the monsters in any case.

Nor did she have the physical strength to begin to fight back. She grabbed the mummy's wrists with her hands, but she might as well have been trying to tear an old oak tree out of the ground.

She managed a glance at Olgerkhan, who was thrashing with another pair of the horrid creatures, and that one glance told the woman that her friend would likely join her in the netherworld.

The mummy pressed harder, forcing her head back, and somewhere deep inside she hoped that her neck would just snap and be done with it before her lack of breath overcame her.

Then she staggered backward, and the mummy's arms went weak in her grasp. Confused, Arrayan opened her eyes then recoiled with horror as she realized that she was holding two severed limbs. She threw them to the ground, gasped a deep and welcomed breath of air, and looked back at the creature only to see the whirlwind that was Artemis Entreri hacking it apart.

Another mummy grabbed at Arrayan from the side, and she cried out.

And Entreri was there, rolling his extraordinary sword up and over with a left-to-right backhand that forced the mummy's arms aside. The assassin turned as he followed through, flipped his dagger into the air and caught it backhand, then drove it right to the hilt into the mummy's face as he came around. Gray dust flew from the impact.

Entreri yanked the dagger free, spun around so that he was facing the creature, and bulled ahead, driving it right over the railing.

Arrayan sobbed with horror and weakness, and the assassin grabbed her by the arm and guided her toward the stair.

"Get down!" he ordered.

Arrayan, too battered and overwhelmed, too weak and frightened, hesitated.

"Go!" Entreri shouted.

He leaped at her, causing her to cry out again, then he went right by, launching himself with furious abandon into another of the stubborn gnoll mummies.

"Now, woman!" he shouted as his weapons began their deadly dance once more.

Arrayan didn't move.

Entreri growled in frustration. It was going to be hard enough keeping himself alive up there as more creatures poured in, without having to protect Arrayan. A glance toward the door inspired him.

"Arrayan," he cried, "I must get to Olgerkhan. To the stair with you, I beg."

Perhaps it was the mention of her half-orc friend, or perhaps the calming change in his voice, but Entreri was glad indeed to see the woman sprint off for the stairs.

The mummy before him crumbled, and the assassin leaped ahead.

Olgerkhan was losing badly. Bruises and cuts covered him by then, and he staggered with every lumbering swing of his heavy war club.

Entreri hit him full force from behind, driving him right past the pair of battling mummies, and the assassin kept pushing, throwing Olgerkhan hard against the back of the opened door. The door slammed, or tried to, for a gargoyle was wedged between it and the jamb.

But Entreri kept moving, right into the incoming creature. He ignored the mummies he knew were fast closing on him and focused all of his fury instead on that trapped gargoyle. He slashed and stabbed and drove it back.

Olgerkhan's weight finally closed the door.

"Just hold it shut!" Entreri yelled at him. "For all our sakes."

The assassin charged away at the remaining two mummies.

Ellery instinctively knew that she was in grave danger. Perhaps it had been the tone of Mariabronne's plea for help or even that the legendary Rover had called out at all. Perhaps it was the closed door at the bottom of the staircase before her, or maybe it was the sound.

For other than her footsteps, and those of the duo behind her, all was silent.

She lowered her shoulder and barreled through the door, stumbling into the room, shield and sword presented. There she froze, then slumped in horror and despair, her fears confirmed. For there lay Mariabronne, on his back, unmoving and with his neck and chest covered in his own blood. Blood continued to roll from the neck wound, but it was not gushing forth as it had been, for the ranger's heart no longer beat.

"Too many," Athrogate said, rambling in behind her.

"Guardian daemons," Jarlaxle remarked, noting the demonic heads, all that remained of the creatures, lying about the room. "A valiant battle."

Ellery continued to simply stand there, staring at Mariabronne, staring at the dead hero of Damara. From her earliest days, Ellery had heard stories of that great man, of his work with her uncle the king and his particular relationship with the line of Tranth, the Barons of Bloodstone and Ellery's immediate family members. Like so many warriors of her generation, Ellery had held up the legend of Mariabronne as the epitome of a hero, the idol and the goal. As Gareth Dragonsbane and his friends had inspired the young warriors of Mariabronne's generation, so had he passed along that inspiration to hers.

And he lay dead at Ellery's feet. Dead on a mission she was leading. Dead because of her decision to split the party to explore the tunnels.

Almost unaware of her surroundings, Ellery was shaken from her turmoil by the shout of Athrogate.

"That's the priest!" the dwarf yelled, and he charged back out of the room.

Jarlaxle moved near to Ellery and put a comforting hand on her shoulder.

"You are needed elsewhere," the dark elf bade her. "There is nothing more you can do here."

She offered the drow a blank look.

"Go with Athrogate," said Jarlaxle. "There is work to be done and quickly."

Hardly thinking, Ellery staggered out of the room.

"I will see to Mariabronne," Jarlaxle assured her as she stumbled back up the corridor.

True to his word, the drow was with the ranger as soon as Ellery was out of sight. He pulled out a wand and cast a quick divination spell.

He was surprised and disappointed at how little magic registered on a man of Mariabronne's reputation. The man's sword, Bayurel, was of course enchanted, as was his armor, but none of it strongly. He wore a single magical ring, but a cursory glance told Jarlaxle that he possessed at least a dozen rings of greater enchantment—and so he shook his head and decided that pilfering the obvious ring wasn't worth the risk.

One thing did catch his attention, however, and as soon as he opened Mariabronne's small belt pouch, a smile widened on Jarlaxle's face.

"Obsidian steed," he remarked, pulling forth the small black equine figurine. A quick inspection revealed its command words.

Jarlaxle crossed the ranger's arms over his chest and placed Bayurel in the appropriate position atop him. He felt a moment of regret. He had heard much of Mariabronne the Rover during his short time in the Bloodstone Lands, and he knew that he had become party to a momentous event. The shock of the man's death would resonate in Vaasa and Damara for a long time to come, and it occurred to Jarlaxle that it truly was an important loss.

He gave a quick salute to the dead hero and acknowledged the sadness of his passing.

Of course, it wasn't enough of a regret for Jarlaxle to put back the obsidian steed.

"Aw, what'd ye do?" Athrogate asked Pratcus as soon as he came upon the dying priest.

Pinned to the corridor wall, his chest shattered and torn, Pratcus could only stare numbly at his counterpart.

Athrogate grabbed the spike and tried to pull it back, but he couldn't get a handhold. It wouldn't have mattered anyway, both of them knew, as did Ellery when she moved in behind the black-bearded dwarf.

"Bah, ye go to Moradin's Halls, then," Athrogate said. He pulled a skin from around his neck and held it up to the priest. "A bit o' the gutbuster," he explained, referring to that most potent of dwarven liquid spirits. "It'll help ye get there and put ye in a good mood for talking with the boss."

"Hurts," Pratcus gasped. He sipped at the skin, and even managed a thankful nod as the fiery liquid burned down his throat.

Then he was dead.

CHAPTER 19

CLEARING THE PATH

Leaning on each other for much-needed support, Arrayan and Olgerkhan inched down the staircase. Entreri came up and moved between them, pushing Olgerkhan more tightly against the railing and forcing the half-orc to grab on with both his hands.

Entreri turned to Arrayan, who was holding on to him and swaying unsteadily. He shifted to put his shoulder back behind her, then in a single move swept her up into his arms. With a glance at Olgerkhan to make sure that the buffoon wouldn't come tumbling behind him, the assassin started away.

Arrayan brought a hand up against his face and he looked down at her, into her eyes.

"You saved me," she said, her voice barely audible. "All of us."

Entreri felt a rush of warm blood in his face. For just a brief moment, he saw the image of Dwahvel's face superimposed over the similar features of Arrayan. He felt warm indeed, and it occurred to him that he should just keep walking, away from the group, taking Arrayan far away from all of it.

His sensibilities, so entrenched and pragmatic after spending almost the entirety of his life in a desperate attempt at survival, tried to question, tried to illustrate the illogic of it all. But for the first time in three decades, those practical sensibilities had no voice in the thoughts of Artemis Entreri.

"Thank you," Arrayan whispered, and her hand traced the

outline of his cheek and lips.

The lump in his throat was too large for Entreri to respond, other than with a quick nod.

"That'll hold, but not for long," Athrogate announced, coming to the railing of the balcony overlooking the keep's main floor. From below, the dwarf's six remaining companions glanced up at him and at the continuing pounding and scratching on the door behind him. "More gargoyles than mummies," Athrogate explained. "Gargoyles don't hit as hard."

"The room is far from secure," put in Canthan, who still stood by the open book. "They will find a way in. Let us be on our way."

"Destroy the book?" Olgerkhan asked.

"Would that I could."

"Take it with us, then?" Arrayan asked, and the horror in her voice revealed much.

Canthan snickered at her.

"Then what?" Ellery chimed in, the first words she had spoken in some time, and with a shaky voice. "We came here for a purpose, and that seems clear before us. Are we to run away without completing—"

"I said nothing about running away, my dear Commander Ellery," Canthan interrupted. "But we should be gone from this particular room."

"With the book," Ellery reasoned.

"Not possible," Canthan informed her.

"Bah! I'll tear it out o' the ground!" said Athrogate, and he scrambled up on the railing and hopped down to the stairs.

"The book is protected," said Canthan. "It is but a conduit in any case. We'll not destroy it, or claim it, until the source of its power is no more."

"And that source is?" Olgerkhan asked, and neither Canthan nor Jarlaxle missed the way the half-orc stiffened with the question.

"That is what we must discern," the wizard replied.

Jarlaxle was unconvinced, for Canthan's gaze drifted over Arrayan as he spoke. The drow knew the wizard had long ago "discerned" the source, as had Jarlaxle and Entreri. A glance at his assassin friend, the man's face rigid and cold and glaring hard Canthan's way told Jarlaxle that Entreri was catching on as well and that he wasn't very happy about the conclusions Canthan had obviously drawn.

"Then where do we start?" Ellery asked.

"Down, I sense," said Canthan.

Jarlaxle recognized that the man was bluffing, partially at least, though the drow wasn't quite certain of why. In truth, Jarlaxle wasn't so sure that Canthan's guess was off the mark. Certainly part of the source for the construction was standing right beside him in the form of a half-orc woman. But that was a small part, Jarlaxle knew, as if Arrayan had been the initial flare to send a gnomish fire-rocket skyward before the main explosion filled the night sky with its bright-burning embers.

"The castle must have a king," the drow remarked, and he believed that, though he sensed clearly that Canthan believed it to be a queen instead—and one standing not so far away.

It wasn't the time and place to confront the wizard openly, Jarlaxle realized. The pounding on the door continued from above, and the volume of the scratching on the keep's main doors, just past Canthan and the book, led Jarlaxle to believe that scores of undead monstrosities had risen against them.

The room was no sanctuary and would soon enough become a crypt.

Jarlaxle will peruse the book and you will guard him, Canthan's magical sending echoed in Ellery's head. *When we are long gone, you will do as you were trained to do. As you promised you could do.*

Ellery's eyes widened, but she did well to hide her surprise.

Another magical sending came to her: *Our victory is easily achieved, and I know how to do it. But Jarlaxle will stand against my course. He sees personal gain here, whatever the cost to Damara. For our sake, and the sake of the land, the drow must be killed.*

Ellery took the continuing words in stride, not surprised. She didn't quite understand what Canthan was talking about, of course. Easily achieved? Why would Jarlaxle not agree to something like that? It made no sense, but Ellery could not easily dismiss the source of the information and of her orders. Canthan had found her many years ago, and through his work, she had gained greatly in rank and reputation. Her skill as a warrior had been honed through many years of training, but that added icing, the edge that allowed her to win when others could not, had been possible only through the work of Canthan and his associates.

Though they were the enemies of the throne and her own relatives, Ellery knew that the relationship between the crown of Damara and the Citadel of Assassins was complicated and not quite as openly hostile and adversarial as onlookers might believe. Certainly Ellery had quietly profited from her relationship with Canthan—and never had the wizard asked her to do anything that went against the crown.

In her gut, however, she knew that there was something more going on than the wizard was telling her. Was Canthan seeking some personal gain himself? Was he using Ellery to settle a personal grudge he held with the dark elf?

Now!

Ellery jolted at the sharp intrusion, her gaze going to Canthan. He stood resolute, eyes narrow, lips thin.

A hundred questions popped into Ellery's head, a hundred demands she wanted to make of the wizard. How could she follow such an order against someone who had done nothing out of line along the expedition, someone she had asked along and who had performed, to that point, so admirably? How could she do this to someone she had known as a lover, though that had meant little to her?

Looking at Canthan, Ellery realized how she could and why she would.

The wizard terrified her, as did the band of cutthroats he represented.

It all came clear to Commander Ellery at that moment, as she admitted to herself, for the first time, the truth of her involvement with the Citadel of Assassins and its wizard representative. She had spent years justifying her secret relationship with Canthan, telling herself that her personal gains and the way she could use them would benefit the kingdom. In Ellery's mind, for all that time, she thought herself in control of the relationship. She, the relative of Tranth and of both King Gareth and Lady Christine, would always do what was best for Damara and greater Bloodstone.

What did it matter if the dark tendrils of her choices delayed her from that "moment of miracle" her relatives all enviously awaited, that release of holy power that would show the world that she was beyond an ordinary warrior, that she was a paladin in the line of Gareth Dragonsbane?

At that moment, though, the nakedness of her self-delusion and justification hit her hard. Perhaps Canthan was imparting truthful thoughts to her to justify her killing of the drow. Perhaps, she tried to tell herself, the dark elf Jarlaxle truly was an impediment to their necessary victory.

Yes, that was it, the woman told herself. They all wanted to win, all wanted to survive. The death of Mariabronne had to mean something. The Zhengyian castle had to be defeated. Canthan knew that, and he apparently knew something about Jarlaxle that Ellery did not.

Despite her newest rationalization, deep in her heart Ellery suspected something else. Deep in her heart, Ellery understood the truth of her relationship with Canthan and the Citadel of Assassins.

But some things were better left buried deep.

She had to trust him, not for his sake, but for hers.

His eye patch tingled. Nothing specific came to him, but Jarlaxle understood that a magical intrusion—a sending or scrying, some unseen wave of magical energy—had just flitted by him.

At first the drow feared that the castle's king to whom he had referred might be looking in on them, but then, as Ellery remarked to him, "Do you believe you might be able to find some deeper insight into the magical tome? Something that Canthan has overlooked?" Jarlaxle came to understand that the source of the magic had been none other than his wizardly companion.

The drow tried not to let his reaction to the question show him off-guard when he lied, "I am sure that good Canthan's knowledge of the Art is greater than my own."

Ellery's eyes widened and her nostrils flared, and the drow knew that he had surprised and worried her with his tentative refusal. He decided not to disappoint.

"But I am drow and have spent centuries in the Underdark, where magic is not quite the same. Perhaps there is something I will recognize that Canthan has not."

He looked at the wizard as he spoke, and Canthan gracefully bowed, stepped aside, and swept his arm to invite Jarlaxle to the book.

There it was, as clear as it could be.

"We ain't got time for that," Athrogate growled, and the thought "on cue" came to the drow.

"True enough," Ellery played along. "Lead the others out, Athrogate," she ordered. "I will remain here to guard over Jarlaxle for as long as the situation allows."

Ellery nodded toward the book, but Jarlaxle motioned for her to go first. He passed by a confused-looking Entreri as he followed.

"Trouble," he managed to quietly whisper.

Entreri made no motion to indicate he had heard anything, and he went out with Canthan, Athrogate, and the two half-orcs, moving down the tunnel Mariabronne had taken on his final journey.

Jarlaxle stood before the open book but did not begin perusing it. Rather, he watched the others head down the tunnel and stayed staring at the dark exit for some time. He felt and heard Ellery shifting behind him, moving nervously from foot to foot. Her focus was on him, he understood; she was hardly "standing guard for him." Over him, more likely.

"Your friend Canthan believes he has figured out the riddle of the castle," the drow said. He turned to regard the woman, noting especially how her knuckles had whitened on the handle of her axe. "But he is wrong."

Ellery's face screwed up with confusion. "What has he said to you? How do you know this?"

"Because I know what he discerned from the book, as I have seen a tome similar to this one."

Ellery stared at him hard, her hand wringing over the handle, and she chewed her lips, clearly uneasy with it all.

"He told you to keep me here and kill me, not because he fears that I will prove an impediment to our escape or victory, but because Canthan fears that I will vie with him for the book and the secrets contained within. He is nothing if not opportunistic."

Ellery rocked back and seemed as if she would stumble to the floor at Jarlaxle's obviously on-the-mark observation. Jarlaxle wasn't fool enough to think he could talk the woman out of her planned course of action, though, so he was not caught off-guard when, just as he finished speaking, Ellery roared and came on.

A dagger appeared in the drow's hand, and with a snap of his wrist, it became a sword. He flipped it to his left just in time to parry Ellery's axe-swipe and he back-stepped just fast enough to avoid the collision from her shield rush. A second dagger spilled forth from his bracer, and he threw it at her, slowing her progress long enough for him to extract a third from his enchanted bracer and snap his wrist again. When the initial assault played out and the two faced each other on even footing, the drow was holding a pair of slender long swords.

Ellery launched a backhand slash and pressed forward as Jarlaxle rolled around the cut and thrust forth with his sword. Her shield took that one aside and a clever underhand reversal of her cutting axe deflected the thrust of the drow's second blade, coming in low, aimed for the woman's leading knee.

Ellery chopped down with her shield, spun a tight circuit behind it, and extended as she came around.

Jarlaxle threw back his hips then started in yet again behind the flashing axe. He stopped and flung himself out to the side as Ellery cut short her swing and came ahead in a rush, her powerful axe at the ready. She stayed right with him, step for step. An angled sword moved aside her powerful chop. Her shield tapped down on one sword, driving it low, came up to take the second high, then low again, then . . .

Jarlaxle was too quick with his second blade, feigning high once more but thrusting it down low instead.

But Ellery was quick as well, and the shield tapped down appropriately.

On came the woman with a growl, and Jarlaxle had to step back fast and spin out to the side. He brought both his swords in one desperate parry and accepted the shield bash against his arm, glad that the momentum of it allowed him to put some distance between himself and the surprisingly skilled woman.

"If I win again, will I find your bed?" he teased.

Ellery didn't crack a grin. "Those days are long past us."

"They don't have to be."

Ellery's response came in the form of another sudden charge and a flurry of blows that had Jarlaxle furiously defending and backing, stride after stride.

Entreri rushed out past Athrogate. "I have the point," he explained. "Follow with caution, but with speed."

He sprinted down the corridor, pushing through the door and into the room where Mariabronne lay still, his sword held in both hands over his chest, its blade running down below his waist.

Entreri shook his head and dismissed the tragic sight. He went across the room to the other door, did a cursory check for traps when he saw that it had not recently been opened, and pushed through to find another curving, descending tunnel.

He sprinted down and carefully set the first torches burning by tapping the pressure plate. Then he turned and rushed back to the door, scrambling up beside it to the top of the jamb. Using just that tiny lip and the ceiling above him, the assassin pressed himself into place.

A few moments later, Athrogate moved out under him, followed closely by Olgerkhan and Arrayan, with Canthan moving last. They passed without noticing the assassin, and before they had even disappeared around the tunnel bend, Entreri hooked his fingers on the lip of the door jamb and swung down, launching himself and landing lightly back in the room with Mariabronne. He hit the ground running and ran back up the corridor.

Her movements were very much in line with the fighting style and skill level she had shown to him in their sparring match those days before at the Vaasan Gate. Ellery was no novice to battle and had practiced extensively in single combat techniques. Her efforts tested Jarlaxle at every turn. He had beaten her then, however, and he knew he could beat her again.

She had to know that too, as Canthan, who had sent her, had to understand.

Unless . . .

They were the "Citadel of Assassins," after all.

Ellery continued the flow of the fight, working her axe with quick chops and cuts, generally playing out more and more to Jarlaxle's right. She followed almost every swing with a sudden popping thrust of her shield arm, leaving no openings for the drow's swords and also balancing herself and her turns to keep her feet properly aligned to propel her side-to-side or forward and back as required.

She was good but not good enough, and they both knew it.

It almost slipped past the observant drow that Ellery had crossed her feet, so smooth was the transition. Even noting that, Jarlaxle was taken aback at how efficiently and quickly the woman executed a sudden spin, so that as she came around, her axe chopping hard, she was aiming back at the drow's left.

And he couldn't stop it.

Jarlaxle's eyes widened and he even smiled at the "kill swing"—that one movement assassins often employed, that extra level of fighting beyond anything any opponent could reasonably expect to see. Jarlaxle had expected something of that nature, of course, but still, as he saw it unfolding before him, he feared, he *knew,* that he could not stop it.

Ellery roared and chopped hard at the drow's shoulder. Jarlaxle grimaced and threw his swords across in an effort to at least partially defeat the blow and threw himself aside in a desperate effort to get out of the way.

But Ellery's roar became a scream, and in mid-swing her axe wobbled, its angle pulling aside, her arm falling limp, as Charon's Claw slammed hard atop her shoulder. Her fine silvery breastplate rattled and loosened as the shoulder cord tore apart under the force of Entreri's blow.

She staggered and turned, trying to come around and get her shield up to fend off the assassin.

Entreri's other hand was under her shield, however, and his dagger easily found the seam in her breastplate and slid in between the woman's ribs into the left side of her chest.

Ellery froze, helpless and on the precipice of disaster.

Entreri didn't finish the movement but held her there, his dagger in place. Ellery glared at him and he called upon the life-drawing powers of the weapon for just an instant, letting her know the complete doom that awaited her.

She didn't persist. She was beaten and she showed it. Her

weapon arm hung limp and she didn't try to stop the axe as it slid from her grip and clanged against the floor.

"An interesting turn of events," Jarlaxle remarked, "that Canthan would move against us so quickly."

"And that a relative of the King of Damara would be an instrument for an assassin's guild," Entreri added.

"You know nothing," Ellery growled at him, or started to, for he gave the slightest of twists on his dagger and brought the woman up to her tip-toes. The commander sucked in her breath against the wave of pain.

"When I ask you to answer, you answer," Entreri instructed.

"I told you that Canthan was fooled," Jarlaxle said to her. "He believes that killing Arrayan will defeat the tower." He turned to Entreri. "She is the Herminicle of this castle, so Canthan believes, but I do not agree."

Entreri's eyes widened.

"This is beyond Arrayan," Jarlaxle explained. "Perhaps she began the process, but something greater than she has intervened."

"You know nothing," Ellery said through her gritted teeth.

"I know that you, the lawful representative of King Gareth in this quest, were about to kill me, though I have done nothing against the crown and risked everything for the realm's sake," Jarlaxle pointed out.

"So you say."

"And so you deny, without proof, because Canthan would be rid of Jarlaxle, would be rid of us," the drow added, "that he might claim whatever secrets and power Zhengyi has left in this place and in that book. You are a pawn, and a rather stupid one, Lady Ellery. You disappoint me."

"Then be done with me," she said.

Jarlaxle looked to Entreri and saw that his friend was hardly paying attention. He yanked free the knife and darted toward the tunnel exit and the four he realized he had foolishly left alone.

Her magical shield absorbed much of the blow, but still Canthan's lightning blast sent Arrayan flying back against the wall.

"It will hurt less if you drop your wards and accept the inevitability," the wizard remarked.

To the side, Olgerkhan once again tried to get at Canthan, and again Athrogate was there to block his way.

"She is the foundation of the castle," Canthan said to the large and furious half-orc. "When she falls, so falls this Zhengyian beast!"

Olgerkhan growled and charged—or tried to, but Athrogate kicked his ankles out from under him, sending him face-down to the floor.

"Ye let it be," the dwarf warned. "Ain't no choices here."

Olgerkhan sprang up and swung his club wildly at the dwarf.

"Well all right then," the dwarf said, easily ducking the lumbering blow. "Ye're making yer choices ye ain't got to make."

"Be done with the stubborn oaf," Canthan instructed, and he calmly launched a series of stinging glowing missiles Arrayan's way.

Again, the half-orc wizard had enacted enough wards to defeat the majority of the assault, but Canthan's continuing barrage had her backing away, helpless to counter.

For Olgerkhan, disaster was even quicker in coming. The half-orc was a fine and accomplished warrior by Palishchuk's standards, but against Athrogate, he was naught but a lumbering novice, and in his weakened state, not even a promising one. He swung again and was blocked, then he tried an awkward sidelong swipe.

Athrogate went below the swinging club, both his morning stars spinning. The dwarf's weapons came in hard, almost simultaneously, against the outsides of Olgerkhan's knees. Before the half-orc's legs could even buckle, Athrogate leaped forward and smashed his forehead into the half-orc's groin.

As Olgerkhan doubled over, Athrogate sent one morning star up so that the chain wrapped around the half-orc's neck, the heavy ball smacking him in the face. With a twist and a sudden and brutal jerk, one that snapped bone, Athrogate flipped Olgerkhan into a sideways somersault that left him groaning and helpless on the floor.

"Olgerkhan!" Arrayan cried, and she too staggered and went down to her knees.

Canthan watched it all with great amusement. "They are somehow bound," he mused aloud. "Physically, so. Perhaps the castle has a king as well as a queen."

"The human is coming," Athrogate called, looking past Canthan to the corridor.

Enough musing, the wizard realized, and he took the moment of Arrayan's weakness to fire off another spell, a magical, acid-filled dart. It punctured her defensive sphere and slammed into her stomach, sending her sitting back against the wall. She cried out from the pain and tried to clutch at the tiny projectile with trembling hands.

"Kill him when he enters," Canthan instructed the dwarf.

The wizard ran out of the room along one of the side corridors just as Entreri burst in.

Entreri looked at Athrogate, at Olgerkhan, and at Arrayan, then back at the dwarf, who approached steadily, morning stars swinging easily. Athrogate offered a shrug.

"Guess it's the way it's got to be," the dwarf said, almost apologetically.

Ellery held her hands out to her sides, not knowing what she was supposed to do.

"Well, gather up your weapon and let us be off," Jarlaxle said to her.

She stared at him for a few moments then bent to retrieve the axe, eyeing Jarlaxle all the while as if she expected him to attack.

"Oh, pick it up," the drow said.

Still Ellery paused.

"We've no time for this," said Jarlaxle. "I'll call our little battle here a misunderstanding, as I'm confident that you see it the same way now. Besides, I know your trick now—and a fine move it is!—and will kill you if you come against me again." He paused and gave her a lewd look. "Perhaps I will extract a little payment from you later on, but for now, let us just be done with this castle and the infernal Zhengyi."

Ellery picked up the axe. Jarlaxle turned and started away after Entreri.

The woman had no idea what to do or what to believe. Her emotions swirled as her thoughts swirled, and she felt very strange.

She took a step toward Jarlaxle, just wanting to be done with it all and get back to Damara.

The floor leaped up and swallowed her.

Jarlaxle turned sharply, swords at the ready, when he heard the thump behind him. He saw at once that those weapons wouldn't be needed. He moved quickly to Ellery and tried to stir her. He put his face close to her mouth to try to detect her breath, and he inspected the small wound Entreri had inflicted.

"So the dagger got to your heart after all," Jarlaxle said with a great sigh.

Entreri wasn't certain if Athrogate was incredibly good or if it was just that the dwarf's unorthodox style and weaponry—he had never even heard of someone wielding two morning stars simultaneously—had him moving in ways awkward and uncomfortable.

Whatever the reason, Entreri understood that he was in trouble. Glancing at Arrayan, he realized that her situation was even more desperate. Somehow, that bothered him as much, if not more.

He growled past the unnerving thought and created a series of ash walls to try to deter the stubborn and ferocious dwarf. Of course, Athrogate just plowed through each ash wall successively, roaring and swinging so forcefully that Entreri dared not get too close.

He tried to take the dwarf's measure. He tried to find a hole in the little beast's defenses. But Athrogate was too compact, his weapon movements too coordinated. Given the dwarf's strength and the strange enchantments of his morning stars, Entreri simply couldn't risk trading a blow for a blow, even with his own mighty weapons.

Nor could he block, for he rightly feared that Athrogate might tangle one of his weapons in the morning star chain and tear it free of his grasp. Or even worse, might that rusting sludge that coated the dwarf's left-hand weapon ruin Charon's Claw's fine blade?

Entreri used his speed, darting this way and that, feigning a strike and backing away almost immediately. He was not trying to score a hit at that point, though he would have made a stab if an opening presented itself. Instead, Entreri moved to put the dwarf into a different rhythm. He kept Athrogate's feet moving sidelong or had him turning quickly—both movements that the straightforward fighter found more atypical.

But that would take a long, long time, Entreri knew, and with another glance at Arrayan, he understood that it was time she didn't have to spare.

With that uncomfortable thought in mind, he went in suddenly, reversing his dodging momentum in an attempt to score a quick kill.

But a sweeping morning star turned Charon's Claw harmlessly aside, and the second sent Entreri diving desperately into a sidelong roll. Athrogate pursued, weapons spinning, and Entreri barely got ahead of him and avoided a skull-crushing encounter.

"Patience . . . patience," the dwarf teased.

Entreri realized that Athrogate knew exactly his strategy, had probably seen the same technique used by every skilled opponent he'd ever faced. The assassin had to rethink. He needed some space and time. He came forward in a sudden burst again, but even as Athrogate howled with excitement, Entreri was gone, sprinting out across the room.

Athrogate paused and looked at him with open curiosity. "Ye running or thinking to hit me from afar?" he asked. "If ye're running, ye dolt, then be gone like a colt. But be knowing in yer mind that I'm not far behind! *Bwahaha!*"

"While I find your ugliness repellant, dwarf, do not ever think I would flee from the likes of you."

Athrogate howled with laughter again, and he charged—or he started to, for as he began to close the ground between himself and Entreri, an elongated disk floated in from the side, stretching and widening, and settled on the floor between them. Athrogate, unable to stop his momentum, tumbled headlong into the extra-dimensional hole.

He howled. He cursed. He landed hard, ten feet down.

Then he cursed some more, and in rhymes.

Entreri glanced at the tunnel entrance, where Jarlaxle stood, leaning.

The drow offered a shrug and remarked, "Bear trap?"

Entreri didn't respond. He leaped across the room to Arrayan and quickly tore the magical dart from her stomach. He stared at the vicious missile, watching with mounting anger as its tip continued to pump forth acid. A glance back at Arrayan told him that he had arrived in time, that the wound wasn't mortal, but he could not deny the truth of it when he looked into Arrayan's fair face. She was dying, with literally one foot in the nether realm.

Desperation tugged at Entreri. He saw not Arrayan but Dwahvel lying before him. He shook the woman and yelled for her to come back. Hardly thinking of the movement, he found himself hugging her, then he pulled her back to arms' length and called to her over and over again.

Lying on the floor to the side, the dying Olgerkhan saw the fleeting health of Arrayan and understood clearly that much of his dear companion's current grief was being caused by her magical binding with him. As the rings had forced Olgerkhan to share Arrayan's burden, so they had begun to work the other way. Olgerkhan knew his wounds to be mortal, knew that he was on the very edge of death.

And he was taking Arrayan with him.

With all the strength he could muster, the half-orc pulled the ring from his finger and flicked it far to the side.

His world went black at the same time Arrayan opened her eyes.

Entreri fell back from her in surprise. She still looked terrible, weaker than anyone he had ever seen before, more—he could only describe it as thin and drained of her life energy—frail than any human being could be, much more so than she had been before the fight.

But she still had life, and consciousness, and so the assassin learned, rage.

"No!" the woman cried. "Olgerkhan, *no!*"

The tone of her voice showed that she was scolding the half-orc, not denying his wound. That, combined with her sudden return from the grave, had the assassin scratching his head. Entreri looked again to Jarlaxle, who studied the pair intently but seemingly with just as much curiosity.

Arrayan, so weak and drained and sorely wounded, dragged herself past Entreri to her half-orc companion

"You took off the ring," she said, cradling his face in her hands. "Put it back! Olgerkhan, put it back!"

He didn't, couldn't answer.

"You think to save me," Arrayan wailed, "but don't you know? I cannot be saved to watch you die. Olgerkhan, come back to me.

You must! You are all I love, all that I have ever loved. It's you, Olgerkhan. It was always you. Please come back to me!"

Her voice grew weaker, her shoulders quivered with sobs, and she held on dearly to her friend.

"The ring?" Jarlaxle asked.

Arrayan didn't answer, but the drow was figuring it out anyway. He thought of all the times the two had seemed to share their pain and their weariness.

"So the castle does have a king," Jarlaxle remarked to Entreri, but the assassin was hardly listening.

He stood staring at the couple, chuckling at himself and all of his foolish fantasies about his future beside Arrayan.

Without a word of explanation, Artemis Entreri ran out of the room.

CHAPTER 20
JUST BECAUSE

Though he was confident that his job was done regarding Arrayan and Olgerkhan and that Athrogate would dispatch the assassin, Canthan glanced back many times as he ran down the descending corridor. Though his gaze turned to what lay behind him, his thoughts were on the future, for he knew that there was a great prize to be found in the pages of the Witch-King's book. His perusal of the tome had shown him possibilities beyond his imagination. Somehow within that book loomed the secret that would grant him ownership of the castle, without it taking his life-force as it had Arrayan's. He was certain of that. Zhengyi had designed it so. The book would trap the unwitting and use that soul to build the castle.

But that was only half the enchantment. Once constructed, the fortress was there for the taking—for one wise enough and strong enough to seize it.

Canthan could do that, and certainly Knellict, among the greatest of wizards in the Bloodstone Lands, could too. Had the Citadel of Assassins just found a new home, one from which they might openly challenge King Gareth's claim of dominion?

"Ah, the possibilities," Canthan muttered as he approached the next door.

The castle was either dormant or soon to be, he believed, or at least it was beyond regeneration given the fall of its life sources. Still the wizard remained at the ready.

He threw a spell of opening that swung the door in long before he physically entered the room. In the large chamber beyond, he saw movement, and he didn't even wait to discern the type of creature before he began his spellcasting.

A gnoll mummy came to the threshold. It served as the first target, the initial strike point.

A bolt of lightning arced onto its head then shot away to the next target, and on again. It diminished with each successive strike but jumped about several times. That first mummy smoked and unwrapped into a pile of smoldering rags, and Canthan was fast to the point, next spell ready. A quick survey of the large room showed him the course of his first strike, the chain bouncing across five targets, mummies all. The healthiest remaining creature had been the last hit, so Canthan reversed his line and made that one the first.

In the instant it took the second lightning chain to leap across the remaining mummies, all four went down, reduced to smoking husks.

Canthan rushed in and braziers flared to life. The wizard looked upward at the ceiling ten feet above and saw the tell-tale egg shapes of the guardian daemons nestled above each of the four braziers in the room.

Grinning, Canthan filled the upper two feet of the room, wall-to-wall, with strands of sticky webbing. It was a precaution only, he believed, for the castle had to be dead. The already animated monsters, like the mummies, might remain, so he thought, but with Arrayan gone, no others should animate.

The wizard paused to catch his breath and consider the situation. He hoped Ellery was done with the troublesome drow and Athrogate with the equally troublesome assassin. Mariabronne's death was good fortune for the Citadel. The troublesome but loyal ranger would have most assuredly handed Zhengyi's great gift over to King Gareth and the other fools who ruled Damara.

Canthan knew he still had to approach things with great care, though. He hoped his guess about the qualities of the castle was correct, for his task of truly deciphering the secrets of the book would be much more difficult if he had to spend half his time destroying monsters.

The wizard had to quickly gather Athrogate and Ellery back to his side and take some rest. He had nearly exhausted his magical spells for the day, and even though he believed the battle to be won, Canthan didn't like feeling vulnerable. His wizardry was his armor and his sword. Without his spells, he was just a clever but rather feeble man.

He didn't appreciate the view, then, when a solitary man stalked with great determination into the chamber.

Far from being dead, as Canthan had presumed, the outer walls of the great structure teemed with life. Gargoyles, regenerated from their previous night's battle on the hill, flew off with the sunset, speeding across the few miles to the walls of Palishchuk.

There the defenses had been set, and there the desperate battle began. But walls proved little impediment to the winged creatures, and they swarmed the city in search of easy targets.

In her room, Calihye heard the commotion beginning on the streets, the cries of alarm and the sounds of battle joined. She looked over at Davis Eng, his eyes wide, his breathing heavy with anticipation and stark fear. A twinge of sympathy went through her, for she could only imagine his terror at being so completely helpless.

"What is it?" he managed to whisper.

Calihye had no answer. She moved to the room's one window and pulled aside the drape. Out on the street below her, she saw the fighting, where a trio of half-orc guards slashed and rushed wildly after the short hops and flights of a single gargoyle. Calihye watched for a while, mesmerized by the strange sequence and dance.

Then she gave a shout and fell back as a gargoyle crashed through the window, scattering shards of glass, its clawed hands reaching for her throat.

The woman let herself fall over in a backward roll, and she came up lightly to her feet, reversing her momentum and leaping forward as the foolish gargoyle charged ahead, impaling itself on her blade.

But another was at the window, ready to take its place.

"Help me," Davis Eng cried out.

Calihye ignored him, except to think that if the situation got too desperate she might be able to use the man as an offering to the beasts while she made her escape out the door.

She was a long way from that unpleasant possibility, however, and she went forward to meet the newest invader, working her sword with the skill of a seasoned veteran.

"Be reasonable, my friend," Canthan said as he backed away.

Artemis Entreri, his face perfectly expressionless, walked toward him.

"The girl is dead?"

No answer.

"Be reasonable, man," Canthan reiterated. "She was the source of power for this place—her life-force was feeding it."

No answer. Soon Canthan had a wall to his back, and Entreri was still coming on, sword and dagger in hand.

"Ah, but you fancied her, did you not?" Canthan asked.

He laughed—a sound he had to admit to himself was for no better reason than to cover his sincere discomfort. For Canthan didn't have many spells left to cast, and if Entreri had found a way to defeat Athrogate, he was a formidable foe indeed.

Still no answer, and Canthan cast a quick spell that sent him in an extra-dimensional "blink" to the other side of the room.

Entreri did nothing but turn and continue his determined approach.

"By the gods, don't tell me that you slew Athrogate?" Canthan said to him. "Why, he was worth quite a bit to the Citadel—a favor

I do for you in killing you now. However we might talk, I cannot forgive that, I fear, nor will Knellict!" He finished with a flourish of his arms, and launched a lightning bolt Entreri's way.

But it wasn't that easy. Entreri moved before the blast ensued, a sudden and efficient dive and roll out to the side.

Canthan was already casting a second time, sending a series of magical missiles that no man, not even Artemis Entreri, could avoid. But the assassin growled through their stinging bites and came on.

Laughing, Canthan readied another blast of lightning, but a dagger flashed through the air, striking him in the chest and interrupting his casting. The wizard was of course well warded from such mundane attacks, and even the jeweled dagger bounced away. He quickly refocused and let fly his blast at the man—or at what he thought was the man, he realized too late, for it was naught but a wall of ash.

Growing increasingly fearful, Canthan spun around to survey the room.

No Entreri.

He spun again, then stopped and muttered, "Oh, clever."

He didn't even have to look to understand the assassin's ruse and movement.

For in that moment of distraction from the dagger, in that reflexive blink of the wizard's eye, Entreri had not only swiped the sword and put forth the ash wall, but he had leaped up, catching himself on Canthan's webbing.

The wizard glanced up at him. The assassin was in a curl, legs tucked up tight against his chest, his hands plunged into the secure webbing. He uncoiled and swayed back, then toward Canthan. As he came forward, he flicked something he held in one hand—a simple flint and steel contraption. The resulting spark ignited the web and burned the entire section away in an instant, just as Entreri came to the height of his swing.

He flew forward, falling over into a backward somersault as he went, extending his legs and arms to control the fall. He landed lightly and in perfect balance right in front of the wizard, and out came his sword.

The skilled wizard struck first, a blast of stunning lightning that crackled all over Entreri's body, sparks flying from his sword. His jaw snapped uncontrollably, his muscles tensing and clenching, the fingers of one hand curling into a tight ball, the knuckles of the other whitening on the hilt of Charon's Claw.

But Entreri didn't fly back and he didn't fall away. He growled and held his ground. He took the hit and with incredible determination and simple toughness, he fought through it.

When the lightning ended, Entreri came out of it in a sudden spin, Charon's Claw flying wide. Given the sheer power of that blade, beyond the defenses of any wards and guards, Entreri could have quite easily killed the horrified wizard, could have taken the man's head from his shoulders. But Charon's Claw came in short in a diagonal stroke, cutting the wizard from shoulder to opposite hip.

Stunned and falling back, Canthan could not get far enough away as Entreri, his face still so cold and expressionless that Canthan wondered briefly if he was nothing more than an animated corpse, leaped high in a spin and came around with a circle kick that snapped Canthan's head back viciously.

Entreri retrieved his prized dagger and wiped the blood from his nose and mouth as he again stalked over to the prone Canthan. Face down, the man squirmed then stubbornly pulled himself up to his elbows.

Entreri kicked him in the head and kicked him again before Canthan settled back down to the floor. The assassin put his sword away but held the dagger as he grabbed the semi-conscious wizard by the scruff of his neck and dragged him back to the corridor.

"Surely you'll be reasonable in this regard," Jarlaxle, on his hands and knees and peering over the edge of the hole, said to

Athrogate. "You cannot get out without my help."

Athrogate, hands on hips, just stared up at him.

"I had to do something," Jarlaxle said. "Was I to allow you to kill my friend?"

"Bah! Well I wouldn't've fought him if he hadn't've fought meself."

"True enough, but consider Olgerkhan."

"I did, and I killed him."

"Sometimes acts like that upset people."

"He shouldn't've got in me friend's way."

"So your friend could kill the girl?"

Athrogate shrugged as if it did not matter. "He had a reason."

"An errant reason."

"What's done is done. Ye wanting an apology?"

"I don't know that I want anything," Jarlaxle replied. "You seem to be the one in need, not I."

"Bah!"

"You cannot get out. Starvation is a lousy way for a warrior to die."

Athrogate just shrugged, moved to the side of the hole, studied the sheer wall for a moment, and sat down.

Jarlaxle sighed and turned away to consider Arrayan. She was still cradling Olgerkhan's head, whispering to him.

"Don't you dare leave me," she pleaded.

"And only now you realize your love for him?" Jarlaxle asked.

Arrayan shot him a hateful look that told him his guess was on the mark.

Noise from the corridor turned Jarlaxle's head, but not the woman's. In came Entreri, muttering under his breath and dragging Canthan at the end of one arm. He moved around the hole to Arrayan and Olgerkhan.

The woman looked at him with a mixture of surprise, curiosity, and horror.

Entreri had no time for it. He grabbed her by the shoulder and shoved her aside, then dropped Canthan before Olgerkhan.

Arrayan came back at him, but he stopped her with the coldest and most frightening look the woman had ever seen.

With her out of the way, Entreri turned his attention to Olgerkhan. He grabbed the large half-orc's hand and pulled it out over the groaning Canthan. He put his dagger into Olgerkhan's palm and forced the half-orc's fingers over it. He glanced at Arrayan then at Jarlaxle, and he drove the dagger down into Canthan's back.

He slipped his thumb free, placed it on the bottom of the dagger's jeweled hilt, and willed the blade to feed. The vampiric weapon went to its task with relish, stealing the very soul of Canthan and feeding it back to its wielder.

Olgerkhan's chest lifted and his eyes opened as he coughed forth his first breath in many seconds. He continued to gasp for a moment. His eyes widened in horror as he came to understand the source of his healing. He tried to pull his hand away.

But Entreri held him firmly in place, forcing him to feed until Canthan's life-force was simply no more.

"What did you do?" Arrayan cried, her voice caught between horror and joy. She came forward and Entreri did not try to stop her. He extracted his dagger from Olgerkhan's grasp and moved aside.

Arrayan fell over her half-orc friend, sobbing with joy and saying, "It was always you," over and over again.

Olgerkhan just shook his head, staring blankly at Entreri for a moment. He sat up, his strength and health renewed. Then he focused on Arrayan, upon her words, and he buried his face in her hair.

"Ah, the kindness of your heart," Jarlaxle remarked to the assassin. "How unselfish of you, since the contender for your prize was about to be no more."

"Maybe I just wanted Canthan dead."

"Then maybe you should have killed him in the other room."

"Shut up."

Jarlaxle laughed and sighed all at once.

"Where is Ellery?" Entreri asked.

"I believe that you nicked her heart."

Entreri shook his head at the insanity of it all.

"She was unreliable, in any case," Jarlaxle said. "Obviously so. I do take offense when women I have bedded turn on me with such fury."

"If it happens often, then perhaps you should work on your technique."

That had Jarlaxle laughing, but just for a moment. "So we are five," he said. "Or perhaps four," he added, glancing at the hole.

"Stubborn dwarf?" asked the assassin.

"Is there any other kind?"

Entreri moved to the edge of the hole. "Ugly one," he called down. "Your wizard friend is dead."

"Bah!" Athrogate snorted.

Entreri glanced back at Jarlaxle then moved over, grabbed Canthan's corpse, and hauled him over the edge of the hole, dropping him with a splat beside the surprised dwarf.

"Your friend is dead," Entreri said again, and the dwarf didn't bother to argue the point. "And so now you've a choice."

"Eat him or starve?" Athrogate asked.

"Eat him and eventually starve anyway," Jarlaxle corrected, coming up beside Entreri to peer in at the dwarf. "Or you could come out of the hole and help us."

"Help ye what?"

"Win," said the drow.

"Didn't ye just stop that possibility when Canthan put it forth?"

"No," Jarlaxle said with certainty. "Canthan was wrong. He believed that Arrayan was the continuing source of power for the castle, but that is not so. She was the beginning of the enchantment, 'tis true, but this place is far beyond her."

The drow had all of the others listening by then, with Olgerkhan, the color returned to his face, standing solidly once more.

"If I believed otherwise, then I would have killed Arrayan

myself," Jarlaxle went on. "But no. This castle has a king, a great and powerful one."

"How do you know this?" Entreri asked, and he seemed as doubtful and confused at the others, even Athrogate.

"I saw enough of the book to recognize that it has a different design than the one Herminicle used outside of Heliogabalus," the drow explained. "And there is something else." He put a hand over the extra-dimensional pocket button he wore, where he kept the skull-shaped gem he had taken from Herminicle's book. "I sense a strength here, a mighty power. It is clear to me, and given all that I know of Zhengyi and all that the dragon sisters told me, with their words and with the fear that was so evident in their eyes, it is not hard for me to see the logic of it all."

"What are you talking about?" asked Entreri.

"Dragon sisters?" Athrogate added, but no one paid him any heed.

"The king," said Jarlaxle. "I know he exists and I know where he is."

"And you know how to kill him?" Entreri asked. It was a hopeful question, but one that was not answered with a hopeful response.

The assassin let it go at that, surely realizing he'd never get a straight answer from Jarlaxle. He looked back down at Athrogate, who was standing then, looking up intently.

"Are you with us? Or should we leave you to eat your friend and starve?" Entreri asked.

Athrogate looked down at Canthan then back up at Entreri. "Don't look like he'd taste too good, and one thing I'm always wantin' is food." He pronounced "good" and "food" a bit off on both, so that they seemed closer to rhyming, and that brought a scowl to Entreri's face.

"He starts that again and he's staying in the hole," he remarked to Jarlaxle, and the drow, who was already taking off his belt that he might command it to elongate and extract the dwarf, laughed again.

"We'll have your word that you'll make no moves against any of us," Entreri said.

"Ye're to be takin' me word?"

"No, but then I can kill you with a clearer conscious."

"Bwahaha!"

"I do so hate him," Entreri muttered to Jarlaxle, and he moved away.

Jarlaxle considered that with a wry grin, thinking that perhaps it was yet another reason for him to get Athrogate out and by their side. The dwarf's lack of concern for Canthan was genuine, Jarlaxle knew, and Athrogate would not go against them unless he found it to be in his best interests.

Which, of course, was the way with all of Jarlaxle's friends.

CHAPTER 21
AN AUDIENCE WITH THE KING

Athrogate and Entreri eyed each other for a long, long while after the dwarf came out of the hole.

"Could've ruined yer weapon, ye know," Athrogate remarked, holding up the morning star that coated itself with the rust-inducing liquid.

"Could've eaten yer soul, ye know," the assassin countered, mimicking the dwarf's tone and dialect.

"With both yer weapons turned to dust? Got the juice of a rust monster in it," he said, jostling the morning star so that the head bounced a bit at the end of its chain.

"It may be that you overestimate your weapons or underestimate mine. In either case, you would not have enjoyed learning the truth."

Athrogate cracked a smile. "Some day we'll find out that truth."

"Be careful what you wish for."

"Bwahaha!"

Entreri wanted nothing more than to drive his dagger into the annoying dwarf's throat at that moment. But it wasn't the time. They remained surrounded by enemies in a castle very much alive and hostile. They needed the powerful dwarf fighting beside them.

"I remain convinced that Canthan was wrong," Jarlaxle said, moving between the two.

He glanced back at the two half-orcs, leading the gaze of the dwarf and the assassin. Arrayan sat against the wall across the way, while her companion scrambled about on all fours, apparently searching for something. Olgerkhan looked much healthier, obviously so. The dagger had fed Canthan's life energy to him and had healed much of the damage of Athrogate's fierce attacks. Beyond that, the great weariness that had been dragging on Olgerkhan seemed lifted; his eyes were bright and alert, his movements crisp.

But as much better as he looked, Arrayan appeared that much worse. The woman's eyes drooped and her head swayed as if her neck had not the strength to hold it upright. Something about the last battles had taken much from her, it seemed, and the castle was taking the rest.

"The castle has a king," Jarlaxle said.

"Bah, Canthan got it right, and ye killed him to death for it," said Athrogate. "It's the girl, don't ye see? She's wilting away right afore yer eyes."

"No doubt she is part of it," the drow replied. "But only a small part. The real source of the castle's life lies below us."

"And how might ye be knowin' that?" asked the dwarf. "And what's he looking for, anyway?"

"I know because I can feel the castle's king as acutely as I can feel my own skin. And I know not what Olgerkhan is seeking, nor do I much care. Our destiny lies below and quickly if we hope to save Arrayan."

"What makes ye think I'm giving an orc's snot rag for that one?"

Entreri shot the dwarf a hateful look.

"What?" Athrogate asked with mock innocence. "She ain't no friend o' me own, and she's just a half-orc. Half too many, by me own counting."

"Then disregard her," Jarlaxle intervened. "Think of yourself, and rightly so. I tell you that if we defeat the king of this castle, the castle will fight us no more, whatever Arrayan's fate. I also tell you that we should do all that we can to save her, to keep her alive now, for if she is taken by the castle it will benefit the construct and hurt us. Trust me on this and follow my advice. If I am wrong, and the castle continues to feed from her, and in doing so it continues to attack us, then I will kill her myself."

The dwarf nodded. "Fair enough."

"But I only say that because I am certain it will not come to that," Jarlaxle quickly added for the sake of Olgerkhan, who glared at him. "Now let us tend our wounds and prepare our weapons, for we have a king to kill."

Athrogate pulled a waterskin off and moved toward the two half-orcs. "Here," he offered. "Got a bit o' the healing potions to get yer strength back," he said to Arrayan. "And as for yerself, sorry I breaked yer neck."

Olgerkhan offered nothing in reply. He hesitated for a moment by Arrayan's side, but then moved back toward the side passage and began crawling around on all fours once more, searching.

Entreri pulled Jarlaxle to the far side of the room and asked, "What are you talking about? How do you know what you pretend to know, or is it all but a ruse?"

"Not a ruse," Jarlaxle assured him. "I feel it and have since we entered this place. Logic tells me that Arrayan could not have constructed anything of this magnificence, and everything I have seen and felt since only confirms that logic."

"You have told me that all before," the assassin replied. "Could you offer something more?"

Jarlaxle patted his button pocket, wherein he had stored the skull. "The skull gem we took from the other tower has sensitized me to certain things. I feel the king below us. His is a life-force quite mighty."

"And we are to kill him?"

"Of course."

"On your *feeling?*"

"And following the clues. Do you remember Herminicle's book?"

Entreri thought on that for a moment then nodded.

"Do you remember the designs etched upon its leathery cover, and in the margins on the page?"

Again the assassin paused, and shook his head.

"Skulls," Jarlaxle explained. "Human skulls."

"And?"

"Did you notice the designs on the book up the ramp, the source of this castle?"

Entreri stared hard at his friend. He had not actually looked at the book that closely, but he was beginning to catch on. Given his experiences with Jarlaxle, where every road seemed to lead, his answer was as much statement as question: "Dragons?"

"Exactly," the drow confirmed, pleased that Entreri resisted the urge to punch him in the face. "I understand the fearful expressions of our sister employers. They knew that the Witch-King could pervert dragonkind as he perverted humankind, even from beyond the grave. They feared the apparent opening of Zhengyi's lost library, as evidenced by Herminicle's tower. They feared that such a book as the one that constructed this castle might be uncovered."

"You doubt that Arrayan started this process?"

"Not at all, as I explained. The book used her to send out its call, I believe. And that call was answered."

"By a dragon?"

"More likely an undead dragon."

"Wonderful."

Jarlaxle shrugged against his companion's disgusted stare. "It is our way. An adventurous road!"

"It is a fatal disease."

Again the drow shrugged, and a wide grin spread across his face.

They continued on their way down the side passage Canthan had taken to the room where Entreri had defeated the battle mage.

The magical webbing Canthan had created to prevent the daemon eggs from falling remained in place, except for the small area Entreri had burned away in his fight with the mage. Still, the five went through the room quickly, not wanting an encounter with those powerful adversaries. They all believed that the "king," as Jarlaxle had aptly named it, awaited them, and they needed no more wounds and no more weariness. The order of the day at that time was avoiding battles, and so with that in mind, Entreri took up the point position.

They made good progress for a short while along the twisting, winding corridor. No traps presented themselves, only the pressure bars that kept lighting the wall torches, and no monsters rose before them.

Around one particularly sharp bend, though, they found Entreri waiting for them, his expression concerned.

"A room with a dozen coffins like those of the gnoll mummies," he explained, "only even more decorated."

"A dozen o' the raggy ones?" Athrogate replied. "Ha! Six slaps each!" he said and sent his morning stars into alternating swings.

The dwarf's cavalier attitude did little to lift the mood of the others, however.

"There is another exit from the room, or is this the end of our path?" Jarlaxle asked.

"Straight across," said Entreri. "A door."

Jarlaxle instructed them to wait then slowly moved ahead. He found the room around the next bend, a wide, circular chamber lined, as Entreri had said, with a dozen sarcophagi. The drow took out the skull gem and allowed it to guide his sensibilities. He felt the energy within each of the coffins, vengeful and focused, hating death and envying life.

The drow fell deeper into the skull gem, testing its strength. The gem was attuned to humans, not the dog-faced humanoids wrapped in rags within the coffins. But they were not too far removed, and when he opened his eyes again, Jarlaxle drew forth a slender wand from its holster inside his cloak and aimed it across the room at the door. He paused a moment to consider the richly decorated portal, for even in the low light of the torches burning in the wall sconces behind him, he could see the general make-up of its design: a bas relief of a great battle, with scores of warriors swarming a rearing dragon.

The drow found the design quite revealing. "It was made of memories," he whispered, and he looked all around, for he was talking about more than that door; he was talking about the whole of the place.

The castle was a living entity, created of magic and memories. Its energy brought forth the gargoyles and the doors, the stone walls and tunnels complete with the clever designs of the wall torches and the traps. Its energy recreated its former occupiers, the gnoll soldiers Zhengyi had used as staff, only trapped in undeath and far more powerful than they had been in life.

And its energy had unwittingly tapped into the other memories of the place, animating in lesser form the many bodies that had been buried on that spot. Jarlaxle suspected then that those undead skeletons that had arisen against them in the courtyard were not of Zhengyi's design but were an inadvertent side effect of the magical release.

He smiled at that thought and looked ahead at the design on the door. It was no haphazard artist's interpretation. The scene was indeed a memory, a recording of something that had truly occurred.

The drow had hoped that the suspicions festering within him since crawling through the portcullis would prove accurate, and there was his confirmation and his hope.

He pointed his wand at the door and uttered a command word.

Several locks clicked and a latch popped. With a rush of air the door swung open. Beyond it, the corridor continued into darkness.

"Remain in a tight group and be quick through the room," Jarlaxle instructed the others when he returned to them a moment later. "The door is open—make sure it remains so as we pass. Come now, and be quick."

He glanced at the half-orcs, Olgerkhan all but carrying Arrayan, who seemed as if she couldn't even keep her head from swaying. Jarlaxle motioned for Athrogate to help them, and though he gave a disgusted sigh, the dwarf complied.

"Are you coming?" the drow asked Entreri as the others started away.

The assassin held up his hand, looked back the way they had come, and said, "We're being followed."

"Press ahead," Jarlaxle instructed. "Our road is ahead of us, not behind."

Entreri turned on him. "You know something."

"You hope I do," Jarlaxle replied, and he started after the trio. He paused a few steps down and glanced back at his friend and grinned sheepishly. "As do I."

Entreri's expression showed that the humor was not appreciated.

"We cannot go out, unless we are willing to let the castle win," Jarlaxle reminded him after they had taken a few steps. "And in that victory, the construct will claim Arrayan. Is that acceptable to you?"

"Am I following you?" Entreri remarked.

They passed through the chamber quickly and no sarcophagi opened and no eggs fell, releasing daemons to rise against them. Through the other door, they found a long descending staircase and down they went into the darkness.

Entreri took the lead again, inspecting every step and every handhold as the light diminished around them. Near to the bottom, he was relieved to see another of the pressure plates, and torches soon flared to life on the opposite walls at the sides of the bottom step.

The light flickered and cast long, uneven shadows across stone that was no longer worked and fitted. It seemed as if they had come to the end of the construct, to a natural winding tunnel, boring down ever deeper before them.

Entreri went ahead a short distance, the others moving close behind. He turned and went back past them to the last two torches. He inspected them carefully, expecting a trap or ten, and indeed on the left-hand one, he removed several barbed pins, all wet with some sort of poison. Then he carefully extracted the torches and carried them back to the others. He handed one to Olgerkhan and had thought to give the other to Arrayan. One look at the woman dissuaded him from that course, however, for she didn't seem to have the strength to hold it, and indeed, had it not been for Olgerkhan's supporting arm, she would not have been standing. He offered the torch to Athrogate instead.

"I got dwarf eyes, ye dolt," Athrogate growled at him. "I ain't needing no firelight. This tunnel's bathed in sunlight next to where me kin've dug."

"Jarlaxle needs both of his hands and Arrayan is too weak," Entreri said to him, thrusting the torch back his way. "I prefer to lead in the darkness."

"Bah, but ye're just making me a target," the dwarf growled back, but he took the torch.

"Another benefit," Entreri said, turning away and moving out in front.

The corridor continued to bend to the left, even more sharply, giving the assassin the feeling that they were in the same general area from which they'd started, only far below. The caverns were all of natural stone, with no more torches and no pressure plates or other traps that the assassin could locate. There were intersections, however, and always sharp turns back the other way as the other winding tunnels joined into this one, becoming one great spiraling corridor. With each joining, the passage widened and heightened, so that it seemed almost as if they were walking down a long sloping cavern instead of a corridor.

Trying to minimize the feeling of vulnerability, Entreri kept them near to the inner bending wall as he edged ahead, sword in one hand, dagger in the other. Their progress was steady for some time, and they put many hundreds of feet between themselves and the staircase. But then Olgerkhan's cry froze the assassin in mid-stride.

"It's taking her!" the half-orc wailed.

Entreri spun and ran back past the turning Athrogate. He shoved by Jarlaxle, needing to get to Arrayan. By the time he spotted her, she was down on the ground, Olgerkhan kneeling over her and whispering to her.

Entreri slid down beside her opposite the large half-orc. He started to call out to her but cut himself short when he realized that he was calling the name of a halfling friend he had left far back in the distant southern city of Calimport. Surprised and unnerved, the assassin looked from Arrayan to Jarlaxle, his expression demanding answers.

Jarlaxle wasn't looking back at him, though. The drow stood facing Arrayan with his eyes closed and his hand over the center of his waistcoat. He was whispering something that Entreri could not make out, and in looking from him back to the fallen woman, Entreri understood that the drow was trying to somehow intervene. Entreri thought of the skull gem and guessed that Jarlaxle was somehow using it to disrupt the castle's possession of the woman.

A moment later, Arrayan opened her eyes. She seemed more embarrassed than hurt, and she accepted Olgerkhan and Entreri's help in getting back to her feet.

"We are running out of time," Jarlaxle stated—the obvious for the others, but his tone explaining clearly to Entreri that he could not long delay the inevitable life-stealing process. "Quickly, then," the drow added, and Entreri gave a nod to Arrayan then left her with Olgerkhan and sprinted back to the front of the line.

He had to hope that there would be no more traps, for he did not slow every few feet to inspect the ground ahead.

The corridor continued to bend and spiral but began to narrow again, soon becoming a mere dozen feet across and with a jagged ceiling often so low that Olgerkhan had to crouch.

Entreri felt the hairs on the back of his neck tingling. Something was ahead, he sensed, whether from some smell or perhaps a sound barely audible. He motioned for the dwarf behind him to halt, then crept ahead on all fours and peered around a sharper bend.

The corridor continued for another dozen feet, then the stone floor fell away as it opened into a great chamber. He remembered Jarlaxle's words about the "king" of the castle, and he had to take a deep, steadying breath before going forward.

He crept ahead, belly-crawling as he exited the corridor into a vast cavern, on a ledge high up from the uneven floor. To his right, the ledge continued for just a short distance, but to his left, it continued on, sloping down toward the unseen cavern floor. It was not pitch black in there, as some strange glowing lichen scattered about the floor and walls bathed the stone as if in starlight.

Entreri crawled to the edge and peered over, and he knew they were doomed.

Far below him, perhaps fifty feet, loomed the king of the castle: a great dragon. But not a living dragon of leathery skin and thick scales but one made mostly of bones, with only patches of skin hanging between its wings and in patches across its back and head. The gigantic dragon carcass, mostly skeleton, crouched on the floor with its bony wings tucked in tight atop its back. If Entreri had any doubts that the creature was "alive," they were quickly dispelled when, with a rattle of bones, the great wings unfolded.

Swords, armor, and whitened bones littered the chamber all around the undead beast, and it took Entreri a few moments to sort out that that had been the spot of a desperate battle, that those weapons and bones belonged to warriors—likely of King Gareth's army, he realized when he gave it some thought—who had done battle with the wyrm in the time of Zhengyi.

Entreri started to back up then nearly jumped out of his boots when he felt a hand on his shoulder. Jarlaxle moved up beside him.

"He is fabulous, is he not?" the drow whispered.

Entreri shot him a hateful look.

"I know," the drow said for him. "Always dragons with me."

Down below, the dragon of bones and torn skin swung its head to look up at them, and though it had no physical eyes, just points of reddish light, its intimidating gaze rattled the companions.

"A dragon cadaver," Entreri said with obvious disgust.

"A dracolich," Jarlaxle corrected.

"That is supposed to sound better?"

The drow just shrugged.

And the dragon roared, its throaty blast reverberating off the stone walls with such power that the assassin feared the ledge he lay upon would collapse.

"That ain't right," Athrogate said when the echoing blast at last relented. The dwarf had come up as well, but unlike Entreri and Jarlaxle he wasn't lying on the stone. He stood at the lip of the ledge, staring down, hands on his hips. He looked at Jarlaxle and asked, "That the king?"

"One would hope."

"And what're we supposed to do with that thing?"

"Kill it."

The dwarf looked back down at the dracolich, which hunched upon its hind legs, sitting upright, head swaying, two-foot long teeth all too clear with little skin covering its mouth.

"Ye're joking with an old dwarf," said Athrogate.

He didn't rhyme his words, and Entreri knew that no "bwahahas" would be forthcoming.

Jarlaxle pulled himself up. "I am not," he proclaimed. "Come now, our time of trial is upon us. Run along, mighty Olgerkhan, for the sake of your lady Arrayan. And you, good Athrogate, fearless and powerful. Those brittle bones will turn to dust before your mighty swings!"

Olgerkhan roared and came out onto the ledge, then with strength and power they had not seen from him before, he took up his heavy club and charged down along the ledge.

"Ye're really not joking with an old dwarf?" Athrogate asked.

"Shatter its skull!" Jarlaxle cheered.

Athrogate looked at the drow, looked down at the dracolich, looked back at the drow, and shrugged. He pulled his morning stars over his shoulders and whispered to his weapons alternately as he ran off after Olgerkhan, bidding their enchantments forth.

"Fill yer teeth with half-orc bread," the dwarf yelled to the waiting beast, "while Athrogate leaps atop yer head! *Bwahaha!*"

"And now we leave," Entreri remarked, coming up beside Jarlaxle and making no move to follow his two warrior companions.

But then it was dark, pitch black so that Entreri couldn't see his hand before his face if he'd waggled his fingers an inch in front of his eyes.

"This way," Jarlaxle bade him, and he felt the drow's arm around his waist.

He started to protest and pull away, sheathing his dagger to free up one hand, though he dared not move too quickly on the ledge. But the assassin was caught by surprise when Jarlaxle pushed against him hard, wrapping him in a tight hug. The drow then fell the other way, off the ledge.

The dragon roared.

Entreri screamed.

But then they were floating as the drow enacted the power of his levitation, and as they set down on the cavern floor, Jarlaxle threw aside the stone he had enchanted with radiating darkness and let go of Entreri.

Entreri rolled to the side, putting some distance between himself and the dark elf. He got his bearings enough to realize that the dracolich wasn't looking at him and Jarlaxle, but was focusing on the half-orc and the dwarf as they continued their raucous charge down the sloping stone ledge.

Entreri had his chance to strike with the element of surprise. With the beast distracted, he could get past its formidable defenses and score a mighty blow.

But he didn't move, other than to look down at his weapons. How could he even begin to hurt something like that?

He glanced to the side and considered leaping over and stabbing

Jarlaxle instead, but he found the drow with his eyes closed, deep in concentration.

Jarlaxle had some hidden trick to play, it seemed—or at least, that's what Entreri hoped.

But Entreri still did not charge in against the beast, as it was no fight that he wanted. He rushed away from the wall, weaving toward the far side of the cavern, putting as much distance between himself and the half-orc and dwarf as possible.

He glanced back as Olgerkhan cried out, and he nearly swooned to see a line of black spittle spraying from the dracolich's skeletal mouth. Though he was still fully twenty feet from the floor, the half-orc desperately leaped from the ledge ahead of that spit, which engulfed the stone and immediately began to melt it away.

"Once a black dragon," Entreri heard Jarlaxle explain in reference to the acidic breath weapon, trademark of that particular beast.

"It can breathe?" Entreri gasped. "It's a skeleton, and it can breathe?"

But Jarlaxle had closed his eyes again and was paying him no heed.

Entreri ran along faster, heedless of Olgerkhan's groans. He did glance back once to take note of the poor half-orc, crumpled on the floor, one leg bent out at a disturbing angle, obviously shattered. How ridiculous, he thought. For the first time, the half-orc had seemed as if he might be ready for battle, and there he was, out of the fight yet again before it had even begun. And he was Arrayan's "hero" and true love?

The momentary distraction cost the assassin dearly, for when he looked back, he saw the great bony tail swiping his way.

Arrayan, too, fought a great battle, but hers was internal and not carried out with sword or wand. Hers was a test of will, a battle as one might wage with a disease, for like a cancer did the darkness of the Zhengyian construct assail her. It clawed at her life energy with demonic hands. For days it had pulled at her, thinned her, sapped her, and now, so close to the king of the castle, the monstrous beast she had inadvertently awakened, Arrayan had come to the final battlefield.

But she had no way to fight back, had no strength to go on the offensive against the dracolich and the continuing intrusions of the book. That was a physical battle for her companions to wage.

She had to just hold on to the last flickers of her life, had to cling to consciousness and identity. She had to resist the temptation to succumb to the cool and inviting darkness, the promise of rest.

One image, that of Olgerkhan, carried her in her battle though she knew it to be a losing cause. For all those years he had been her dearest of friends. He had tolerated her pouting when she couldn't unravel the mysteries of a certain spell. He had accepted her selfishness when all of her thoughts and all of her talk had been about her own future and dreams. He had stayed beside her, his arm offered in support, through every setback, and he cheered her on from afar through every victory.

And she had accepted him as a friend—but just as a friend. She had not understood the depth of his devotion and love for her. He had worn that ring, and though Arrayan had not been in on the placement and explanation, she understood the properties of physical arbitration the matched set had created. He had suffered, terribly so, so that she could get where she was, so that she would have her one chance, feeble as it seemed.

She could not let him down. She could not betray the trust and the sacrifice of the half-orc she loved.

Yes, loved, Arrayan knew beyond all doubt. Far beyond her friend, Olgerkhan was her partner, her support, her warmth, and her joy. Only when she had seen him near death had Arrayan come to fully appreciate that.

And she had to fight on.

But the darkness beckoned.

She heard the ruckus in the far room and managed to open her eyes. She heard the approach of someone from the other direction, but she hadn't the strength to turn her head.

They passed her by, and Arrayan thought she was dreaming, then feared that she had gone over to the netherworld. For those three, Ellery, Mariabronne, and Canthan, had certainly died, yet they walked past her, ran by her, the warrior woman hefting her mighty axe, the ranger holding his legendary sword, the wizard preparing a spell.

How was it possible?

Was this the reality of death?

"*Bwahaha!* Ye got to be quicker than that, ye bony worm!" Athrogate bellowed as he dodged past a slashing claw, dived under the biting fangs, and came up with a smashing swing that cracked hard against the dracolich's foreleg. Bone dust flew, but the leg didn't give out or crack apart.

Athrogate had put all of his weight behind that strike, had let fly with all of his magically enhanced might, and had used the enchantment of the morning star, the oil of impact coating it, for maximum effect.

He hadn't done much damage.

He hit the leg again, and a third time, before the other foreleg crashed against his shoulder and launched him into a flying roll. He bounced through the heap of bones, weapons, and armor, finally coming back to his feet just in time to leap aside to avoid the snap of the dracolich's powerful and toothy jaws.

"A bit o' help, if ye might!" the dwarf yelled, and that was as close to a call of panic as had ever been uttered by the confident Athrogate.

The dracolich bit at him again, and he dodged aside, and even managed to snap off a one-two routine with his morning stars, their glassteel heads bouncing alternately off the thick dragon bone.

The creature showed no sign of pain or fear, and the head

pressed on, snapping at him over and over. He retreated and dodged, jumped back, and when the dracolich finally caught up to him, the dwarf leaped up high, just high enough to get above the thing's snapping maw. He was spared a deadly bite but was thrown back and to the floor.

When he landed and slid down onto his back, he noted Olgerkhan, still squirming and grabbing at his shattered leg.

"By the gods, ye dolt, get up!" Athrogate pleaded.

Entreri wasn't quick enough. He jumped and turned sidelong but got clipped by the swinging tail and spun halfway over. He kept the presence of mind to tuck his head and shoulders and turn all the way as he landed among the bones, but when he came back to his feet, he found that one ankle would hardly support his weight. He gave it a cursory glance to see blood staining the side of his boot.

He hopped and limped along, though, and still his thoughts were to simply find a way out of there. All along, Entreri had expected that Jarlaxle's thirst for adventure would eventually put them in a position where they could not win. That time had come.

He stumbled on a tangle of bones then threw himself flat as the dracolich's tail swung back his way but higher off the ground. He glanced back across the length of the undead beast to see Jarlaxle standing quietly off to the side, to see Athrogate's desperate struggle against the more dangerous weapons of the dragon, to see Olgerkhan squirming in agony, and to see . . .

The assassin blinked repeatedly, unable to comprehend the scene before him. Running down the slope to join in the fray was Ellery. Ellery! Supposedly dead at his hand. And behind her came Mariabronne, also dead.

Entreri snapped his glare back at Jarlaxle, thinking that his friend had deceived him. He hadn't seen Ellery's corpse, after all. Was it all just a lie?

Even as he contemplated abandoning his flight and rushing back to slaughter Jarlaxle, however, he realized that he had indeed seen Mariabronne lying in the utter stillness of death.

Entreri's gaze was drawn up to the small landing at the top of the ramp. There stood Canthan, waving his arms.

Now that man was dead, Entreri knew. More than dead, his soul had been destroyed by the jeweled dagger.

Yet here he was, casting a spell.

Farther down, still forty feet from the ground, Ellery took up her axe in both hands and leaped out into the air.

Suicidal, Entreri thought. But could it be suicide if she was already dead?

She soared from on high, her body snapping forward as she crashed down beside the dracolich, her axe slamming into a rib with tremendous force, taking a chunk of bone and tearing a long line of tough skin all the way down to the ground. She landed hard but came right back to her feet, swinging with abandon, without concern for any semblance of defense.

Behind her came Mariabronne, leaping far and wide. He slammed down on the dracolich's back face-first, and somehow held on, eventually bringing himself to a sitting position straddling the beast's huge spine. He locked his legs around a vertebra, took up his sword in both hands, and began slamming away.

The dracolich reared—and from above came a sudden and blinding stroke of lightning that crackled around the creature's head.

But if the lightning hurt the dracolich at all, the beast didn't show it.

It all made no sense to Entreri, so of course he glanced back at Jarlaxle. The drow just stood there, serene, it seemed, with his eyes closed in concentration. Entreri shook his head. That one always had a trick to play.

His sigh was one of disgust, his shrug one of helplessness, but Entreri changed direction and lifted Charon's Claw above his shoulder. Perhaps it wasn't the end after all.

The dracolich was focused on Canthan, and Athrogate charged back in from the front as Entreri limped in at the back. Ellery and Mariabronne pounded away with abandon. The assassin still shook his head, though, doubting that it would be enough.

He watched the serpentine neck lift the head fast toward the wizard. Canthan let loose a second spell and the dracolich's skull momentarily disappeared within the flames of a fireball. It came through smoking and blackened in spots.

With his free hand, Entreri pulled out the side of his cloak and whispered, "Red" into a pocket, then grabbed Charon's Claw with both hands, determined to make his first strike count.

Up above, the dracolich's head snapped Canthan from the ledge, its powerful jaws taking in the wizard to the waist and clamping hard. The beast swung its neck side to side and Canthan's lower torso fell free from on high as his upper body was ground into pulp.

Entreri wanted to scream.

But he growled instead and came up on the dracolich's rear leg, throwing all of his weight behind his strike.

He did some damage, but hardly enough, and it occurred to him that he would have to hit the creature a thousand times to kill it.

Canthan was already gone. The dracolich fell to all fours and swiveled its head around to spit forth another stream of acid, one that engulfed Mariabronne and melted him in place.

Entreri reconsidered his course.

Beside him, a skeleton rose, lifting a rusting broadsword. The assassin slashed at it, felling it with a single stroke. But all around him, more bones rattled, collected themselves, and rose. Entreri looked everywhere for some way out. He moved to strike at the next nearest skeleton, but he stopped short when he realized that he was not their enemy.

The skeleton warriors, formerly men of the Army of Bloodstone, attacked the dracolich.

Stunned, Entreri looked again to Jarlaxle, and his mind whirled with the possibilities, the insanity, as he noted that Jarlaxle stood with one hand extended, a purple-glowing, skull-shaped gemstone presented before him.

"By the gods!" Athrogate yelled from in front, and for the first time Entreri was in full agreement with the wretched little creature.

All around the great chamber, the Army of Bloodstone rose and renewed the battle they had waged decades before. A hundred warriors stood tall on skeletal legs, lifted sword, axe, and warhammer. They had no fear and only a singular purpose, and as one they rushed in at the beast. Metal rang against bone, leathery skin tore apart beneath the barrage.

Athrogate had no idea what was happening around him or why. He didn't stop to question his good fortune, though, for had the dead not risen, he undoubtedly would have met a sudden and brutal end.

The dracolich's roar thundered through the room and nearly felled the dwarf with its sheer power. A line of acidic spittle melted one group of skeleton warriors, but as the beast lowered its head to breathe its devastation, another group of warriors charged in.

Athrogate saw his opening. He called forth more oil of impact on his right-hand morning star and charged in behind the group of skeletons, pushing through them and letting fly a titanic swing.

The explosion shattered dragon teeth and took off a large chunk of the dracolich's jawbone, but before the dwarf could swing again, the great skull lifted up beyond his reach.

Then it came down, and hard, and Athrogate cried out and dived away. Skeletons all around him got crushed and shattered, and the dropping skull smacked him hard and sent him sprawling, his weapons flying from his grasp. He tried to rise but could not. He sensed the dracolich coming in at his back and knew he was doomed.

But first he was grabbed by the front by a stumbling half-orc who yanked him aside and drove him to the ground then fell atop him defensively.

"Ye still smell bad," the dwarf muttered, his voice weak and shaky.

Olgerkhan would have taken that as a thank you, except that the half-orc was barely conscious by that point, overwhelmed by the lines of agony rolling up from his broken leg.

Entreri slashed and bashed with all his strength, his mighty sword having some effect. The cumulative efforts of all the fighters was their only chance, he knew, and he played his part.

But not too well, for in Entreri's thoughts, first and foremost, he did not want to draw the dracolich's attention.

Wherever that attention went, the beast's enemies crumbled to dust.

And the great creature was in a frenzy by that point, its wings beating and battering, its tail whipping wildly and launching warriors through the air to smash against the chamber's distant walls.

But metal rang out, on and on, snapping against bones, tearing rotting dragon skin. One wing came down to buffet Ellery, but when it reached its low point, a dozen undead warriors leaped upon it and hacked away, and bit and clawed and tugged on bones with skeletal arms. The dracolich roared—and there seemed to be some pain in that cry—and thrashed wildly.

The skeletons hung on.

The dracolich rolled, and bones splintered and shattered. When it came around, the skeleton warriors were dislodged, but so was its wing, snapped right off at the shoulder.

The creature roared again.

Then it bit Ellery in half and launched her torn corpse across the room.

Stubbornly, relentlessly, the skeletons were upon it again, bashing away, but Entreri recognized that the ring of metal on bone had lessened.

A line of spittle melted another group of charging skeletons. Forelegs tore another undead soldier in half and threw its bones at yet another. The dracolich flattened another pair with a downward smash from its great skull.

All hope faded from Entreri. Despite the unexpected allies, they could not win out against that mighty beast. He looked over to Jarlaxle then, and for the first time in a while the drow looked back. Jarlaxle offered an apologetic shrug, then tugged on the side of his hat's wide brim. His body darkened, his physical form wavered.

The dark elf seemed two-dimensional more than three, more of a shadow than a living, breathing creature. He slipped back to the wall, thinned to a black line, and slid into a crack in the stone.

Entreri cursed under his breath.

He had to get away, but how? The ramp was no good to him with the large section burned out of it.

So he just ran, as fast as his wounded ankle could carry him. He stumbled across the room, away from the dracolich as it continued its slaughter of the skeleton army. He looked back over his shoulder to see the creature's massive tail sweep aside the last of the resistance, and his heart sank as those terrible red points of light that served as the beast's eyes focused in on him.

The monster took up the chase.

Entreri scanned the far wall. There were some openings but they were wide—too wide.

He had no choice, though, and he went for the narrowest of the group, a circular tunnel about eight feet high. As he reached its entry, he leaped to a stone on the side, grimacing against the stinging pain in his ankle, then sprang higher off of it, catching the archway with both hands. He worked his hands fast, hooking a small cord, then let go and ran on into the tunnel.

But it wasn't a tunnel, only a small, narrow room.

He had nowhere to run, and the dracolich's head could easily snake in behind him.

He turned and flattened himself as much as possible against the short tunnel's back wall. He drew his weapons, though he knew he could not win, as the creature closed.

"Come on, then," he snarled, and all fear was gone. If he was to die then and there, so be it.

The beast charged forward and lowered its head in line. Its serpentine neck snapped with a rattle of bones, sending those terrible, torn jaws forward into the tunnel, straight for the helpless Entreri.

The assassin didn't strike out but rather dived down, curled up, and screamed with all his strength.

For as the dracolich's skull came through the archway, came under the red-eyed silver dragon statuette that Entreri had just placed there, the devilish trap fired, loosing a blast of fire that would have given the greatest of red dragonkind pause.

Flames roared down from the archway with tremendous force, charring bone, bubbling the very bedrock. The dracolich's head did not continue through to bite at Entreri, but the assassin knew nothing but the sting of heat. He kept curled, his eyes closed, screaming against the terror and the pain, denying the roar of the flames and the dracolich. He felt his cloak ignite, his hair singe.

The defenders of Palishchuk fought bravely, for they had little choice. More and more gargoyles came in at them from out of the darkness in the latest wave of a battle that seemed without end. After the initial assault, the townsfolk had organized into small, defensible groups, tight circles surrounding those who could not fight. To their credit, they had lost only a few townspeople to the gargoyles, though a host of the creatures lay dead in the streets.

In one small room, a lone warrior found less luck and no options. For, like some of the other townsfolk who had fallen that night, Calihye had been cut off from the defensive formations. She battled alone, with Davis Eng helplessly crying out behind her.

Three gargoyles were dead in the room, with two killed in the early moments of the long, long battle. After an extended lull, the third had come in against her, and it had only just gone down. Its cries had been answered though, with the next two crashing in, and Calihye knew that others were out there, ready to join the fray.

She dodged and stabbed ahead, and she thought she might win out against the pair, but she knew she couldn't keep it up much longer.

She glanced over at Davis Eng, who lay there with the starkest look of terror on his face.

Calihye growled as she turned her attention back to the fight. She couldn't leave him, not like that, not when he was so utterly helpless.

So she fought on, and a gargoyle went spinning down to the floor. Another came in, then another, and Calihye spun and slashed wildly, hoping and praying that she could just keep them at bay.

All thoughts of winning flew away, but she continued her desperate swinging and turning, clinging to the last moments of her life.

The gargoyles screeched so loudly, so desperately, that it stung Calihye's ears, and behind her, Davis Eng cried out.

But then the gargoyles were gone. Just gone. They hadn't flown out of the room. They hadn't done anything but disappear.

The gargoyle corpses were gone too, Calihye realized. She blinked and looked at Davis Eng.

"Have I lost my mind then?" she asked.

The man, looking as confused as she, had no answers.

Out on the street, cheering began. Calihye made her way to the broken window and looked down.

Abruptly, without explanation, the fight for Palishchuk had ended.

From a crack in the wall across the chamber, Jarlaxle had seen the conflagration. A pillar of fire had rained down from above, obscuring the dracolich's upper neck and head. The great body, one wing torn away, shuddered and trembled.

What trick had Entreri played?

Then it hit the drow. The statuette he had placed over their apartment door in Heliogabalus, the gift from the dragon sisters.

My clever friend, Jarlaxle thought, and he thought, too, that his clever friend was surely dead.

The flames relented and the dracolich came back out of the hole. Lines of smoke rose from its swaying head and neck, and when it turned unsteadily, Jarlaxle could see that half of its head had been melted away. The creature roared again or tried to.

It took a step back across the room. It swayed and fell, and it lay very, very still.

Jarlaxle slid out of the crack and rematerialized in the chamber—a room that had grown eerily quiet.

"Get off o' me, ye fat dolt," came Athrogate's cry, breaking the silence.

The drow turned to see the dwarf roll Olgerkhan over onto the floor. Up hopped Athrogate, spitting and cursing. He looked around, trying to take it all in, and stood there for along while, hands on his hips, staring at the dragon cadaver.

"Damned if we didn't win," he said to Jarlaxle.

The drow hardly heard him. Jarlaxle moved across the room quickly, fearing what he would find.

He breathed a lot easier when Artemis Entreri walked out from under the archway, wisps of smoke rising from his head and torso. In one hand he held the crumpled, smoldering rag that had been his cloak, and with a disgusted look at the drow, he tossed it aside.

"Always dragons with you," he muttered.

"They do hold the greatest of treasures for the taking."

Entreri looked around the bone-filled but otherwise empty room, then back at Jarlaxle.

The drow laughed.

CHAPTER 22
TO THE VICTOR...

Olgerkhan grunted and groaned and held his breath as Athrogate tied a heavy leather strap around his broken leg. The dwarf looped the belt and held one end up near the half-orc's face.

"Best be biting hard," he said.

Olgerkhan looked at him for a moment, then took the end of the strap in his mouth and clamped down on it.

Athrogate nodded and gave a great tug on the strap, yanking it tight and forcing the half-orc's leg in line. The strap somewhat muffled Olgerkhan's scream, but it still echoed through the chamber. The half-orc's hands clenched and he pounded them on the stone floor.

"Yeah, bet that hurt," Athrogate offered.

The half-orc lay back, near to collapse. He flitted in and out of consciousness for a few moments, black spots dancing before his eyes, but then through the haze and pain, he saw something that commanded his attention. Arrayan appeared on the ledge. She stood straight, for the first time in so long, leaning on nothing.

Olgerkhan came up to his elbows as she met his gaze.

"And so it ends," Jarlaxle remarked, he and Entreri moving to the dwarf and half-orc. "Help him up, then. I will levitate you up to join Arrayan on the ledge one at a time."

Athrogate moved to help Olgerkhan stand, but Entreri just moved away to the wall, where he quickly picked a route and began climbing. By the time Jarlaxle made his first trip up, easing Olgerkhan down beside Arrayan, Entreri was nearly there, moving steadily.

When he finally pulled his head above the ledge, he found Arrayan fallen over Olgerkhan, hugging him tightly and professing her love to him. Entreri hopped up beside them, offered a weak smile that neither of them even registered, and moved off to check the ascending hallway.

He sprinted up some distance but found no enemies and heard no sounds at all. When he came back, he found the other four waiting for him, Olgerkhan leaning on the dwarf with Arrayan supporting him under his other arm.

"The corridor is clear," he reported.

"The castle is dead," Arrayan replied, and her voice rang out more strongly than Entreri had previously heard.

"Ye can't be sure," Athrogate replied.

But Arrayan nodded, her confidence working against the doubts of the others. "I don't know how I know," she explained. "I just know. The castle is dead. No gargoyles or mummies will rise against us, nor daemons or other monsters. Even the traps, I believe, are now inert."

"I will ensure that, every step," Entreri assured her.

"Bah, but she can't be sure," Athrogate reiterated.

"I do believe she is," said Jarlaxle. "Sure and correct. The dracolich was the source of the castle's continuing life, was giving power to the book, and the book power to the gargoyles and other monsters. Without the dragon, they are dead stone and empty corpses, nothing more."

"And the dragon was giving the book the power to steal from me my life," Arrayan added. "The moment it fell, my burden was lifted. I do not understand it all, good dwarf, but I am certain that I am correct."

"Bah, and I was just starting to have some fun."

That brought a laugh, even from Olgerkhan, though he grimaced with the effort. Jarlaxle moved out before the trio to join Entreri.

"We will move up ahead and ensure that the way is clear," the dark elf said, and he and Entreri started off.

They trotted along swiftly, putting a lot of distance between themselves and the others.

"The castle is truly dead?" Entreri asked when they were well alone.

"Arrayan is a perceptive one, and since she was inextricably tied to the castle, I would trust her judgment in this."

"You seem to know more than she."

Jarlaxle shrugged.

"No gargoyles and no mummies," Entreri went on. "Their source of power is gone. But what of the undead? Will we find skeletons waiting for us when we get back to the keep?"

"What do you mean?"

"Their master, it would seem, walks beside me."

Jarlaxle gave a little laugh.

"When did you become a necromancer?" Entreri asked.

Jarlaxle took out the skull gem.

"It was you back there, of course," the assassin said. "All of it."

"Not completely true," Jarlaxle replied. "I brought in our three lost companions, true. You did indeed hear them following us down."

"And left the fourth hanging on a spike?"

Another laugh. "He is a dwarf—the gem grants me no power over dead dwarves, just humans. So if you fall in battle. . . ."

Entreri was not amused. "You have the power to raise an army of skeletons?" he asked.

"I did not," the drow explained. "Not all of them. The dracolich animated them, or the castle did. But I heard them, every one, and they heard me, and heeded my commands. Perhaps they harbored old grievances against the dragon that had long ago slaughtered them."

They crossed the room where Entreri had battled Canthan and moved steadily along. No eggs fell from the ceiling carvings, releasing guardian daemons to terrorize them, and no sarcophagi creaked open. When they at last reached the main chamber of the keep, they found that the monsters had broken through the doors. But none remained to stand against them. Bones littered the floor, and a pair of gnoll mummies lay still on the stairs, but not a gargoyle was to be seen. Outside it was dark, for it was well into the night by then.

Jarlaxle paid it all little heed. His prize was in sight, and he was fast to the book, which still stood on its tendril platform. No mystical runes spun in the air above it, and the drow felt no tingles of magical power as he moved to stand before it. He looked over at Entreri then tore out a page.

He paused and looked around, as if listening for the rumble of a wall crumbling.

"What?" Entreri asked.

"The castle will not crumble as did Herminicle's tower."

"Why?"

"Because, unlike that structure, this one is complete," Jarlaxle explained. "And because the life-force that completed this castle is still alive."

"Arrayan? But you said . . ."

Jarlaxle shook his head. "She was nothing more than the one who began the process, and the castle leeched her for convenience, not for survival. Her death would have meant nothing to the integrity of the structure, beyond perhaps slowing the growth of the gargoyles or some other minor thing."

"Well, if not Arrayan, then who?" Entreri asked. "The dracolich?"

Jarlaxle tore out another page, then another. "Dracoliches are interesting creatures," he explained. "They do not 'die' as we know it. Their spirits run and hide, awaiting another suitable body to animate and inhabit."

Entreri's eyes went wide and despite himself he glanced around as if expecting the beast to drop upon him. He started to ask Jarlaxle what he meant by that but paused when he heard the others shuffling into the chamber behind him.

"Well met," Jarlaxle said to them. "And just in time to witness the end of the threat."

He stepped back from the book as he finished and tapped the

tips of his thumbs together. Fingers splayed before him, he called upon the power of one of his magic rings. Flames fanned out from his spread hands, washing over the magical book and igniting it. Laughing, Jarlaxle brought a dagger into his hand and began tearing at the tome, sending blackened, burning parchment flying.

In that show, the drow found his treasure, and he slipped it into his sleeve under the cover of his slashing movements. He was not surprised by the sight of the prize: a purple glowing gem shaped like a skull. Not a human skull, like the one Jarlaxle already possessed, but the skull of a dragon.

Immediately upon closing his fingers on the gem, the drow felt the life-force of the great black dragon contained within.

He felt the hate, the outrage.

But most of all, he felt the dragon's fear.

He enjoyed that.

The five remaining party members did not have to go far to find more allies. With the defeat of the dragon, the defeat of the Zhengyian artifact, had come the defeat of the gargoyles. Guessing that something positive and important must have happened out there, Wingham had quickly led a contingent of half-orc soldiers out of Palishchuk's northern gate.

How pleased they were to see the five exiting through the hole in the portcullis Athrogate had earlier made.

Pleased and concerned all at once, for four were missing, including a man who had been a friend to Palishchuk for decades.

Arrayan ran to Wingham and wrapped him in a great hug. Cheers went up all around the pair—for Arrayan and for Olgerkhan, with the occasional reminder thrown in to salute the other three.

Those cheers were fast tempered however, when Olgerkhan confirmed the deaths of Canthan and Ellery, of good Pratcus and of Mariabronne the Rover.

So it was a muted celebration, but a celebration nonetheless, for the threat had passed and Palishchuk had survived. After a short while of cheering and many prayers offered for the dead, Wingham demanded a complete recounting.

"There will be time for that when we return to Palishchuk," Jarlaxle responded, and the others, even ever-curious Wingham, quickly agreed. The castle might have been dead, but they were still deep in the Vaasan wilderness, after all.

"We almost lost her," Jarlaxle later said to Wingham, for he had made it a point to walk beside the old half-orc on their journey back. "Olgerkhan threw off his ring, and the sudden shock of bearing all the burden nearly overwhelmed the poor girl."

Wingham cast him a curious glance and nearly blurted out, "How do you know about that?" Jarlaxle figured, for he read it clearly on the old weapon dealer's face.

"When we could not find Olgerkhan's ring, we knew we had to move quickly. Fortunately, by that time, we were ready to do battle with the true king of the castle, a black dracolich of enormous size and power."

That widened Wingham's eyes. "You have a few stories to tell," he said.

"It has been a long day," Jarlaxle replied.

All of the city turned out that night, the old, the very young, and everyone in between, to hear the tales of the fall of the dracolich. Jarlaxle served as storyteller for the five, of course, for few in all the world could weave a tale better than the strange old dark elf. Athrogate got in a few rhymes and seemed to take particular delight in the groans of the onlookers.

Through it all, Entreri moved to the far side of the common room, trying to remain inconspicuous. He didn't really want to talk to anyone, didn't want any pats on the back, and had little desire to answer questions about the deaths of Ellery and Canthan in particular.

But he did see one face among the crowd, in the back and over by the door, which he could not ignore.

"Davis Eng?" he asked when he arrived by Calihye's side.

"Resting well," she curtly replied. "He nearly died when the gargoyles attacked the town, but I was there."

"Ever the hero."

Calihye turned a glare over him. "That would be your title, would it not?"

"We asked you to come along."

"To lie dead beside Ellery, no doubt."

Entreri merely smiled, bowed, and took his leave.

The cheering faded behind him as he walked out into the Palishchuk night. He was alone with his feelings, including a few that he hadn't even known he possessed. He pictured Arrayan's face then thought of Dwahvel Tiggerwillies. He considered his anger, his hurt, when Arrayan had professed her love to Olgerkhan.

Why had he felt that? Why so keenly?

He admitted to himself that he was indeed attracted to Arrayan, but he had been to Ellery and Calihye, as well, on that level. He didn't love the half-orc—how could he, when he didn't truly know her?

It all had him shaking his head, and as he considered it, with time to think and reflect, with no danger pressing and no distractions, he found his answer.

He drew out Idalia's flute and stared at it, then gave a helpless little laugh.

So, the dragon sisters—and his drow friend, no doubt—had conspired to manipulate him.

Strangely, at that moment of reflection, Artemis Entreri was not angry with them.

A wagon rolled out of Palishchuk three days later, carrying Entreri and Jarlaxle, Calihye, Athrogate, and Davis Eng. A handful of Palishchuk soldiers had agreed to serve as guards and drivers. Behind it came a second wagon, bearing the bodies of Pratcus and Commander Ellery. Of Mariabronne, they hadn't found enough to bury, and Canthan's lower torso, though supposedly retrieved by the Palishchuk guards who had returned to the castle, had not been placed in the cart. Whispered rumors said that it had been claimed and removed in quiet the day before, but even the ever-suspicious Jarlaxle and Entreri had put little credence in the confused reports.

"You would be wise to keep all curiosity seekers out of the castle," Jarlaxle told Wingham, who stood with Arrayan and Olgerkhan and a much older half-orc, who had been introduced as an old and renowned bard. "The book is destroyed, so the place should be dead, by all reasoning. But it was a Zhengyian artifact, after all, and we do not know what other surprises the Witch-King left in place."

"The soldiers who went in have told everyone of the fate of Pratcus," Wingham replied, "and that there was apparently no treasure to be found. The castle will remain as it is until King Gareth can send an appropriate force to investigate."

"Farewell then," the drow said with a low bow and a sweep of his great hat. "Expect my return here at Palishchuk, at a time when I might more fully peruse and enjoy the town."

"And you will be welcomed, Jarlaxle," Arrayan put in. "Though we'll not likely see you until the spring melt."

Jarlaxle smiled at her and held up the magical ring she had given him, on his request that he might study it further and perhaps replace its lost companion. Arrayan had no problem in handing it over after Wingham had agreed, for neither knew that Jarlaxle already had the sister ring in his possession. As soon as the others had left that room of battle, a quick spell had shown Jarlaxle its location, and the drow was never one to let such items go to waste.

"Winter is fast approaching," Wingham said. "But then, up here, winter is always fast-approaching, if it is not already here!"

"And you will be welcomed, as well, Artemis Entreri," Olgerkhan added.

Entreri locked stares with the half-orc then turned his gaze over Arrayan. Her smile was warm and friendly, and full of thanks.

Entreri reached into his cloak and pulled forth the flute of Idalia, then looked back to the pair. Feeling Jarlaxle's curious gaze upon him, he turned to the drow.

There was apprehension there, and Entreri got the sense that his friend was about to be quite disappointed.

He held up the flute but didn't toss it to Olgerkhan, as he had intended.

"Perhaps I will learn to play it well enough to entertain you upon my return," he said, and he saw the smile widen on Jarlaxle's dark face.

Entreri wasn't sure how he felt about that.

"I would like that," said Arrayan.

The wagons rolled away. Artemis Entreri spent a long time staring back at the half-orcs, and a long time letting his hands feel the craftsmanship of Idalia's work.

The rest of the day proved uneventful. Even Jarlaxle was quiet and left Entreri pretty much alone. They set their camp for the night, and Entreri chose one of the wagon benches as his bed, mostly because then no one was likely to sleep too close to him. He wanted very much to be alone again and only wished that he had been far enough away from all the others that he might take up the flute and try to learn more of its magic.

He found himself wishing he could be even farther away when, a short while into the quiet night, Calihye climbed up to stand beside him.

At first, he feared she might make a move against him. His dagger in hand, he knew he could easily defeat and kill her, but he did not wish to do that.

"The road will not be clear tomorrow," the half-elf said to him.

Entreri put on a puzzled look and swung around to sit up.

"Before mid-day, perhaps sooner, we will find pursuit, a band of riders coming with questions and accusations," she explained.

"What do you know?"

"The Citadel of Assassins wishes to know about Canthan," Calihye explained. "He was no minor player in that dark association, and now he is dead. Rumors say by your hands."

"Rumors say many things."

"Olgerkhan told of his near-death experience in the castle. He told of a dagger and of the fall of Canthan. Many ears beyond the small group of friends sitting beside the half-orc heard that tale."

Entreri stared at her hard.

"Archmage Knellict is not Canthan," Calihye went on. "Whatever success you found against that wretch will not easily be replicated where Knellict is concerned. Nor will he come alone, and the men beside him will not be novices to the art of murder."

"Why are you telling me this?"

The woman stared at him for a long while. "I will not live indebted to Artemis Entreri," she said and turned away.

Not for the first time, Entreri was glad that he had not killed her.

Dawn was still long away when Entreri and Jarlaxle moved out from the wagons.

"The word is 'Blackfire,' " Jarlaxle explained as he handed the obsidian figurine over to his companion.

"Black—" Entreri started to ask, but the drow interrupted him with an upraised hand and a word of warning.

"Do not speak the summons until you are ready to ride," Jarlaxle explained. "And place the figurine on the ground before you do, for it will summon an equine beast from the lower planes to serve you. I found it on the body of Mariabronne—a curious item for a goodly ranger of the Army of Bloodstone to carry."

Entreri started at him, then at the figurine.

"So if you are ready, we should go," Jarlaxle said.

"You will ride behind me?"

"Beside you," said the drow, and from yet another of his many pouches, he produced an identical item.

Entreri couldn't find the heart to even shake his head.

The cries of the nightmares split the night, awakened the others at the wagons, and reminded those who were supposed to be guarding the troupe that they were supposed to be guarding the troupe. By the time any of them got to the south side of the encampment, though, Entreri and Jarlaxle were long gone.

The wind whipped Entreri's hair and buffeted his cloak as the nightmare charged on, fiery hooves tearing at the soft tundra.

When dawn broke, the companions were still running, their steeds showing no sign of tiring though they had put many, many miles between themselves and the wagons.

Even with that, however, they found that they were not alone.

"The woman spoke truthfully," Jarlaxle remarked when a line of horsemen appeared behind them and to the side, riding hard and with purpose. "Let us hope that the Bloodstone Lands are filled with places to hide!"

The horses would not catch them, however hard their riders drove them. The hellish steeds were too powerful and did not tire. Soon the pair were running free again, and they knew they were much closer to the Vaasan Gate.

"We could seek the protection of King Gareth," Jarlaxle remarked.

"Until he learns that we killed his niece."

"We?"

Entreri turned his head, and if Jarlaxle hadn't been grinning at that moment, Entreri would have leaped across and throttled him.

"If the Citadel of Assassins hunts us, then King Gareth will likely embrace us even more," said the drow. "I am not fond of relying on such things, but until we can sort out the potential of our new power, it will have to do. Well, that and the dragon sisters, who I'm sure will look upon us with new respect."

"Respect or hatred?"

"They are not as different as you seem to believe."

Entreri moved to reply, but before he could get a word out, the air around the riding pair shimmered weirdly, like a wave of soft blue cloth.

Their summoned horses disappeared out from under them.

Entreri hit the ground hard, bouncing and rolling, scraping his face and nearly shattering his jaw. As he at last came around, finally controlling the roll, he saw Jarlaxle drift by, the drow still upright and levitating through the momentum of the fall.

"That was no accident, nor did the duration of the magic of the mounts run out simultaneously," the drow called back, from far ahead.

Entreri looked around, his hands going to his weapons.

"To the foothills, and quickly," Jarlaxle insisted. "The Citadel mustn't catch us out in the open."

They rushed back to retrieve their mounts, merely obsidian figurines once more. Then they scrambled to the west, where the ground began to slope up, and great tumbled boulders from the Galenas offered them some cover. They were still climbing when far in the distance to the north, they spotted the unmistakable dust and movement of many galloping horses.

"How did they do that?" Entreri asked when they pulled up with their backs against a huge stone for a much-needed break. "Was it an ambush? Is there a wizard about?"

"Was it even them?" Jarlaxle asked.

"If not, then this troupe should ride right past us," Entreri reasoned.

Both he and Jarlaxle took that cue to peer around the boulder down to the flat plain, where the truth of it all became quite evident. For the pursuers had slowed, with some already turning to the west and filtering into the foothills north of their current position.

"We should find a defensible spot," Jarlaxle suggested.

Entreri didn't blink. "When they close on us, you will just turn to shadowstuff and melt into a crack in the stones, no doubt," he said.

Jarlaxle considered the words for a moment, but given the incident in the dracolich's cave, he really wasn't in any position to promise differently.

"Come," the drow offered. "All hope is not lost. There are caves, perhaps."

"None that will suit your needs," came a voice, and the two turned their heads very slowly to see an older man, well-groomed and dressed in splendid robes of purple and red, and with not a speck of mud on him. The way he held himself, the tilt of his head, and the obvious reverence with which those several guards around him, including a dwarf both of them knew too well, told them exactly who he was before he even introduced himself as Archmage Knellict.

"I do not know that I would name Canthan as a friend," Knellict said. "He was an annoying one, who seemed to find even more annoying companions."

"That'd be me," Athrogate proudly announced, and no one was amused.

"But he was an asset to my organization," Knellict continued. "A valuable one, and one lost to me."

"If I had known that, I would have let him kill me," Entreri quipped.

"Bwahaha!"

"Shut up, dwarf," said Knellict, and when Athrogate immediately buttoned his lip, shifted nervously, and averted his gaze to the ground, it occurred to Entreri and Jarlaxle that the archmage was all his reputation claimed, and more.

"Commander Ellery was no small asset, as well," Knellict said. "A liaison to the happenings of the crown—mostly an unwitting and stupid asset, but an asset nonetheless."

"Ah, and now you seek to reclaim that which you have lost," Jarlaxle replied.

"Do I?" Knellict began walking around to the side, studying

them both as he went. "You were stronger than Canthan, obviously, since you vanquished him," he said. "And no doubt King Gareth will now welcome you into his court, since you have saved Palishchuk and defeated the magic of Zhengyi."

"I think we just volunteered," Entreri remarked.

"You prefer the alternative?" Jarlaxle came right back.

"I need not explain the details to you, of course," Knellict said. "You are both well aware of the rules. We understand each other?"

"I have created such organizations," Jarlaxle assured him.

Knellict burst into movement. Entreri went for his weapons, but Jarlaxle, recognizing the gesture, grabbed his friend's arm.

A great wind came up and dust swirled around them, blinding them momentarily. And when it was gone, the two stood alone.

"They were never really here," Jarlaxle said. "Knellict projected the image and sounds of the entire group to us. He is a powerful one."

"But we really had that conversation?"

"We heard them and they heard us," Jarlaxle assured him. The drow cast a few quick spells and tapped his eye patch more than once.

"And now we work for the Citadel of Assassins?" Entreri asked.

"And the dragon sisters. We would not be wise to forget that pair."

"You seem pleased by it all."

"The easiest road to gaining control is one walked beside those who currently rule."

"I thought it was Jarlaxle who was always in control," Entreri remarked, and his voice took a sudden sharp edge to it.

The drow looked at him curiously, catching that razor line.

"Even when he should not be in control," the assassin went on. "Even in those instances when he is taking control of something that does not concern him."

"When did you take to speaking in riddles?"

"When did you presume to so manipulate me?"

"Manipulate?" Jarlaxle gave a little laugh. "Why, my friend, is that not the nature of our relationship? Mutual manipulation for personal gain?"

"Is it?"

"Are we to spend this entire conversation asking questions without answers?"

In reply, Entreri pulled forth Idalia's flute and tossed it at Jarlaxle's feet.

"I did not give you that," the drow stated.

"Truly?" asked Entreri. "Was it not a gift from the sisters, with Jarlaxle's understanding and agreement?"

"It is a precious instrument, a gift that most would appreciate."

"It is a manipulation of the heart, and you knew it."

The drow put on an innocent look but couldn't hold it and just gave a little laugh instead.

"Did you fear that I would not go into the castle unless I felt something for Arrayan?"

"I had no idea that there was an Arrayan," Jarlaxle pointed out.

"But you enjoyed the manipulation."

"My friend . . ." Jarlaxle began, but Entreri cut him short.

"Don't call me that."

Again Entreri's tone caught the drow by surprise, as if that knife's edge in his voice had developed a wicked, serrated blade.

"You still cannot admit the obvious, I see," Jarlaxle said. He took a step back, almost expecting Entreri to draw his sword on him.

The assassin looked around.

"Knellict and his minions are long gone," Jarlaxle assured him, and he tapped his enchanted eye patch to accentuate his certainty.

"Jarlaxle knows," Entreri remarked. "Jarlaxle knows everything."

"It keeps us both alive."

"And again, that is by the choice of Jarlaxle."

"You are beginning to bore me."

Entreri rushed up to him and grabbed him by the throat.

Jarlaxle dropped a knife from his enchanted bracer into one hand, ready to plunge it home. But Entreri wasn't pressing the case, other than to shout in Jarlaxle's face, "Are you my father, then?"

"Hardly that."

"Then what?" Entreri asked, and he let go, sending Jarlaxle stumbling back a step. "You manipulate and carry me along, and for what? For glory? To give a dark elf credibility among the humans? For treasures that you cannot carry alone?"

"No such treasures exist," came the dry reply.

"Then for what?" Entreri yelled at him.

"For what," Jarlaxle echoed, with another of his little laughs and a shake of his head. "Why, for anything and for nothing at all."

Entreri stared at him with a puzzled expression.

"You have no purpose, no direction," Jarlaxle explained. "You wander about muttering to yourself. You walk no road, because you see no road before you. I would be doing you a favor if I killed you."

That brought a look showing a complete acceptance, even an eagerness, for the challenge.

"Is it not the truth?" Jarlaxle asked. "What is the point of your life, Artemis Entreri? Is it not your own emptiness that led you all those years into desiring a battle with Drizzt Do'Urden?"

"Every time you mention that name, you remind me how much I hate you."

"For giving you that which you desired? For facilitating your fight with the rogue drow? Ah, but did I steal the only thing in your life giving you meaning, by giving you that which you said you desired? A pitiful state of the heart, would you not agree?"

"What would you have me say? I only know that which I feel."

"And you feel like killing me."

"More than you would understand."

"Because I force you to look at yourself and you do not like what you see. Is that a reason to kill me, because I am offering to you a chance to sort through your own emotions? That is all the magic of the flute did to you, I suspect. It offered you the opportunity to look past your own emotional barriers."

"Did I ask for your help?"

"Friends help when they are not asked."

Entreri sighed and shook his head, but he could not deny any of what the drow had said. His shoulders slumped a bit, and Jarlaxle let the dagger fall to the ground behind him, certain then that he would need no weapons.

A few moments passed between them until finally Entreri looked up at the drow, his face calm, and asked, "Who are you?"

Jarlaxle laughed again, and it was a sincere expression of joy, for that was where he had hoped it would all lead.

"Why, Artemis Entreri, do you not yet know? Have you not come to understand any of it?"

"I understand less each day."

"I am your muse," Jarlaxle announced.

"What?"

"I am he who will give meaning to your life, Artemis, my friend. You do not even begin to understand the breadth of your powers. You know how well you might skulk through the shadows, you know all too well your prowess with the blade, but you have never understood what those well-deserved, well-earned powers can bring you."

"You assume that I want anything."

"Oh, you do. If you can only dare to wish for it."

"What? Athrogate's Citadel of Assassins? Shall we move to dominate them?"

"Of course, to begin."

"Begin?"

"Think large, my friend. Make your goal expansive. Athrogate will give us the insight and bona fides we need to find a strong place within the Citadel's organization—we will quickly learn whether it is worth our time to overtly dominate the place or merely to covertly exert enough control to render them harmless to us."

"Couldn't we just kill the annoying little dwarf instead?"

Jarlaxle laughed. "There has been a void of power up here for many years."

"Since the fall of Zhengyi."

"Vaasa is ours for the taking."

"Vaasa?" Entreri could hardly repeat the word, and for one of the few times in all his life, he actually stuttered. "Y-you would go against King Gareth?"

Jarlaxle shrugged. "Perhaps. But there are other ways." He ended by holding up the dragon skull gemstone. "The sisters will learn of a new balance of power between us, to begin with. And within this stone lies control of the castle and a new ally."

"An ally that will bite us in half."

Jarlaxle shook his head. "Not while I am in possession of his phylactery. He and I are already in communication, I assure you. If I choose to let him out again, he will only do so with great trust in me, for if I destroy the phylactery, I destroy the dracolich's spirit. Utterly."

"Gareth will send soldiers to the castle."

"And I will let them stay for a while."

"Vaasa?"

"At least."

"You will go against a legendary paladin king?"

"Come now, can you not admit that it might be fun?"

Entreri started to speak several times, but nothing decipherable came forth. Finally he just shook his head, sighed, and turned away, moving back down toward the flat ground.

"Trust me," said Jarlaxle.

"My muse?"

"Your friend."

EPILOGUE

Did the fool human pass your silly little test?" Kimmuriel Oblodra asked Jarlaxle a few days later, off in the shadows beneath the Vaasan Gate.

"Do not underestimate Artemis Entreri," Jarlaxle replied, "or the value he brings to me—to us."

"And you should not overestimate the power of the skull gems you have found," Kimmuriel warned, for he had just finished inspecting the pair at Jarlaxle's request. He had spoken with the dracolich, Urshula by name, and had confirmed Jarlaxle's suspicions that the beast would not dare to go against the possessor of the phylactery.

"They are but the beginning," Jarlaxle said with a grin. "Artemis Entreri and I have an audience with the paladin king in two days, just south of here in Bloodstone Village. We will be received as heroes for our efforts in Vaasa and as solemn witnesses to the end of Gareth's heroic niece."

He couldn't help but chuckle at the irony of that last statement. If King Gareth only knew!

Kimmuriel looked at Jarlaxle, wary, recognizing that look of confidence and grandiose schemes in his eyes, for he had seen that look from his former master dozens of times over the centuries. But they were not in the Underdark, in Menzoberranzan where Bregan D'aerthe and Jarlaxle had held many secret trumps.

"Have you found another Crenshinibon?" the psionicist asked with obvious disgust and concern.

"I have found opportunity," Jarlaxle corrected.

"Bregan D'aerthe will not come forward in force against the likes of King Gareth Dragonsbane."

Jarlaxle stared at him with appreciation and said, "Glad I am that I had the wisdom to put Kimmuriel in control of my band," he said. "Of course you are correct in resisting this bold move. You are a fine leader, and I urge you to continue with all caution, but too with an open mind. There are many events yet to play out up here in this untamed land, and I am in control of most of them." He brought forth the dragon statuette. "My relationship with a pair of living dragons just changed in ways they cannot understand."

"More allies for your battle?"

"Allies? We shall see."

Despite himself, Kimmuriel could not help but offer a wry grin.

"You might find a way to fit in as events play out," Jarlaxle said to him. "I pray that Kimmuriel remains an opportunistic leader. The point of Bregan D'aerthe is more than survival, is it not? It is to grow in power."

"You nearly destroyed us in Calimport."

"Nay," Jarlaxle corrected. "It was an inconvenience to you. It was myself that I nearly destroyed."

"You and Entreri will take down a paladin king?"

"If it comes to that."

Kimmuriel didn't reply, other than to dip a respectful bow.

Muddy Boots and Bloody Blades had long since emptied out for the night, but Entreri had tossed the innkeeper enough gold to get the key for the door. He sat alone with his thoughts and a beer, considering the emotions that had accompanied him all the way to Palishchuk and back. On the table beside his flagon lay

Idalia's flute, and Entreri wasn't yet certain if he hated the item or prized it.

It was all so very new to him.

He was to leave in the morning with Jarlaxle for a meeting with the king, where they would receive a commendation and an offer to join the Army of Bloodstone, so Honorable General Dannaway had informed them. As intriguing as it all was, however, Entreri's thoughts were much smaller in scope. He thought of the women who had accompanied him to the north, of how that innocent looking flute had given him a different way of viewing them.

That new viewpoint hadn't stopped him from killing Ellery, at least, and he took some comfort in that.

A soft footstep behind him told him that he was not alone, and from the sound of it, the assassin understood much. She had been watching him from across the room for most of the night, after all.

"I did not kill your friend," he said, not turning around. "Not with intent, at least."

The footsteps halted, still half a dozen strides behind him. Finally he did turn, to see that his reasoning was correct. Calihye stood there, her face very tight. Entreri was relieved to see that she did not have any weapon in her hands.

"Accept it as truth or do not," he said to her, and he turned back to his beer. "I care little."

He started to raise it to his lips, but Calihye came over quickly. Her hand grasped his wrist, stopping him and making him look back up at her.

"If you do not care whether I believe you or not, then why did you just tell me that yet again?" she asked.

It was Entreri's turn to stare at the half-elf.

"Or is it that you're simply afraid that you do care, Artemis Entreri?" Calihye teased, and she let go and stepped away.

Entreri stood up, his chair skidding out behind him, and said, "You flatter yourself."

"I am still alive, am I not?" Calihye reasoned. "You could have killed me back in Palishchuk, but you didn't."

"You were not worth the trouble," Entreri said. "A soldier of the crown was under your care."

"You could have killed me any time, yet I am still alive, and still, perhaps, a threat to you."

"You do flatter yourself."

But Calihye wasn't even listening to him, he realized as she stepped right up to him, her bright eyes staring into his.

"I assure you, Artemis Entreri, that I am always worth the trouble," she said, her voice turning husky, her breath hot on his face, her lips practically brushing his as she spoke.

"I did not kill your friend," Entreri reiterated, but his voice was not so strong and not so steady at that moment.

Calihye brought her hand gently up, brushing his chest and settling on his collar, where she grasped him tight.

"I accept that," she said, and she pulled him closer, pulled him right into her.

She kissed him hard and bit at his lip. Her arms went around him and pulled him even closer, and Entreri didn't resist. His own arms went around the half-elf, crushing her into him. He brought one hand up to grab at her thick, silky black hair.

Calihye pulled him with her as she fell atop the table—or tried to, for the pair were too far to the side and the flimsy table overturned, dumping them against a chair, which went bouncing away, and they dropped down to the floor.

Neither cared or even noticed. They fumbled with each other's clothing, their lips never parting.

Artemis Entreri, surviving on the wild streets of Calimport from his boyhood days, had known many women in his life but had never before made love to a woman. Never before had the act been anything more to him than a physical release.

Not so this time.

When they were finished, Entreri propped himself up above Calihye and stared down at her in the quiet light of the low-burning tavern hearth. He brought his hand up to stroke the line of her facial scar, and even that didn't seem ugly to him at that moment.

But it was just a moment, for noise out in the corridor reminded the couple where they were and told them that the night had nearly ended. They jumped up and dressed quickly, saying not a word until they stood facing each other, with Calihye fastening the last buttons on her shirt.

"You are looking at my face and regretting your choice?" she asked.

Entreri put on an incredulous expression. "Do you think yourself ugly?"

"Do you?"

Entreri laughed. "You are a combination of talent and beauty," he said. "But if your vanity demands of you to coerce such compliments, then why not seek out a wizard or a priest to repair . . ." He stopped short, seeing the woman's scowl.

And Entreri understood. Without that scar, Calihye would have ranked among the most beautiful women he had ever seen. She was trim and fit, slight but not weak. Her eyes shone, as did her hair, and her features held just enough of an elf's angular traits to make her appear exotic by human standards. Yet she kept the scar and had worn it for years, though she certainly had the financial means, by bounties alone, to be long rid of it. He thought back to their lovemaking, to the frantic beginning, the very tentative middle, and finally, the point where they both simply let go and allowed themselves to bask in the pleasure of each other. That had been no easy break-point for Entreri, so too for Calihye, he realized.

So she could draw her sword and battle a giant without fear, but that more intimate encounter had terrified her. The scar was her defense.

"You are beautiful, with or without the scar," he said to her. "How ever much you wish it was not true."

Calihye rocked back on her heels, but as always, she was not long without a response.

"I'm not the only one hiding behind a scar."

Entreri winced. "I have killed people for making such presumptions about me."

Calihye laughed at him and stepped closer. "Then let me make another one, Artemis Entreri," she said, and she put her hands on his shoulders, then slid them up to cradle his face as she moved very near.

"You will never kill me," she said softly.

For one of the few times in his life, Artemis Entreri had no answer.

FORGOTTEN REALMS®

R.A. Salvatore

The Sellswords
Book III

ROAD OF THE PATRIARCH

An Excerpt

Tazmikella was out of the city in short order, moving far from the torchlit wall toward the lonely hill where she kept her modest home. At the base of that hill, in nearly complete darkness, she surveyed all the land around her, ensuring that she was alone. She moved to a wide clearing beyond a shielding line of thick pines. In the middle, she closed her eyes and slipped out of her clothes. Tazmikella hated wearing clothes, and could never understand the need of humans to hide their natural forms. She always thought that level of shame and modesty to be reflective of a race that could not elevate itself above its apparent limitations, a race that insisted on subjugating itself to godly concepts instead of standing as their own gods, in proud self-determination.

Tazmikella was possessed of no such modesty. She stood naked in that unnatural form, basking in the feel of the night breezes. The change came subtly, for she had long ago perfected the art of transformation. Her wings and tail began to grow first, for they were the least painful—additions were always easier than transformations, which included cracking and reshaping bone structure.

The trees around her seemed to shrink. Her perspective shifted as she grew to enormous proportions. For Tazmikella was no human. She had crawled from her egg centuries before beside her sister and sole sibling in the great deserts of Calimshan, far to the southwest.

Tazmikella, the copper dragon, lifted into the night air. She gained altitude quickly, flying away from the human city. The leaders of the land knew who she was, and accepted her, but the commonfolk would never comprehend, of course. If she revealed herself to them, King Gareth and his friends would be left with no choice but to evict her from the Bloodstone Lands. And she really didn't want a fight with that company.

She moved directly north, across the least populated expanse of Morov and into the even less densely populated Duchy of Soravia. She flew between the Goliad and the Galena Snake, the two parallel rivers running south from the Galena Mountains. And she continued to climb, for the thin air and the cold did not bother Tazmikella at all. A person on the ground might catch a fleeting glimpse of her, but would that person know her to be a dragon flying high, or think her a nightbird, or a bat, flying low?

She was not concerned. She was naked in the night air, above such concerns. She was free.

She crossed the mountains easily, weaving in and out of the towering peaks, enjoying the play of the multidirectional air flows and the stark contrast between the dark stones and moonlit snow. She entered Vaasa just to the west of Palishchuk, and turned east as she came out of the mountains. Within moments, she noted the lights of the half-orc city.

Tazmikella stayed way up high as she overflew the city, for she knew that the half-orcs, living amidst the Vaasan wilds for so many years, knew how to protect themselves from any threat. If they saw the form of a dragon overflying their city at night, they wouldn't pause to consider the color of the wyrm—nor would they be able to determine that in any case, under the light of the half-moon and stars alone.

Tazmikella used her extraordinary eyesight to scrutinize the city as she passed. It was late, but many torches burned and the town's main tavern was bright and noisy. They still celebrated the victory over the castle, she realized.

She banked right, to the north, and began her descent, confident that none of Palishchuk's citizens would be out and about. Almost immediately, she saw the dark and dead structure, an immense fortress, a replica of Castle Perilous, only a few miles to the north of the city.

She came down in a straight line, too intrigued to pause and take a survey of the area. As she alighted, she changed back into a human form, thinking that anyone who subsequently spied her wouldn't feel threatened by the sight of a naked, middle-aged woman. Of course, if any lurking onlookers had watched her more closely, that image would have created more confusion than comfort, for she strode up to the huge portcullis that barred the front of the structure without pause. She considered the patchwork grate that had been chained over the break in the gate, where Jarlaxle and his companions had apparently entered. She could have removed that patch easily enough, but that would have meant stooping to crawl under.

Instead, the woman slipped her arms between two of the thick portcullis spikes, then pushed outward with both, easily bending the metal so that she could simply step through.

Unconcerned, Tazmikella strode right through the gatehouses and across the courtyard of torn, broken ground, littered with the shattered forms of many, many skeletons.

She found the great doors of the main keep repaired and secured by a heavy chain—one that she grabbed with one hand and easily snapped.

She found what she was looking for in the main room just beyond the doors. A pedestal stood intact, though blackened by fire near its top. The remnants of a large book, pages torn and burned, lay scattered about. Her expression growing more sour, Tazmikella went up to the ruined tome and lifted the black binding. Most of it was destroyed, but she saw enough of the cover to recognize the images of dragons stamped there.

She knew the nature of the book, a tome of creation, and of enslavement.

"Damn you, Zhengyi," the dragon whispered.

The clues of Jarlaxle and Entreri's progress through the place were easy enough to follow, and Tazmikella soon entered a huge chamber far below the structure, where lay the bones of a long-past battle, and the debris of a more recent struggle. One look at the dracolich confirmed everything Tazmikella and her sister Ilnezhara had feared.

October 2006